WOLF OF THE TESSERACT

WOLVES OF THE TESSERACT BOOK 1

CHRISTOPHER D. SCHMITZ

TreeShaker books

TREESHAKER BOOKS

CONTENTS

SPECIAL OFFER!

Stay up to date on the world of Wolves of the Tesseract... you'll get access to a bunch of special freebies, bonus content, and the author's newsletter. You can unsubscribe at any time.
To get access to this exclusive group, just follow this link:
https://www.subscribepage.com/wolvesofthetesseract
and add your email to be added immediatley!

Chapter One

"You know I never take it off," Claire Jones told her fiancé, James. She twirled a finger absentmindedly around the antique-looking pendant on the filigree chain. The ancient piece hung there, always. "It reminds me of my father and where I came from."

James said little more, but closed the hinged case with the pearl necklace. So far, all attempts to update the jewelry had failed.

"You look ravishing in anything," the waiter confirmed to Claire. "It could be twine and your fiancé would love it," she winked at the man opposite Claire at the table of the fancy restaurant. "It doesn't matter if Mister Shianan is famous or not. You're lovely."

James gave her a disappointed look as the waitress carried their orders back to the kitchen.

Claire might have normally been a pajama bottoms and hoody kind of girl, but today she wore a skintight dress from some fancy designer in Hollywood and had done her makeup. She hadn't seen her boyfriend—her fiancé, actually—in weeks. He was in pretty high demand for commercials, television, and movie shoots. She was still barely used to his jet-setting schedule.

James had dropped in for the weekend in between trips. He'd planned to come back for a longer period soon, but that wasn't for several weeks, still. But that gave Claire time to finalize wedding plans; James wasn't big on ceremonies and so he'd left those details up to his fiancé and her wedding party.

Wedding aside, Claire had plenty of her own interests that kept her busy. In addition to continuing her education, she considered herself something of an amateur sleuth. She could trace her love of that, most recently, to true crime and paranormal podcasts. Longer-term, her father had imparted that same passion that had propelled him into archeology.

"Did you hear about the local news?" Claire asked.

James raised a brow.

Claire leaned forward and spoke in a conspiratorial tone. "The murders. Bigfoot has been killing people in the state parks."

James almost choked on the drink he was sipping. He finally coughed with a splutter. "I'm sorry, what?"

Duluth, Minnesota, was furthest north city of any size in the state. It rested upon the western tip of Lake Superior and was surrounded by rugged woodlands and millions of acres of forest. Four of the largest state parks were directly adjacent to the city, and there were many more natural zones and woodlands than just those. It was a great place to get lost if one so desired, and it had also spawned a number of cryptid sightings. Everything from Native American wendigo to dog men, and, of course, sasquatch.

Claire pulled a bi-fold periodical from her over sized purse; it was only a few pages, but presented itself as a legitimate publication, nonetheless. She slid it across to James. He picked it up and rolled his eyes.

"You're still reading this?"

"It's a real story. They interviewed eyewitnesses and everything," Claire insisted. *The Unexplained* was a small, monthly journal local to the area. A couple of Claire's old classmates had started it after becoming disillusioned with the state of journalism. James had once noted their inability to get jobs in their field, and cited quality issues in their reporting, suggesting they were unhireable for any real media.

He read the by-line. "I have no idea who this Henry Clifton fellow is. Must be new, maybe another one of your college mates? Do you know him?"

"Um, kind of, yes. We shared all the same classes." She played it cool, not yet ready to share that she'd been moonlighting for *The Unexplained* as a freelancer.

Claire wasn't particularly close to any of those classmates who'd started the paper up—but she found the idea of the unknown to be intriguing. "I... I do think I agree with you," she told him. "I've always thought there were rational reasons to explain most things like ghosts and psychics and stuff." She gave him a wry grin. "Except for bigfoot. Bigfoot is real. But still, I'd like to see these murders solved."

James gave her a skeptical look. "And where do you draw the line? Aliens? Lizard men in the white house?"

"Well, I mean, all politicians are basically reptiles, so no argument there. But I draw the line at the Loch Ness Monster. I'm fifty-fifty on that one," said Claire.

James scanned the paper again. More than half of the space on each page was devoted to advertisers. "Eyewitness accounts are always compelling," he said. "You should maybe stick close to me, Claire-bear."

"I'm *always* close to you," she said. "Whenever you're in town, anyway."

"I mean it," he said more seriously. "There are some things out there more dangerous, and a lot more real, than sasquatches."

Claire smiled and wrinkled her nose in cute, pixie fashion. "You're always worried about the crazies in the paparazzi," she said. "And I keep telling you, Minnesota is too cold for them. They'd all freeze to death before they ever get their film developed."

James laughed. "*Film?* What is this film you speak of? I swear sometimes I think you're the same age as my grandmo—"

The door to the kitchen behind them burst open. Their waiter stepped forward with hesitant steps and with her hands held up.

Tears streamed down her face. A man behind her held a gun to her head and walked in short stutter steps to keep his hostage directly in front of him for use as a human shield.

Gasps rose from the other diners who slouched down in their chairs, trying to make themselves smaller potential targets. Glasses crashed as someone knocked them over, splashing water and ice as they tried to hide on the floor.

"James," the man said, locking eyes on Claire's fiance. There was a manic note to his voice, and he spoke with a British accent. "James Shianan. Did you get my letters?"

James was stiff, but held the man's gaze. Claire looked at him, ready to react to whichever way the situation went. She'd heard professors talk about fight vs. flight reflexes, and she was not one to freeze up when things took a turn.

She looked across the restaurant and spotted a middle aged woman hiding under a table with her mobile phone pressed up against her ear. The woman barely kept her composure as she whispered into the receiver.

At least someone has gotten off a call to the authorities.

"Are you G.G.?" James asked.

"Geoff. Geoff Gaines," he confirmed, with a slight warble creeping into his voice. "You got my letters?"

"I did." James gave the waitress a reassuring look, as if he had the situation well in hand.

The waitress brightened slightly, though Claire knew the situation was poised a knife's blade. *Was this what James meant—did he suspect this was going to happen?*

"I got every letter you sent, Geoff. I read them all," James said. "You've been sending them since I still played—since before I started acting."

Prior to a career in Hollywood, James had been a very successful soccer player. That had propped him up to worldwide fame, despite his humble ties to the mid-west fly-over states.

"I—I tried to get an autograph from you after your last match. But you... you missed the signing table." He held the gun at James now. His hand wobbled as he pointed the weapon, which was both less likely and more likely to do serious damage because of that. "I—I just wanted a picture with you."

"I know," James said, rising very slowly. Making deliberate motions to keep his hands low. "We can take that photo now, if you like." His eye contact seemed to keep the gunman focused with laser precision.

"You. Lady," he fumbled in his pocket and produced a digital camera. He handed it to Claire. "I want you to take our picture."

Geoff released the waitress and took James by the arm.

Claire took a position to try to get the photo for her fiance's stalker.

James smiled as affably as ever as Claire took several shots. "You want some video, too? Maybe record the time you got to meet me... I know you're my biggest fan. You said it in your letters."

As Claire fumbled for the smart-phone's camera features, she heard the man whisper.

"I... I can't move. What... what's wrong with me?"

And then Claire got the camera into video recording mode. A moment after the device began recording, James sprang into motion. He slapped Geoff's gun away and then swept the man's legs out from under him with a sliding kick.

Once on the ground, James wrapped him up in a restraining hold. He locked his hands and feet around their assailant, and Claire kept the camera on them.

Within a few minutes, the police arrived and took over. They led Geoff Gaines off in handcuffs, and the news crews began arriving shortly after.

By that time, James had gotten Claire safely into his vehicle. He'd always remained adamant about shielding her from the press as much as possible until she was ready to take on the challenges of life in the limelight. Claire had always thought it best to take that part slow.

A police detective was speaking to the press several feet away and James leaned against the car, speaking to Claire through the mostly closed window. That afforded them some measure of privacy.

"This is what I meant by needing to keep you close," James said. "Maybe I should hire some security for you to—"

Claire spat a raspberry. "No thanks. This guy came across the country—probably across the ocean—to get your attention. He was after you, not me. He didn't even know who I was."

"But all the same," James began to say.

Claire glowered at him. "I can take care of myself," she insisted.

He held up his hands in defeat. "Okay. But maybe someday you'll see it differently."

"And maybe you'll believe in the bigfoot murders," she said.

James shrugged and headed for the driver's seat of his car once the detective signaled he was cleared to leave. "I guess you could say that date night was a bust."

"Are you kidding?" Claire said. "This is the most exciting my life has been in quite a while."

The archaeologist looked up from the work on his desk. A photograph of his daughter, Claire, sat near a name plaque that read Dr. Sam Jones. She wore the pendant around her neck, which she always did; he'd bought it for her one summer when she'd accompanied him to a dig site.

His field office wasn't much to write home about, but he wasn't writing to Claire. Sam addressed the shipping label to one of his peers, an old friend back home.

He wrote *Miles Jecima* at the top, followed by the address in northern Minnesota. Sam wiped the sweat from the back of his neck and wished for the cooler climes of the north-most state of the union. It was a far more comfortable place than the high heat and humidity of the third world country of Chiriqui in central America.

The archaeologist discovered something he knew Jecima, a language scholar, would appreciate. Jecima had spent much of his career trying to decipher mysterious texts such as the infamous Voynich manuscript, and lately, a new and mysterious text—a text written in a language which Sam thought he could shed some light on.

He neatly folded up the rubbings he'd made within the dig site. Given enough content, Jecima would eventually be able to isolate a word or phrase he could use to develop a cypher, and then he could begin to decode the mysterious book which he'd been researching.

Something crashed in the distance where the workers had a problem with some malfunctioning equipment. He stood and peered out the tent flap.

Sam slipped his rubbings and a quick note into an envelope and sealed it before slapping his shipping label onto it. Stepping outside, he dropped the package into the outgoing mail bag, which an intern would drop off at the post later that day, and then Sam headed for his workers and the gear that needed to be fixed before they could continue to explore.

"Make it out to Pietro," said the older man at the front of the line.

Jacob Sisyphus nodded and absentmindedly scribbled To my biggest fan, Pietro. He hastily did a bunch of others as well. The line was mostly teens: children of important people and make a wish kids who'd been brought backstage at the pro wrestling event by Thomas Chelish.

Sisyphus didn't know anything about the rest, but Chelish owned half the television stations. At least, the half that were worth watching, in Sisyphus's opinion. When Chelish gave an order to sign autographs, you signed autographs.

The angry man in the center of the ring quit screaming into the microphone and then threw it out of the ring. Sisyphus's entry music boomed over the speakers and the massive man rushed out and onto the stage, leaving behind Chelish and his line of fans.

Dark heavy metal blared and Sisyphus posed as a minor flare of pyrotechnics went off. He wore mostly dark leather with buckles and straps and he curled his lips up to brandish fanged surgical dental implants he'd had for years. A jumbo-tron behind him turned from his fanged visage and zoomed in on goth kids in the crowd who held up signs with his name on it.

Sisyphus may have been a heel, a villain character in the drama that was pro wrestling for most of his career, but he had a dedicated fan base, and he'd been around for decades—he was an icon. Those people erupted in cheers when he ran down the ramp and towards the ring where Pretty Boy Roy stood waiting, all baby oiled muscles and blond hair.

"I'm going to rip that stupid mustache off your face," Sisyphus howled as he slid below the ropes and traded blows with Roy almost immediately.

A turn on the ropes later, the two grappled center ring, bear hugging. Sisyphus towered above Roy by several inches.

Roy was more of an iconic wrestler and a classic face, or good guy character. The crowd went nuts as they traded positions setting up for each wrestler's signature move meant to finish their opponent's struggles.

"What are you doing?" Sisyphus growled as Roy slapped his hands away from him as he set up to perform his highly illegal variant of a pile-driver. "This ain't how we rehearsed it."

"Sorry," Roy growled, with no hint of remorse. "I talked to management last minute. They liked my idea better."

Sisyphus gave him a genuine shove, separating them by a step. He gave him a menacing glare. "This was supposed to be my time... I was gonna go out on top, retire with the belt."

Roy flashed him a smile. "Not anymore." And then he head-butted him, splitting his lips and drawing blood.

Sisyphus reeled, still barely reacting to the news, let alone Roy's sudden antics in the ring. Red dripped down his chin, slicking his chest and neck as Roy tripped him and rolled him into a surprised cradle maneuver and pinned him to the mat, where the ref slapped the ground three times, perhaps a little more quickly than normal.

Jumping to his feet, Roy leapt onto the turnbuckle and pointed at the cheering crowds while wearing a victorious grin.

Sisyphus stood. He curled his bloodied lips in a sneer. *Crowds always love blood—don't matter who draws it.*

He growled a bunch of juvenile curses as he slunk away back towards the locker rooms. Another of the up-and-coming personalities lifted his mirrored sunglasses and gave him finger guns while grinning manically.

"Dark and edgy wrestling personas are a thing of the past, brochacho. Adapt or die," the kid quipped.

Sisyphus gave him a flashy wrestler called Rocker, a look that could skin cats. He and his twin brother, Roller, stood with a member of the management staff discussing how the match was about to go down. The storyline was that the feuding brothers, each a half of the circuit's most popular tag team, would have an in-ring brawl, and then make up.

"Really?" Sisyphus wiped blood from his face as he complained to the manager. "We're going with Pretty Boy Roy and Rocker and Roller plot lines? Come on, Tim. This was supposed to be my last big run!"

Tim sent the younger athletes off towards the ring. "I gotta level with you, Jacob. You're a thing of the past—"

"I can still compete with any of these kids you bring in."

"Oh, I know," Tim said. "You're venerable. And you've stayed in good shape. But honestly, you don't jive well with the new blood. Most of em are creeped out by you. I keep getting reports of weird stuff in the locker room, back stage, wherever."

Tim looked Sisyphus up and down. "I thought this gothic, wizard, vampire schtick was a gimmick, man."

His rage boiled up deep within and Sisyphus licked the blood from his hand and snarled at him, more like an animal than a man.

"Whatever," Tim said, shaking his head. "I'm sitting ringside for this one. Good luck in retirement," he said sarcastically.

Sisyphus bared his teeth, but Tim had already left.

He muttered as he headed for the lockers. They were empty and mostly dark and so he withdrew a black candle from his gym bag and a few powerful texts he kept with him always.

"I'll show you," Sisyphus growled. He lit the candle. "I'll show you all!"

Minutes later, on live television, a hole opened up center-ring and the ropes collapsed as Rock and Roll grappled with each other. They yelped and fell into the crack just before the squared circled collapsed in on itself as if pulled by gravity. And then the ceiling and roof gave way overhead, obliterating the ring, the cameras, and everything in their immediate vicinity.

"No, Barbara," Clark hissed. "We are not going home. I don't care what the old man at the bait store said."

Barb crossed her arms in a huff. "Three dead campers over a week just sounds super suspicious to me."

Clark set his jaw. They'd only had to drive from their campgrounds to the crusty old bait store to get an over priced loaf of bed and a few other food items which Barb had forgotten to bring.

That had started a fight between them. Another fight. Clark was beginning to suspect she'd been sabotaging their entire vacation.

"It's bad enough we gotta eat this off brand crap, but let's not put too much stock in rumors from some old convenience store owner at the edge of nowhere. That guy was practically a Scooby Doo villain," he said.

Barb pouted as they pulled back into their campsite.

By the time they'd gotten back, the sky had turned dark already. Their fire was barely more than coals, since they hadn't tended it since starting it a few hours earlier.

"Jim? Jenn?" Clark called out to their neighbors in the site next to theirs. The group of four friends went back several years—they'd met on their honeymoons, actually—both couples had been married at about the same time and had much in common. "We got the food—now let's get those burgers cooking... Jim... Jimbo?"

Their tent was dark, and both sites were quiet.

"Clark?" Barb asked. Her voice wavered with fear.

"They probably just went hiking or something," Clark insisted.

A twig snapped nearby. Clark whirled. "Jim?"

Barb screamed as a furry figure tore through Jim and Jenn's tent. Long hair spattered with fur covered the humanoid creature.

Clark dove back into the car and hit the accelerator.

"Clark—Clark, get back here," Barb screamed at the bright red taillights as her husband sped off. "Clark, you asshole!"

And then she screamed again as he turned and spotted the murderer bounding down upon her.

CHAPTER TWO

The Prime Dimension...

"There!" Zabe shouted to his men. "They're coming in at our side!"

Explosions ripped through the western wall of the fortress—not at the main gate where the army had expected it! Shrapnel and debris scattered through the army's unprepared flank. The royal military had amassed at the castle's front gate, expecting an attack at the least durable barrier, but the enemy came in at the side walls instead and threw the plans into disarray.

Zabe barked orders to his troops atop the parapet and they swung the massive laser battery to target the encroaching enemy: the vyrm. The reptilian soldiers swarmed to the breach in the wall. These walls were supposedly impenetrable, and yet the warlock's troops had managed to rip them open with some new alchemy the vyrm forces brought from another dimension.

The scaly, humanoid race traveled from a forsaken dimension far beyond the Prime and brought their poison with them to besiege the Prime's capital. Enemy forces poured through the yawning hole in the bastion wall, trampling over the wounded. They violently dispatched those still resilient enough to resist.

Zabe whirled in a panic to assess the situation from his post high on the wall. The armor clad enemies crashed in waves against the royal forces as they streamed through the broken side-wall of the royal keep. His instincts tore at him. His first impulse was to drop from above and rush to aid his overwhelmed comrades.

His eyes darted to his father, Zahaben, master at arms and personal security chief to the royal family. Zahaben led the Guardian Corps: those charged with protecting the heirs of the Architect King and all the royal secrets. Stuck at the main entrance where they'd expected the brunt of the assault to occur, his father struggled to position the elite forces towards the newly drawn battlefront.

Zabe rejected his instincts and turned back to the laser turret. It pummeled the forces surging beyond the wall, flinging hot energy bursts which tore through the enemy. A fiery blast crippled a crude trebuchet in the distance. Scorched wreckage erupted near impact craters, ripping seams through the endless array of marauding vyrm. A black banner of their nega-god, Sh'logath, wavered and fell as debris cut down the standard bearers. The vyrm hissed defiantly as they collapsed.

Another detonation rocked the fortress' foundations. Dust flew up, caking Zabe's sweaty face as he struggled to keep his balance. He hesitantly stole attention from his post again and turned to the main gate. The royal forces had repositioned to defend against the ruptured wall of the castle flank.

Dire groans followed a minor eruption at the gate, and the immense front entry shifted on its hinges. An alchemical bomb eked destructive reagents in massive spidery webs of corrosion. The doorway crumbled into a heap of chunks burned by acerbic fire.

Zabe coughed as the acrid dust invaded his lungs even at this distance. His eyes searched eagerly for his father amongst the dust-borne silhouettes. Those seconds proved too long, and the raging battle demanded his full attention. He whirled back and gave the order for his troops to unload their full complement of munitions on the mass pressing in upon the bastions.

"But sir! They're too close to us!"

"Rain hell upon them! I know the risks, Wulftone," Zabe spat the order at his cousin, even as their entire rampart shook from another explosion. Such heavy damage to the battlefield at so little range might weaken the integrity of a wall that still afforded some protection to the castle. "All towers, full barrage!" He growled the order into his communications array. "Empty your reserves and then fall back! The perimeter is already lost to that snake. Protect the interior!"

Even as he spoke, Zabe's eyes locked on the enemy commanders at the edge of the battlefield; he put a scope to his eye to double check. Their leader, the inter-dimensional warlock, Nitthogr, and he were no strangers. The figure in the distinct crimson cloak could be none but the sorcerer; the tall and muscular vyrm to his side would likely be his chief general, Regorik. At this distance, even with the scope, it was impossible to tell, but he could swear that his enemy grinned at him from beneath his scaly red hood.

Nitthogr shimmered and suddenly disappeared. *No! He could be anywhere*, Zabe thought. His mind panicked only slightly as his eyes darted across the war-torn battlescape. He had to be somewhere nearby. For all the power of the crafty sorcerer, the arcane arts were still a kind of science, and likewise had rules to obey. Nitthogr was present somewhere—and likely very near!

The thundering of the tower defense cannons' heavy shelling matched the rapid beating in his chest. Zabe's heart sank deep into his gut. His metallic gauntlet clacked against the breastplate of his Guardian Corps' uniform as his fist rapped upon his breast and bowed slightly in salute. "Wulftone! You're in charge of the cannonade."

Wulftone gave him a nod and a serious look. Both knew that this might be the last time they saw each other alive. He turned back and barked orders to the men under his command, hoping to open a hole for his cousin to escape by.

Zabe drew the sword from across his back and checked the holstered sidearm strapped to his thigh. Then, with a whirl, he leapt from the ledge and hurled himself towards the frenzy below.

His emotions raged unchecked. He could only think of the safety of the Princess. Just before the vyrm army encircled them, he had been with her, asking her the most important question. Zabe had to make haste in order to arrive before the evil sorcerer who had long set his intentions upon the daughter of the Architect King. *I've got to get to Princess Bithia!*

Zabe whirled around the corner and quickly spun back the way that he had come. Vyrm soldiers flooded the passageway leading to the royal chambers. Smoke crawled along the ceiling, spilling upwards and seeping through the archways, nagging at Zabe's nostrils. The vyrm paid it no mind; oily fumes rolled off their scaly skin.

He peeked around the corner once more and counted them: too many! He steeled himself for a mad charge that would likely be his last service to the crown. Zabe exhaled a stiff huff; he straightened up, poised for a zealous dash.

"Psst!" A loud, distinct tone grabbed his attention.

Zabe caught sight of a hand motioning behind the edge of a broken and blackened portcullis. Clad in the colors of the Guardian Corps, the armored forearm insistently waved for him.

Cautiously, quietly, Zabe snuck behind the wall to join his comrade. Only once crouched safely behind cover did he recognize General Zahaben. "Father," he whispered, "what do we do?"

Zahaben jerked and tugged at the armor pieces covering his large forearms. He unstrapped a simple, leather wristband that was branded with a variety of their family sigils—the figure of the wolf branded most prominently. Zahaben flopped the simple yet precious heirloom onto his son's lap.

Zabe looked at his grim-faced father. He knew what it meant.

Zahaben stood and winced, skillfully masking any further admission of pain behind his tight lips. As chief of the royal guard, charged with protecting the monarchy, he had earned his position by both trial and birthright. In that moment, as he stood straight, battered and bleeding, yet determined, Zabe understood the meaning of duty and honor.

The elder checked the charge pack on his pistol and tore a thin piece of metal from the zipper on his boot. "I know what I have to do. But you, son," he glanced at his eldest from the corner of his eye as he worked, "you must find the princess. Rescue Bithia; preserve the royal line at all costs! If the line fails, falters, or if you fail, then all may be lost. We must keep the vyrm, especially that hybrid Nitthogr, out of the Chamber of Mysteries. The survival of the multi-verse depends on it."

They stood and faced each other for what seemed a long pause. Their moment ended abruptly when a nearby vyrm explosives unit overwhelmed a nearby blast door. The ground buckled and shook with the detonation; dust flakes and debris rained from the ceiling.

Zahaben picked up a length of metal wire from the ground and jammed the metal splinter into a tiny port on the blaster's charge pack. He put a palm upon his son's shoulder, ignoring the shrill whine his hand-cannon emitted. Zahaben nodded to his son, and then spun around the corner and charged into the enemy group, bowling over the surprised vyrm and scattering the squad. The whine peaked, chirping urgently as he fought them with his hands, sword, and whatever he could.

Zabe stood frozen and watched him chuck the complaining device into the thick of the crowd while slashing with his sword. The blaster exploded in a concussive burst, flinging smoldering vyrm warriors to the floor. Zabe finally looked away from the fray as his father took on twenty soldiers simultaneously in martial combat.

His father's last order repeated in his mind, and he darted down a nearby hall as stealthily as possible. His father's sacrifice would not be in vain.

Pressing onward through the castle grounds like a wraith, Zabe slashed through each pocket of resistance within the keep with cold, hard precision. They hadn't penetrated so deeply into the fortress yet, at least, not in significant numbers.

He sprinted across the observation deck he'd just cleared of vyrm troops and leapt across a yawning chasm that divided the defensive perimeter from the castle wall. Sailing across the opening, he fell several feet before colliding with the stonework of the tower. His hands grabbed a firm hold on the lattice-like vines that ensconced the spire.

Urgently, he scaled the vertical wall until he arrived at the level where Bithia's window overlooked the embattled stronghold. He worked horizontally until he verged upon her casement. He could see her there, standing rigidly, facing down some unseen enemy. Her eyes barely darted to meet Zabe's; he was certain she was aware of his presence.

Voices. The wind and sounds of the fighting below muddled the words, but he could hear the tone of them and recognize the notes of Bithia's distinct voice. It brimmed with defiance, so like her! *The warlock must have found her first!*

Zabe's eyes scanned the small, visible part of the room he had vantage of and spotted a small vanity mirror. The reflection showed a group of soldiers led by Nitthogr. Zabe's strong hands squeezed the vines in frustration. Rage swelled in his heart, urged him to fly into the room at her defense, and the wrist strap his father had given him seemed to burn with warm energy as it responded to his emotions.

As if Bithia knew exactly what he had in mind, her eyes darted to their corner once more. They warned him against that course of action. *There has to be another way.*

The breeze died just enough for Zabe to make out the ageless sorcerer's voice. "Take her to the dungeon." This time, he could not avert his eyes from the tragedy. Vyrm soldiers shackled the insubordinate princess and led her away.

Moments later, the room emptied and Zabe crawled into her room, seething with impotent fury. *There has to be another way.*

Claire Jones angled her smartphone to keep her best friend connected to the video stream. Despite living far from each other after high school, throughout college, she and Jackie kept in regular contact and spoke often.

"I'll send you links to the places we're going to go dress shopping at when you get here," Claire said.

"I can't wait," Jackie said, holding up her plane ticket so that the video camera picked it up.

A chime interrupted their call as Claire's calendar beeped at her. "Oh, I just remembered I've got to go to an interview."

Jackie quirked an eyebrow. "I thought you were happily unemployed? Something about being engaged to the rich and famous." She did her best impression of a snooty voice for the last sentence.

"Actually, I'm the one doing the interview," Claire said.

"Straight to the boss's chair. No time in the Mc-Trenches for you. Straight to McManagement."

Claire smiled. "I'll tell you a secret, but don't tell anyone. Not even James knows."

"I'm listening," Jackie said, holding her phone closer.

"There have been a bunch of murders around here lately. Mostly in the parks, usually by the campgrounds, wherever there is forest land and people. Have you heard of them—maybe keeping tabs on your folks?"

Jackie's face was grave. "You're not... you know?"

Claire narrowed her eyes. "Not what?"

"Oh, good Lord. I thought you were confessing to being a serial killer." Jackie breathed a sigh of relief.

"What? How could you think I was—"

"I've seen you mad, honey. I'd believe a confession," Jackie laughed.

"That was one time," Claire laughed off the time she'd lost her cool over something stupid in high school. She barely remembered it except that it involved a boy whose name she couldn't even recall any longer.

"No," Claire continued. "There have been Bigfoot sightings lately. A bunch of them. And a few of the witnesses got fleeting looks at the murderer—and they claim it was Bigfoot."

"Okay." Jackie stretched the word out with confusion.

Claire explained, "I started writing for *The Unexplained* in some of my free time."

"Claire Jones," Jackie said with equal parts pride and surprise, "you're a journalist... for a crackpot newspaper read by schizos and psychos. You're not turning into one of those tinfoil-hat-people, are you?"

She shook her head. "No. It started after I read the paper and saw some huge problems in a story, some kind of haunting story. It was easily explained, and so I reached out and told the editors as much. Before long, I wound up writing for them, explaining the likely causes behind local weirdness. But this... the Bigfoot murders? So far, I'm having trouble rationalizing anything."

Jackie laughed. "They'll make a true believer out of you yet. Claire Jones: ace reporter for *The Unexplained*."

"Oh, I dunno. I'm still super skeptical. And just because I think something is interesting doesn't mean I think it's true. Halloween is fun and I also like Christmas—but I don't believe in Santa Claus," she responded.

"Touche."

Claire shrugged. "But still, some things... the jury is out on. But I *definitely* don't use my real name when I write articles. It might make for bad publicity for James—last thing I need is more paparazzi concerns."

"Ohmygodyouright," her hurried words came out as one. "I just read about that—the incident at the restaurant."

Claire shrugged. "Just another hazard of dating the rich and famous," she mimicked Jackie's pretentious voice. "But I got to go."

Jackie said her goodbyes, and the call ended.

Earth...

Vikrum Wiltshire stood in front of a hot dog cart in front of Rockefeller Center. He paid the vendor and walked the remaining block to St. Patrick's Cathedral in downtown New York City. Wiltshire polished off the hot dog on his way and then sipped the coffee as he entered the massive, stone church and snuck into the compartment where he accessed the secret stairs that descended to the Red Order's New York City headquarters, a location known as the Red Keep.

Several years prior, Wiltshire had turned from police detective work to investigator of the paranormal. The Red Order was a secret society funded by the Vatican and with one purpose: to keep the paranormal away from the normal. Humankind wasn't prepared to mentally and emotionally deal with the knowledge that the universe was much bigger than our immediate surroundings... and that it included universes, plural, if one considered all the attached dimensional realities.

Atticus Sexton, Wiltshire's partner, sat in a chair with a hot cup of coffee of his own. It was early still, and he leafed through the mail. He mumbled something about it being too early in the morning to have a rational conversation.

Wiltshire raised his cup in salutary agreement. "Instructions from the Praetor, yet?"

Praetor Jon Russo was in charge of the United States' entire east coast. Russo was both their Vatican contact and their direct boss.

Wiltshire didn't mind having a boss—but he and Russo were never going to be good friends, something Wiltshire assume was connected to his background. Wiltshire's history was checkered, if anything, and he'd been a cop, not an altar boy. If it hadn't been for being pulled into the Order by Quintin Hall, a former detective for the Red Order, Wiltshire would be just one more unemployed former policeman.

"Oh hey," Sexton said. "Envelope from Quintin." He handed it to Wiltshire.

The package was a plain manila envelope. Inside, Wiltshire found a newspaper that read *The Unexplained*. He scanned a quick handwritten letter.

"What's he been up to lately?" Sexton asked. "I've heard nothing about him since he left the Order a few years back, before you joined."

"He's working privately," Wiltshire said, turning to the newspaper. The top headline read, *Bigfoot Murders Continue to Plague the Northland*. A sticky note clung to the paper with a note where Quintin had scribbled, I thought this might be up your alley.

A smart phone rang nearby. It was a dedicated line from Praetor Russo and it rested face up in a cradle so that they could video chat.

Sexton answered, and Russo's visage filled the screen.

Wiltshire and Sexton had completed their reports and all the busywork normally associated with wrapping up their most recent few cases, so Russo only had one reason to contact them: a new assignment. On the screen he lifted a print out of the digital files from *The Unexplained.*

"We don't often deal with cryptids," Russo said, "except for when they have paranormal elements, but I want you to look into this potential sasquatch event."

Wiltshire raised a brow. "Minnesota is a little out of our coverage zone."

Russo scowled. "I know that. I have my reasons."

Wiltshire's nostrils flared. *Because I said so* was never a good reason as far as Wiltshire was concerned, but he kept his mouth shut, regardless.

"And no contact with the local chapter of the Order," Russo insisted. A printer hummed and began queuing up as it received data from a connected network. "Your assignment is incoming by the usual channels."

Before either of Wiltshire or Sexton could ask any questions, Russo ended the connection.

"As friendly as ever." Sexton shrugged.

Wiltshire picked up the plane tickets as they printed and showed them to his partner. "Well, at least he didn't put us in coach. Business class, baby."

"That's basically the same as coach on almost all flights since I was a kid," Sexton pointed out.

"Yeah," Wiltshire sighed. "I'm just trying to take my mind off what Russo's instructions imply."

"No contact with local with the local chapter?"

Wiltshire nodded. "Whatever the reasons, it can't be good."

Chapter Three

The Prime...

Zabe scrambled through the muddy pit under the cover of night. He wore his family's crest, the symbol of Vangandra, strapped proudly around his wrist as he crawled behind a tall stack of supplies deep within the enemy encampment.

With the princess captured, the invaders knocked most of the fight out of the army, and they'd been able to coax many into surrendering. General Zahaben would have been embarrassed, but he was no longer with them.

Zane knew he couldn't attack the army head on. That would have gotten him killed without a plan, and something about the look Bithia had given him urged him to find another path. His path led him to secret passages only known to the royal family and their closest protectors: the Guardian Corps. The war had gutted the corps, and Zabe and his father were the only survivors as far as he knew.

I may be the last, he corrected his thoughts with grim determination and then slipped out of the secret passage, exiting the fortress wall.

The vyrm had control over the castle, but much of their army still remained in siege formation around the perimeter of their prize. They kept an additional buffer between the royal family's hereditary home and any rag-tag resistance groups that would surely form.

Zabe shook away the guilty thought that he ought to be leading that resistance. Surely they assembled even now in the highlands beyond the castle. He turned his eyes to the mountains. With the princess captured, maybe the Veritas would finally intervene? The mystic order had an army of their own, and they'd been recluses for generations now.

Bithia's rescue, however, was more important than fighting vyrm, though. It was his father's last order, and it was not an undertaking any militia could accomplish on its own. Reclaiming her would be delicate work, and he still had to survive the night.

He stepped lightly, cautiously, keeping to the shadows of the vyrm encampment and hugging the edges of the stacked boxes. Zabe keenly understood the gravity of his situation. One misstep and the entirety of the vyrm army would flock to him in a heartbeat.

Zabe saw his chance in the distance; a lone patroller in a vyrm ranger's cloak walked a lazy path that would inevitably meander past Zabe's hiding spot behind the muddy supply crates. Scooping up handfuls of the muck that he'd just crawled through, Zabe caked himself wherever he wasn't already covered in the dark, grimy stuff in order to better camouflage himself.

Hiding in the shadows, he remained perfectly still and waited for the guard to drift nearer. Zabe could see the vyrm from the edge of his eye; the soldier was also covered from the knees down in the pasty, tenebrous mud. As soon as he took a full step past, Zabe leapt out and silenced the enemy, choking him out and dragging the struggling vyrm out of sight.

Moments later, Zabe emerged from the darkness wearing a hood and cloak that identified him as a ranger of The Black's army. The black were the lowest caste of the vyrm species, but they were the largest group. They were the ones to throw in their lot with

Nitthogr. Most of the others, the tarkhūn, followed Nitthogr's brother, and the two had been embroiled in a civil war for ages.

Zabe's improved concealment let him travel quickly. He moved purposefully through the enemy tents, searching for the nondescript tabernacle of his chief enemy.

Skirting the perimeter of the tent, Zabe spotted the markings which identified a tent as Nitthogr's personal quarters.

Zabe's disguise didn't need to fool many enemies. Most of the important members of warlock's entourage had moved inside the castle, plying their wills toward whatever plans the dread sorcerer had devised this time. There were still low ranking vyrm to be wary of, however. And followers of the sorcerer had appetites for promotion within their ranks; they were hungrier and perhaps more vicious than any other soldier.

Zabe wasn't looking for a fight, though. He needed information, and conquerors rarely wasted time cleaning up during the aftermath of their battles. That was always a task for left for the proles: the lowest ranking members who chased scraps for approval.

Hopeful that Nitthogr's tent might hold some clue to his next step, Zabe sat several paces away from the tent flap, watching, waiting for his moment. He planned to slip inside and locate notes, strategies, anything that could give him an idea of Nitthogr's nefarious scheme as soon as he was sure the coast was clear. Those notes might show Zabe how he could rescue Bithia.

He saw a woman coming from a distance and knew exactly who she was: Caivev—a former ally.

Despite their victory, Caivev still moved stealthily through the grounds; a former member of the royal shadow guard, those habits did not die easily. She'd defected years ago, right before an entire regiment of corrupted shadow guards attempted a coup under Nitthogr's direction.

Zabe narrowed his eyes at the raven haired woman. His father had foiled the plot, for sure, but casualties had mounted high, nonetheless. Caivev had been part of the enemy's inner circle ever since, and she'd make a better source of information than ransacking Nitthogr's tent.

He rolled to his feet and walked a lazy intercept course. Moments later, he fell in step two paces behind her. Mid-step, he made sure he had firm footing and then pounced towards her, silently slipping an arm around her neck. Caivev struggled for a few seconds, thrashing in the mud.

Zabe cast a wary glance in all directions as the hold rendered her unconscious. Relieved that he hadn't been seen, Zabe snatched the cords off a tent flap and tied her up. He knew of a safe place nearby, and he dragged his prisoner off to the nearby cave.

Zabe splashed his prisoner with the cold, bitter water he'd collected from a pool in the deep, rocky cave. She groaned and thrashed.

He let the water drip down her face; everything looked black. He dared not light a torch, but he could surmise that the fetid seepage which formed the pools had probably drained from the vyrm army's hastily dug latrines.

"I'm going to take the gag out in a minute." He warned in a stern voice, "You're going to tell me the truth. You will accurately answer all my questions. If you don't, things won't remain so pleasant for you. He yanked the gag down her chin. She spat and gagged; her stomach retched.

"Who are you?" she croaked into the darkness. "We have everybody of importance already taken care of! Nitthogr's plan is fool-proof! None remain who are capable of stopping what has been thrust into motion!"

"I'm glad you're so chatty, Caivev."

"I recognize your voice. You're Zahaben's son."

A pause in the darkness.

"I'll take your silence as a confirmation."

"What is Nitthogr's plan?" Zabe asked.

Silence.

"What is Nitthogr's plan?" Zabe asked again, calmly.

"Look at you. Keeping all that rage in check. Daddy would be proud. And where is he now?"

"What is Nitthogr's plan?" Zabe asked. He couldn't keep all the tension out of his voice this time, his tone rumbled more insistently.

"Your father was the same, you know. He single-handedly dismantled an entire squad inside the keep. Clever man; rigged his blaster to blow and took out many vyrm before they even knew he was there." She paused just long enough to test if she'd hooked him with the story. "It was the same in the end... in the interrogation rooms. He stayed calm until the end."

The blackness flashed with light. Caivev's head rocked back as Zabe's blow struck her from the dark. She laughed and then spat, tasting blood.

Something wet and hard hit Zabe's face and stuck to his cheek; she'd spat on him. He wiped the spittle off and turned the object over in his fingers: one of her molars. He took a little pride in that.

"There's that rage. Everyone knows it. Your father knew it well. But he so rarely uncaged it. He couldn't, not as the wearer of his crest. Do you wear your father's wristband? He did not wear it when we found him. Can you control your emotions as well as he, or will you unleash the beast of Vangandra?"

"What is Nitthogr's plan?" He ignored whatever distraction she had tried to feed him.

"I'll give it up," she toyed. "But only because you can't possibly stop him. And also because the warning beacon embedded in my tooth activated when you knocked it out. I'm curious to see if my rescue arrives before I can share all the gruesome details."

Her voice echoed off the wall, and she spoke loudly and clearly, trying to echo-locate Zabe's position based on the subtle shifts in tone. She couldn't discern it. He'd either fled or been more adept at stealth than she'd ever given him credit for.

"Nitthogr's going to use her up, you know: the princess. He wants what he's ever wanted, control of the Tesseract—domination of all the aligned realms. And he'll force a marriage to get it! The sealed royal chamber of power and secrets will only open to one with both the will and the blood to do it. If your princess has the blood, but lacks the will, that makes it obvious! This contingency has been running for years, you know. The sorcerer is a patient one; he will eventually gain access to the Architect King's cache—even if he must marry the princess and wait for it. His future child could grant him access, you know."

"But the royal blood, the arcane element that seals their power, will not pass to an heir without marriage—and Bithia would die before she marries him!"

She grinned in the blackness. His voice came from far off. He'd bet his evasive skills against the clock.

"But what if she loves him? What if a child is born before her Prime spirit passes from one body and bonds to a new one of Nitthogr's choosing? The child could be his," she cackled.

She heard footsteps in the distance. "Do you really think you stand a chance against a plan ten years in the making?"

"One would have to be sick to love that monster," Zabe spat.

The words hung in the air. It was no secret to those in the court that Caivev pined for the twisted warlock; it was the catalyst to her fall.

"The more Bithia hates him, the more her non-prime variant will love him," she stated with a mocking, sing-song voice. "The variant wears an amulet."

The Dimensional Inversion Pendant! Zabe realized its theft a decade ago must have been tied to Nitthogr's long-term plans.

"He will marry the earth girl, and after their child comes, Nitthogr will bring his wife here and then kill the princess. Bithia's spirit will take hold of the earth girl, and then she will be the prime and the child will be an heir."

A light flashed! Blinding in its brilliance, it washed everything in white illumination as a troop of vyrm guards swarmed the chamber of the cave. Flares burned through the veil of darkness, maintaining a constant but low level visibility. Chaos ensued; vyrm scrambled through the chamber. Some wielded guns and others held blades in preparation for whatever scenario they might encounter.

The only thing they found was Caivev. Dirty and bleeding, she sat tied on the stony floor. They helped her up as she scanned the ill lit cavern for her captor. Crevices and fissures broke off at many random junctures.

It was not likely they would find him, at least, not immediately, and not in these caves. "Go ahead and run," she hissed, hoping Zabe could still hear him. "There is no chance that you can save her, now."

Zabe stalked the edges of the city, now overrun with vyrm. The city had mostly emptied out with its citizens thrown into prisoner camps, where they'd likely be tortured and killed to try and force Bithia to bend to Nitthogr's will.

If what Caivev had said was true, it explained the sorcerer's long absences these last several years. Nitthogr was an expert at traveling the multiverse and whenever he was absent, Regorik or the liches, vyrm with psychic abilities, directed The Black. Many of them were also arcane practitioners to some degree.

Bithia was also a powerful psychic—far more advanced than anything the vyrm had thrown at them over the years. *She must have gleaned the details from their minds when they captured her—it's why she warned me off—hoping I'd stop the snake's plan. She wants me to go to the forbidden realm and save this earth girl!*

He crept across the roof of an archaic building. The immense, multi-level villa stood as a testament to the Prime's architectural tastes. He rolled his feet gently so that the clay roof tiles wouldn't click and crack, alerting the guards posted below.

Peering over the edge, he spotted the two sentries posted near the front door of the museum. They stood barely alert, as expected after days spent guarding the tactically insignificant location. Even posting guards here might have been a show of force by Nitthogr as the armies of The Black spread out across the countryside following the capture of the capital. Guarding ancient, artistic relics and historic documents of The Prime made very little sense except to demonstrate that the vyrm's takeover was utterly complete. The historical records would likely be destroyed once the takeover was complete, anyway.

Standing resolute as a stone gargoyle, Zabe perched on the ledge and waited for his prey to move close together. They drew close for a moment, undoubtedly sharing some joke at the expense of the royal family or making a derogatory jest at Princess Bithia's honor.

His keen ears picked up the conversation. "It's the new TRX718 cellular disruptor I told you about." The guard brandished a matte black pistol. "Very limited production—very expensive. Twice the energy cycling rate and larger battery: bigger boom." He fiddled with the weapon's components. "It's not standard, but I've wanted one of these babies for so long. There's no way I was leaving it behind during the assault—"

Zabe pounced over the edge and hurtled two stories towards the ground. He crashed down upon the two guards, and they collapsed under the force of their shadowy assailant. Their heads cracked against the milled stone tiles of the reception area with thunderous force.

Swinging to his feet, Zabe skulked to the door and reached for the handle. *Locked.* He rifled through the enemy's belongings until he located the key. Zabe also picked up the hefty TRX718 and slipped it into his waistband.

The door opened silently, and Zabe hopped from shadow to shadow, skulking through the corridors and slinking around the displays. He cast his eyes to a giant mural and the relics adorning the hall; they had taught a million schoolchildren about the origins of reality, the multiverse, and beyond. Zabe's eyes caught hold of the grand creator, depicted in mosaic form. He appeared as a mighty, benevolent humanoid, giving the royal family the keys to the Chamber of Mysteries: the most secure location in all creation, and the origin point of the Tesseract. Zabe sent up a quick, silent prayer to the Architect King and continued through the dark.

He ducked into a wing branching off the middle-histories section. The archway had the title of "The Dark Years," and a free-standing sign warned sensitive visitors of the graphic content.

Zabe slipped past the bio-summaries of Basilisk and Nitthogr; his heart rate thumped high as he skulked around the full-sized replica of Nitthogr. He remained ever watchful, as if the realistic mannequin might spring to life at any moment.

Deeper inside, full wall-sized images from the Syzygyc War splashed across the walls: images of an entire planet laid waste with its population incinerated or turned to living stone. Nearly all surviving members of the reptilian dimension's race, the vyrm, pledged fanatic loyalty to the Brothers of the Apocalypse. Images showed the power of the great and vast vyrm army. Most terrifying of all, however, was an artist's rendering of the Tesseract's membrane being pressed in upon by Sh'logath, "The Great Devourer." An actual, grainy image taken in The Desolation inset from the diagram sent a chill up Zabe's spine. He shuddered and continued; he knew he was on the right path for what he sought.

At the nexus of all the histories rested a heavily secured glassine enclosure. Leaned upon a display rack lay a bundle of papers ripped out from the Grimmorium Nitthogr prior to the Syzygyc War; in fact, their removal may have been the premiere cause of the event. Displays pointed out the danger of inter-dimensional travel, pioneered by Nitthogr prior to his fall from grace as the chief cleric to the King, over a thousand years ago.

Recognizing the danger inherent in his writings, they had been taken from Nitthogr's personal collection. The knowledge was too dangerous to remain at large; they were an easily understood guide to traveling the corridors of the multiverse, a map of sorts.

The verdict to rip out the writings had sent the traveler-cleric into a spiral of depression and madness: a corruption already begun by his older brother, the founder of the Cult of Sh'logath. He was already a fallen monk who betrayed The Architect King's service long prior.

None could have known that the depraved warlock had committed his records to memory. Hundreds of years later, he would later fling wide the gates during the celestial alignment, pouring vyrm armies out in the first sortie of the war: a battle that would last nearly another century, renaming an entire dimensional reality as Desolation. The Syzygyc War pitted the Prime reality against the Brothers of the Apocalypse, unrelenting until a dark bargain had been struck in the reemergence of the Architect King himself.

For many generations, this forbidden text, scrawled by Nitthogr's own hand, had been secreted away inside the Chamber of Mysteries by the royal family. Only in recent centuries had it been made into an object of archaeology: a historiological warning to those who would dabble with the corrupting influence of Sh'logath: Agod of Destruction.

Zabe examined the case where the forbidden writings lay. For nearly an hour he tried to break past its security, constantly rejected by the sophisticated protocols programmed into the near-sentient system. Finally, frustrated, he slid the TRX718 out of his waistband and dialed in a low power setting. Zabe put the barrel up to the security interface and pulled the trigger. An electric crackle of energy erupted from the weapon; sparks and shrapnel blew out from the hole and the corner of the enclosure broke open.

He reached in and snatched the chapter of the profane text. Tucking it away alongside his powerful pistol, he promptly fled the building, only pausing long enough to locate his next destination. He cross-referenced a crude star-chart made in his enemy's handwriting. Within hours, he could use the texts to flee The Prime for Earth.

Earth...

Wiltshire and Sexton stood near the policeman at the edge of the crime scene. The officer hung up his phone and shouted over the crunch of tires on gravel behind him. "The Chief says to let them work," he pointed at the two investigators.

"Actually, hang on a minute." The officer rummaged through his squad car and located a pair of clip on ID badges. They were laminated printouts of a badge with the brightly lettered words *special consultant.* "These should get you around the crime scene without too much hassle."

"Thanks," Wiltshire said, clipping his to his chest as a second van pulled into the dirt drive near the campsite.

"Looks like the feds showed up," the cop said. "About time. This last one makes the kill count nine." He nodded towards the crime scene.

A van door slammed shut, and a slender woman stepped out. She looked like she was in her mid twenties, maybe. Her skin was pale and her dark hair hid much of her face.

"Crap," Wiltshire muttered as the woman approached.

She stepped between the Red Order investigators and the cop. And then she yanked off their laminated badges as she handed over her identification to the officer. "Special Research Division," she said, as if that was enough authority to do whatever she wanted. "This is my crime scene now."

"The chief already cleared them," the cop informed her. "They are—"

"They are not getting in," she barked, giving the policeman a withering glare. He nodded, offered the investigators an apologetic glance, and then backed away to secure the border with more yellow caution tape.

"Vivian," Wiltshire greeted her. "It's been a little while."

"Not long enough," she growled.

Vivian stood there staring at them. A few moments passed in awkward silence.

"Are you really not going to let us in there?" Sexton asked. "Even after the incident with, *you know?*"

"The werewolf," Wiltshire spoke in hushed tones. He and Sexton agreed they would not speak of the incident after it had happened. They'd done what was necessary to protect the public, *and* the unfortunate soul who'd born the curse.

Vivian merely glared a second longer. "No."

Wiltshire held her gaze. "Okay, then. We're gonna make a few calls in the meantime."

"Who are you gonna call? it's not like you can get a warrant," Vivian scoffed.

"Oh please," Wiltshire said. "It's not like the Red Order bothers with warrants. The stuff we deal with goes way beyond humans and their petty rules. You know that."

"You're not getting through to mess with my investigation."

"The Order's got lots of resources," Wiltshire said. "It'd be unwise to turn them down."

The Red Order was a kind of secret investigative society. They were secret players with interests in many areas. But while they didn't have direct authority, they had the backing of the Vatican, and as such, they could pull a lot of strings.

Vivian made a shooing motion. "Good luck with all those resources... elsewhere."

Wiltshire shrugged as Sexton withdrew his phone and began dialing. "Most of all, their resources are favor and good will with the one-percenters." He joined Sexton as they walked back towards their car until they could get clearance. He called back to Vivian, "And everyone's got a boss somewhere up the chain of command."

Franklin caught a glimpse of himself as the museum's glass enclosure briefly reflected his image under the flashlight beam. "Momma always said a woman loves a man in uniform," he mumbled to himself. "At least a security guard's outfit is better than a burger flipper's."

He panned a swath of light from left to right across the dusty exhibits as he meandered through the labyrinth of sarcophagi, ancient monuments, and glass-boxed artifacts. He normally did rounds only out of sheer boredom and habit. He thought that doing them might be yet another way he had lied to himself: it was the only task that made him feel like he had any real significance to his employers.

"Who would rob a museum anyway?" he asked aloud. Franklin always assumed that the sort of person who robbed museums was probably independently wealthy already. *She could just buy whatever she had her mind and heart set upon.* He assumed all museum thieves would be women. Cute women. He sucked in his gut the next time he caught his reflection. *Maybe I'll get lucky and find an intruder, then? It'd do wonders for my love life.*

Still, despite his braggadocio, something started to buzz in the back of his mind. He thought he heard the shuffle of feet in the dark as he neared the research labs. His hubris suddenly fled.

"Man," he muttered under his breath. "Why did I ever pick up this stupid night shift?" he swung the beam from his flashlight in a wide arc. His breath came shallow, now, as he held half of it in. "Oh yeah, to pay for my wildly expensive college classes," he reminded himself, while also chiding his younger version for partying away his first three semesters at the University—the kind of lifestyle that landed him in extra courses and with no student aid.

He shuffled slowly towards the language research pod. Franklin's peripheral vision kept playing tricks on him; shadows seemed to loom just outside his blind spot every time he turned his head. A single bead of hot sweat rolled down his right temple.

That internal buzzing kept niggling at the edge of his consciousness. Something was not quite right.

His instincts spun and tightened his guts; he stepped gingerly into the document room. That buzzing—his heartbeat thumped in his ears—if there was an intruder, she must be very near! His eyes jumped from shadow to shadow. Franklin slapped the light switch just as his senses locked onto the ethereal, humanoid form he was sure had invaded. Illumination ripped through the darkness with all its fluorescent glory.

Nothing. Shadows. Desks piled high with notes, books, and research materials.

Franklin spat a giddy sigh and his arms tingled with the aftermath of the adrenaline surge. Finally releasing the full contents of his lungs, he felt ridiculous for chasing ghosts through the night. He turned with a chuckle, reaching again for the switch.

A man cloaked in a red hooded robe suddenly barred his path. Franklin's endorphins coursed through his veins in an instant; his heartbeat nearly deafened him. He was poised for action, but Franklin couldn't move—couldn't even breathe! The intruder's glowing, yellow eyes had fixed upon him so fiercely that the security guard fell under his utter control. Even breathing was impossible without the stranger's permission.

The mysterious figure regarded Franklin with curiosity as he walked a slow circle around his prisoner. "You are not Gerald," his gravelly voice stated the obvious.

Franklin's eyes pleaded for mercy. His lips locked shut and his chest burned under the asphyxiating gaze.

With a wave of his finger, he released Franklin's lungs. He looked over the guard's body for some identifying mark, yet ignored the faux gold nametag. "And you are not one of my other Heptobscurantum."

Air rushed into his chest with a wheezing gasp. He coughed, "Gerald called in sick."

"Most unfortunate." He paid him no further mind, leaving the guard immobilized. He shuffled through the stacks of ancient manuscripts, papyri, and books on the research benches. The intruder worked methodically, but remained nonchalant about his prisoner. He spoke in a rhetorical tone. "I'm looking for something. A book that once belonged to me. Something that was stolen from me by my brother... long, long ago."

"Who are you?" Franklin asked, against his better judgment.

The invader had a sudden look of delight as he uncovered an old manuscript. He pushed the nearby materials away and gently dusted off the book labeled Grimmorium Nitthogr. Lazily leafing through the pages, he smiled at each turn. He frowned ever so slightly as he fingered the slight gap where a swath of pages was missing. Caressing the tome's wound, he bit back his rage at the defilement of the ancient text; it contained information he didn't need at the moment, however—information he'd pioneered millennia ago—forbidden knowledge he'd acquired at great expense.

Franklin could feel the air crackle with magic. He hadn't believed in it until now—when it suddenly found root and blocked his lungs.

The intruder took the heavy, leather bound volume and slipped it within his crimson robes. Leaning close, he whispered, "I am

Nitthogr," and then he was gone, vanishing, and taking with him the poor security guard's ability to breathe.

Chapter Four

"Ugh, why don't you cheer for a real sport?" Vivian rolled her eyes in disgust as she plowed her way into Claire's apartment in the early morning hours. Claire had barely opened the door to her apartment, and Vivian shoved a box of Krispy Kreme donuts and the morning paper into Claire's hands and walked in like she owned the place.

Wiping the crust away from her eyes, Claire untangled the strands of hair kinked into the fine chain around her neck. The strange, locket-like pendant had never left her neck. Not even for sleep.

"Who even subscribes to the printed newspaper anymore?" Vivian muttered.

Claire had just barely gotten out of bed; she shook off the comment about her tattered Minnesota Vikings pajama pants. They had been the last gift she'd ever received from her mother before she passed away several years ago. Claire wasn't always late to rise, but she'd dreamed so vividly last night, and rising before the doorbell had proven difficult.

She scowled and tossed the pastry box onto her counter top. *Another one of Vivian's subtle plans to sabotage my wedding... making me too fat for my dress.* Claire only barely tried to hide her displeasure that Vivian was the first bridesmaid to arrive for the wedding planning party. She was only a bridesmaid because her brother was the groom. *Sometimes you have to take one for the family*, her father had told her via telephone a week ago. If she'd been less diplomatic and had her own way, only Jackie would have been a wedding attendant.

Vivian had never quite gotten along. They'd known each other only a little in their high school days, but they hadn't moved in the same circles. Vivian had been something of a bully, in fact, and so the swollen spot on her cheek where it looked as if she'd been smacked in the face brought her a little joy.

I know she's got some kind of top-secret kind of government job. Maybe someone decked her in the face?" Claire smiled. *But then again, she's probably just some kind of tax enforcer and paper pusher—but still... maybe someone decked her in the face.*

Claire flipped through the newspaper absentmindedly, stopping when she recognized a photo. "Hey, I know that guy!" She turned to Vivian as she spoke, but Vivian didn't pay her any attention as she organized the wedding periodicals scattered haphazardly on Claire's coffee table. Claire prattled on anyway, partly to spite Vivian.

"It says he was murdered last night in the museum." She scanned further. "It happened just down from my dad's office! That's where I've seen him before."

"Good thing Daddy's away on that archaeological dig, hmm?" She didn't even look at Claire as she spoke.

Something that Claire had learned about her soon-to-be sister-in-law was that she always payed attention. Claire was pretty sure, though, that she couldn't see her scowling at her back. A few years older than her, they'd attended the same high school. Now, Vivian worked for some obscure government agency that Claire knew nothing about. She was pretty sure Vivian preferred it that way.

"He worked in the same wing near Dad's office," she continued. "The coroner ruled it a homicide; a hand print on his throat makes it look like he was choked and he died of asphyxiation, but..." she trailed off.

"But?"

The doorbell buzzed. Claire turned to answer.

"But there was no crushing damage to his neck. Just the hand print. No other trauma. That's weird, right?"

"Not as weird as your morbid obsession with forensic analysis. Maybe back off on the CSI marathons?"

Claire rolled her eyes at what might have been a friendly ribbing, as if Vivian had ever acted friendly. She opened the door.

"Yay!" Jackie leaned in for a hug, practically falling through the door to squeeze Claire into her bubbly embrace. Jackie caught a glimpse of her disheveled, yawning friend. "Oh my God. You haven't had any coffee yet, have you?"

Claire only grimaced in reply to her ever-peppy friend. She'd been waiting for Jackie to arrive for days now.

Jackie held up a single digit to indicate she should wait a moment. Jackie spun around and bent to get a drink tray she'd set on the floor outside the apartment door as she'd adjusted her luggage. She happily turned back with a smile that betrayed the early morning hour.

"I got you an extra shot to help you deal with—Oh hi, Vivian!" she exclaimed. Jackie squeezed past Claire and into the apartment.

Claire smiled as she took one of only two cups from the cardboard cup holder. Her best friend since high school knew the rules well: true friendship meant an unspoken alliance against anyone who didn't properly appreciate your best friend.

"I smell doughnuts!" Jackie snatched up the box and raised her drink in salute. "Say what you want about Seattle," she referenced her original home state, "but they've got nothing on Caribou." She'd spent her high school years with Claire before relocating back west for college, even though her family remained in the area.

"Ugh." Vivian rolled her eyes. "But the snow?"

Claire smiled subversively as she sipped her giant sized Turtle Mocha. Vivian always complained about the cold, like she was some kind of reptile; Claire hoped that one day she'd up and relocate to a warmer climate. "Oh, I don't know." She walked to the patio door and opened it to the late-spring morning air. She left it open intentionally and glimpsed Vivian pulling her arms around her. "I've always liked it."

Gazing across the skyline, she pondered how Duluth was unlike the larger metropolitan areas; it existing only minutes away from actual wilderness. It offered many of the comforts of a tiny city, but without the soullessness she felt engulfed by whenever she visited Minneapolis or worse, Chicago. Those were jungles of concrete, but she preferred the adventure of the real wild. Even if that notion resided mostly in her head; she'd rarely left the city since beginning college, and before then her experiences mostly centered on helping her father at archaeological sites which were rugged, but there was no real danger. Her father would never bring if that had been the case.

She took another deep, satisfying sip from her cup and leaned over her railing, gazing out at the cold bay the city rested upon. Claire took in the morning view; traffic had not yet awoken in her part of the city. She glanced down and did a double take.

A wild-eyed and bedraggled homeless man stared up at her. She looked away when their eyes met, but caught sight of him again from her peripheral vision. He didn't even try to hide his gaze; he stared at her for long moments while Claire pretended to focus on other things. She finally locked eyes with him again, hoping he would notice the stern look on her face and turn away.

As their eyes met, Claire's plan backfired. Her nerves failed; she backed away, discomfort overwhelming her. Blushing, she retreated back inside her apartment. "Jackie, I've got to tell you about this crazy dream I had last night." She tried changing the subject of her inner dialogue to ignore her little defeat on the terrace. But still, something about the man rang uncannily familiar in her memories.

"Oh, I love dreams," Jackie said, stuffing the last bite of pastry into her mouth. "Was it a hot one?" She winked.

With a slight nod, Claire glanced across the room. "Yeah. But remind me later. After lunch." Nodding at her nemesis on the couch, she picked up a bridal magazine and yellow legal pad, hoping Jackie would understand her subtle plea for privacy. It might have partly been due to the content of the dream: she hadn't dreamt of James, her fiancé last night—a fact which both embarrassed and intrigued her—real "best friend" kind of material. Scribbling at the top of the tablet the topic: *Wedding Plans,* she said, "We've got a lot to do for now."

Vivian stood abruptly and walked towards them. Claire blanched as if she'd just been caught with her hand in the cookie jar. Her soon-to-be-sister-in-law bit her lower lip as she scanned the screen of her phone. "I got a text from work. They're making me run to... a thing."

She didn't say much. Vivian simply headed for the door. And once she was gone, the mood suddenly improved.

And then Jackie cocked her head. "I thought she worked for the government. Should I, you know, call my insurance agent or something?"

Vikrum Wiltshire examined the body. It lay in pieces within a tent, yanked apart with the head and torso cast aside to bleed out without its limbs. Little was left of a tent. The camping structure was little more than a tattered mess of anti-moisture canvas and busted fiberglass poles.

Blood dripped off the fabric scraps and spattered the grass and bracken near the tent. A fire had dwindled to nothing but smoldering coals overnight.

Atticus Sexton stood several feet away, taking photos and jotting notes.

"Are you guys almost done?" Vivian growled with her arms crossed over her breasts. She was evidently unhappy that Wiltshire and Sexton had gone over her head and called her director.

Wiltshire waved her off as he stared at the grisly scene. Using a pencil, he played with the edges of the flesh where the body had been dismembered.

"Hey," Vivian yelled at Wiltshire as he got down on his hands and knees and prodded the joints with a pencil, poking at the edges where synovial fluid made the joint infinitely slippery.

"I don't care if my director gave you jerks clearance to investigate in tandem with the Agency or not—but you can't just desecrate a corpse!" Vivian barked.

"Investigate," Sexton responded. "Investigate the corpse. None of this is blasphemous... at least, not beyond what's been done already."

Vivian's nostrils flared. "I don't care. If you want to muck about with the corpse, you can go downtown with the coroner."

"That's okay," Wiltshire said in his British accent. He stood up. "We're done here. I've seen what I need to."

Vivian stared at him. A few moments of awkward silence passed. "And?" she finally asked. "Are you going to share your assumptions?"

"Are you going to share yours?"

Her eyes narrowed. "The department is not in the habit of giving out that kind of information."

Wiltshire shrugged. "I guess turnabout's fair play, then, but I'll play nice."

"Wonderful. You're a testament to diplomatic relations between our countries," Vivian hissed.

"He's an American," Sexton pointed out. "He emigrated with his family years ago."

"Whatever," she said. "Out with it."

Wiltshire nodded. "The Red Order got wind of rumors up here. Bigfoot on killing spree, they said. And that's why *you're* here, isn't it, Miss Shianan?"

"Agent Shianan," Vivian corrected. "And no. I'm here, coincidentally."

"Mmhmm," Wiltshire rubbed his jaw and made a disbelieving sound. He leveled with her. "This is supposed to be a sasquatch murder. It's not."

"Yeah, well, maybe tell those guys over there." Vivian motioned to a small cluster of eye witnesses who huddled together sipping hot drinks in the cool, morning air.

Wiltshire and the others quieted enough to hear them give detailed descriptions of the cryptid that had viciously torn their friend to pieces. It matched the stereotypical description of a sasquatch. Vivian headed towards her crew, who debriefed the witnesses.

She called back over her shoulder as she went, "I'm glad your investigation has ended. Now, how about you go back to New York and get out of my hair?" The words made a question, but it sounded more like an order.

Sexton sighed. "We're not going anywhere, are we?"

Wiltshire shook his head. "No, we are not."

"Thank God Vivian had to go do a work thing," Jackie laughed. "She really is the worst!"

"I know." Claire matched her giggle. "I don't appreciate being made fun of." She impersonated the flat tone of her fiancé's sister.

Jackie laughed so hard she snorted. She quickly covered her nose; her eyes watered. "I don't know how she keeps her face so blank and expressionless. I don't know how you can do such a good impression, either!"

"Oh, easy," she laughed. "I binge watched a bunch of Kristen Stewart movies last week."

"Yeah, I figure that's the only qualifying talent that got Vivian her job with the CIA, or FBI, or whatever it is she works for. What is her title? Special Research Division Consultant? Her title sounds pretty meaningless, if you ask me."

Claire nodded, politely laughing. Despite the slight lingering chill, they sat in the outdoor seating area of a restaurant in the trendy waterfront district. Her eyes, however, darted back towards the traffic. Something felt off, like she was being watched.

"Honestly, I understand we didn't know her very well in high school because of the age difference, but we knew enough: she had a super-hot, semi-famous half-brother, and she was a shallow, soulless vampire of a human being. Ohmygodyourright!" She covered her mouth in a mock gasp. "She *is* Kristen Stewart!"

Claire laughed, despite the distracted feeling in her mind. And then her eyes spotted *him*. The shaggy man: the homeless wanderer from outside her apartment building. He stood next to the bus stop, watching the small crowd in her direction. Her eyes fixed on him like lasers for a long moment.

"Claire. Claire? Earth to Claire?"

She shook her head and looked back at Jackie. "Huh?" She realized her friend had been talking for a while and she'd zoned out. "Sorry, this bum across the street was staring at me."

"Oh, is he cute?" she blurted out, leaning across the table for a better view.

Claire looked back, but he was gone.

"Well, if he *is* cute, send him my way. I still have a plus-one to fill for your wedding, and Tinder is only full of creepers. Say, when is James coming back to town, anyway?"

Night came early, but not as early as Jackie's snores. She'd fallen asleep on Claire's couch, even though she had intended to return to her parents' home for the duration of her stay. They both knew it was likely that she'd sleep most nights on Claire's couch, and Claire had prepared accordingly. The television's volume remained barely audible; neither had paid much attention to their *Say Yes to the Dress* Netflix marathon, which still flickered on the nearby screen.

Claire glanced sidelong at her best friend and smirked. It was good that she'd come back for the summer. They hadn't had much time together since college; there was always something else vying for attention: boys, education, careers, possibly graduate school, but she felt confident that nothing could ever truly come between them. They'd always be connected.

She glanced at the TV and wondered if she felt as deeply connected to James, too. *Maybe I'm just in love with the idea of being in love?* She asked herself the honest, hard question. *A former professional athlete, turned celebrity actor... what's not to love about him? But am I in love, or do I just want to be married to a good option?* Her private reflections stretched long, penetrating her deepest fears and hopes. Was she making her best choice? Is a good choice always necessarily the best one? Claire groaned into a pillow. *I think I've been reading too much Jane Austen... freaking Darcy is ruining the curve for the rest of mankind.*

On the counter nearby, her phone vibrated repeatedly, indicating a phone call. The device's insistent buzz snapped her out of the reverie.

Claire pushed those momentary doubts and thoughts far from her and chalked them up to cold feet. She dispelled them with a smile and quick thought of the ways her husband would make her happy. She reached for the phone, already knowing it would be her father. Most of her other friends would simply text her, and James was still filming a piece on the west coast which had him tied up with his busy schedule.

"Hello daddy," she answered. Claire could tell that the signal was weak by the laggy quality of his voice.

"I was just checking in to see if everything was okay? I mean, I'm sure there is no danger, but Professor Jecima told me about a security guard who was murdered in the museum."

Claire reassured him that everything was okay. He tended to worry more when he was far away and couldn't respond to emergencies. But that would be her new husband's job, anyway... as if anyone could ever be such a vigilant protector as a father over his only daughter.

"It's all so very mysterious," he commented. "The murderer left so many priceless items behind; he or she only stole an ancient text that Professor Jecima had been decoding, the Grimmorium Nitthogr he'd called it. He figured it was the earliest work of some ancient religious fiction—that or it must've been from another planet." Her father chuckled nervously. "It referenced a being of immense power called the Sh'logath. It was all so very Lovecraftian, and I helped with the research... I found some carvings that may have been a cipher.

"It's mythology and theology doesn't match any others from any time-frame or any culture known to man. Probably why Jecima made the alien joke. We'll never know, I guess. He'd only just begun his translations, really; it's a shame. And too bad about Franklin. He was an okay kid."

As he digressed from the tragedy, Claire asked, "How is everything going on the dig?"

"It's okay, but I thought it more important to call and talk about what was happening in the land of the living instead of the realms of the dead."

She chuckled. He always talked like that. Even if he let his work consume him at times, especially in those years following her mother's passing, he'd always made it a point to stay connected to family. He valued the things that were important to Claire—even when those things weren't really all that significant. She smiled and reflected on that between his laggy, long distance questions about wedding plans.

He reassured her that they would talk again soon. She promised to pick a flattering color scheme so he could hit it off with the single ladies at the wedding dance. He vowed not to dance, unless the musicians played Beyoncé. They both agreed, laughing.

The Prime...

Princess Bithia sat clad in chains, firmly affixed to the stiff chair inside the tiny cell. Even with her hair matted and her clothes dirty, she still looked regal and maintained an air of nobility.

She hung her head, masking her anguished face behind the veil of falling locks. The hair softened the blows as Nitthogr slapped her again with the back of his hand.

"Give me what I want, Princess."

"By all the power our Creator has given me, *I will not*," she hissed through her teeth. "If I could grant you what you wished, I would resist you until the end."

The warlock grinned at her defiance. "I am a patient man, Princess Bithia," he remarked casually. And then he slapped her again in a brief flash of rage.

Bithia shuddered under the blow. She looked up at him and smirked; her defiant personality peeked through.

"Oh, you think you can hold out until you expire, sealing all your precious royal secrets and powers away forever in the royal tomb?" He pounded on the door, signaling a vyrm soldier outside.

The guard pushed in a metallic contraption. Its wheels squeaked beneath the conical base, which supported a shimmering orb.

"I've been playing the long game for decades now," he spat, activating the artifact. It emitted an ominous, vibrating hum.

Bithia glared at the image flaring to life above the active sphere. It pulled its signal from across the planes of reality, opening a visual portal to the Earth realm. She stared at her reverse image in dawning horror. In this different dimension, her alternate persona talked into a flat, rectangular communication device. She talked with some other person... *her father?* Bithia's mind touched briefly with her doppelgänger, even spanning the planes of reality. Her spirit confirmed that it was indeed her dimensional variant.

Within most planes of existence, a person had a different version of himself or herself. But the *prime* version was the truest version of a person. The collective whole of all the multiverses' variants could be summed up in the prime variant, and Bithia stared now at one of her iterations from a different realm.

Nitthogr grimaced and manipulated the image, pulling its focus in closer. "Do you see it, Princess?"

Bithia stared in horror at the long lost relic which the girl absent-mindedly toyed with as she spoke into her device. *The dimensional inversion pendant!*

As the dawning comprehension spread across her face, a smile crept across the ageless sorcerer's. "The long game is mine: the more you hate me, the closer she comes to being mine! Your feelings for me here on the prime readily reverse and find root in your inter-planar self!"

The sorcerer grinned wickedly. "I've planned for this now for decades."

Nitthogr struck Bithia again for good measure, and then left her to sulk in her lonely, dark cell. With her psychic ability, she'd seen glimmers of the plan in Nitthogr's mind during her capture, and she hope Zabe was up for the challenge... and she hoped that he didn't jump to conclusions about the pendant—while it would make her doppelganger susceptible to manipulation, removing it from her would be a critical mistake.

CHAPTER FIVE

Claire's nightmare had returned in all its vivid glory! No stranger to reoccurring dreams, last night's vision came back with full fury, and even though Claire knew she dreamt, she winced and writhed anxiously under her sheets, trapped by the reverie. She sighed and slowly relaxed into a fitful slumber. Immediately, she began having the chronically reoccurring dream where she was helpless and hunted by a ravenous wolf.

Struggling against violent winds which tore through her, Claire strained against the unknown spiritual forces that clutched her and she clawed against the air. Her voice was barely audible over the shrieking winds. Her father's ancient locket had pulled free from her neck and threatened to fling itself into the maelstrom that spun her about. Claire was at the eye of the storm, standing trapped in the center of tornadic activity.

She squinted against the gale that spun her around... her and this unknown man—her true love. Claire's eyes dried out and blurred as their bodies spun within the void. She couldn't make out his face, but in her heart she knew it was her life's great love, and then guilt washed over her. *It wasn't the man who whose proposal she'd already accepted.*

The man yelled for her to hold on, but Claire's heart went numb. Hand in hand, her iron grip weakened where her engagement ring from James bit into her finger, the massive rock pressed into her flesh. *Guilt.*

Claire looked at the man. He felt all too familiar. She only knew this wasn't James. The shame of that realization stole her breath. As she looked at the man, her mind turned fuzzy and her breathless lungs screamed. Her hand slipped from his, and the cyclonic wind threw her across the horizon.

Suddenly gasping for air, Claire sat up in her bed. "Stupid sleep apnea," she muttered, punching her pillow. She flipped her phone to check the time, squinting at the phone's lit screen. *Four in the morning.* Claire rolled over, tried to return to her slumber. "At least it wasn't that stupid wolf dream again."

Vikrum Wiltshire nearly pissed on his own leg.

He and Sexton had set up tents and surveillance equipment in a remote campground, hoping to get some kind of reading. Well, actually, they hoped *not* to get a reading, but to calibrate any sort of their sensitive equipment to a base-line in case they needed it later.

At the moment, they were not ready to handle any sort of encounter. Which pretty much guaranteed that they'd run into something unnatural.

Wiltshire had gotten up in the wee hours to take a leak and wandered inside the tree line to do it. A twig had snapped, making him whirl around, trying to pinch off the flow as he did so while simultaneously cursing beneath his breath.

In a flash, Wiltshire had a pistol in his hand, and he scanned the trees as he fumbled at his crotch.

He'd just gotten his pants zipped when he heard a voice in the trees, a low and rumbling voice. "You there, human. I would not have snapped the twig had I meant to kill you."

The voice was resonant and seemed to come from all around, as if speaking in surround sound.

"Show yourself," Wiltshire ordered the voice's owner.

"As soon as you lower your weapon."

Hesitantly, Wiltshire lowered his handgun. A tall form peeked out from behind a massive tree trunk. The figure had been practically melded to it in the low light.

"Are you Red Order types always so jumpy?" he asked. "It was the same when I first met those in my chapter."

Wiltshire asked, "You are a sasquatch?"

The figure came closer, near enough that Wiltshire could see the long gossamer hair that covered him and smell the thickly pungent odor of the forest wafting off him. His form was strangely matte, and he seemed to somehow look even more like a shadow in the direct moonlight.

"My name is Grandfather Tlugv. You may call me Grandfather."

Wiltshire eyed him skeptically and spoke in halting words. "And... you know about the Order?"

Grandfather chuckled. "I *work* for the order. They ask me for information. I provide it. I am a resource for the local brothers of the Order, and they know how to contact me."

Wiltshire cursed. *No wonder they don't want us talking with the local Order. The Praetors needed an outside investigation just in case bigfoot really is killing people—they didn't want locals influencing the findings.*

"I've got to say, I'm kind of surprised to find you," Wiltshire told him.

"You thought I'd be hiding because of the murders," Grandfather said. "Wouldn't that make me look guilty?"

"You know about the murders?"

"I do. Of course I do," the creature said. From some folds of his fur he produced a printed copy of *The Unexplained*; however he got it was anybody's guess. "This writer, the Clifton fellow, he is not a bad writer, though I'm not happy with how he's characterized me or my kind. Even those of us who eat meat seldom kill, except for sustenance."

Wiltshire cocked his head. "Bigfoot reads the newspaper... well, I'll be."

"I am quite well read, and I'm very observant—especially being so good at obfuscation. And I've been watching you since you arrived, you know."

Wiltshire looked Grandfather Tlugv up and down. He was tall. Very tall. "So, you're here to provide an interview for the investigation?"

"I am."

"Okay, then. Where were you at the time of the murders?"

"Nowhere near here," Grandfather said. "I only came down when I heard someone was trying to frame me."

Wiltshire looked Grandfather in the eyes. "I have a pretty good sense about folks. Did you do it? Did you kill those campers?"

"I did not."

Wiltshire shrugged. "Well, that's good enough for me."

"You are a strange man," Grandfather said. "And I like it... You asked the questions, but you already knew I am innocent."

"Of course," Wiltshire said. "Never play chess with a wookie."

Grandfather cocked his head.

"Star wars. Ever see it?" Wiltshire thought he'd asked a stupid question.

"Yes, in fact, I have."

Wiltshire's eyebrows rose.

"*Everyone's* seen Star Wars," Grandfather told him.

"Right." Wiltshire shifted back to the topic at hand. "The victim's wounds were wrong for your hands."

The sasquatch turned his paws over to look at them in the moonlight.

Wiltshire continued. "The victims were dismembered, all of them. Arms and legs ripped off their bodies—or so it seems. But the flesh should be torn and frayed where the limbs were ripped free. These were, but only partially. At the joint, they were cut."

He stepped closer, closing the gap, and put one hand up against Grandfather's, holding palm to palm.

Good lord, those hands are huge.

"The killer used something sharp. And I don't see any talons or claws on your big hairy mitts," Wiltshire told him.

Grandfather nodded. "Very observant. So you know it is a were-wolf?"

Wiltshire crooked his jaw. "God, I hope not. My partner and I dealt with one before."

"It went well?"

"So well that we decided to never speak of it again... but this one is different. The last one was unlike any others in the Order's records. I mean, we know there are different types of them, but this... it was..."

Grandfather let Wiltshire trail off. "Was what?"

He kept his voice low. "It was from someplace... *else*."

The sasquatch also kept a low voice. "Trans-dimensional?"

Wiltshire remained silent.

"Oh. I see," Grandfather said. "And you think this one could be the same?"

"God, I hope not." Wiltshire turned at a new voice.

"Who are you talking to?" Sexton asked with a yawn as he emerged from the tent.

Wiltshire turned back and re-holstered his weapon. There was no one there.

Claire yawned, as if that could chase away the lingering fatigue that clung to her. She clutched her large, double-shot espresso drink as if it alone could provide her salvation.

The air was crisp on this bright, sunny morning, and people walked everywhere in the busy shopping area atop the hill. The shopping area rested a lofty height above the Great Lake Superior, giving them a gorgeous morning view. Claire watched the shoppers bustle to and fro, waiting for her bridesmaids at an outdoor table at the café.

Jackie plopped down in the metal chair, laying the daily newspaper in front of her friend. She set down a napkin-wrapped scone and glared at it. Jackie didn't trust scones. "Where *is* Vivian? She always brings junk food, and they were all out of the good stuff inside."

Claire smiled over her hot cup of goodness. She knew Jackie would eat it, anyway.

"I mean, look at it." Jackie nudged it as if it might be alive. "It's hard like a rock. I don't know if it's animal, vegetable, or mineral."

"You know, Vivian doesn't eat that stuff. I think she's just trying to poison us with it."

"Well, the jokes on her," Jackie laughed as Claire leafed through the paper. "I was going to buy that junk, anyway. I might as well let her do the honors for me and at her expense."

"So much weird stuff in the headlines lately," Claire mumbled absentmindedly.

Jackie talked over her, already in full-blown monologue mode. "It's not like I have a man I need to be skinny for—and besides, who decided that skinny is what's in, anyway? Probably some *man*! I don't even think I ever want to get married..."

"Hold up." Claire raised a hand to pause her. She tried to concentrate on the paper.

"Why? You have a single friend? Because I was totally lying. Is he cute? Tell me he's cute..."

"No. I mean yes. I know a couple of guys, but that's not what I meant."

Jackie pushed the scone away from her. "Stupid, skinny Vivian," she muttered. "If she was here, I'd punch her right in the thyroid gland. But the joke's on her—our little ladies get together tonight is gonna be fun, and a girl her weight is gonna get tipsy real fast."

"This is what I meant." Claire turned the paper so that her friend could see the article. The paper reported a massacre nearby. A group of campers just south of the city in the state park were found murdered. "It's not the first, either," Claire mentioned. "There've been a number of these recently—animalistic, or even ritual-like in nature. Who could do something like this?" She scanned the headlines. "Four more dead. It's over a dozen bodies as of this morning."

"Minnesota nice," Jackie noted, "it only goes so far and then," she motioned as if cutting a throat. "That's when they snap!"

"Speaking of murderers, where is Vivian?" Claire checked her clock. "She was supposed to be here forever ago."

Claire's phone chirped loudly.

"Speak of the devil, right?" Jackie said.

Claire read the message. "She's actually at the murder scene right now and offered to finally show us what it is she does for work, if we can stomach the macabre. Apparently, this is the kind of stuff her office works on."

"I'm in." Jackie scooped up the scone and shrugged at Claire's goofy expression. "Hey, until you introduce me to my dream guy, I'm eating whatever the heck I want. And if he's really my dream guy, he'll let me eat it, anyway."

They squeezed into Claire's tiny car and headed south.

Claire's silver Jetta hopped and jerked on the pot-holed road as they left the city via the freeway. The further they got from it, the less polished the roads became. Not that they'd ever been smooth in downtown Duluth, either.

"So these weird dreams..." Jackie let the statement trail off as a question.

"Yeah, I had it again," Claire said. "But it's been different lately. I used to have this recurring dream that I was alone in a wilderness-wasteland and this wolf was protecting me. It kept me safe, guarding me from giant snakes."

Jackie and Claire both shuddered. It was a mutual hatred of snakes that originally brought them together so many years ago. They shared a memory of a teenage bully putting a snake into the locker they'd shared.

Teenage pranks were seldom as harmless as people remember. Another boy had rescued them: a strange kid who nobody paid any attention to, even after he'd been bit by the poisonous reptile.

"Ugh," Jackie shuddered. "I hate snakes," she stated the obvious.

"Things have just been so weird lately. In the last year or so, that dream changed. It's almost the same dream, except that the snakes aren't attacking me—the wolf is. And now the snakes are my friends—it makes my skin crawl to say it out loud." She grew quiet for a moment. "I die in my dreams... every night."

They let the heavy statement hang in the air until it could eventually evaporate.

Gravel crunched under the wheel treads, and her silver automobile eventually turned into the parking lot.

Vivian conversed with three different people in a small knot of official looking people wearing scowls and matching jackets. She motioned to the officer patrolling the edge of the crime scene, where Claire and Jackie stood. She signaled schat they were okay to cross the yellow-taped border. Vivian wore the same disinterested look on her face she normally did. She scrawled some notes on a tiny notepad as the two approached.

Drawing just within earshot, they heard the surreal statements from campers who had been witnesses to the massacre. Claire gave

Jackie an incredulous look as the family of three recounted their story to an obviously skeptical Vivian.

The interview reminded Claire of an interrogation guide for the FBI, which she'd read. They had lots of techniques to tell when someone was being untruthful. She'd used some of those in the past. There were a few obvious tells, such as rapid blinking and looking away and to the right when someone was developing a story—the right side of the brain contained the imaginative mind. Looking away and to the left meant an interviewee was accessing their true memories.

But she didn't need an interrogation field guide. Claire could smell the pungent green aroma of marijuana, even from a distance.

"It came out of nowhere," the unshowered man stated in his enthusiastic, southern drawl. "Almost eight feet tall, hairy and manlike! It trampled the other campers' tents and ripped the poor folks limb from limb!"

"It's true," the child piped up. "Tell em, pa! Tell em it was Bigfoot!"

Vivian rolled her eyes. "Sir, have you used drugs at all in the last twenty-four hours?"

"My boys wouldn't lie to you," the female argued.

"It was one o' them whatcha-call-it, sasquidditches," he stood his ground.

"Drugs, sir?" Vivian repeated. "You smell like you've been smoking pot. Recently."

He stared at her dumbly for several seconds. "I have a prescription." He barely managed the correct pronunciation.

"Thanks." Vivian said. "I think I have enough here." She walked away from the trio, face expressionless.

"You've got to believe em!" The woman called after her. "We'll sell our story to the newspapers!"

Claire and Jackie busted a gut, laughing as soon as they were beyond earshot.

"And this is what I do," Vivian said as she guided them through the roped off area. "I work with a team that chronicles, tracks, and discredits news of the weird. I was close enough that they called me in, even though I'm technically on vacation."

Jackie scanned the scene of carnage, trying not to focus on what were obviously human remains. Most bodies had been collected into black bags or covered; some were just too mangled to even recognize which parts belonged to which bodies. A severed human hand lay within a cordoned off area; a heavy gold ring on one finger displayed an ornate seven-pointed star.

"I'm sorry," Jackie said, suddenly covered her mouth, trying to keep her scone down. "You're here because?"

"Didn't you catch what the hippie said? Bigfoot just murdered eleven people."

The statement hung there for a moment.

"Come again?"

"There were a few witnesses. Most of their stories corroborate it. They all describe some kind of animal-like humanoid as the perpetrator. Six said Sasquatch, two said werewolf, one said alien."

"Are these killings all related?" Claire speculated. "I mean this one and the others that have been dotting the countryside the last few weeks? Most of them were also on, or near, other state parks."

Vivian didn't make eye contact. After a pause, "We're not at liberty to make any kinds of statements or conjecture to that effect."

"So Bigfoot is in the northland and he's killing Minnesotans?" Claire asked.

Jackie tapped herself on the chest. "I'm from Seattle! I'm immune."

"Obviously, there is something behind it. These people didn't accidentally die; maybe it's a feral bear or some kind of group hallucination." Vivian explained, "That's what we do: get to the bottom of mysteries and disprove the crazy theories."

Jackie whispered to Claire, "She's not Kristen Stewart. She's Daphne from Scooby Doo!"

Claire chuckled quietly.

"Jinkies," Vivian said flatly. "Maybe you could whisper more quietly."

Jackie Blushed.

"I know what we're watching tonight," Claire said. They still had another long afternoon before James got back from his press tour.

"I guess that means Jackie is Velma and James is Fred," Vivian commented.

Claire was glad for the attempt at humor on Vivian's part. She was a little unsure how to take it, though. It meant Claire was either Shaggy or Scooby, and neither seemed a particularly flattering comparison.

Vivian took Claire by the arm and escorted her a few steps away so that Jackie could not overhear. "Listen, Claire. This is my job: I'm here to tell people what they need to hear—that there is no such thing as the boogeyman. The agency I work for helps preserve order by giving rational explanations."

"Okaaaayyy," Claire said. "So, what's the big deal, then?" She looked past Vivian to where Jackie was left out of the loop.

"I know that you're writing for *The Unexplained* under the name of Henry Clifton."

Claire gave her a shocked look.

"I just thought you should know that I know your secret," Vivian said. "I want things to actually be explained, and not sensationalized. This thing... it's killed at least thirteen now. I'm afraid any new speculation could start a panic."

"That's the same thing that I want," Claire said. "All the articles... that's what I'm trying to do. If you've got any answers about who or *what* did this, I'd write the article in a heartbeat."

Vivian nodded measuredly. "Deal."

Claire looked at her with serious eyes. "Vivian? Don't tell James."

She'd set her jaw, but Vivian nodded and accepted her request.

Claire separated from her and headed back towards Jackie. Her friend called out, "Don't forget tonight, Vivian! You're responsible for bringing the drinks!"

"Claire!" Jackie sat on her friend's couch and yelled with remote control in hand. She pointed it at the television and continued scrolling through the streaming services. "Your popcorn's burning!"

Claire stepped back into the living room and sniffed. "That smell's not food." She nodded to her patio door. Vivian stood just outside, dragging deep off the cigarette in her hand.

"Oh. Disgusting," she noted, as Vivian opened the sliding door and reentered the apartment.

"Not as disgusting as the great unwashed down on the street," Vivian remarked. She touched a spot on her temple and massaged it gently and then looked at her fingertips to see how much make-up she'd smudged. Vivian took a compact from her pocket and touched it up.

Claire gave her a quizzical look.

"There's a gross hobo down on the street. He was staring at me the whole time... gave me the stink-eye."

Jackie jumped to her feet. "Where is he? I'm the only one who hasn't seen him yet, and Claire says he's cute!"

"What? I did not! And don't look right at him! Peek out this window, here." She cracked the drapes.

The three girls huddled close to the opening and gazed at him. He was watching everything, scanning traffic and the surroundings, glancing occasionally back at the apartment. He wore a tattered, hooded sweatshirt that covered his face and he'd obviously staged the boxes and bins nearby as his bed.

"He *is* kinda cute," Jackie stated. "I see a dimpled chin and stubble. That's all I need."

The others looked at her but didn't disagree. "What? I like the rugged look."

She jumped back from the window. "I think he saw me!" she squeaked. She leaned back in. "Oh, no. We're fine." She exhaled with a shudder. "My heart is racing. Maybe it's love." She laughed.

Vivian chuckled. "Looks like Claire has her own personal stalker... and your stalker has a stalker of his own. Do you suppose he's dangerous? Maybe he's trying to get close to my brother?" she reminded Claire that she was betrothed.

Claire rolled her eyes, but kept observing the scene on the street. "I'm sure he's no threat," she lied. "He's probably just passing through to a warmer city."

He peeled the hood back from his face.

"Ohmygod!" Jackie jumped again. "I *know* him. That's Robert Somethingorother... You know, that weird kid from high school. Rob, he went by."

The other two pressed their noses to the glass and scrutinized him. "Who?"

"The snakes?" Jackie explained. "Remember when I first moved here in the middle of tenth grade and they made me share a locker with Claire? He was the kid that saved us from the snake that Jeffrey Bremer put in the locker!"

"Oh yeah!"

Vivian tried to hide a mischievous smile. "Jeffey B. I paid him a dollar to put that snake in there when I was a senior."

The two stood aghast at her omission.

"What. It's not like I *knew* it was poisonous! *Jeez.*"

"I remember," Claire stated. "He got bit and went to the hospital. I had a few classes with him. Quiet. I didn't know anything about him." She leaned back towards the window again. "Yeah, that's definitely him."

"I am going to call someone." Vivian had her phone in hand.

"No," the other two shot her down, speaking in unison.

They observed him for a few more minutes on the street. Rob watched the cars pass. Something made him tense. He stopped and shrank back towards the alley, crouching down to avoid detection, even though the girls could see him plainly from their level.

Rob glanced up at the apartment once more and then darted down the alleyway behind his viewing post. After a few more moments of watching and waiting for any return, a knock came at the door.

"Maybe it's him?" Jackie whispered giddily.

Claire walked across the room. She tensely checked the peephole, then pushed the door open. "James!" She flung himself into his arms.

He wrapped his arms around her, roses in one hand. "I'm glad to see you, too!"

Chapter Six

Claire struggled to raise her head off the table and squinted against the morning light. She groaned as she reached for the cup of coffee and struggled to keep her throbbing head upright enough to see her foam cup. There wasn't enough caffeine on the planet to help with the hangover she battled.

Girls' night... erg. Girls' nights suck.

She turned her face to Jackie, who sat slumped in the adjacent chair. The outdoor table's undersized umbrella provided little help against the early rays. Claire grinned stupidly; her friend looked dead: pale, slouched, and motionless. Jackie's broad sunglasses hid most of her face from the late morning sun, which had heated the table to the same approximate temperature as magma.

Grimacing, Claire felt the crosshatched metalwork of the hot tabletop searing her cheek like a griddle. Moaning, she slumped back into her own hang-over pose and raised the cup to her lips.

Claire glanced right. Vivian remained straight faced as ever while she sipped an espresso. In that moment, Claire knew Vivian wasn't human; she'd drank enough tequila at last night's impromptu bachelorette party to make a buffalo blind. Yet, here she sat. Claire could feel Vivian's judgmental eyes scan her critically.

"Shut up," Claire croaked as she held her head in her hands.

"I didn't say anything," Vivian remarked coolly.

Claire groaned again. "You were thinking it."

She merely nodded.

Jackie snorted a half-asleep snore and then sat straight up—waking herself. She mumbled something unintelligible and reached for her cup on the table.

Vivian's phone chirped a few times. Claire winced at the shrill noise.

"I've got to go," Vivian stated, eyes scanning her text message. "There's been another... incident."

They let her leave in silence, save for the scraping of her chair on the concrete. A few minutes later, slightly sobered by the coffee, Claire and Jackie laughed about the previous evening's events. The conversation quickly descended into another Vivian bashing session, but eventually turned back to other issues.

"How is your dad doing, anyway?"

Claire absentmindedly twirled her pendant around her index finger. "He's not able to get away for long, but he'll be at the wedding. The local government at the dig site is in some political disarray, and that means they've got to dig as much as possible and as quickly as they can. They're trying to ignore the hostile activity all around, but if the rebels have their way, there would be a civil war," Claire glanced down at the paper. There was a small, world-news headline about Chiriqui and a foiled coup in that country on page thirteen. "If there is a war, all their work will be lost, even if their town misses any hostilities, which would be unlikely. By the time it's sorted out and the archaeologists can get back to business, he might be..."

She trailed off. Jackie finished her sentence for her. "Retired." Nobody wanted to think of another option, and Jackie knew how important of a figure he'd always been in her life.

A grating noise startled the two girls: metal chair-feet scraping on the sidewalk. The homeless man, Robert, had snuck up on them unnoticed. He quickly took a seat across the small outdoor table.

Both girls sat frozen. They were not terrified, but rather stunned at his incredible audacity; neither knew quite how to react.

For several long moments, he stared at Claire. "Amazing," he finally said. "You look just like her—in so many ways, *you are* her."

Claire responded, "Of course I am. Uh, Robert?" She threw out the leading question, trying to make sure they had properly identified him. She looked him up and down, finally close enough to see him clearly. He was not unattractive, despite his longish hair and several days' worth of stubble; he clearly possessed all the qualities that had Jackie sighing wistfully to her left.

He exhaled and furrowed his brow, searching his mind introspectively. "Robert... Robert? Yes. That's my name. Call me Rob."

"We all went to school together," Jackie interjected.

He seemed only slightly confused. "Yes. You're right about that, too. Here in this town." The last statement almost came off as a question rather than a statement.

"What do you want?" Claire asked bluntly, keenly aware that Rob was a homeless man who'd followed her for several days now.

Rob met her brash remark with a hard stare of his own. "I want you to stay safe."

"Okay," she led. "But you're acting kind of stalkery."

"What do you know about me?" Rob cut her short.

"Well," she looked him over. "You look like you've maybe fallen on some hard times lately. Maybe you heard I was marrying some famous guy—"

"Famous, cute guy," Jackie added.

"—and you maybe thought there was a way you could bail yourself out?"

"I wasn't asking you to speculate. What do you *know* about me?"

The tension in the following moment was palpable. "Very little," Claire admitted at last.

He motioned for her to continue.

"I know that you're a little... different." She softened the blow, choosing a word other than 'weird.' "I know you once rescued me from what turned out to be a poisonous snake and you got bit instead—but then you kinda disappeared a few weeks after that.

Nobody knows if you moved, or joined a terrorist group, or what. You are a ghost, Robert Schaeffer," Claire remembered his full name at the last second.

Rob suddenly looked fidgety and distracted. "Yes," he responded as he stood. "I am a ghost. But are all ghosts evil? You be careful, Claire Jones," he begged her as he turned and departed.

"Ohmygod, ohmygod, ohmygod," Jackie burst out once he'd left earshot.

Claire nearly melted as well. Her adrenal glands felt like they'd just exploded. The potential danger of such an encounter left them both giddy.

"You handled that so well!" Jackie gushed. "And oh my God. He got so hot!"

"Who's hot?" a familiar voice asked over their shoulders. James sat down, steaming cup of black in his hand.

"You are," Claire stated emphatically. She gave Jackie a warning look to try to change the subject.

"Oh really?" James pressed. It was obvious he hadn't been fooled.

"Just some guy we knew in high school," Claire offered. "Jackie's got a crush."

"I do," she confirmed. She laughed, more serious this time, "I think I really do."

Claire wore makeup and had dressed up. She was on her way to a date with her fiance and left Jackie to mind her apartment. She'd promised to keep an eye out for their favorite stalker.

Her heels clicked and echoed in the parking garage attached to her apartment building, and she stood straight, stiffening when she found a strange man leaning upon her car. He was obviously waiting for her.

The man grinned when he saw her. "I thought you'd be taller, and way more masculine, Mister Clifton," the stranger said with a slight British accent that was either fake or watered down by decades of living in the states.

"I'm sorry," Claire lied, "but I don't know who you're talking about."

"Of course you do. You're the reporter from *The Unexplained*." He clarified, "You're not in any trouble, Miss Jones. My name is Vikrum Wiltshire. I'm a... a kind of private investigator."

Claire kept her voice low and insistent. "How did you find out that I am Henry Clifton?"

"We interviewed a lot of the same people about this sasquatch story," Wiltshire told her. "It wasn't hard to put two and two together once I had a description and a few details about you. I think that we—" He stopped mid sentence, staring at her pendant.

Claire gave him a quizzical look.

"Atticus," Wiltshire called. "Are you seeing what I'm seeing?"

Atticus Sexton got out of the adjacent parked vehicle and introduced himself. He'd stayed in the car so that it wouldn't appear to Claire that she was being ambushed.

"My father gave it to me," she told them. "Found it at a little tourist shop near an archaeological dig."

Wiltshire pointed at Claire's necklace, and his partner nodded solemnly. They ignored the mundane explanation she'd given them. "Darque metal."

"What? What do you mean?" Claire asked. "What is that?"

"It's a strange metal that we've encountered before." Wiltshire shook his head as he searched his memories. "Sexton and I vowed to put the topic to rest, but..." he flashed an apologetic glance to his partner. "It's made of the same substance that someone we know fashioned into a bullet that killed a friend. He was a... a kind of cryptid we encountered. You work for *The Unexplained*, so I'm sure I don't have to tell you what a cryptid is."

Claire nodded along. "And you don't want to talk about this... this person, or thing, or whatever it was? Why not?"

Sexton said, "We have our own unexplainables. But we don't like it when we've got zero knowledge about something."

Wiltshire agreed with him. "But the more and more we keep exploring, this metal, and the thing—our friend—keeps coming back up."

"Okay, but why are you here? I don't know much—and I think I think I know even *less* now that you're telling me this." Claire was frustrated by the pair of investigators.

"We're just here to tell you that Bigfoot is definitely *not* killing people in the area."

She cocked her head and crossed her arms. "And how do you know that?"

"Simple," said Wiltshire. "I asked him. Also, there's some forensic evidence to the contrary. *Someone is trying to frame Bigfoot.*"

"That sounds crazy, you know?" Clarie asked.

Wiltshire merely shrugged.

"Does Bigfoot have any suspects as to *who* has been doing these actual murders?"

With a sigh, Wiltshire admitted, "A werewolf. Or werewolves. The jury is out."

"Werewolves?" Claire barely batted an eye.

Sexton noted, "Yes, but we had our detection equipment set up, and there was another murder last night. We're certain that this is a natural occurring phenomenon or else some kind of cryptid. That is outside of our normal domain. Werewolves are often paranormal—and that's something we might have been able to help with."

"Wait, I'm confused," Claire said. "I thought you said it *was* a werewolf? Are you just making up rules as you go along?"

"Sorry," Wiltshire explained. "There are several kinds of werewolves. Some are naturally occurring conditions such as lycanthropy: raving madmen who are animalistic lunatics. Some are arcane curses which come from dark magic, usually. And others are a naturally occurring hereditary line of shifters, and there are skinwalkers, too, which is a mystic variation on that. We only deal with the arcane kind."

"So you think this is the madman kind?" Claire asked.

"We do," Sexton said. "And that means your local law enforcement is capable of handling it."

"Goodbye, Claire Jones. Hopefully, this will point you in the right direction for your next article. In the meantime, lay off of Bigfoot. He's one of your fans, you know."

With that, they turned and departed, leaving Claire behind, and flabbergasted. *Bigfoot reads my articles?*

James leaned across the dinner table at the fancy restaurant and took Claire by the hands. She had just brought him up to speed on the details of their wedding plans, but kept away any details of her secret work life—and avoided all talk of sasquatches and paranormal detectives.

Besides, there are much more pressing matters at hand. I've got a whole freaking wedding to plan!

The flickering candlelight played across his face and highlighted his starkly handsome features. "It's so nice to be back." His mellow baritone voice rattled a sweet spot deep inside her.

Claire smiled politely. It was sincere, but she and James had just talked about living arrangements. "Are you really back, though? I mean, where is home for us? We don't really have a place for *us*. We have *your* bachelor pad on the west coast and we have *my* apartment here."

James smiled and slid a business card across the table. "I know you really hate Los Angeles and that the Hollywood scene isn't really your thing. So let me propose something new."

She picked up the card. "A real estate agency?" She turned it over in her hand. James had written an address on the back. "What's this?"

"I have to be at a table reading tomorrow morning, but I've arranged for you and my sister to walk through this house." He smiled. "I think you'll absolutely love it. If you do, it will be our home. I've already had papers drawn up."

"Oh, James..." Claire was speechless.

"I just want you to be happy. I'll commute. There will be some periods of distance because of the travel, but honestly, that would be the case regardless of wherever our home is. Hollywood can only invade on your terms." He smiled. "Plus I can certainly see the upside to this," he joked. "It's like you said: the paparazzi would freeze to death up here if they tried following you."

Claire could only smile. Having to bring Vivian along was only a small concession in light of such a gift. It would be difficult to find a moment in her life more perfect than this.

Vivian knocked on the apartment door. It swung open to reveal a disheveled Jackie, holding a rumpled blanket over herself.

"Oh. I was expecting Claire."

"I was expecting pizza," she yawned. Jackie stepped aside so Vivian could enter the apartment. "She's on some swanky date with your brother."

"You're not at home?"

"Claire's apartment is as much my home as my parents' place is."

"Fair enough," Vivian said flatly. "I was just going to bring Claire these." She lifted a manila envelope.

"Oh, what's this?" she asked inquisitively. Jackie took the package and pulled out a small stack of drawings and articles.

"I knew she was... interested in this thing. I always did say she read too much—it couldn't possibly be good for her." Vivian played coy with her words.

"I know," Jackie said.

Vivian squinted, playing dumb.

"About Henry Clifton. That Claire's been writing for *The Unexplained*."

"Oh. Okay." Vivian turned over an artist's composite sketch of a hairy, lanky beast. "This was from our most recent event. An eyewitness described this to the artist who drew it up."

Jackie recognized this as some kind of peace offering between Vivian and her soon to be sister-in-law. "It looks like Bigfoot with claws... except he's maybe been working out a little. I don't get it. Is Bigfoot hitting the roids?"

Vivian shook her head with a grimace. She cycled through to a few new stills: grainy photographs. The creature looked almost exactly as described, although the photo was low resolution and from a distance. "There was an ATM at the bait-shop down the road. We were able to pull these couple of images." She'd finally managed to silence Jackie.

"Wow," was all she could manage.

"I have no idea what this is, or how to disprove it. I'm not certain that it *can* be disproved." She wondered aloud. Letting her thoughts hang in the air. "Whatever this thing is, it might be the real deal."

Chapter Seven

Can't breathe! Claire struggled against the beast that gripped her throat. She lashed and clawed at the wolf as it tightened its grip further. She was impotent against its locked jaws. Just as her eyes bulged and lungs nearly burned out, she coughed and sat up straight in her bed—yanked out of the vivid dream.

She took a deep, raspy gulp of air and blinked against the burgeoning light that crept through her window. Claire's sweaty nightclothes were cold and slick and her panting breaths calmed momentarily; she swung her legs over the edge of the bed.

The toilet flushed and a zombie-like Jackie surrendered the restroom. Jackie shambled towards the kitchenette and declared the obvious. "Coffee."

Claire leaned over the lavatory sink and looked at herself in the mirror. A long mark arced across her neck where she'd scratched herself, thrashing in her sleep. She looked closer; two reddened handprints, bigger hands than her own, faded from her neck as her color returned. She blinked away the crud from her eyes and looked again, but they'd disappeared entirely, and she wondered if they had been a hallucination.

"Rough night?" Jackie asked from the doorway, sipping the first cup of the morning.

Toothbrush in mouth, Claire nodded and rolled her eyes.

"With all that thrashing last night, I thought that maybe James had followed you in," she suggested.

Claire glared at her friend's crass comment and spat her foamy mouth of paste into the sink. "You know he's a perfect gentleman. James is very proper and has his upright public image to protect."

"Oh, I know," Jackie said. "But he's also a boy."

Claire rinsed the sink quickly. "He's more of a man, that way." She stole Jackie's cup mid-sip and claimed it as her own.

"Well, I'm glad you've been lucky enough to find the last remaining well-mannered man on the planet."

"Ha ha, I know, right?" She took a deep draught of coffee. "It's like he's not even from Earth."

Jackie sighed. "If I only had your luck." She ticked off points on her finger. "Your fiancé is famous. Gorgeous. Wealthy. Sweet. Gorgeous. Confident. Giving."

Claire waved her hands away.

"I could go on."

"You forgot that his sister is a bit of a monster. You'll find your prince; I'm sure of it. Rob's probably down on the park-bench as we speak—show some initiative."

"I think you might be wrong on all counts."

Claire raised her eyebrows.

"I've seen the way Rob watches you. I don't think he'd ever look at anyone else like that. And even if he could, he's a hobo... and also, he's in the alley, not on the park bench. I already checked." Jackie went to the kitchen again and clicked the brew button for a new cup. "And you never know, Vivian might turn out okay, too."

During their visit last night, Jackie and Vivian shared an honest discussion about Claire and relationships. For her part, Vivian seemed genuine in her efforts to be a better human being, at least to Claire and Jackie.

They sipped their coffee in relative silence, waiting for the gray to burn off the sky with the advent of a full morning sun. It had no sooner crested than someone knocked at the door.

Claire opened the door to Vivian. She held a full drink tray. No pastries.

"Ready for the big viewing?"

"Just give me a few more minutes to get ready."

"We are meeting the real estate agent at the house. Do you want to tag along to the showing, Jackie?" Vivian offered. She understood Claire would be more at ease with a friend tagging along and understood it might help her build that bridge she worked towards with her soon-to-be family.

"That would be great. I'd like that. I'll grab my stuff and get ready."

"These are incredible," Claire remarked from the passenger seat as she shuffled through the sketches and photos that Vivian had brought over on the previous evening. Vivian was driving them in her rental car, which had more space than Claire's.

"I thought you would find them interesting, even if I don't understand your exact fascination with the supernatural."

"But isn't it your job to?" Jackie asked. "At least in a general sense?"

"It's actually to search for the rational answer from a viewpoint of skepticism. Someone says 'ghost' and the instant reaction or position my office takes is that we should find a way to discredit it as a potential threat—keep away the sort of thing that starts those UFO cults that mix poison in their Kool-Aid. We're a small niche inside DHS dedicated to keeping paranormal fear in check. But I don't know how they're going to handle... that." She motioned to the images in Claire's hands. "At least, not without a gag order."

Claire shuffled the printed images. She could see how there were similarities between a sasquatch's stereotype and that of a werewolf. She had no first-hand contact with either, so she felt woefully under-qualified to make a definitive judgment on the images' contents.

"I am always skeptical," Claire admitted. "But I grew up with my dad visiting dig sites all summer long, surrounded by artifacts from ancient civilizations. I've seen everything from cursed mummy sites to supposed ancient alien landing pads and other-worldly hieroglyphics. I don't know," she trailed off. "Maybe I just loved Halloween too much as a kid. But I think that it's because I've seen the collective sum of cross-cultural, historical superstitions and I find it all so... interesting. Not necessarily valid—just interesting. I mean, I believe in *something*... I'm definitely not an atheist. I'm just not entirely certain where the line between reality and fiction intersects. I think my father's curiosity is deeply ingrained in me."

"Yeah," Vivian noted, "I wonder if this... thing... in the photos might just be that intersection."

Vivian pulled the car into the private cul-de-sac below a sprawling Tudor; it rested upon a blanket of carefully manicured landscaping. Claire and Jackie exited the car. The sheer size of it silenced even the passionate conversation they'd been engaged in.

Claire turned her head in panoramic fashion, taking in the scenery. The entire estate was flanked with an old-growth forest abutting one of the many state parks in the area. The wild greenery's border was kept in careful check against the carpet of grass that covered the expansive yards.

A middle aged woman wearing a wide smile and a pencil skirt rushed out the front entry to greet them. Claire recognized her photo from the business card as the real estate agent.

"Welcome!" she greeted them over-warmly. "I'm Emily Washington, at your service. Your fiancé said you would need a full tour." She beamed as if she already knew the deal was as good as inked.

The agent guided them on a detailed tour of the bedrooms and other amenities. Starry-eyed, both Claire and Jackie practically staggered through the immaculate halls of the mini-mansion.

When they got to the large den, the agent sat on one of the loveseats and motioned for them to join her. The three girls each took a seat and surveyed the comfortably staged and appointed room.

Emily handed them each a binder filled with information, photo sheets, and disclosures. The packets highlighted the acreage, features, and floor plan as well as details and dimensions on the house's niceties.

"Just take a moment to imagine yourself right here. Imagine your belongings and furniture; perhaps envision a party or a gathering of your close friends. Envision your family, and *family to be*, pictured in those photo frames..." she trailed off to let the moment of imagination take over.

Claire sighed, focusing on a large gilded frame nearby, and thought of her favorite photo. She imagined the picture of her and her father, taken at a dig-site outside of Thebes, filling its decorative edging.

"I think my father would love seeing me here," she found herself saying. Beneath her smile, her mind imagined a million simultaneous scenarios, each filling the home's grandiose proportions. She thought of raising future children here; graduation ceremonies and garden parties. She imagined her father visiting between his expeditions. *She thought of going on her own expeditions.* Claire suddenly panicked, wondering if settling down was truly the nature of her heart—the most alive she'd ever felt was journeying through strange and foreign lands on adventures of discovery: a researcher on the trail to uncovering ancient, lost truths!

Her thoughtful digression evaporated as a nearby floor beam groaned loudly, like a stressed galleon mast beneath a heavy gale. Silence—everyone froze in shock. One breath passed silently. The fleeting moment of quiet erupted in flame and chaos as the finely crafted hardwood flooring erupted in splinters, propelled by the detonation.

Claire flung herself to the side. Her couch flipped backwards with Jackie still on it; she could hear her friend's scream as it tipped. Vivian had already fled through the door.

Fire shot up through the hole in the ground and spread to everything within seconds. Claire crawled backwards as a curtain of flames draped itself between her and the exit. It seemed to move supernaturally, not flickering in rapid and random succession, but a constant conflagration designed to isolate her from any help or exit.

Claire screamed in terror. The roaring inferno muted Jackie's pleas as the spreading pyre forced her near the door; the acrid stench of burning hair and fear enveloped the room as the real estate agent flailed about, fully immolated, like a living torch. She cried with an otherworldly shriek and crumpled to the floor. Jackie screamed and fainted as Emily Washington collapsed into a burning heap.

The wall of living fire pressed against Claire. Soot caked her face, and the heat blew her hair back and dried any fearful tears that would have otherwise streamed down her face. A solid pillar of fire burst up from the floor. It spun like a whirlwind, taking on humanoid features.

It singed Claire's hair and buffeted her to the side. As the fire demon pressed towards her, seeming to reach for her with an arm-like tendril, Claire was sure she could hear a dark laugh coming from its core.

The ceiling suddenly collapsed, crushing and dissipating the flame demon as another monster entered the fray. A massive beast smashed through the upper level and fell down into the room, roaring as it dropped through.

Scorching the debris, the renewed column of fire shot upwards again. The intense prison of flame that trapped them burned ever hotter as the blazing fiend swatted the animalistic humanoid. It howled in pain. A blackened and singed swath burned across his snout.

Claire shuddered with shock. The raging noise of the hellish chamber choked out her groans. The beast's ears perked at her pained sound and whirled to face her.

She immediately recognized its lupine features from a million movies. Perhaps more horrific than the mythical Sasquatch, the beast which locked its gaze on her was a hulking werewolf. Claire couldn't stop staring as it approached, shrugging off the ferocious lashes of the animated flame mephit. She did all she could do to keep her eyes from rolling back inside her skull. Claire clung to her only hope: maintaining consciousness. She turned and tried to crawl away, but collapsed under the thin, smoky air, doomed to watch helplessly as the wolfman rushed forward and scooped her up.

More ash and smoke whirled. The enraged, living fire seemed to scream and burst forward, rattling the ceiling, threatening to bring the whole house down on them. Claire could barely see her friends through the flame wall.

Growling with pain, the beast leapt through the pyre, charging through. He busted through the sheetrock wall and stumbled into the adjacent room. The smell of burning canine fur and flesh filled Claire's nostrils; she hung limp in his rippling muscles.

The fire chased after, allowing only a moment for the two to catch their breath. Tendrils of flames grabbed a hold of the massive hole and pulled the blazing entity into the next room as it gave chase.

Tensing for action, the werewolf leapt away and rushed towards the window. He lowered his head and used his body to protect Claire from any cuts as he soared through the massive panes of glass. Breaking through to the rear yard, the beast bound ahead, aiming for the forest.

Only three giant-steps away from the edge of the wood, Claire's vision blurred. Her sight went black, and she slipped beyond consciousness.

CHAPTER EIGHT

Claire awoke with a start. Even unconscious, her heart had been pounding a hundred beats per minute. She hadn't dreamt at all—and she hoped that her most recent recollections had been nothing more than a new, intense nightmare—hoping it had merely been the worst ever variant of her "wolf dream." Claire ached all over and her head was foggy; the pain in her body told her that it had all been very real.

A moment of acute panic struck her, and she felt as if something was missing—something important. Her phone was gone, sure, but that could be replaced. Her fingers glanced against her bare neck and rubbed the phantom itch as if there should have been a necklace there. And then it hit her—*where was her...* her mind went blank. *What was I looking for again?*

The unmistakable chirping of medical instruments and the strong scent of expensive men's cologne informed her of her location and told her she was not alone. Claire turned her head, searching the hospital room for her fiancé. *Where was he? Is that what I am missing?* She called, "James?"

His coat lay over a chair nearby. Past that, muted by the door and distance, she could see James through a window, clearly angry at whomever he was speaking with. She hadn't seen him wear a look of worry very often, but it clung to him now.

She hurt all over. The radiant ache of minor burns spotted her skin. Claire touched the wounds and wiped away the sticky topical ointments she'd been treated with. More than the pain, though, she felt anger. She couldn't pinpoint the source of her rage, but a feeling of helplessness made her want to lash out.

The frustration mounted as she lay there, unable to get comfortable because of her burns. She listened to the beeping machines. Beep. Beep. Beep. Minutes on end. Finally, her calm broke, and she started ripping the sticky sensors off her body, making the machines lose their calm as well. Beep. Beep. Breeeeeeeeeeeee!

Nurses came storming into the room, trailed closely by James. "What are you doing? You can't do that!" they chided.

"Are you holding me here against my will?" Claire snapped.

"No, but you're not well," a large nurse replied. Claire was pretty sure the large nurse could hold her against Claire's will if she'd wanted to. The other nurse and a doctor stood near the door, only one step closer than James.

"If I stay here a minute longer, I swear I'll lose my mind," Claire threatened.

The nurses and the doctor traded sagacious glances. James interrupted their silent conversation. "Doctor Smith, is she well enough to check herself out?"

"Wait." Claire stopped him. "I want to know. What do you mean by that? I said 'I feel like being in here is making me crazy' and everyone freaks out."

The long pause after her demand hung palpably. Finally, Doctor Smith said, "Miss Jones, when they admitted you, you were raving about fire demons and werewolves. They found you in the woods early this morning suffering a psychotic break from reality."

Silence again. None dared break it. Only Claire had that right.

"The fire. The burns," a confused Claire stammered.

"Yes." James helped her. "There was an explosion at the house. A gas line ruptured, the fire marshal says. It was very traumatic; the real estate agent died, but Vivian and Jackie got out the front door. Vivian dragged Jackie to safety, but when she came back, you'd escaped out the back entry of the room and apparently fled into the woods."

"Right!" she exclaimed. "Vivian saw the whole thing! She can tell you, something big—a creature, saved me. He scooped me up and carried me to the woods!"

Her physician regarded her coolly. His white coat sported a gold star-shaped lapel pin and a name tag identifying him as Ryan Smith, M.D.

Doctor Smith watched her carefully as she repeated the same details she'd arrived raving about. "You do appear more coherent this time," he said, only stating the facts of his observation, avoiding any diagnosis.

Claire grimaced at him. James had slid in closer and now had his hand on her shoulder in full support of her. Crazy or not.

"Can you tell me, Miss Jones, did you lose consciousness at any time?"

"Well, yeah," she said, unclear why the doctor didn't have that written on his little notepad too. "Right before I got to the woods; that's why I had to be carried." Her frustration mounted again. James met her frustration with a gentle shoulder rub. "What did Vivian say?" Claire demanded, looking at James.

James shook his head negative very slightly, as if it was an answer he was sorry to give. He spoke gently. "She didn't see anything, Clairebear. Just the fire and chaos."

Claire withdrew into her shell for a few quiet minutes, leaving the doctor to stand there while she took stock of herself. The nurses switched the machines off and dutifully wrapped the cords, further quieting the room.

"How is Jackie?" she finally asked.

"She's okay," said James. "She was treated for minor injuries and burns, and then went to her parents."

The doctor nodded and then turned to leave, but motioned to James. "A brief word, Mr. Shianan?" They stepped into the hall.

After one minute, the nurses left. Claire waited in silence; her frustration waned, morphing into resign. She couldn't even bring herself to think—only stare at the white wall. Two minutes later, James returned.

Claire looked at him hopefully. Her eyes asked for news.

"The doctor says that he just wants to keep you overnight for observation, but that you can go home tomorrow as long as I keep a close eye on you."

She nodded at the news.

"Whatever you saw," he led cautiously into the subject, "has the doctor concerned, but he's ruled out neurological damage. Except for the blackout, there aren't any physical indicators. He thinks it was a stressed induced state, almost like a PTSD fugue. I mean, my god, a woman burned alive right in front of you," he said sympathetically.

Claire's mind started wandering. She wondered if there was any truth to their concerns for her mental state. After all, she worried more about the possibility that her mind was unreliable than the fact that a human being burned to death only feet away from her. She nodded, submitting to Doctor Smith's verdict.

"Listen," James slid in next to her, "I'm right here with you. Every step of the way," he promised. Something in his voice soothed her anxiety; even as Claire felt like she slipped away from her grip on reality, she knew that James could keep her grounded.

Claire squeezed his hand to respond with gratitude. James leaned in and kissed her forehead.

"Get some rest."

She suddenly felt very relaxed, as if a sedative had kicked in. *No... I can't believe anyone would drug me against my will... would they?* Claire closed her eyes and nodded off.

The rest of her hospital stay passed uneventfully. Claire had awoken the following morning fully rested. Oddly, she had not dreamt. Perhaps her body needed every scrap of brainpower to continue healing, or maybe it simply couldn't handle another surreal, recycled psychological encounter.

She passed the remaining time watching television reruns and reading a trashy novel she borrowed from the nurses' station. James acted admirably. He handled everything, and despite the fatality in the accident, he was able to run interference with the police, so she hadn't had to relive the encounter by giving a statement.

Nothing demanded that she engage it with her brain. It was as if her thoughts cycled in neutral, spinning freely.

A foreboding sense that she'd lost control of her life, and perhaps her mind as well, seemed to envelop her. Claire followed and did as told, as if in shell-shock.

Sometime after a soft, bland hospital lunch, she signed the discharge paperwork that an orderly brought to her. She neatly packed her few belongings and prepared to return to her apartment. Her mobile phone had been destroyed in the ordeal and so she pulled the memory card from its back and tossed the smashed device in the wastebasket and then met James, who waited to drive her home.

The remainder of her day passed like a gray cloud; everything felt tainted by the dull, murky wash. Claire and James went over wedding plans, discussed other houses, and talked about guest lists; he changed her wound dressings, but they did not speak about what happened.

She felt like she watched her life as a passenger, looking in from a window but helpless to intervene. The only thing she needed to complete the scene were the three ghosts of Christmas: past, present, and future.

Evening crept up. James drifted off to sleep on her couch. Claire retired to her bedroom, laid her head on her pillow, and let go. Her mind slipped off, and she, too, slept.

Claire awoke with the sun. She looked over where she would have normally left her phone charging and in alarm-clock mode, but she no longer had it. It was very early still, but she knew returning to sleep would be impossible for her.

Standing in front of her bedroom window, Claire greeted the daylight with silence. She dressed herself and peeked in on James. He snored almost inaudibly on the couch, and Claire picked up her keys and her wallet and slipped quietly out the front door.

Longing for some sense of normalcy amidst the haze of uncertainty that enveloped her, she wandered towards the coffee shop on the corner near her apartment. After crossing the road, she very nearly tripped over a pair of feet sticking from the alleyway. A homeless man sat bent at a ninety-degree angle against the brick building as he rested his back.

She'd almost stepped around him when he sleepily called her name. "Claire?"

Claire didn't recognize him. "Sorry. I don't have any change," she lied, trying to walk past.

"Claire Jones," He stated.

The fact that the man knew her full name startled her, called her mind to attention.

"He's got you enthralled, you know. The warlock, the sorcerer. But I don't think he sent the fire demon."

Claire chided herself for being fooled. Clearly, this hobo was insane, rattling off the kind of crazy talk one expected from his kind. Maybe she'd merely misheard her name being spoken. Still, compassion had always intertwined around her innermost being. She put a hand in her pocket, searching for some money.

Her eyes searched vainly for a change cup, or somewhere to drop coins. He didn't have any such thing.

"Nitthogr's *in your mind*, Claire Jones. But this will protect you. He thought it would trap you, but it has some resistant power as well. The amulet helps you resist his magics, even if it endears you to him." The bum held up a necklace pendant. *Her pendant*, the one her father had given her. It dangled from his fingertips as he freely offered it to her.

Claire looked into his eyes, suspicious of him. They contained not a shred of deception or threat; she snatched the necklace from his outstretched arm. "Nith-who?"

As soon as she grabbed it, the fog in her mind lifted. Her sight seemed to clear and things became more apparent to her state of mind, as if it had been struggling to wake up this entire time. Her brain felt tingly, like a foot one sat on too long before suddenly having blood restored.

"Rob?" she asked, bewildered, but suddenly recognizing the vagrant. "What happened?" She stared at his scarred and bandaged forearms; a puffy, red burn mark raked across his face and nose. Soot and grime ringed his face and hairline.

Rob nodded as she latched the clasp of her necklace behind her head. "Don't lose that." He suddenly looked over her shoulder at something.

Claire turned to see James opening her patio door. He walked onto her balcony and rubbed his eyes, yawning.

"There you are," he called out loudly, putting enough force behind his voice for her to hear him across the street. "What are you doing out here?"

She turned back, but Rob had disappeared. She touched the jewelry hanging from her neck. Yesterday she might've questioned if Rob was even real; she might've believed he'd been a figment of her imagination or a delusion. Now? Now she knew better.

Claire turned to shout back, "I'm just getting coffee. Do you want any?"

"I'll be right down and join you. You know; doctor's orders and all. I've got to keep an eye on you."

His voice was different... somehow insincere, like he was acting. Claire immediately felt suspicious.

Throughout the day, Claire regularly checked over her shoulder, trying to spot Rob. She still didn't have him figured out. Her seeming paranoia kept prompting James to ask her what she was looking for; it forced her to concoct any number of tiny, white lies as she placated her fiancé's protective doting.

Nearing evening, she finally twisted James' arm enough to drive her to a cell phone dealer; she hadn't replaced her destroyed mobile yet. Until she'd retrieved her necklace, she hadn't even realized how much she'd been thrust into complete isolation, and if Rob's crazy story was right, mental control.

She understood James' hesitation to venture out, though. Everywhere they went, people snapped selfies with him and tried to engage him in conversation. Claire made the stop quick, however; she told the first person inside the door exactly what model she needed and merely replaced her previous phone and inserted her memory card.

They weren't there long, and they'd planned it for as close to the store's closing as possible to minimize any kind of circus. She'd explained to James that she simply couldn't wait another day or two if she ordered one and had it delivered. What if her father needed to call?

"Here's your device," the salesman stated, handing the device over to her as it powered up. "It should be activated, and your service automatically transferred over. Can we help you set it up or show you its features?"

She snapped it away as the alert signal began to chirp repeatedly. "No. I'll do it myself." She quickly gathered her materials and she and James departed for her apartment.

Claire did feel a twinge of guilt as she ignored her fiancé, even though he could've been more on top of this matter. James couldn't get in a word with her; she'd fixed her gaze on the screen, attempting to update and sync all its services so that she could get back up to speed.

The notes from her friends and acquaintances who had tried contacting her these past few days reminded her of who she was. It felt like she had been restored, much like the software on a device. Jackie had especially freaked out, sending a flurry of messages. But her first call would be to her father.

Once back at her apartment, James sat on the couch and asked how she felt. He resigned himself as a mere observer as she spread her wings and returned to her former life.

"I'm fine," she reassured him, even as she dialed the out-of-country phone line. "I'm finally back; I feel well." She smiled apologetically. "I'll probably be up late." She shrugged at her phone to indicate the reason. "I've got to call my dad and bring everybody up to speed, assure them I'm okay."

James smiled neutrally. He picked up his own mobile and thumbed the screen over to the internet. "Just promise me you won't read the news from the past few days? TMZ aren't the only ones who like to throw wild, yellow-rag speculation around when celebrity news is concerned, and you probably don't need the added stress that garbage can bring."

"I promise," she said, clicking the green dial icon. She slipped into her room and lay on her bed, conversing with her father.

She calmed him down and reassured him that everything was okay. Claire caught up with Jackie immediately after. She followed that with a blast of text messages to other people and then read the news. James had been right. Bloggers and instigators had been critical, blasphemous, and downright unkind, especially since one of the first responders had quoted her raving about a fire demon and a werewolf rescuer. There were even a slew of internet memes comparing her with a raving lunatic and comparing James with previous famous actors who had married mentally disturbed people.

Claire scowled at her news feed and then peeked out her door. It had been several hours since she'd gone to her room; time had flown without much notice, and James had fallen asleep long ago.

Her thoughts turned inward as she absentmindedly fingered the amulet under her chin. What had Rob meant by his comments? What about a sorcerer? It all sounded so crazy—the ravings of a madman! ...just like her. They'd said she was crazy at the hospital: that her experience was a total break from reality.

Claire pulled up the website for the real estate agency they'd contracted through. The front page featured a short memorial for Emily Washington and a link to her obituary. Claire clicked to the listing for the home where the fire had occurred; as hoped for, it hadn't been taken down quite yet.

She poured over the data online. As a high dollar listing, it contained large amounts of detailed information in an effort to appeal to the most discriminating of potential buyers, either informing them or weeding them out in agented efforts to whittle down the prospect pool to only the most qualified buyers.

Finding the information Claire wanted, she clicked on the floor plan and layout tab. She zoomed in and located the room where the incident had occurred.

She ran her fingers through her hair and bit her lip, not wanting to believe what she'd seen. But not wanting to believe the opposite either.

They'd said that she fled through a back door to escape; that story meant she'd gone crazy. The opposite account, that some monstrous creature had saved her and there was no other route of escape, meant that she was perfectly sane—and everyone was lying to her.

Claire snapped a screenshot and emailed the image to herself. She stared at the tiny screen showing the wrecked home's blueprints. Here was her proof: the room had *only the one door.*

For the first time since she was a teenager, Claire Jones felt terror. At fourteen, she'd been in a hostile, foreign country with her father, and a member of the corrupt local military had planned to kidnap her. Her father intervened and prepaid a small ransom to secure her safety. Right now, he felt so far away—and, if Rob was right, her new captor might just be her fiancé.

She peeked out her window and down to the alley. Sure that she spotted the shine of Rob's eyes deep in the alley as a car's headlights passed, she sighed. Could she trust him? *Was he the beast?* And if he was, then what about all the local killings? Is Rob the murderer? Could she really trust James?

Claire laid down with more questions than ever before. She only knew for certain that she could not tell anyone.

The shrill vibrations of her cell phone jolted Claire from her fitful sleep; it rattled noisily against the polished wood of her nightstand. She reached across and checked the LCD screen on her device. It was awfully early for Jackie to call. *It must be very important,* she thought, swiping to answer the call.

"Hey," Claire croaked.

"Don't speak," the gravelly male voice commanded her. "Just listen. I... found this phone and I would like to return it to your friend. You know where to find me, down in the alley."

Claire recognized the voice as Rob's. She answered him with the silence he'd ordered her to.

"I'm sorry to wake you so early, but you mustn't bring your fiancé. This was the only way I could think to get you away from him. I have to tell you something in private: you were right. Come down. Tell no one." He ended the open line.

Staring dumbfounded at her phone, Claire quickly weighed the pros and cons. Warning sirens blared in her mind, cautioning her against what Claire knew she was eventually going to do in the end. *Damned foolish curiosity*, she chided herself.

She pulled on a pair of pants and threw a hoodie over her tousled hair. Creeping out into the apartment, she kept a cautious eye on James as he snoozed on the couch. Claire cradled her keys in her palm and slipped out the door.

In a few short moments, she found herself in the middle of the crosswalk. Streetlamps glowed above as the sun had yet to bulge against the horizon.

Walking with purpose, she strode right in front of him and jammed her hand out, as if to demand that he return the cell he'd most likely stolen from Jackie. He gently placed it in her hand; the burn marks on his wrist obviously causing him discomfort.

"So, you have something to tell me?" she demanded. "Maybe we start with those burns?"

Rob sighed, relenting. "First, let me see that you're wearing it." He indicated her neckline.

Claire jangled the necklace for him to see.

"Good, good. The amulet is from my realm; it dispels much of the influence that Nitthogr has over you. It has... some magically resistant properties."

"Say what?" Claire asked skeptically. "That's not even English."

"I'm sorry," he continued. "I keep forgetting that things are so very different here. But I confess, I did get these burns, saving you from that fire demon. And I'm not sure of its allegiance yet."

"I knew it!" she hissed. "And you're the monster, too? The one killing people in the parks! Or was that some kind of hallucination?"

Very somber and serious, he stated, "I am no monster. I am not sure exactly what I am. I never transformed until I left The Prime. I never knew I could do that." He glanced at his leather wristband. It was embossed with a wolf logo imprint.

"The Prime? Nitthogr? Fire demons?"

"Let me try to start again. I don't come from this land, Claire Jones. I came here from The Prime—the ultimate reality—and while you barely recognize me, I know *you*. We are very connected."

"Now you're just talking gibberish," she accused as she wagged Jackie's phone at him. She made to leave, her anger at his thievery motivating her curtness.

"Please," he pleaded.

Something about the urgency in his voice made her pause and listen.

"We have to protect the Tesseract."

She crossed her arms over her breast. "What is a Tesseract?"

"Think of all reality like a giant crystal. This is the Tesseract: a crystalline cube within a cube with many facets and vertices—the lens of an ancient machine that creates reality. This giant gem's facets each make up a reality: a different realm of existence." He grabbed his shirt and tugged, as if to indicate the material facticity of the world. "If each face is a different reality, or dimension, then the substance, the essence of the jewel at its thickness, what it's made of, that is the Prime."

"And what?" Claire chided. "You want me to drink some magic Kool-Aide and ride on your magic rocket ship into an alternate reality?"

He looked at her quizzically, not understanding her euphemism.

"Next, you're going to tell me that you are from The Prime? You're probably on some special mission or you are a very important person there?"

"Yes," he stated, still confused as to her use of sarcasm.

"I swear I must've been hit in the head," she talked to herself, further confusing the man in her alleyway. "That would sure explain everything." She paused. "It might be the only rational answer to all of these questions."

"You are not losing your mind, Claire Jones. At least, not exactly. There are powerful forces at work—a sorcerer has been trying to wrest your mind from you."

It was Claire's turn to give a quizzical look.

"The amulet," he pointed. "You began to question your sanity after you lost it at the fire, correct?" He understood her silence as a confirmation. "It has been since then that you began to question your judgment, your sanity, and your mind has felt vapid and elusive? That is the work of Nitthogr. The amulet has kept him at bay, even if it works toward his ultimate cause. It is something even older than the warlock—something he stole from the vaults of the royal family, an artifact collected by the Veritas—a religious order from my world. It cannot be so totally bent to the will of the warlock and so it protects you as he twists its purpose.

"Once it was returned, did you not feel your old self come back? You became less timid, more confident. You share these strengths of character with your Prime: Princess Bithia. You are defiant, strong, wise, and stubborn. These things returned, did they not?"

Claire nodded measuredly, seeming to agree, and then she quickly turned on him. "You're insane, and you're stalking me." She put up a finger of warning. "You need to back off. I don't care if we did go to school together; I'm not going to let you suck me into your delusion."

Rob suddenly slunk up against the wall of the alley and crouched against the dumpster. He pointed to a black van that pulled into a parking space beside Claire's apartment. "I know that one, too," he said. "And she knows me."

Claire turned and spotted Vivian in the passenger seat. The driver was watching Claire. "Yeah. I know her, too."

"She is not who you think. She is allied with him: one of his lieutenants."

"She works for this evil Nitthogr dude?"

"Yes, but worse in some ways. She only serves him because of her blind devotion to Sh'logath."

"Oh, now there's a Sh'logath too?" Her words dripped with sarcasm.

"I know I sound very confusing. Please, it's all too much to take in over just a few minutes. We need to get away from here. Let us leave, go somewhere far away where I can properly explain it all to you. You can't go back to him."

"Um, yeah. That's not going to happen." Claire turned and began to return under the watchful eye of the van driver.

"Don't tell your fiancé, or that woman, what I've told you!" he called after her. "Don't trust either of them; they're not who you think they are. Say nothing!"

"Yeah," she hollered over her shoulder. "Don't worry. That ain't gonna happen. They already think I'm losing my marbles. I'm not going to start talking Sh'logaths and Nitthogrs on them!"

"They are lying. Ask the woman—whatever name she's using, how she got her bruise," Rob said.

Claire paused, but resisted giving any indication she knew what he was talking about.

"She got it from me when I knocked her tooth clean out of her face," Rob said.

Claire acted indifferent to his words. She waved Jackie's cell in the air. "Whatever. Stop stealing my friend's stuff!" Claire turned to warn him as she spoke. "I seriously don't want to see you around here anymore."

As she looked back at the alley. Rob was already gone, like he'd vanished into thin air.

Claire turned back as Vivian slammed the van door shut. Vivian looked surprised to see her out and about. Claire suspected it might have been an act; the driver couldn't seem to hide his intentions.

"Are you staking me out or something?"

Vivian shook her head and pointed to the corner of the block. "Best coffee in town, and they serve us early risers. What's got you up?"

She held up Jackie's phone, though convinced that Vivian was lying. "Just retrieving Jackie's phone from an old friend. I'm on my way back inside now."

Claire paused and leaned against the van. "Where's the rental car?" She glanced at the driver, who she recognized from her trip to the massacre scene several days prior.

Vivian sipped her coffee. "Had a work thing. I have another one shortly. Agent Brock was just driving me around for the day between appointments."

Brock gave Claire a casual two-finger salute.

Claire saw the bruising on Vivian's cheekbone where her foundation makeup had smudged. It looked blueish. "Hey? What happened to your eye? It looks like someone clocked you, good? Bigfoot, maybe?"

Vivian's eyelids fluttered, and she turned to glance at her face in the mirror of the van. She fumbled for her makeup compact in her pocket, opened it, and reapplied just a dab to cover the mark.

She looked up and away, to her right, as if recalling what happened. "I bonked it getting out of that rental car. It's got a little less clearance than I'd like."

"Bummer," Claire said, wincing. "Well, I've got to let Jackie know we found her phone." She turned and headed back home.

Vivian nodded and watched as Claire crossed the road back to her apartment building.

I don't know what's really going on, she thought, *but it can't be half as crazy as the story Rob fed me!* She glanced back at the empty alleyway. *Don't go back to him!* His words still rang between her ears.

But Vivian was definitely lying to me... for what that's worth. But werewolves and alternate dimensions? Come on! She paused as she mulled over her thoughts. *It's crazier than a Bigfoot murder mystery... isn't it?*

Claire briefly weighed the options and considered going to Jackie's instead. She could always stay with her friend and with Jackie's family. She shook her head and ducked inside her apartment. This was home. She'd made her choice, and James was a part of that. No number of crazy ghosts from her past could change that.

Chapter Nine

James slipped back inside Claire's apartment, bearing his gift. It was late in the morning, but he knew how his fiancé liked to sleep late whenever possible. Besides, she had gotten up early yesterday and then stayed up all day pretending she wouldn't be tired. She'd spent most of the day making wedding plans with Vivian; they planned to scout some wedding reception locations today. The event needed an area big enough to accommodate the crowd a celebrity would inevitably draw.

Checking the clock, he snipped the ends of the flowers he'd stepped out to purchase so they'd stay fresh longer. He knew he could still arrive in time for his meeting, but it wasn't likely that he'd see Claire before he had to leave. Vivian was quite capable of keeping close tabs on her, however.

He arranged an empty breakfast plate on the table he'd adorned with the flowers and affixed a Post-It note to it. "Frozen Waffles in the freezer. You are my everything!" James smirked; he put serious effort into being charming for his betrothed.

James took his car keys and a door key from the table near the entry and closed it gently behind him. He had a group that he needed to meet with, and he didn't expect it to go very well.

Even though he wore a warm, Hollywood smile on his face as he walked through the apartment complex's hall, his mood turned considerably darker. James knew that he had some minor hiccups to iron out with his comrades, and he anticipated smoothing out at least one wrinkle this very morning. What vexed him most was another situation that had crept up. James was pretty sure Claire had been seeing another guy, someone she knew from several years ago.

James didn't feel insecure. Vivian had informed on him; there was no real threat, and he knew exactly who this person was, even more so than Claire did. What troubled him was that Claire hadn't said anything to him about it. That seemed so unlike her; perhaps the nature of their relationship was not exactly as deep and secure as he thought. James would have liked nothing better than to resolve that issue this morning too... but not with Claire. He hoped to have that encounter as soon as he was able—if he could ever locate the other guy.

Still fuming, James crossed the street and peeked into the alley-way. There was no sign of the interloper. James hadn't foreseen him as capable of showing up here, of all places. He grimaced and returned to his car in the underground parking ramp.

He didn't expect he'd find that meddler today, anyhow. It would sort itself out. He had a team of experts put on the matter.

Pulling a sleek cell phone from his pocket, he thumbed in his sister's contact. He typed a quick message. "Meeting with them soon. Keep Claire safe."

He clicked the fob to unlock his Lexus, then got in and sped away. Today would be his. He was James Shianan. He was Hollywood's darling. And he knew that he was so much more than just that. Soon, the whole world would know who James Shianan truly was.

Claire strolled through the verdant, manicured park flanked by her two bridesmaids. With her face beaming, she spun slow circles as she took in the scenery,

imagining the setup she had planned for the wedding reception and how it would look on these park grounds.

Vivian took fastidious notes and drew a diagram on her clipboard. Jackie kept close, providing emotional support and positive feedback. She'd grown quite worried for her friend since the fire and the subsequent but temporary communications blackout.

Walking near a pond fed by a babbling brook, Vivian took a call on her cell and meandered just out of earshot. Jackie, bubbly as ever, crept close to her friend while Claire threw a few bread scraps to the geese that paddled nearby. They honked and demanded the scraps whenever she held a piece for too long.

Jackie asked, "So, have you seen Rob these last few days?"

Claire didn't seem to have much of an opinion on the matter, judging by her blank expression. "I haven't seen him since I got your phone back from him." She paused long.

"That's too bad. He seemed like he was looking out for you—er. You know, as much as a stalker can. Maybe he moved on?"

"Maybe," Claire mused. "Or else, something happened to him."

The statement hung in the air like a lead balloon.

Jackie caught the look on Claire's face. "Something's on your mind, Clairebear. What's bothering you?"

Claire looked over her shoulder at Vivian.

"Is it a cold feet thing? Spill it. I'll help you talk it through." She did a goofy move with her hips. "We can even dance it out if you need to."

"It's just... I've been very tense since the incident. I'm still trying to work it all out in my head. Doctor Smith told me that my mind was confused, but what I experienced was so vivid." Another tense pause. "Do you think James would ever lie to me?"

"Of course," Jackie spat out immediately. "To protect you, though," she followed. "He's in Hollywood. I'm sure certain things get said to keep you from worrying, like when your dad tells you everything is safe in the areas near his expeditions. He's a man—we *want* our men to tell us certain lies. Like, if I ask a man if my favorite Ramones T-shirt makes me look fat, there's only one right answer."

"Not that kind of lie," Claire said. "Do you remember the layout of the room where the fire started?"

Jackie shook her head. "No. I still barely remember anything. I hit my head pretty hard during the explosion."

"I asked James and Vivian again yesterday, but not overtly, or they'd think I was losing it again. They insist that there was another door leading out the back of the room that I used to escape."

Jackie nodded. She'd heard the talking points.

"See, the more I think about it, the more I can see the room in my mind—I relive every detail, right down to the smells and the screams. And I'm telling you that there was only the one door. That's the kind of lie I'm wondering about."

"Do you have any way to check? I mean, the house was destroyed in the fire, but maybe the previous homeowners had some photos or something you can check."

"There's no way to contact them. But there is this." She motioned her friend to take her cell phone. Claire clicked on a book-marked link on the mobile browser.

A blank page came up. One line summed up the situation. "Content unavailable; property of the Heptobscurantum Group. All rights reserved." Moments later, the page redirected to a larger real estate directory.

"What am I looking at?" Jackie asked.

Claire took her phone back. "It was the original listing for the property, complete with blueprints, floor plans, photos, you name it. Whoever this Heptobscurantum Group is, they bought the agency, the content, everything, and shut it all down. The records are even unavailable through other channels like public works."

She tapped through a few screens on her device and turned it back to Jackie. "But not before I got this screenshot."

Jackie cradled the LCD screen and stared at the picture. Clearly, the room had only one door. She handed the phone back. "What does this mean?"

Vivian started walking back. With her almost in range, Claire muttered under her breath, "It means someone is lying to me, and I don't know who else I can trust anymore."

Instantly changing her demeanor like a chameleon, Vivian switched from a dour expression to her happy sister-in-law's face she'd been wearing since the fiery incident. "I like this spot for the reception," she gushed. "Lots of natural light and plenty of space for guests. Plus, there's a nearby pavilion for the band to set up in."

The three ladies simultaneously turned to look at the covered pavilion. A skinny man wearing a hood pulled low over his face sat at one of its shaded picnic tables. Something about him unnerved all three of them.

"He looks more like a washed-up hip hop artist than a band member." Jackie tried to defuse her nerves with humor.

"Yeah," said Vivian. "Let's go check out the other side of the park. Maybe see how far we are from the guest parking."

They moved as a small unit. Claire looked back at the pavilion and spotted the mysterious man. He followed them from a distance, walking intentionally, urgently, as he pursued. All three picked up the pace, speeding to a brisk walk.

Continuing to shoot furtive glances backwards, they barely noticed the other man in the ratty, thrift store poncho. He leaned suspiciously against the concrete block restroom building along the walking path. They rushed past him, almost jogging now, while he ducked around the corner, keeping hidden from the trail.

The skinny hood broke out into a sprint. Jackie squealed, and the girls tried to accelerate.

From around the corner of the utility building, the second man launched out and tackled the skinny one, dropping him with a shoulder spear. The cowl of his poncho flung back to reveal Rob's face.

"Run, Claire!" He urged her forward while the lithe stalker grappled him.

None of the girls moved. They stood riveted by the brawl.

The skinny one kicked free from Rob. He pulled his arms back and stiffened, contorted them before clapping his hands together. Flames sprang to life between his palms and he shot a column of fire at the girls' protector, blasting Rob across the lawn and knocking him over a grassy berm.

Turning back to the girls, the fire in his eyes burned as intensely as the flames flickering between his tightly balled fists. For a moment, his eyes shimmered animalisticaly, like a reptilian blink.

A roar snarled from the other side of the lush knoll where Rob had been thrown. The air seemed to crackle, like the oxygen vibrated at a molecular level under the stress of so much supernatural power colliding in such close proximity.

Streaking across the green like an arrow, the massive lupine charged the slender man who had fixed his evil gaze upon the girls. Seizing him by the torso, he suplexed the fire wielder caught in his massive paw, smashing him into the concrete of the walking path, shattering the cement tiles below. The beast stuck his snout down into his prey's face and bellowed a warning. His hot breath blew his victim's hair backwards, flecking him with spittle.

Claire could barely see the skinny one's face, but she could swear that the cheek where he'd been hit was covered with scales; his pale, pasty makeup had been scraped away by the werewolf's fist. She cringed as the thin man screamed back at the werewolf's face, spewing a wave of caustic heat.

The wolf snarled, his face singed, and he flung the man the entire distance back to the pavilion. Skinny heat-miser crashed into the wooden structure and it collapsed upon him while the beast turned his face to the girls. He bellowed again and launched into a sprint towards their position.

Vivian drew a semi-automatic handgun and began firing rounds into the lycanthrope. Claire watched in horror as the beast closed the gap; Vivian practiced her marksmanship with cold, hard precision. Claire spotted something in the monster's eyes and she instantly knew that he was Rob—not a doubt remained in her—but his eyes contracted with terror, and not from the hollow point rounds, which barely seemed to phase the beast. A split second later, Claire was yanked off her feet from behind!

Claire could barely hear her own screams over the ringing gunshots and the sounds of the other fleeing park-goers. Tipped sideways, before she could spot her attackers, she saw the rubble of the pavilion explode in flames and the skinny man walking from the pyre.

Rob, the wolf, peeled off in another direction, crashing through the brush nearby. Vivian leaned into a shooter's stance and squinted down her sights, firing hot lead at the fleeing lycan.

Jackie shrieked, pointing to the approaching pyromancer.

Vivian paid him no mind, but pushed Jackie back. "We've got to go!"

"But where's Claire?" She turned and spotted two burly, well-dressed men in the distance. One had Claire under an arm, barely containing her as she fought and writhed to escape. The other held a pump-action shotgun in his grasp. He looked ready for anything; walking backwards, he provided cover for his occupied partner.

"They've got her!" Jackie insisted.

"Yeah. I see them." She paid them little attention, instead focused on retreating to the car. In a rare display of bravery, Jackie broke with Vivian and rushed towards her friend.

Rob burst out of the underbrush nearby. He leapt over the first blast of shotgun fire and pounced towards the backpedaling mercenary. He ducked under a second blast that tore through the space above his head. The acrid, sulfuric smell of gunfire hung in the air; Rob leapt past his enemy, dragging his razor-sharp claws across the man's midsection as he pursued Claire's handler. They'd almost made it to the white cargo van that waited for them in the parking lot with doors open.

Claire screamed for help just as Rob caught her kidnapper and dashed him to the ground with a sickening thud. He gingerly lifted Claire to her feet, even as he shielded her from the small arms fire. Vivian continued to approach with extreme prejudice.

Jackie shrieked as she almost reached her friend, but both were thrust to the ground under the shockwave from a nearby explosion. The white van detonated with a colossal fireball, throwing flame and broken glass everywhere.

Rob turned and growled. Vivian stood only fifty yards in the distance. Another fifty beyond was the skinny pyro fiend. He dashed forward as Jackie helped her friend to her feet. They fled to the parking lot, watching over their shoulders.

The werewolf slugged Vivian as he sped by. The force of the blow tossed her twenty feet away, where she crumpled like a rag doll. Jackie was in shock and barely managed to find her car keys while tracking the battle just beyond the lot.

As she watched their lupine savior fall upon the fire wielding maniac, she tore out of the parking lot, spraying gravel behind her as she turned the corner faster than common sense dictated. Both girls hyperventilated uncontrollably; tears streamed down their faces as they hit the freeway. Neither had any plan beyond simply drawing their next breath.

James smashed his fist down upon the ornate wooden table at the room's center. It hit with unearthly strength, nearly shattering the finely crafted, heavy surface. The decoratively engraved seven-pointed star suddenly looked less resolute beneath his raw rage.

"What do you mean, you lost her?" James hissed ominously. He paced the room, cradling his beloved mystic book.

None of the stalwart seven men seated at the table flinched. They each stared at him as if ice water ran through their veins.

Peter Greyson spoke up. "We had assurances that the men we sent were more than capable and they had done numerous jobs for the Heptobscurantum in the past. They are agents of The Seven."

"This is the best you have available?" James hissed.

"We deemed them," Greyson said calmly, "adequate."

"Adequate?" James calmed himself. "Did I not stress the high importance and sensitivity of this mission?"

"Quite. And besides, these were soldiers that *your* contact introduced us to. Also, you gave us very little notice in order to make proper arrangements. These agents were ready and on hand. And while you expressed the dangers of the mission, you failed to inform us of the exact nature of the mission. Had we known of the supernatural components, we might have been better prepared—"

"Do you know so little, Greyson? *Every* supernatural thing is *natural* to me!"

Greyson spoke with more authority and volume. "You expected us to anticipate a rogue vyrm agent and a werewolf? You forget who you speak to!"

James stood straight. He towered over The Seven and seemed to grow in size as he shouted with a booming voice. "You forget who *I am! I am Nitthogr, the great warlock and Herald of Sh'logath: Beast of the Tesseract!*"

All members of the secret council fell speechless. James adjusted his tie in the uncomfortable silence that immediately followed. He calmed himself again. "You each live by my own good pleasure. If this council fails to live up to the title of Illuminati, then it will be replaced with new adherents of almighty Sh'logath who appear more capable."

James paced a bit more, well aware that some of these men had begun to suspect his true loyalties. Each had been selected because of their skills, and none of these men were prone to stupidity. James set the heavy tome on the table. "Lest any of you think my heart is anything but fully committed to the Awakening, I will leave here the mythic Grimmorium Nitthogr—which contains the only recorded guide to enacting the Awakening. It contains the very words spoke to me by the Voice of the Thousand Elders at the Plains of Neggath. The Seven may do their best to perform the rites in my absence."

Following the moment of tense quiet that came after the unspoken challenge, Victor Adams leaned forward at the table. In his thick Persian accent he asked, "None dare deny the powers or position Sh'logath has bestowed upon you, but why does the almighty Nitthogr not merely snatch up this Claire Jones in the middle of the night? Why involve The Seven? It seems that we might be better served in making preparations for the Great Awakening while you are obviously close to the girl."

James paced at the head of the table. "There is some mystic force preventing me. Mark my words, Claire Jones is the key to this all. The blood that courses through her veins is the final reagent needed to open the door and unlock the Void. The Agod of Destruction cannot be summoned without her. She must be captured prior to the completion of the next two synodic months in order to cause the Awakening this year," he referenced the lunar calendar, which had just restarted. "She is the child of prophecy: the key. She wears a certain ancient artifact on her neck that prevents any physical interference with her while I remain on this plane of existence. My extra-planar efforts are... different in nature."

The members of The Seven nodded as he explained. "So you need human help in this matter?" Greyson pressed his point. "You need the members of the Heptobscurantum."

"I have legions of vyrm warriors at my disposal. Human efforts or otherwise, I have many tools at my command. And all my tools are replaceable." He narrowed his eyes at Greyson. "However, I do suspect that there may be a traitor amongst The Seven." James scanned the room, meeting each one's gaze in turn. "And this vyrm flame-caster concerns me; he is not one of my faction: the vyrm of The Black. If he is truly a member of the Tarkhūn, then my suspicions would be confirmed."

"And the Lupine?" Charles Summers interjected.

"He concerns me less," James said flatly. "I know his origins. My sources have traced him back to my own dimension. He is a discursive anomaly, although his presence does not exactly surprise me. I have plans for him. But there are not many factionless vyrm, fewer yet with any significant powers, and so this rogue takes priority."

"Then what comes next?" asked Andrew Thornton. "How do we find Claire Jones?"

"She's in the wind," Thomas Chelish noted. "She will be difficult to locate unless she wants to be found."

James noted. "The Lupine did not leave with Claire and her friend."

"If you like," Chelish interjected, "I can use broadcast media to locate her? Maybe a story about her failing mental health? It would certainly go viral. It might change your influence; there could be unforeseen repercussions to your public image. It is difficult to anticipate the result, but it would certainly generate leads as to her location."

James paused and thought about it. "Do it," he ordered. "Every day she remains at large means we risk failing our grand orders: the release of Sh'logath." James pointed to Bruce Cannon and Jonathan Trask. "Cannon, secure another team for Claire's acquisition... equip my team of vyrm hunters so they are capable of handling this usurper wolf. Trask, get another team of men from within the ranks of the Heptobscurantum; I want this Tarkhūn firelord caught. I want this rogue vyrm *and* Claire, and I want them both alive!"

Trask and Cannon each nodded. Trask interjected, "Do you really think that this vyrm is with the Tarkhūn?"

James did not dignify the question with an answer—the only reason any vyrm would openly defy Nitthogr was that they were a part of the Tarkhūn: his brother's Vyrm faction, which derived from the old ruling caste. He finished his final thoughts, instead, "Do not spare the werewolf. He must be destroyed."

The warlock watched his puppets use a ceremonial gavel to adjourn the meeting. Sullen, he watched the seven humans depart, each a powerful lord of men in their own right; he had groomed them for a place on this council. They silently walked away, back to their own empires and lives. He grinned with an evil, deceptive smile. He needed Claire Jones, and he was, thus far, true to Sh'logath... just not as any suspected.

He was James Shianan. James Shianan was Nitthogr.

Chapter Ten

“Ohmygodohmygodohmygodohmygod...” Claire's face sank into her hands while Jackie spun a sharp corner around the freeway exit.

“This is crazy!” Jackie yelled, agreeing with her. “I believe everything you've ever said after this. Fire demons and unicorns? I'm drinking the Kool-Aid, too! I'm seeing whatever you're seeing.”

“Did you see the way that Vivian just started shooting at that thing?” Jackie paused as she mentally connected the dots. “Wait! Was that thing Rob?”

Claire nodded.

“I didn't even know Vivian had a gun!”

“Rob saved me the last time. He's the only one who's been trying to save me all along.”

“But hasn't he been terrorizing the wilderness and killing people and animals? Isn't lycanthropy some kind of occult curse?”

Claire shrugged. “I only know that he's saved me twice now from whatever that thing is, and Vivian tried to murder him for it... I think she and James might be trying to kill me. Or at the very least, make everyone else think I'm a lunatic.”

“But why?”

Shrugging, Claire barely managed, “I don't know.” She caught sight of the amulet that hung from her neck. “It might have something to do with this? Rob said to never take it off. He said it helped protect me."

Jackie glanced at it. "Girl, you're involved in some weird juju." She cocked her head at something on the radio and turned up the volume. The signal crackled and a news report repeated itself.

An announcer read the emergency bulletin. "Claire Jones, local fiancée of Hollywood golden boy James Shianan, is nowhere to be found. Witnesses report a violent, psychotic break with reality that sent her on a violent rampage, which included arson and property damage. Any persons with knowledge of her whereabouts are urged to contact the authorities. She was last seen in a—"

Jackie flipped it off and pulled a hard U-turn. "I guess we're not going to my parents. Somebody, whoever is behind this, really has it in for you."

"Where can we go?" Claire shuddered, holding her head again, trying to blink back hot tears of anxiety. "God, I wish my father was here."

Jackie pulled into an alley behind a decaying building where she braked hard. "I just saw a patrol car. Let's wait here for a couple of minutes."

Claire sobbed for a few quiet moments. The tension wore on her, and she searched her brain for anywhere else she could go. "I think I know someone who can help."

James paced the floor of the old basement. Lavishly appointed, yet spacious, it used to be a raucous speak-easy owned by Al Capone in the prohibition era. A negative energy lingered in the place and so it served his purposes perfectly.

His phone vibrated insistently, and he turned the screen over. A wicked smile crept across his face. The sounds of a skirmish echoed within the old subterranean access tunnel.

The distinct thudding sound of fists against flesh confirmed that his hit squad had returned with a struggling prisoner. James slid the heavy steel door open and granted them access.

Dressed in black and heavily armed, the human mercenaries dragged into James's lair a noncompliant, hooded, bound, and gagged prisoner. The burly, mustachioed mercenary walked up to James; James handed him a sealed manila envelope stuffed with cash.

The man nodded with a grin and gave him the keys to the manacles which bound the skinny, writhing man. "Watch out for that one," he warned. He whistled to his crew of five and they slipped out the door.

Standing resolute, yet in chains, the slender man stood at the edge of the room, where he tried to get a sense of his surroundings despite the blinders. James sauntered over to him and yanked the hood from his head and leaned in to look his prey in the eyes; he put a hand over the pyromancer's face and raked his hand in a downward motion. The caked-on flesh-tone makeup wiped away in deep streaks, revealing the concealed, scaly skin of the vyrm assassin.

"As I suspected," James whispered. He stared deep into his enemy's eyes. "Do you know who I am?" James' eyes flickered as a clear lens slid sideways, revealing his own half-serpentine nature. James's skin dried and shriveled, becoming momentarily scaled and tinted olive.

"Nitthogr," he replied.

"And who are you?"

"Rashaka. Keeper of the flame."

"Who sent you?" Nitthogr demanded.

Rashaka stood stoic. He refused to surrender any new information.

James waved his hands in a dismissal. "I already know who sent you," he accused. Nitthogr caught the look in the vyrm's eyes, noting that he had his ear. He continued, "I have known all along and planned for all possible contingencies."

He casually approached Rashaka and slashed across his chest with a razor sharp fingernail. Blood seeped out of the wound, but the rogue vyrm barely winced, remaining indifferent and removed.

"I anticipated the possibility of Zahaben, or one of his clansmen, parting the veil and finding the Earth realm. I took precautions for their presence. I know that Princess Bithia has been interfering on the astral plane, even from her captivity, and so I've sent her earth doppelganger an interference dream so that she is less likely to trust him. I've also planted enough evidence to incriminate this would-be hero as the danger she dreamt him to be."

Nitthogr cocked his head at the stiff-necked rogue. "But none of that matters to you," he bragged, demonstrating his strategic prowess. "Because you are not connected to the royal line—you're no friend to Bithia. You're not even loyal to the old, divergent vyrm bloodline. You are an agent of my brother, Basilisk. You are one of his Tarkhūn." He yanked down on the cut fabric at Rashaka's chest and revealed a large tattoo: a crude octagonal shape which loosely resembled a lizard. "Funny. You're quite small for a Tarkhūn."

Rashaka didn't rise to the baited insult.

"I just find it so odd," the sorcerer continued. "I can tell by your features that you are not a genetic Tarkhūn. Perhaps you are one of The Black, but you converted? Possibly a defector to Basilisk, just like General Regorik has been to me?"

The warlock got in his captive's face. "You sold out your heritage, your loyalties, for some kind of wrong-headed idealism? Perhaps you seek to escape your caste and rise above it, or maybe your desire is that Sh'logath slumbers forever?"

The accusation came so confidently that Rashaka turned his head to answer with his full attention. "You're no brother to the true Herald. You are a mere pretender. The Tarkhūn have the truth! The Tarkhūn were the first adherents who called to him from Neggath! We are the true followers of Sh'logath, and Basilisk is his herald!"

Smiling, James struck the Vyrm in the mouth with his fist. "Fool. *I* am his chosen one. I do not understand why my brother opposes me when I act in accordance with the divine will of the great Agod."

"Basilisk plays spoiler." Rashaka spit a mouthful of dark blood from his lips. "You do not serve Sh'logath! You serve only Nitthogr—pretender of the apocalypse. You think no one sees you working your machinations in the shadows? Even now, you work *against* Sh'logath's release, as if you could hold the apocalypse in your back pocket like some trump card to save you from boredom or failure. Your elder brother has seen all! You are nothing; you are no longer Nitthogr! You are James Shianan—an ambitious pretender and a false acolyte, flying the black flag of the vyrm army in vain."

James merely grinned in response. It was a cocky, brutish smile as he read from his handwritten notes—a copy of the Grimmoirium Nitthogr which he'd left with The Seven. He mumbled along under his breath, making a show of how little attention he paid to Rashaka. He mixed the last couple of reagents into a beaker on the nearby table and dipped his fingertips into the fizzing solution.

Next to the mixing beakers, his phone buzzed with a text message from his secondary tactical team. *Wolf got away, but not unscathed. Following the blood trail. Expect capture soon.*

James turned his gaze to the prisoner. "Are you quite finished? Because there is no power you or my brother wields which can stand against me." He flicked the fingers from his dry hand in a horizontal motion and Rashaka's restraints fell to the floor.

The vyrm bellowed a battle cry, and his eyes flared like emblazoned coals. Fire enveloped his body, and he hurled orbs of napalm-like flame.

James didn't even look at him. He held up a hand, and the attack dissolved against the shimmering force shield his dark magics erected.

The pyromancer stood in surprise at the complete ineffectiveness of the firestorm.

Mumbling a quick incantation from the forbidden book, James turned his gaze to the slender man. He flicked the liquid from the other fingers at his enemy and on contact, the rogue vyrm instantly exploded, leaving behind only a vaporous wisp of smoke and a mound of bloody gore. The rest of him caked the stony basement walls of the speakeasy like wet confetti.

He taunted the festering pile of super-heated, liquefied flesh and reveled in the carnage. Nitthogr spoke as if his brother could hear him. "Your Tarkhūn are not the chosen ones, *either*. You pretend you are waiting for Sh'logath's perfect timing, waiting for the revelation of the Architect King—but I know you. *You will never act*. You think you can balance reality like some kind of god! Even the Tarkhūn will not wait forever, brother. The Black follow me because I act!" He spat upon the molten pile and his spittle sizzled in the heat.

James smiled. He'd played this game of wills with his brother for centuries now, and this specific gambit had been decades in the making; he'd been careful enough not to tip his hand in all this time. For the first in a long while, he knew that he was clearly winning this game.

"Plenty of weirdness here in the Big Apple," said Vikrum Wiltshire, leaning back in his chair as his partner sifted through the messages. They'd had to wrap up the Minnesota job once they'd concluded that the murders were little more than humans trying to scare the local folks.

The reasons *why* they were doing it weren't of interest to the Red Order. That was a human concern, and the Order had more than enough supernatural concerns to deal with.

"Another package from Quintin," Sexton said. "That's strange. Two messages in as many months after more than a year of silence?
"

Wiltshire shrugged. "When it rains, it pours, right?" He took the envelope and spilled its contents onto the table. Documents and photographs—developed film—slid out.

A few documents detailed an illuminati cult called the Heptobscurantum: the secret seven. Wiltshire scanned the documents. It was light on data, most of it Wiltshire already knew from their archives. But Quintin had identified at least three of its members and worked up dossiers.

"Oh my God," Wiltshire said, prompting Sexton to join him at the table. "The Seven includes the real estate tycoon Peter Greyson and Thomas Chelish."

"Who's that?" Sexton asked.

"He owns half the premium channels on cable and a bunch of other media, too," Wiltshire said, sliding out the third image. "Also Bruce Cannon. The philanthropist art collector. He's in charge of, like, half the world's museums." Another photo, this one of former pro soccer player turned actor James Shianan, had a sticky note on it with a question mark and the number 4.

Quintin had hand-written a note detailing a string of kidnapping, explaining that heptobscurantum cultists were using people for blood rites and also scientific experiments.

He wrote: *Whatever they are doing, it can't be good, and it's way above my pay-grade... gotta call this one into the Order. Stole some computer files identifying the next target. See photo.*

Wiltshire shuffled to the next item in the stack: a photograph printed from the Internet of Claire Jones.

He looked Sexton in the eyes. "We've got to get back to Minnesota."

Chapter Eleven

Gravel crunched under the wheels of Jackie's car. It came to a stop at the spacious home nestled in a private, wooded area on the outskirts of town. The weathered mailbox read "Jecima."

The two girls sat in the vehicle for a long moment. "You're sure about this?" Jackie asked.

Claire exhaled a tense breath. "Yes. He's a friend of my father's. I know my dad would trust him. I just hope he's home." She looked at the phone on her lap. It lay in pieces with the battery separated. They hoped it would help prevent being tracked.

They steeled their nerves and approached the front door. A heavy, antique style knocker adorned the door, and it made an ominous *boom* as it struck.

Long seconds passed before the door creaked open to reveal a wizened old man. He wore his wispy hair and gold-rimmed spectacles with a sort of disheveled charm; age had shrunk him since Claire had last seen him. He asked, "Can I help you?"

"Professor Jecima? Miles Jecima?" Claire was surprised that he didn't recognize her.

"Yes. Can I help you?"

"It's Claire, Claire Jones. Sam Jones's daughter."

"Oh, right! I'm so sorry. I have a terrible way with names and faces." He chuckled. "I can immediately identify a thousand ancient texts... but people? I'm not so good with those. If you could ask my late wife, she'd tell you that for a fact. Do come in." He opened the door wider.

They followed him inside, watching over their shoulder as they closed it behind them. The old home bore the distinct markings of a widower; it had once been well maintained with a woman's touch, but obviously suffered at the hands of scholastic bachelorhood in the years since… at least from the professor's diminutive reach and downward. Stacks of books, loose papers, and maps lined the edges of the hallway.

"Right this way." He led them to his parlor, where a few sitting chairs still remained available without the prerequisite stacks of research materials piled atop. Jecima seated them and asked, "What brings you by? I'm not used to receiving many visitors. Oh dear! Is your father alright? I told him that zone was hostile."

"Yes. Yes, he is doing well. We spoke a few days ago." She paused for a moment, unsure of quite how to go about asking for help or explaining her situation. Claire didn't even know what kind of help she was looking for exactly.

As she wordlessly worked her mouth for a few seconds, the old man interjected, "Goodness. I'm a terrible host. Millie would have had my hide, bless her. Let me get you girls some tea." He rose quickly and shuffled out the door. He would clearly hear no argument on the matter.

No sooner had he left the room than a sudden peace fell over the girls. Claire felt like she might literally melt into the leather wingback chair. Something about the surroundings—old books and dusty artifacts—made Claire feel safe and protected.

"This reminds me of your dad's place growing up," Jackie observed.

Claire's eyes caught sight of a photo of her father and the professor taken over a decade ago, when Claire was still young and her mother still alive. She smiled at it and looked at another frame.

Next to the photo, she found a photocopied still: a double-paged spread copied from something obviously old; the ragged page edges zig-zagged down the image inked with a jagged toner mark. She took it into her hands and stared at the hand-drawn charcoal print.

She turned it to face Jackie. Jackie's jaw dropped, and she stared in disbelief.

Professor Jecima pushed a small cart into the room. A teapot, cups, and small plate of sugar cookies rode atop; Greek reference manuals weighed down the bottom rack. He noticed them looking at the image. "Ah, you have found 'The Brothers' I see. At least, that's what I think the small print says at the bottom."

"Where is this from?" Claire asked.

"That came from an ancient text I'd been working on until late. The book was stolen only recently: the Grimmorium Nitthogr. A very odd book, almost otherworldly—if such a statement didn't make me sound like I'd given up scholasticism in favor of joining a UFO cult. But it's a strange text: one unlike any other on the planet, both linguistically and archaeologically. It dates to ten thousand years old or more by our best measuring devices, and yet no culture we know of preserved bound books at such an early date. The language is certainly a linguistic anomaly; it is similar to the famous Voynich manuscript which scholars have tried to decode for over a hundred years to no avail.

"That drawing is a copy from the book. It appears right before a missing selection that had been cut from the text. I'd been working on that image title in order to develop a cypher to the text. It literally seemed to be the key. And yet, it's all for naught, now. And a pity, too. I'd just begun to make some serious progress in my translations based on it after your father sent me some stuff from central America. Very interesting stuff: the Sh'logath cult it was about...

"But you didn't come here to listen to an old man's woes. What brings you by?"

Jackie offered, "That's not your book's key. It's Claire's fiancé."

Jecima returned a quizzical look.

Claire pointed at one of the two men drawn in a reclining pose against an unfamiliar backdrop. "This man right here is the spitting image of my fiancé, James Shianan."

He stared back blankly. The name clearly didn't ring any bells.

"You don't know who James Shianan is?" Jackie asked incredulously. "Do you ever go to the movies?"

"Not in many years," he admitted.

Jackie asked, "Do you maybe have an iPad or something with Wi-Fi?"

He fumbled through a stack of things nearby. At the bottom of the pile of small household items was an iPad. "My sons gave me this as a gift a long while ago. I never really took the time to figure the blasted thing out."

Jackie thumbed it on. It had very little battery left and the network signal was weak, but it was enough. She did a quick search for James Shianan and pulled up a Hollywood gossip article and turned it over to the Professor.

"Well... this is quite an uncanny resemblance," he admitted. "But connecting him to an ancient, obscure text is a little..."

"Crazy?" Claire offered. "Let me tell you a little about crazy." She launched into a forty minute narrative of the last few weeks. She unloaded the entire story on the old man, ending with their arrival on his doorstep.

Professor Jecima followed the entire story, sometimes asking for more details. He suspended disbelief and gave her story a thoroughly analytical consideration.

"So I don't know what to believe," Claire concluded, exasperated, but feeling strangely good after venting all her tangled thoughts and emotions into the air. "I really have three options, as far as I can tell. The first option: James is after me for some unknown reason and the seemingly supernatural things are all coincidence. Number two: Vivian has been manipulating this whole ordeal as some kind of devious villain master-mind. Or thirdly: I'm hallucinating, delusional, or just plain off my rocker—I could be imagining all of this from a rubber room as far as I can tell. What do you think, Professor?"

The wise old man approached her where she sat in the chair. He bent over but slightly so that he could look her in the eyes. After gazing into them for a few seconds, he slapped her across the face; the palm of his hand cracked against her cheek hard enough to redden it.

"Whoa!" Jackie yelled incredulously.

Claire held her throbbing cheek. "What was that for?"

"Did that hurt you? Did you feel pain?"

"Yes!"

"And did you see it coming or have any kind of intuition or impulse that warned you it was coming?"

"No..."

"Then you can safely eliminate the third option; this is not a product of your mind. Furthermore, I'd just like to say that my entire history and life story would resent the implication that it was nothing but deluded snippets from an insane person's imagination. I think we can safely assume you are quite lucid."

"Well, what do you think, then?" Claire asked his opinion. "What is really going on?"

"I don't really believe in the impossible, and like Sherlock Holmes said, 'when you have eliminated the impossible, whatever remains, however improbable, must be the truth.'" He paused long as he gave it some thought. "Something supernatural is happening here; not unscientific, just not yet explainable by it. I guess I would like to know more about this Rob fellow."

Jackie chuckled. "You and her both."

Claire gave Jackie a dirty look. The nonverbal communication was not lost on Jecima. He raised his eyebrows. "Oh? Do tell."

Stone faced and about to give a rational response, Jackie butted in. "Well, he reminds me an awful lot of her dad... except homeless and cute. All signs point to a pair of star-crossed lovers."

Jecima mused, "Ah. A relationship like a Shakespearean Tragedy?"

"Say what?" Jackie was confused. "How does Shakespeare relate to astrology?"

Claire intervened and changed the subject. "I'm a little too preoccupied with staying alive to fall in love, thank-you very much. And I still don't know what's really going on just yet." Her defense was filled with bluster, but her blushing cheeks betrayed her.

The momentary lull afforded them a moment to sip hot tea and turn their thoughts to the next step. As Claire reached for a cookie, Jecima's eyes caught her pendant.

"I notice you're still wearing that artifact your father picked up in South America."

Claire nodded. "I never take it off."

"I was with him when he found it."

"At a dig site?" Jackie asked.

"In a junk store," the Professor corrected. "Like the Grimmorium Nitthogr, I'm not sure of its mysterious origins. Then again, I'm not sure that it's real, and that could account for the mystery. But it is pretty to look at."

"Oh," she said, "it's real."

Just then, an exterior door burst open with a loud crash on the other side of the house. The wall hangings shifted and clattered under the impact. A porcelain dish fell from its high perch and shattered as the threesome immediately jumped to its feet.

A loud scratching and smashing sound echoed down the hallway; the cacophony aimed straight for them and moved in fast. They barely had a moment to breathe and no time to react.

The door to the sitting room tore open, breaking off its hinges. A monstrous, lycan shape fell to the floor, skidding to a stop even as the behemoth form melted away into the smaller form of a ragged, scruffy man.

"Rob!" Claire screamed. She ran to his side where he lay mangled and slumped over, barely clothed, following his transformations.

Blood dripped from his twisted and busted nose. More pooled from what looked like a sword-cut across his chest; bruises and burns mottled the skin all over his body. He looked like he'd just been run over by a Mack truck.

Jackie ran to help. She mashed a throw pillow onto the bleeding wound and tried to staunch the hemorrhaging.

"Rob! What happened?" Claire didn't even think to ask how he found her.

Rob looked up at her, his eyes barely able to focus. He stiffened and whispered with a raspy voice, "Madeline Island." Then, his eyes rolled back, and he slumped limply.

Jackie grabbed his wrist and concentrated, feeling for a pulse. She looked at Claire and shook her head. "He... he's dead."

Claire stared in disbelief. Shellshock blanched her face.

The Professor fumbled in the background, tossing through a cabinet of medical supplies. Jackie urged insistently, "Claire—if he was able to track you, it's possible that whoever is chasing you can, too!"

She needed to act quickly. But her options suddenly became *very* limited.

"Screw the paperwork," said Wiltshire as he began to hastily pack up to follow Quintin's lead back to Minnesota. "We must have missed something—and the cultists are after that girl. We've got to help her."

The phone in the headquarters rang before Sexton could respond. The screen identified the caller as Praetor Russo, which was expected. Few had access to that line.

Sexton opened the channel.

"I got your verbal report," he said. Russo sounded weary, and whenever he got tired, his Italian accent became more pronounced. "I'm calling to tell you that we are upgrading you both to our global team."

Sexton cocked his head. "Like a promotion?"

Russo shrugged. "Your work was good in the Midwest. We are expanding the territory you will cover."

"We won't be able to keep up with the work *here* if we're also supposed to investigate cases in Seattle or Iraq."

"True," Russo said. "And you'll still work out of New York's Red Keep, but you'll get special assignments that will send you all over the world. A new local team will be formed. They'll work out of the same space and take over your region's duties."

"Good," Wiltshire said. "Can they start today?"

Russo gave him a confused look.

"We just got a new lead on the Minnesota case," Sexton said. "There may be more to it than we thought."

"The heptobscurantum may be involved," Wiltshire informed him. "The humans disguising themselves as sasquatches or as werewolves or any other giant hairy monster? We think they were part of the cult and they're after a girl."

Russo shook his head. "No. I need you here."

"You just increased our jurisdiction," Wiltshire said, frustrated.

"Exactly. I need you *here*. In Rome. And I need you here right away," said the Praetor. His voice had dipped an octave, expressing the severity of whatever concerns had motivated his decision. "I will have another Praetor reach out to the Keep in Minneapolis. Their local team will handle it."

The printer whirred to life as Russo hit a button on the other side of the connection. "Your flight leaves soon."

Russo killed their feed and Wiltshire cursed. He hated leaving a job unfinished, especially if it meant someone else was in danger.

Sexton turned his computer screen so his partner could see it. "Looks like the girl's already in the wind."

A news article on the screen showed Claire's photo. *Celebrity's Fiance Flees Mental Health Professionals.* It claimed she was mentally unwell and on the run, giving descriptions of who to call if there were any tips or sightings.

Sexton's hands flew across the keyboard and he pulled up information on the publisher and the company which owned it. A cursor blinked near the name of the primary shareholder in the media company. *Thomas Chelish.*

"Shit!" Wiltshire crumpled up the printed airline tickets. He angrily launched it towards the wastebasket.

His partner intercepted the paper ball and unfolded it, smoothing it out on the desk. "You know what we have to do," he said. "The praetors need us in Rome. So we go to Rome."

Wiltshire's nostrils flared, and he threw a mini tantrum.

"There's nothing we can do if the cult is after her. Nothing that the local brothers can't do if it's not too late for the girl already. But we *can* get to the bottom of whatever has Praetor Russo so rattled."

Wiltshire stood there, fuming for a few moments longer. He cursed again loudly, and then snatched up his bag and finished packing for Rome.

Chapter Twelve

Claire exhaled a sigh of relief as Jackie's car cleared the edge of the city. She'd made it past the far edge of the Wisconsin side of the city. Duluth's twin city over the bay, Superior, shrank behind her and the roads narrowed while the wilderness expanded, thickening. She glanced into the rearview mirror, tilting it down so she could look at her incapacitated passenger.

She'd let Jackie out at a tourist trap near the edge of Superior. Her friend had graciously given up her car and volunteered to find her own way back to her parents' place. Undoubtedly it would be watched, but they weren't pursuing her; they wanted Claire.

Reaching back, she took Rob's wrist and felt for his pulse. The faint beat of his heart reassured her that he still lived. She stole a glance at him. He still looked terrible, but his color slowly returned. Dark blood splattered Jackie's backseat with stains that Billy Mays would have difficulty removing. Most of the serious wounds had clotted by now. At first, she feared he might have simply run out of blood, but Rob proved tougher than anyone else she'd ever met, and he healed unusually fast, even if the burn marks seemed to fade slower than other damage.

Claire turned back to the road. Her head was a mess, and her stomach roiled like a bundle of raw nerves and self-doubt. She wasn't sure why she was even doing this: following some vague clue, the last words of a dying homeless man. Part of her felt she should just go back and tell her fiancé everything—he would surely understand! *My heart tells me that he loves me! This is probably all Vivian's doing. Maybe she's involved in some kind of conspiracy through her government agency?*

She pushed the thoughts from her mind. She couldn't make decisions based on her desire to be back in her relationship of comfort... or because she feared the man in her backseat, either. Her thoughts drifted to the recurring dream of the wolf attack. *I wonder if the dream is a premonition—a warning? Am I running towards even more danger as I'm fleeing?*

There was that self-doubt flaring up again—the words in her head didn't even sound like her voice—she barely knew who she was anymore. Claire didn't know if her sanity was assured, Professor Jecima's hand slap aside.

Rob mumbled something incoherently. Her ears perked up as she tried to make sense of his syllables. She had little desire to listen to the radio, her only other potential distraction.

"...don't understand... Tesseract... Have to tell... know before the end... I love you!" Rob writhed like a man with a fever. He rambled like one, too.

The voyeurism made Claire blush. It felt a bit like reading someone else's diary. His fevered state reminded her of a trip to Africa with her father; he'd caught a virus that gave him such a high temperature that he raved like a madman for two days.

"...going to die... Bithia... Everything's going to burn... will always love you. Claire."

Hearing her name, Claire's resolve broke, and she turned on the radio. But for most of the next hour, Rob lapsed back into a sweaty quiet.

The gentle rocking of waves lulled Rob out of his sleep. His eyes fluttered and then opened. He grimaced against the harsh, white sunlight that blinded him as he came around.

Groaning, Rob recognized that he'd returned to the land of the living. He found himself in the backseat of Jackie's car. His voice barely managed more than a whisper. "Where are we?"

Claire turned around from the driver's seat. "On the Island Queen ferry: Halfway between the mainland and Madeline."

Rob pulled up the remnants of his bloody shirt and looked at his chest and abdomen. They still bore bruises and wounds from his battle with the vyrm assassins. Two fresh, bright red burn patches radiated pain through his rib cage. "What is this?"

"A defibrillator burn. Professor Jecima had an AED installed in the final days before his wife passed. Luckily, it was better charged than his other electronics."

He blinked at her, obviously confused.

"Your heart stopped. AEDs electrocute your heart in order to restart it."

Rob sat back and melted into the seat. "I think I need to rest."

"You look like you need it. But don't take too long. You still haven't told me the plan."

"We need to take you to see a shaman so that we can contact Bithia."

"Bithia? I've heard you say that name before," Claire said. "When?"

Claire blushed slightly. "You talk in your sleep."

Rob paused for thought. "I hope I didn't say anything embarrassing. After everything I've been through, I'd hate for it to be embarrassment that finally kills me."

Claire smiled. She'd never heard him joke before.

"It's very easy for things to get muddled, confused, jumping between worlds. It gets even more intense when one is unconscious."

"What do you mean?"

"Between the Prime and the other realms… memories can become… cloudy. Not all of my memories are mine: if I concentrate, I can feel this realm's memories of myself, search them for answers. It's how I know my other self's name is Robert."

She nodded, accepting his answer, even if she didn't understand it. "I don't really get this whole 'Prime' thing, or whatever the Tesseract is."

Rob, still cloudy from the pain and the toll the healing process took on his body, drifted off as the ferry bobbed in the waves of Lake Superior. Groggily he said, "I'll tell you as soon as I can keep my eyes awake."

As the car pulled off of the ferry and onto the wharf, Claire's anxiety level shot through the roof. Her situation became very real to her at that moment. She had left her home, her former life, and all that she'd ever held dear. Here she was: engaged to a wealthy, famous, A-list actor, but she'd suddenly run away to a tiny, remote island with a homeless man who told her he'd just arrived from another dimension.

"Wait here," she said to Rob as he rubbed the sleepy crust from his eyes. Claire stepped out of the vehicle and ran into a public restroom just one block from the visitors' information area.

Since he'd fallen asleep again, Claire's mind had turned inward again and turned against her. Much like her time in the hospital, it felt like a supernatural invasion: an attack on her mind.

Once inside the bathroom stall, she broke down and sobbed. She already missed her old life, her habits, her father, her friends. She wanted her safety net back! She wasn't ready for this! In a moment of weakness, she pulled a cell phone out of her purse: an anonymous prepaid cell Jackie had bought for her at the truck stop where she'd been dropped. Just in case she absolutely needed to make contact, she had options.

Like it was second nature to her, Claire thumbed in James's number and composed a brief text message. *I'm on Madeline Island with the wolf. Please take me home.* Just about to press send, her resolve took root again. This was not who she was! She clutched the amulet around her neck and all the haziness that had fogged through her mind evaporated like mist in the sunlight.

That's weird. I didn't think I even know James's number by heart, she admitted to herself. She only knew a handful that she could enter without struggling to remember, and those were numbers she learned before ever owning a mobile phone.

She regained her composure and forced herself to think about the last couple days and the decisions she'd made in that time. Claire fought back against the mental invader that tried closing doors in her mind. She wouldn't let it twist up her thoughts and emotions.

Everything within her mind claimed that James was vile—urged her to run. But something in her heart refused to quit loving him, despite that. She squeezed the pendant around her neck again. Claire knew that she was a mess. But she also knew she was strong, and that she was the one in control: she alone chose who she could give her love to.

She pulled the battery from the phone, killing it cold. Then she hardened her heart and checked herself at the mirror before leaving the restroom and returning to the car.

Claire flung the door open and plopped into the driver's seat. "Okay. Tell me everything about the Prime and the Tesseract."

James opened his eyes. His skin smoldered and a light, acrid smoke wafted off of his body. Vivian stood nearby with her arms crossed. She watched him writhe in pain, like he'd been immersed in some invisible, electric current.

He shook off the throbbing sting and smoothed his robes, regaining composure. A thin layer of ash sheathed his skin. "She has figured out how to resist. She must be learning, drawing power from the amulet."

"All these years spent in preparation for the Earth gambit. What is the contingency plan if she cannot be secured?"

"Just find her, Caivev!" James lashed out in frustration. "*There is no contingency*! She is the key!" He seethed as he paced the length of the old gangster's facility. "We've shifted all of our focus to this plan. This is the closest we've ever come in our efforts—this is the *only* plan now!"

"We still have Princess Bithia."

Nitthogr shot her a sidelong look. "Yes. Of course. But she will never bend to my will." He paused. "Return to the Prime. I may not be able to bypass our prey's mental defenses, but at some point, they will make a play for the end game. Claire Jones cannot run forever, and we must be able to anticipate their next course of action. Zahaben's son has never been predictable.

"Have General Regorik reassure the vyrm army that everything goes according to plan. Keep them on our original schedule. We will preserve the original timeline. Return at once and use your contacts in the earth's government to expand our search. Use the humans' own forces against them."

Vivian bowed, but she did not smile. She'd always been jaded by the fact that she had not been given Regorik's appointment. "And Princess Bithia?"

"Make sure Regorik maintains a heavy guard around her; he should include some of the vyrm psychics. Also, all portals to the

Prime must be guarded from within. If our fugitives attempt to access it, we will have them."

"Can I use the nearest dimensional gate?"

"The old cathedral on fourth, at the altar," he confirmed, searching his thoughts for the proper calculations. "The church has been bought by the Heptobscurantum; there are no prying eyes to be wary of."

Vivian nodded and clicked her heels. She turned and departed. If Claire slipped out of their grasp, it wouldn't be her fault.

"Imagine that reality, all the dimensions combined, was like a giant block of Swiss cheese," Rob tried to explain. He'd had more time to compose his thoughts and explain inter-dimensional travel along the planes of reality that made up the Tesseract.

"But I thought it was like a Crystal?"

"That's true, but for the sake of my illustration, think of it like a cube of cheese. Some cheese makers coat the outside in colored wax. Imagine that this six-sided block of Swiss had a wax coating on each side so that each was a different color. That would be a simple way to think about it. Each facet is a different color because each is a different dimension; aspects of reality are different there, even though we're all tied to the greater stuff of reality which makes up the center: the Prime. The way reality is expressed is different from dimension to dimension, like a different color, even though it's still all cheese. For example, the vyrm are the race of people from The Desolation, a realm utterly corrupted by Nitthogr long ago, during the Syzygyc War, when all of reality very nearly was devoured."

"Devoured?"

"Sorry. The Reality Eater is a title given to Sh'logath."

"You mentioned him before."

"He is the anti-god worshiped by the vyrm. Many centuries ago, Nitthogr and his brother, Basilisk, acted as inter-dimensional surveyors; they discovered the methods of travel and recorded it all. But in their time exploring, they were seduced and corrupted by the vyrm and the newly formed cult of Sh'logath."

"And Sh'logath is what, like God's enemy, some kind of devil or Satan?"

Rob chuckled. "Oh, no. Sh'logath is far worse than that. He is the essence of unreality. Satan is hard at work against you, but neither he nor other any mere demon could ever be considered an equal with the Almighty—"

"Wait," Claire interrupted. "You're saying God and Satan are real, too? That doesn't make any sense."

Rob looked far off. "Open your mind, Claire. An eternal, creative force like God did not stop with making only your kind. Humanity, even Earth, is special, but there is more to reality than just this flesh." He pinched his cheek for emphasis. "But I understand your confusion. That is why this realm has always been off-limits to travelers. Eventually, almost all travel was prohibited."

"But something changed?"

"We were overrun. Nitthogr finally acquired enough power and flooded the gates with his vyrm. The Prime is his, now."

"How does he get through?"

"Back to the cheese." Rob winked. "If one wanted to move from the edge of the block to the inside, you must move through one of the holes: go from edge to inside. Once inside, you could then go to another edge."

"Can you go from edge to edge, too?" Claire attempted to follow the analogy.

"Yes, but the destinations are more fixed in those circumstances, but every hole *can also* lead to the inside."

"So how did Nitthogr conquer the Prime?"

"He came all at once. If you were going to push something through this cheese-hole, you would need some kind of force, like, say, a stream of water. It can be pointed from one direction when it is on, and if the angle is right, the force will push whatever you want inside the tunnel. That is how travel works: when the moon phases are right and everything aligns, travel is possible, as the tunnels are free and open. But at certain times, like certain moon phases or cosmic events, all the portals are unlocked.

"If the cosmic and lunar forces are like streams of water that push through, what happened during his invasion is the equivalent of this cheese being plunged deep inside a bucket. He came when all the portals opened wide and we were caught off guard. Vyrm forces came from every portal; they arrived everywhere and all at once.

"We did not foresee such an attack or so many vyrm that he positioned throughout the planes; some of our own had also been corrupted over the years. But still, Nitthogr hasn't made his play for a greater prize: total control of all the Tesseract's power and secrets.

"He kidnapped the daughter of the King to try to gain access. The Creator, the great Architect King, invented such a secure method of access that none can penetrate its defenses. But I fear he will eventually succeed if he acquires you. You are the key, Claire Jones. You and Bithia are both access points for him to break the vault or open the void."

"So if he gets me, the world ends? Perfect."

"That's just one of two options," Rob explained. "The vyrm are fanatical. They seek the unleashing of Sh'logath and the annihilation of reality. Some aspects of God are creativity and the grand song of existence. Sh'logath is Agod: the opposite of God. He is not maliciously evil or malevolent like Satan, a fallen, heavenly being. Sh'logath is The Hunger, the opposite of reality. He is the nether and the nonexistence. Contrary to God, Sh'logath has no power; he does not exist."

"Except that he does, or he wouldn't have a whole planet full of crazed cultists," Claire pointed out.

"That's the paradox, of course," Rob agreed. "By calling Sh'logath into existence, letting him into the Tesseract, into reality, the vyrm would splinter existence, shatter it. Everything would cease to exist: only Sh'logath personified—the great nothing."

"Not even God?"

"Existence and nonexistence cannot dwell together. This goes beyond the Light and Darkness of Lucifer and Jesus. Shadows can be dispelled with the light. But neither shadow nor daylight exist without the Sun."

Claire nodded. "Don't get caught."

"And don't eat the cheese." Rob winked and pointed to the nearby public beach as they drove very slowly through the tiny tourist town of La Pointe. "Pull over there."

"So all of reality ending is option number one. What was the other possibility?"

"I think it far more likely that Nitthogr, your James, is leveraging the awakening of Sh'logath against his own plan. Basilisk was always far more enthralled by the Devourer. And yet, it was Basilisk that ended the Syzygyc War; in the end, his sudden doubts overruled his fanaticism. Nitthogr's heart bent towards a different sort of corruption. He seeks domination and adoration. He is using the vyrm to his own end, I believe; eventually he will need to somehow turn their devotion from Sh'logath to Nitthogr.

"If he cannot have his satisfaction, if Nitthogr cannot subjugate the creation of the Architect King, only then will he release Sh'logath."

Claire nodded. She felt less confused than before, but knew she'd only learned snippets of a grand story which spanned the pages of galactic history. She turned her thoughts to the more immediate situation. "Then what will this shaman be able to do? How will that work?"

"First, we've got to find her." Rob withdrew an elongated crystal almost the size of his thumb from his pocket. He hopped out and waded nimbly into the water, wincing only slightly as the cold water came in contact with his wounds. Rob reached down and retrieved a clamshell almost as big as his hand; he shook it dry as he returned to the passenger seat.

"What's that?"

Rob used the pointy end of the faceted stone to etch a rune into the inside of the shell. He put the crystal into the shell while holding it. The crystal slowly moved to point north. "It's a kind of compass," he said as he navigated them through the village on the south-western side of the island. "Go north east."

Vivian dusted off her clothing as if she could somehow wipe off the Earth stink as she walked through the halls. Her boot heels announced her presence as they clacked and echoed down the cobblestone corridor. She strode up to General Regorik, who sat near the door to the prison cells. Perched atop a stool, he and four other guards engaged in a game of chance.

"Caivev," he hissed from behind his serpent-like tongue. "What news from the earth-front?"

She scowled down at the venerable warrior as he pushed in an ante chip. "Surely there are better uses of your time while our lord is away?"

Regorik laughed. "I'm sure you'll tell me just what those things are! For all your desire and devotion to Sh'logath, you still lack those fundamental qualities that make a good vyrm!"

Caivev rolled her eyes. Deep down, he was correct, but also more wrong than he would ever know. She *was more than vyrm!* Caivev's zeal and devotion burned stronger than any vyrms' because she was not—she did not inherit her faith. Her consecration to Sh'logath belonged only to her.

"Tell me," Regorik pressed, "Have you let all the blood necessary to complete the Dunnischkte?"

Her tight-lipped grimace came as close to a smile as she would give. "I have, when my Earth persona, Vivian Shianan, fell under my knife."

Regorik waved to the drunken priest who sat nearby on the floor. "Charsk! Check her."

Charsk staggered to his feet. He took her by the face and stared deep into her eyes.

Caivev bit her tongue; Charsk was, perhaps, her least favorite vyrm, but as the leader of the priest caste, he held the keys to her completing the Dunnischkte ritual which would merge her human self with the Vyrm physiology, much like Basilisk and Nitthogr had done so long ago. It was the ultimate symbol of devotion to the Cult of Sh'logath—a task that only an outsider and convert could perform. Eliminating all dimensional variants, the Dunnischktet could conceivably live forever—and yet this devotion to the agod demanded that it never come to pass.

Charsk shook his head. "There still remains another. She has not yet eliminated all her forms across the Tesseract. She cannot yet merge." He playfully slapped her face with a drunken grin.

She cursed as her shoulders slumped. Regorik exposed a winning hand and the other players mirthfully spat profanities at him. "What next, then?" he asked her.

Caivev spun on her heels. "I've got more work to do. Get more guards in here on Nitthogr's orders!"

"Nobody's getting in here," Regorik defended.

"Then get some sober ones in here! And call for some psy-vyrm: someone who can defend our prisoner through the ether! He wants a psychic tabs kept on Bithia at all times."

Regorik spat out an amused sigh as he anted up again. "Psssh! Humans."

The small size of the island meant that the car soon closed in on the mystic compass's destination. Claire and Rob sat inside Jackie's car at an overgrown driveway near the north coast, where a rusty chain barred their path. A rickety fence made of rusty corrugated sheet metal waged a war of heights with the unkempt stalks of field grass.

"You're sure this is the place?" Claire asked for confirmation.

The six foot hunk of steel nearest a stray fencepost wore an age-faded Native American eagle symbol. The emblem of the Anishinaabe, though only done in red Krylon, looked like it was once a majestic and artistic piece before the rigors of age set in.

Rob nodded and then got out of the car. He detached the chain and let it fall to the ground. "I see a little shack back there in the woods." He pointed the way.

The little car rocked and bucked on the rutted, earthen driveway. Claire feared it would bottom out and get stuck in one of the potholes. After a jarring bump, the trees opened up into an ill-kept yard. Piles of debris and other assorted junk had been heaped in a variety of manners all around. Their sheer size made distinguishing a mound of twisted scrap from the owner's hovel a difficult task. An intertwined mess of interlaced branches peeked up from behind the shanty house; the owner obviously put more effort into that tangled structure than the home.

They exited the vehicle and walked toward the shack, passing a disturbingly tall pile of weather-checked Jack Daniels bottles. The fading evening sunlight glinted off of the western side of the glass mound.

"Whaddaya want?" a disheveled, old Native American woman crooned from the dilapidated porch as they approached. She attempted to stand up, nearly knocking over her freshly emptied whisky bottle in the process. "I already told em, I ain't paying those back taxes. It ain't like that on the island!"

Rob stepped forward apprehensively and said in a calm tone, "That's not who we are, miss..."

"Kechewaishke," she said arrogantly, as if the name born of her proud heritage should mean something to an outsider. "Besides, I'da had the money if those National Geographic people woulda ever completed that piece on th'island history." Her words held a slight slur, but might have been a product of her hermitage more than the effects of the alcohol. She slumped back into the old rocking chair that propped her up.

Something in her defeated tone indicated it might be okay for them to continue their approach. Rob crept up beside her; he ignored the unpleasant odors lacing the air.

The old woman noticed the look on his face and chuckled. "Don't mind th'smell. An opossum died under the deck last week. It'll quit stinkin in a few days. What do you folks want from me, then?"

Claire interjected, "We were told a great shaman could be found here."

Kechewaishke cackled a great, almost toothless chortle. She laughed so hard she cried. Wiping a tear from her eye, she said, "Honey, I don't know who's been filling your head with such nonsense, but you might've seen Dances with Wolves one too many times."

Claire looked at Rob with hesitation.

"I'm sorry, Miss Kechewaishke..."

"Ma Kechewaishke. Call me Ma."

"Ma. I'm looking for someone who can help my friend on an Hembleciya."

Ma spat at the word and gave Rob a dirty look, as if he'd offended her.

"I'm sorry, Ma." He corrected his verbiage, accidentally using a Sioux term instead of the Ojibwa. "She needs to meet with her Weyekin. Can you help us?" He told her only what she needed to know and might be capable of understanding in her state.

She spat again, but looked at them with a gleam of enterprise in her eye. "D'you got any money?" She picked up the bottle to take a sip, but discovered it empty.

Rob looked apprehensively at Claire. Claire returned his nervous look and pulled out her empty pockets in response.

"Is there anything else we can do to secure your help," Rob asked.

A foul look came over Ma's face. "If you're name ain't Jack Daniels or Benjamin Washington, I ain't listening to ya." She crossed her arms sternly, firmly gripping the glass jug.

Dejectedly, Claire muttered, "Let's just go. We can find another."

Rob whispered back, "No. There's a reason we are here. Nitthogr will have guards near any with the practiced skill to 'send you beyond.'"

Claire gave him an apprehensive look. She still didn't quite understand what she was doing here.

"What if I told you we were on a mission from Gichi-manidoo?"

Ma uncrossed her arms and leaned forward in her squeaky chair. "What did you say?" She almost whispered the question; a long pause followed as Ma looked back into her memories. "He said you would come..." she trailed off, looking away, into the distance, into nothing at all. She looked down at the empty bottle in her hands. "Long ago... so long ago, when my Weyekin brought me into the presence of almighty Gichi-manidoo. He told me to expect you, to aid you. I was a young girl, then."

Her eyes narrowed at her bottle, and she clutched it with white knuckles. "I waited and waited. But you never came. And I couldn't find my Weyekin or Gichi-manidoo, no matter how long or how often I quested through the ether. I was alone; He was silent. And now... here you are, and I'm an old lady."

She stared down, ashamed at her own impatience. "What form does your Weyekin take?" Rob asked gently.

"A wolf."

Ma looked up to see Rob standing there as a mountainous lycanthrope. She choked back her gasp, stood, and threw her bottle at the mountain of empty glassware. It hit with such force that it shattered and caused a violent landslide of empty jugs. The avalanche engulfed her regrets and thrust new life and vigor into her.

"This way," she said, beaming. "I will get the spices and reagents. My sweat lodge is in the back!" She hobbled quickly inside her house.

Rob took Claire by the hand. "Don't be scared. I am sending you to find Princess Bithia like only *you* can. But beware; this journey won't be without its own perils." He squeezed her hand. "You will have to find the Prime from among your own chaos."

Chapter Thirteen

Wincing at the flavor, Claire sipped deep from the cup of bitter, boiled herbs. She wiped her mouth and lay down inside the lodge as Ma Kechewaishke stoked the fire within the sweltering structure. Sweat beaded upon Claire's lip and her nostrils burned; pungent fumes wafting from the wetted weeds Ma carefully arranged upon the coal bed.

"How do you feel?" Rob squeezed her hand as he asked the question.

"So sleepy." Claire's words slurred and her eyelids moved ever slowly.

"Don't disturb her," said Ma, between sips of her own on the herbal concoction. "Not that you would be able to once she has 'gone up the mountain.' But the sooner she sleeps, the sooner she has her encounter."

Rob gave her an inquisitive look, focusing on the old woman's cup.

"Perhaps Gichi-manidoo will finally answer me, too," she said hopefully. The more experienced planes-walker exhaled deeply, as with a contented sigh, and closed her eyes. She leaned back against the wall and her lids shot open to reveal milky white eyes. She'd traveled beyond.

Claire's head lolled to the side, and her jaw slackened. She sighed as every remaining scrap of breath leaked from her lungs. Then, she inhaled and exhaled rapidly, like a panting dog; Claire, too, was gone.

Rob sat in silence between the two unconscious female forms. The roasting heat made his head swim and his new shirt, an over-sized hoody borrowed from Jackie's trunk, quickly soaked with perspiration. He refused to leave the sweat lodge before they'd returned.

James only needed a fraction of his concentration to maintain the open viewing portal. The ethereal opening between the dimensions looked much like a smoky window.

From the other's side of the aperture, Vivian assured Nitthogr that he'd correctly anticipated his enemies' move. "The Vyrm psychics tell me that Princess Bithia's trance is deeper than mere communion with the Architect King. She sent her spirit out into the ether, probing, trying to connect with her other form and interfere with your plans. Thus far, she has been adept at evading the Vyrm eidolons and escaping any traps they have set against her."

Amused, James chuckled. He knew he couldn't simply kill her—with her spirit disconnected from body, the Royal mark her soul bore would be lost forever. She'd made a good move.

"Fools," he grinned again, easily guessing his fugitives' next moves. "Zabe is running straight down the contents of the Grimmorium. It's like he does not realize that *I wrote* this book! There's no way he can beat me at my own game, but it will be fun nonetheless, even if it is barely a challenge.

"Pull the psychics back. Their eidolon projections are not to interfere with Bithia making contact inside the ether."

"As if they could," Vivian spat over her shoulder to the vyrm clairvoyants behind her. "They cannot even locate her now; she's talented, and her will is strong."

James continued. "Have them lie in wait and merely observe. If I'm right, Claire or Zabe will try to contact with the princess. Once that happens, we should be able to locate them. We won't need to find Bithia; if the eidolons can mark Claire in the ether, then we will have them."

Vivian nodded, and the vyrm behind her immediately sank into their positions outside of the prison doors. "I'm ready to return," she assured him. "Regorik will contact you through the runestones once there is news."

Nodding and smiling, James congratulated himself. "The snare is set. We only need to wait for the prey to walk in." He waved a finger and the inter-dimensional window dispelled in a wisp of smoke.

Soon, she would be his again. And time was urgent. The Seven grew restless; astral bodies aligned, and they still required Claire's blood to complete the dark summoning rite to release Sh'logath.

Claire awoke with a violent gasp! *No... not awake... conscious on a different plane...* It felt like a vision, but Claire knew that it was also real in a different sense of the term. Everything appeared silent and still. She spun a lazy circle and observed her surroundings; nothing moved save a gentle dust that floated in the air, kicked up by her slow movements. Shades of blue and grey seemed to paint everything in an otherworldly light: a cool tone of faded sepia.

She called out, but no sound came from her mouth, though she could hear her words echoing through her mind; they seemed to reverberate into eternity. Claire centered herself and moved forward through her surroundings, trying to identify where she was. It all felt so familiar, certainly far removed from the wild growth of Ma Kechewaishke's island.

Concrete and pavement stretched across the ground. From deep within the cracks, dandelions and crab grass shoots sprang up; they wavered in a breeze that she couldn't quite feel. A recognizable building towered nearby: the high school she attended when she was a teenager.

Climbing the front stair, Claire pushed her way through the heavy double doors. The thought stuck in her mind that these doors shouldn't weigh so much. They were difficult to open and so much heavier than she remembered.

The main hallway stretched before her as she bravely entered. Seeing it all again—reliving it—she suddenly began to doubt herself. Claire felt just as she did when she entered that building for the first time so many years ago, unsure and overwhelmed by life. This was a brick ark that preserved her pain and suffering. Emotions bubbled to the surface: doubt and self-loathing, fake friends and the painful, social pecking order, the heartache of losing her mother so shortly after enrollment, the sense that everything in life was uncertain. Everything felt like a threat.

Claire winced against the pain that slowly crippled her heart. She knew she'd buried these feelings so long ago, but she'd thought them dead and far below ground. Now, they threatened to crawl out from that grave she'd put them in years prior.

She swallowed hard and wandered the halls. Empty desks sat like gravestones amid the abandoned rooms. The drab tones only helped conjure old memories, though not all bad. Claire meandered past the drinking faucet where she'd first met Jackie.

Her heart caught in her throat when she looked down at her hands. She held a photo frame that she had made in her introductory wood shop class, and she knew what that meant! *This is that dark day*—the one that nearly broke her! She looked around, but the halls were still empty and silent.

Claire walked forward as if drawn to her locker, knowing that she had to put the frame in her locker before her next class—she had to, like irresistible fate. Claire tried to slow down, to drag her feet, but she could not. This was a fixed memory. She couldn't change it! As soon as she'd get to her locker, the announcement would come for her to report to the office and learn that her mother had died.

She struggled against the forced march towards that tiny, metal door as if she might somehow change the course of history—but her efforts proved futile. Standing before her locker another memory rushed back to her: she didn't even realize it had all happened on this same day... the frame never made it into the locker! There was a snake in there. This was that day, too!

Closing her eyes against the locker that loomed before her, Claire could feel the vibration of the speakers demanding her presence in the administration hall. It all repeated itself, but this time there was no Robert there to save her!

Time seemed to stretch out forever and she slowly, inevitably, reached for the locker handle. She looked around in a panic for Rob, half expecting to see a young Vivian watching her handiwork from a distance, but the halls remained empty. *Claire was on her own.*

The locker latch lifted. The door swung free. And there was her algebra book, tattered and propped up against the side, like it always was. Claire exhaled the tense lungful of air she'd been holding; there were no snakes here. She laid the frame inside and walked to the ladies' room, wiping away the warm tears that rolled down her cheeks.

Her resolve rose up inside her again as she pushed her way into the lavatory and leaned against the walls. Closing her eyes, she dried her cheeks and remembered what her father had told her. *You are strong, and so much like your mother.* Claire rarely thought of her mother; those thoughts were too painful.

She'd always been strong. But perhaps her strength did not come from killing her hurts, or dying to them; maybe denying her emotions was the wrong course? Was it possible that strength came by conquering those emotions and ruling them even amid all the pain they caused?

Feeling childlike, Claire chided herself and looked at her fingers. They had blackened from the mascara when she'd wiped her tears. She walked towards the sink in order to clean herself up, trying to remember exactly what it was that she was supposed to do here.

Scrubbing the dark makeup from her fingers, she looked up at the mirror and caught her reflection. Her reflection moved of its own accord. Standing further back than she was, her doppelganger held a finger to her lips and motioned for her to be silent.

For all the self-talk building up her bravery and strength, Claire's heart skipped a beat, and she bolted for the door. Never a believer in ghosts, she'd never experienced anything like this before! Looking over her shoulder, her reflection pounded on the glass, demanding her attention.

Nearly tumbling into the hall, Claire reevaluated her situation. *I've never experienced anything like this before?* She laughed at herself. *What about living fire demons, werewolf protectors, inter-dimensional warlock fiancées, plus whatever the heck a Sh'logath is?*

Claire's heart rate returned to normal, and she scanned the hallway. A fog had crept in, obscuring much of the tiled floor. She looked at the locker door she'd left hang wide. Snakes poured from the opening; one after another, they fell to the ground like great drops of scaly water leaking from a faulty tap.

Her heart leapt again, but this time it was for a perfectly rational fear: snakes. Wild eyed and worried, Claire rushed to the mirror to meet her other self.

The woman in the mirror nodded knowingly, as if she could tell from Claire's expression that the serpents had arrived. *They are here?* Claire could hear the question echo through her mind.

She confirmed with a head bob.

I am Bithia, she explained through the mirror. *Rob must have sent you?*

Yes, she responded.

Bithia looked excited at the prospect. *If the snakes have found us, then there isn't much time. The darkness has already started.* The tiny window revealed a creeping darkness as dusk had fallen; it grew deeper by the moment. *You must get out and into the light, and you must not let the snakes touch you!*

Why did Rob send me to see you? What is it that I need to know?

Bithia reached into her own chest and pulled out a glowing orb from where her heart should have been. *We must align! There isn't time for me to tell you.* She looked hesitantly to the creeping shadow by the window. *Take this; once we merge you will see it all.* Bithia pushed the radiant sphere to the edge of the glass. It slowly pushed through, like a hot stone sliding through butter.

Claire cradled the orb. She paused only momentarily and then thrust it into her own chest. Memories, realities, information, feelings and emotions all flooded through her, crackling within her nerves and synapses as the collective moments of Bithia's life hit her at once. They washed over her as one. She knew the vast history of the Prime and its importance to all of reality. Everything that Bithia knew Claire now had access to.

She fell to her knees, only slightly trembling. They had merged. Claire touched her cheek. She felt the sting of Nitthogr's backhand strike. Her amulet crackled with energy, polarity confusion caused a ripple of power to radiate off it.

All the warlock's plans lay open before her; the bragging monologues and hours Nitthogr spent lording his scheme over her were exposed via Bithia's memories. The vyrm's Chosen One planned to use her as leverage: he sought the opening of the sacred chamber of the Tesseract so he could claim reality as his own to mold and master.

The vyrm would feel betrayed and possibly revolt if Nitthogr denied Sh'logath his due. And yet, if he seized hold of such power, he could be an even more dread force than the mere annihilation imposed by Sh'logath; he could easily cow them into submission and eventually turn their hearts.

In her mind's eye she saw the prospective fallout of his reign of terror; it spread across the multiverse like a cancer. The Prime would fall under his thrall and all the dimensions would bend and bow before him in domino fashion.

Claire saw her part in intricate detail as Nitthogr became James Shianan in order to bind her to himself and tie his line into the royal lineage. Birthing a child would grant him access after killing Bithia post-birth: Claire would then assume the spirit of the Prime and the power of the royal blood would run through the heir. Nitthogr would create, and then mold the child, in his image—the mother was unnecessary.

He would offer up the blood of either the Princess or Claire and unleash the mighty Sh'logath only as a last resort should his assumption of power fall short. The entire scheme of the warlock hinged upon the proper alignment of the lunar bodies.

The machinations of the evil warlord appeared impossible to delay; the quickest and most immediate option was to flee Nitthogr's forces. As long as they remained hidden, reality would continue to exist despite the Prime's beleaguered state—but if Claire fell into captivity, all would be lost.

Bithia pounded on the glass again, gaining her attention and pleading for her flight. She pushed her hand to the portal and begged her to relay a message. *Please, tell Rob how much I love him!*

Claire touched her hand to the glass and bid a silent farewell. She bolted for the door, where her feet scattered the ankle-deep fog as she sprinted through the haze.

She rounded a corner, armed with the knowledge of Nitthogr's plans and her deep, abiding connection to her Prime. The hiss of a viper alerted Claire, and she dodge-skipped over an area where the snake struck. She doubled down and ran forward.

In the distance, she spied a glowing light at the end of the hallway; the shining exit radiated hope. She bit back against her burning lungs and pressed ahead, ignoring the pain in her chest brought on by the sudden sprints.

Another adder struck, passing through the vapor with a shrill hiss. She paid it no mind, only keeping her eyes on the exit. Her shoes scattered a growing cloud away from her feet, which dashed through the vaporic miasma.

Her soles pounded like drums. The hiss of her assailants' efforts tempted her to take her eyes off the prize. She resisted!

The door grew larger and larger. The light outside shone brighter! Just as she hit the threshold of the door, she felt the sting of a viper as it latched onto the back of her leg. Claire screamed as she tumbled through the door; but she could only hear the hissing of snakes in her ears as she collapsed into the light.

Claire skidded to a halt on her back as the serpent coiled itself around her leg, injecting its venom ever deeper into her soul. She could see blackness crowding her vision, choking the light as she struggled to hold on to everything that Bithia had instilled within her.

As her vision faded, she could feel the sting of Nitthogr's vanity and dark desires; they overruled and dominated her soul, shriveling the glowing orb that Bithia had implanted within. She looked to her leg to see the snake drive its fangs ever deeper. She could swear that it smiled at her. And then everything faded into black.

James Shianan stormed into the dingy room filled with Thomas Chelish's aromatic cigar smoke. He welcomed the surprised faces with a fake smile. Seated at The Sevens' table were high ranking magnates from around the globe: Victor Adams, Peter Greyson, Charles Summers, Andrew Thornton, Thomas Chelish, Bruce Cannon, and Jonathan Trask. Each formidable in their own right, together, they could rule the world... or destroy it.

Greyson rose to his feet and stammered, trying to give a plausible reason for their meeting, which had secretly convened an hour prior to the time appointed by James. James let him ramble while he dumped a box of heat-etched runestones into a pile on the table.

"Sit down," the warlock barked. "I already know why you've assembled without me."

The seven men traded sagacious glances.

"I'm not sure any of you trust me. However, you each *owe me*."

Their glances melted into the inevitability of this knowledge. Each of these men owed James innumerable favors.

Nitthogr touched a finger to his temple as if he could read their minds. "You fear that I am letting Claire escape for my own purposes or benefit?"

Adams chimed in with his thick accent, "You do seem like you have lost care for the Great Awakening! The astral alignment is only days away—we could miss our next opportunity to release the Master."

Whirling around to address him, James explained. "More than any of you, *I know Sh'logath!* I have served him since long before the Syzygyc War and I have worked to release him ever since!"

He scanned the room, looking for a tell on any of their faces. The conniving warlock still suspected that his brother had somehow wormed his way into the group he'd so carefully setup on Earth, a dimension where Basilisk's reach and vision was severely limited. None had overtly betrayed him... not *yet*.

"Then just tell us why you don't just bring the princess here from the Prime!" Trask demanded. "We could easily sacrifice her upon the altar; we don't need Claire Jones."

Even as the runes began to move of their own accord upon the table, James tapped his lower lip. "You know so little about what happens when a Prime is taken from the master realm against their own will," he bluffed. "What you seem to know a great deal of, is my plans... such as how I am holding the Princess in the Prime capital. I had not divulged that information to anyone here."

Trask stuttered. "Well—we can assume that's the case."

"I've long suspected a traitor on the council—one of the Seven feeding information to my brother." He looked down at the runes and smiled. Regorik's message had come through as timely as could be hoped for.

Trask stared at him, both inquisitively and fearfully.

"Our efforts have paid off. Sh'logath *will* rise. Claire has been discovered and marked by my psi-vyrm. She will be apprehended in no time, and the rituals will happen." He leveled a gaze at the other six men seated at the table, and then at Trask.

He circled Jonathan Trask like a predator sizing up his prey. Trask looked around the table for support, but his fellows averted their eyes, rejecting any association with a possible traitor.

Nitthogr raised a curious eyebrow at the tiny octagonal symbol tattooed behind Trask's left ear, an identification mark of the Tarkhūn. It was the last piece of evidence he needed to condemn him. "Oh, but you'll never see it." He made a sign in the air, tracing Trask's silhouette with his index pointer, and then snapped his fingers; Trask burst into flames before he could react.

The traitor sank to his knees amid his screams and crackling of the heat. He quickly reduced to a pile of organic ceramic, cinder, and ash.

Nitthogr turned back to his chosen illuminati. "Make preparations for the Great Awakening! And must I need to reiterate what happens if you betray me to my brother? He works against us from afar."

The sorcerer scooped up his runes and stepped away. Trask's blackened bits crunched and broke under Nitthogr's foot. The sounds brought him deep satisfaction, a happiness he anticipated hearing so much more of very soon.

Chapter Fourteen

Like a jolt of lightning, Claire's eyes rolled forward, and she shot back into the land of the conscious. She sat up with such force that she nearly tumbled into Rob's arms. For a moment, she shook violently as her mind tried to get accustomed to the temperature shock; sweat poured off her trembling frame.

She gazed at Rob with a look of confusion. There wasn't time to address it; old Ma Kechewaishke also rocketed into consciousness, albeit her landing was more graceful.

Ma took a deep gasp and straightened up, stiff for only a moment. Her eyes unclouded, and she rushed to Claire's side. She wore a mixed look of both elation and alarm upon her face. "Did they touch you?"

Claire only stared at her, slack-jawed and unable to string together any words in her muddled mind.

Ma grabbed her by the arm and shook her so hard that sweat droplets flung violently off both of them, like a shaking, wet dog. "Did they touch you?" she called loudly, trying to snap the girl out of her fugue.

Slowly, like a bewildered child, Claire pulled up her moist pant leg and exposed her lower leg. A blackened spot grew like an angry stormhead on her calf. Still catatonic, she stared at the wound with vacant eyes.

Ma Kechewaishke squeezed her eyes tight and sighed with disappointment. When she opened them again, she addressed Rob.

"It's a psychic wound," she stated flatly. Worry permeated every word. "She has been marked by the enemy." Ma patted Claire's face and looked into her eyes for a response. "Tell me, does she have any psychic abilities—even latent ones?"

Rob gave her an unknowing look.

"They might present as intuition, perhaps... we must assume so," Ma said. "It will be worse for her given that is the case."

Rob spotted the difference in Ma. She had become a completely different person since her astral journey. She had undoubtedly made contact with the great Gichi-manidoo. Rob wished he had time to share with her Gichi-manidoo's role in the divine scheme; religious texts of the Prime had much to say about how the manifold realms of the Tesseract often misinterpreted spiritual forces under a pantheistic pretext. But Ma's look of worry and her shortness of breath insisted that their time grew shorter each second.

"They will find us, and sooner rather than later." Her intense eyes nearly burned into Rob's soul.

"Gichi-manidoo told you of the vyrm?" He and Claire had shared so little information with her until now.

"Yes. And I've seen their war raging across the heavens. I've seen the end: I saw through the desolation and into the void where Sh'logath dwells in his nonexistence—he awoke from his slumber and devoured all of Gichi-manidoo's beauty. And then, I too was devoured, but not before Gichi-manidoo told me what you must do!

"You must take the Stone Glaive!" Ma reached over and squeezed Claire's arm. She only stared blankly at her for a long moment.

"There is more?" Rob interjected.

"Her father..." she trailed off.

Rob nodded, understanding how the vyrm operated: swiftly and decisively. He pressed a hand to Claire's face while she looked at both of them, quite confused by their conversation and even by her presence in the rank, sweaty hut.

"Bithia's father remains entombed, so the Princess is the last of the royal blood on the Prime—one piece of the puzzle is already in his possession."

Swallowing hard, Rob looked down at his ward. He knew what that meant: if either Claire or Bithia died, Nitthogr's options in this grand game would become so limited that he would call upon Sh'logath and unleash the Devourer. The sorcerer could afford to play this cosmic game of chicken. Either side needed both pieces in order to win.

Rob scooped Claire up into his strong arms. She looked into his face and squinted, trying to remember. "I know you, I think?"

He nodded. "Yes. Yes, you do."

"I—I can't remember much. I wandered in a giant maze... for years, I think... I just kept forgetting everything. Every time I took a wrong turn, I forgot more and more! Oh, Zabe!" She buried her face in his chest.

"Zabe?" he asked.

She looked at him again, confused. "Robert?"

"Her memories are... folding upon themselves, and unfolding, all at once," Ma tried to explain. "It's the vyrm poison. They will use it try to hone in on your position in order to acquire her. The confusion is like the hobbling poison of a snake; now that she's vulnerable, they will try to constrict around you while she is slowed."

"What can we do?"

"It will wear off in time."

"How much time?"

"Not enough." Ma insisted. "Even now, they come to ensnare you. You must keep moving, always moving, or they will retrieve her and all will be lost." She motioned for them to follow her. Ma Kechewaishke led them back to her hovel. Rob carried Claire the short distance.

Peeling back a tattered, woven rug, Ma lifted a loose floorboard and pulled out an old steel coffee canister. Several empty ones like it littered the crawlspace surrounding this last, full one. She set it down with a loud thud. The sound of its weight betrayed its size, and it gave a decisive "clink" when it moved.

"You must flee. The enemy is already making haste to your location." She nodded to the lidded can even as she shuffled over to the nearby coat rack. Ma threw off the old seaman's raincoat to reveal a twelve-gauge shotgun.

"You're going to need that," Rob assured her.

He picked up the incredibly heavy cylinder she had motioned to and opened it. Two fistfuls of ancient gold coins filled the can. Rob looked at Ma Kechewaishke incredulously.

"How else do you think I could afford all that?" She nodded out the door to the mounds of empty whiskey bottles that buried her yard. "But there's no time for stories. You've got to go. Consider this a gift from Gichi-manidoo."

She finished loading and checking her shells, and then chambered a cartridge. "My neighbor has a fancy speedboat just down the shore. Usually leaves the keys in it."

Rob nodded, understanding she had embraced more than her role as a noble sacrifice as she stood in that doorway with a shotgun in hand. Ma Kechewaishke had seized her destiny—she was buying all of reality a little more time so they could fight the oncoming storm.

From the corner of his eye, Rob spotted an old, faded National Geographic map pinned to the wall. It depicted the sun and different solar and lunar bodies and plotted their orbits.

"They can track her anywhere?" he asked as he stashed coins in pockets and wherever else he could.

"Almost anywhere," she confirmed. "Wherever the Old Snake's power holds sway."

"Do you know what moon phase it is?"

Ma nodded almost apologetically. "Stonehenge?"

Rob nodded resolutely. "Stonehenge," he stated resolutely. "It only makes sense."

"Blessings, and Godspeed," she bid them and then watched them forage through the overgrown brush behind her hovel. The path had grown over, making the way to the beach difficult, but she had no doubt that they could escape.

Ma Kechewaishke gave a long, contented sigh and then turned back to her rocking chair. She sat down in the familiar haunt and rocked gently, a smile upon her face and the shotgun across her lap. Ma Kechewaishke thanked Gichi-manidoo for His many blessings and for giving her such an honored part in the divine plan.

Humming an old tune she learned as a child, she smiled at the setting sun as it neared the horizon. *It won't be long now*, she knew.

Surrounded by her team of government operatives, Vivian sat in her cargo van. Most of them consisted of vyrm operatives who had also infiltrated the secretive military branch under her direction, or that of the Heptobscurantum. She ran operations from the van, parked right in the heart of La Pointe. The town only consisted of a few blocks in any given direction, and the location afforded them a perfect vantage to secretly spy on the ferry in case they tried to escape.

She'd dispatched two agents. One she'd sent to the eastern side of the bay near the old Indian Cemetery; there was a latent portal there that might be used to shift between the realms of the Tesseract if their prey knew how to access it—something Zabe had already proven capable of doing. The other agent had been sent to scout further up the island with a handheld piece of technology brought back from The Prime.

The tracker could detect the psychic disruption which the vyrm psychics had caused in Claire's spirit-journey. They could run, but they could no longer hide, and this was not an overly large island.

Agent Brock, the scout, reported in over his secure channel. "I see them, trying to circle around the back of the house... the guy is carrying the girl—she doesn't look so well." Long pauses punctuated his whispered reports over the com line. "Just a little old lady in a rocking chair nearby... target's car is still in the driveway." The line crackled with a burst of static.

"Man, this place is a dump... moving in to intercept."

"Use caution," Vivian warned.

"Understood." Brock left the channel open and the van load of operatives could hear the swishing of his pants against the tall grass as he moved in.

"Can I help you?" an elderly voice called out, barely audible over the radio line.

"Yes, ma'am. I'm looking for my friends. They own that car over there... I spotted them from the road."

"They're just using my outhouse around back... ate something disagreeable."

A long white ripple of quiet static. More sounds like movement, then a long and loud string of expletives flooded the channel, followed by a shotgun blast and returned gunfire.

Vivian muttered profanities of her own. "Agent Sams, get your ass up there and find out what's going on!"

Chapter Fifteen

Help. Oh God, I think I've been roofied. Vivian read the text on the cellphone she'd recently stolen from Jackie and smiled. Charsk's psychics had delivered on their promise. For the next couple of days, Claire would barely be more capable than a drunken amnesiac.

The tall, blood-splattered grass crunched underfoot. Vivian kicked an empty bottle of Jack Daniels out of the way while she barked orders to her crew at the Kechewaishke property. "Burn the whole place down; eliminate all the evidence." She glanced down at Brock's body; he lay where he'd bled out in the grass. "Including this. I've got a new lead to follow up on."

Jackie's text had come in from a phone number that Vivian didn't recognize: an anonymous prepaid phone, no doubt. She was certain the text had come from Claire. *Where are you? I'm coming to get you!* She responded, pretending to be Jackie.

Nothing makes sense! I think I know this guy, but he's talking crazy! I think I'm hearing voices in my head! The doctors must be right!

Vivian couldn't contain the grin that crawled across her face. Just when the trail had gone cold on the island, she'd caught a break.

Can't tell James! Don't tell him I'm with another guy! Vivian had to credit Charsk's troops. The poison overruling her strong-willed nature must have helped endear Claire to Nitthogr's James persona again.

I'll text when I get back to Duluth. He's driving. Doesn't know I have a phone. Be there soon. Will text a location, Claire's final text read.

Stuffing Jackie's phone into her pocket, Vivian quickly pulled out her encrypted work phone and dialed a contact of her own. If she called in a favor and secured a helicopter, she would probably beat Claire back to Duluth.

Rob led Claire by the hand through the little café and seated her at a table. She still seemed like a walking zombie. Debilitated by the twilight poison, she'd regressed to a mental age of about thirteen years old and suffered random bouts of complete disassociation.

He sat her down and looked out the window, hoping that Ma was right and that it would soon wear off. The nearby sporting goods store closed soon, and he needed to gather a few supplies immediately. He scanned the sidewalks. All seemed relatively calm.

"Excuse me, ma'am?" Rob asked a nearby barista. An older woman, she wore a denim smock and an *Ask me about Jesus* button; she seemed to radiate positivity. Rob thought her a more trustworthy person than any other options.

The middle-aged woman looked up from behind the counter. She smiled warmly in reply. "How can I help you?"

"Can you keep an eye on my friend for just a few minutes while she drinks her coffee?" He pointed to Claire, who sipped on the hot cup and grimaced.

Claire turned to Rob and fixed her befuddled eyes on him. "Are you sure I like coffee?" she called with a drunk-like cadence.

Rob twirled his fingers near his temples, indicating mental disorder to the woman. "I'm trying to get my friend the help she needs, but I need to step across the street for just five minutes. Can you just make sure that she doesn't go anywhere before I get back?"

The woman bobbed her head sympathetically. "Well, it's not too busy at the moment. I'll see what I can do." She leaned forward to whisper in her heavy Scandinavian accent, "but if she insists on leaving, I can't keep her here, you know."

"I know," he commented. Rob assured her, "Five minutes?"

She slipped her hands into the pouch on her apron. "Sure, and I admire what you're doing." She took out two tiny pamphlets from the pocket and slipped them into his hand.

Rob nodded and told Claire he'd be right back. "This nice lady is going to keep an eye on you for the next couple of minutes. I'll be right across the street. If you get bored, you can read these." He gave her the religious tract and the drug rehab clinic pamphlet the barista had given him, and then he jogged across the street.

Claire eagerly watched him go. As soon as he'd stepped off the sidewalk, she impulsively reached for the hidden cell phone and texted the address to her friend. *I'm alone for the next several minutes. Don't know when he comes back!*

A text reply came back: *OMW.* She choked back the dark drink in tiny sips and leafed through the brochures, watching the window for signs of Rob's early return.

Only minutes later, an arm reached over her shoulder and set a warm cup of chai tea before her. Claire looked up. Vivian had set the mug down and sipped a chai latte of her own.

"You didn't look like you were enjoying the coffee," Vivian said politely as she took a seat across the table from her. She carefully angled the chair so that it still afforded her a view of the window.

Claire gave her a confused look, but shrugged, not strong enough to fight through the mental grog, but she recognized the friendly face. "Is Jackie coming?"

"Probably. Drink your tea, dear, and tell me everything." Vivian turned slightly to wave off the barista, nonverbally indicating that she was a friend.

Claire took a big gulp, and the floodgates opened up. She relayed the confusing litany of disjointed events: fleeing from a burning man and a werewolf, an old archaeologist with a dead wife, a trip to the island, and fleeing from snakes in her old school. None of the events connected to each other in Claire's mind, even as she accurately summarized many of her recent trials. To her, they seemed like a series of bad dreams, but barely connected in some manner. "You were in some of them, too," Claire mumbled.

For a moment, the haze began to lift, but only slightly. "I'm not sure why I'm really telling you any of this, even," she said before taking another gulp of chai. "After all, aren't you the snake lady?"

Vivian laughed, noting the concerned look on the hovering barista's face back by the counter. "Are you sure of all these stories?"

"Oh yes," Claire exclaimed like a lush who'd had too much wine. "The shaman on the island warned me not to get bit... I've seen some crazy things the last couple days... but I'm not crazy am I? Jackie knows I'm not crazy."

Under the table, Claire fired off a quick, blind text to Jackie. *Coming? Viv's here.* She slurped down the last of the Chai.

"I don't think you're crazy," Vivian replied with a grin. "But maybe you've been drugged. What did that shaman give you? I think you should come with me right away."

Vivian's breast pocket vibrated and chirped with a distinctive alert tone that Jackie had set for her best friend. Vivian looked down at it with a guilty look on her face.

"Why do you have Jackie's phone?" The fog in Claire's mind had begun to lift as her anger and sense of self-preservation welled up.

"She loaned it to me," Vivian lied.

Claire felt it was a lie, but couldn't quite verbalize that. She looked down at her empty paper cup with suspicion, but her arms felt heavy.

"I certainly did not!" yelled Jackie, who'd just walked into the café. She held a tablet with a tracking app running. "I knew I'd find whoever stole my cell. And it figures!"

The middle-aged barista stood slack-jawed. She worked her voiceless mouth for a few seconds, not quite knowing how to respond.

"Jackie!" Claire slumped her head, suddenly too weary to hold it up. She could only stare at the empty chai cup. Vivian's words echoed in her ears. *Maybe you've been drugged.*

Jackie drew a Taser from her hip pocket and told Claire to get up and run. Claire couldn't pick out the individual words; everything blended together at this point. She tried to flee, spotted the barista panic, and call the emergency line.

Claire's brain swam and spun. She barely made out Jackie and Vivian fighting; Vivian drew a gun. Her vision went dark and her mind swirled like a margarita blender. Head rolling back, Claire blacked out.

Rob saw the altercation through the window before he even got to the sidewalk. He tucked the large duffle under his arm and ran to the door, where he found a frightened barista cowering behind the register and pointing to the nearby catfight.

Jackie fired her taser at Vivian. Vivian dodged the stinger projectiles with uncanny reflexes. She held her gun high in order to whirl around and dodge the stunning wire projectiles. Rob scooped up a nearby ceramic mug and chucked it at Vivian before she could bring her handgun to bear.

The cup glanced off of the assailant's forehead and knocked her to the ground with a loud crash. Rob tossed the large duffel to Jackie just in time to catch Claire before she shifted in her seat and nearly toppled to the floor. "Come with me! Quickly, before backup arrives!"

Even if she didn't understand what that meant, Jackie nodded and sprinted towards the side exit as Rob turned to follow. "This is heavy! What's in here, gold?"

Vivian scrambled to her feet, screaming at them. "Drop the girl!"

He did not slow; Vivian fired three rounds, which lodged squarely in Rob's back.

The force of the bullets' impact knocked the breath out of Rob. The barista screamed and dropped to the floor, where she fainted. Rob staggered and slowed to a stop, still cradling Claire's unconscious form in his arms. With a pained groan, his body bulged and grew as his wolf form burst outward in response to the threat. With a growl, Rob flexed his muscles; the three bullets slipped out of his flesh and clattered to the hardwood floors.

Rob set Claire down gently and turned to snarl at his attacker. Grudgingly, the over-matched agent backed out of the café, keeping her gun leveled the entire time as she fumbled for her mobile.

Whirling around, Rob scooped up Claire in one paw and snatched up a wild-eyed Jackie under his other massive arm. He sprinted away through the night as fast as his giant legs would bear them.

Still in his bestial form, Rob ducked below the rotating spotlight. He held Claire close to him while Jackie scanned the shipping manifests in the dim light. They'd swiped the data sheets only a few minutes earlier.

"I can't seem to make any sense of it at all," Rob admitted.

Jackie shushed him and concentrated on the lists. "I've seen these kinds of papers before. I did a short internship with some corporate sector types, and we used this same format." She tossed the clipboard aside and pointed across the tarmac. "That big cargo plane over there is the one we want: it'll take us to the UK."

"Us?" Rob interjected.

"I'm not letting you take my unconscious best friend half way around the world without me there to protect her!" She stared at the monstrous, toothy behemoth with no fear.

Rob saw the stern look in her eyes and quickly relented. "It will not be easy," he cautioned quietly, trying to bring the volume level back to where security patrols couldn't hear them. His whispers in the low and guttural lupine voice sounded almost like growls.

Jackie shouldered the duffel bag. "Lead the way."

They skulked across asphalt sections of the airport, keeping to the long shadows cast by the warehouse buildings. The sounds of the forklifts loading freight easily alerted them to any potential onlookers in their vicinity, allowing them to easily avoid them.

Several tense minutes later, they peeked around the edge of a cargo building where a freshly fueled plane had just finished receiving the last of its cargo through the rear ramp. Several members of the loading crew loitered nearby, standing just inside the well-lit building. The last of them parked his forklift and joined his peers; any one of them would probably spot the stowaways if they made a break for the plane. They didn't appear highly alert, but neither did they appear to be leaving the area any time soon.

"We need a diversion," Rob whispered.

Jackie had a large stone already in hand. "I'm on it." She snuck through the shadows to the next hangar door several hundred feet down the side of the warehouse. It gave her an angle to see the far end of the facility that the cargo haulers were based out of. She wound up her pitch and chucked the stone, shattering a large bank of fluorescent lights and plunging the far side of the building into darkness.

She jogged back and stuck her thumb in her chest. "Powder Puff League MVP."

They grinned as the workers left their well-lit vantage in order to investigate the sudden lighting failure. Moments later, the three stowaways tucked themselves safely inside the cargo bay and weaved their bodies into the security webbing.

Only one hasty security walkthrough later, and the trio could breathe easy once again. The massive cargo doors closed with a flashing amber light and a shrill, warning klaxon. The plane climbed into the sky with its urgent deadline to keep; airborne, the noise of the rushing wind was deafening.

"These planes were not meant for human travel." Jackie almost had to yell the words into Rob's ear.

The aircraft's steel skin only seemed to amplify the howling engines which kept the plane in the sky. It did nothing to prevent the cold air at that high altitude from sapping their heat.

Rob unzipped the duffel bag and took out some warmer clothing options, water, and vacuum sealed food rations. He took care to keep many of the other survival items mostly out of sight: the rope, hatchets and knives, and especially the TRX718 pistol he still kept handy. He didn't want to worry Jackie any more than she probably was already.

Jackie added whatever layers she could, but still shivered against the howling cold. She almost felt jealous of Claire, who seemed impervious to the low temperatures in her unconscious state; Jackie readily accepted the high-calorie rations, knowing that she'd easily burn them off by shivering, although the taste would be much improved if she'd had her way.

Rob only watched her shiver next to her friend for a few minutes. The lycanthrope laid down next to her and pulled the three together. They huddled together against his furry body.

Jackie felt his intense, radiant body heat, and she shifted until she felt more comfortable; she knew they were safe in his arms. Jackie, too, drifted off to sleep amid the howling, droning engine noise and the frigid cold.

Chapter Sixteen

R ob shuddered and woke, but not from the cold. A subtle shift in the plane's trajectory startled him, woke him up. He shook the crystalline frost from the tips of his mottled charcoal fur and looked down at his two female charges. They still snoozed peacefully despite the circumstances.

The descent took its due course. Jackie and Claire eventually awoke, but little could be done except await touchdown. Conversation proved nearly impossible over the roaring noise box that confined them.

Claire stared at them both, still a little wild-eyed, but she did not panic; Jackie's presence was a big comfort to her. The other two assumed her relative calm was a good sign and that some of her memories must have returned. As soon as the plane bounced down on the foreign pavement and the engines began winding down, the group quickly began formulating an escape plan.

"They're going to park the plane either inside a giant warehouse or alongside one. That's where they will unload the cargo, refuel and check the plane, and then start the process all over again," Jackie stated, drawing on her cursory knowledge of shipping operations.

"I'm still confused," Claire interjected. "What's going on?"

"We'll fill you in when there's time," Jackie said. "Please, just trust me for now. What's your plan, Rob?"

"When they open the door, I'll show them this lycan form, and when they run away screaming, we can escape."

Jackie scrunched up her face at his plan. "Wouldn't stealth be better?"

"Is that an option?"

"I have a plan. Quickly, we've got to move to the front near the pilot's section, so we'll have enough time to pull this off. What time is it?"

"Almost five in the evening, I think, based on time zones and how long we traveled."

Jackie scanned the immense cargo bay and paused for thought. "I think this might work if we get lucky. If we don't, we'll consider your American Werewolf in London idea as a Plan B."

Alfie spun the wheel on his forklift and turned it around quickly. He urged the machine forward even as the ramp lowered from the rear of the immense cargo plane; his ruddy hair flapped in the breeze as he accelerated.

He sighed as he climbed the ramp next to the corrugated steel warehouse and checked his watch. "It's gonna take forever to clear this lot," he muttered to himself as he got to work. Dropping his forks, he picked up the first pallet of freight shipped in from the United States.

Even though it was against company policy, he popped in a set of ear buds and cranked the music up. He had to do something to kill the monotony of his job and help the time pass.

Several pallets deep, he couldn't help reflecting on his life's course. A twinge of guilt for wearing his headphones momentarily niggled at his introspective train of thought; he really needed to keep this job, and he was lucky to have it, especially so soon after his release from incarceration.

Alfie debated pulling the headphones out; everyone else on the floor broke that same rule, though. He cussed at himself for his brooding as he dwelled on what a burden he'd become to his poor mum. He slowed the forklift and checked his iPod. A slow, melancholy song had somehow worked its way to the top; perhaps that had been what prompted the meditation. Alfie cursed whoever invented random-repeat, and skipped ahead to a hard rock offering so he could continue his work without his thoughts interfering.

With the cargo bay cleared to about ninety percent, he slowed the loader to a stop and noted an area where several boxes lay scattered around the floor. Alfie got out and walked around the pallets nearby. They'd all remained properly chained down, and none of the pallet's wrapping plastic had been cut or burst.

Exasperated, Alfie cussed loudly. The damaged, loose boxes meant he had to fill out some paperwork; the report process for things like this was unpleasant. It wasn't uncommon, but he hadn't factored it into his plans and his twisting stomach reminded him that his mum had packed him a bag lunch to celebrate his three-months of sobriety.

He sat back in the machine in a huff and dropped the forks, slamming into the nearest pallet. Angrily biting his lip, he whirled around and sped out the rear of the plane, fully intending to ignore the problem until after supper break.

As Alfie piloted the craft inside the massive building, he heard the whistle blow, alerting him and his fellows of the mandatory break time. He dropped the pallet to the floor, not noticing how this load shifted and wobbled slightly more than usual—as if it were hollow on the inside: a mere shell of shrink-wrapped boxes.

He killed the engine on the forklift and hopped out. Thinking could wait until after the lunch break, and maybe he could win a few quid playing cards in the break-room today. The paperwork would wait, although it would inevitably increase, as would his employer's scrutiny as soon as they discovered the cut packing plastic wrap on his last pallet—cut from the inside, as if something had escaped from within the improperly inspected load.

"And you don't remember anything," Rob overheard Jackie asking Claire as he exited the tiny pawn shop and currency exchange.

"Very little," Claire replied. "It's more like I remember feelings, but anything else is blocked, like it's foggy. Kinda like when you have a dream that felt so real, but when you try to remember it, the details start getting hazy, even when you're sure that you knew them... and some of the memories I *do remember* aren't even mine... it's like they're..." she trailed off.

"Because they are not yours," Rob noted. "Well, not exactly. They belong to you now because your Prime, Bithia, shared them with you. They were meant to give you clarity and knowledge, but the vyrm's psychic toxin is disrupting them."

"Prime?" Jackie asked.

"Her alternate self in the Prime realm: the ultimate reality. The essence of a person, who they are at their core, fills a Prime. All a person's base, prominent character aspects are shared across the realms."

"Realms? Like, it's an alternate dimension or something?"

Rob hesitated to state as such, having seen how people from Earth react to that news with disbelief. "Yes," he said.

Jackie shrugged, easily believing it. Rob shot her an inquisitive look, and she stated, "I watch television. I've heard of string theory. It sounds like the logical conclusion theoretical physicists are leaning towards nowadays. Besides, I've already seen werewolves and a guy who wields fire like an X-man. How hard are multiple dimensions to swallow after that?"

"X-man?" It was Rob's turn for confusion.

"Never mind. What's next?"

"Dear Lord, let it be coffee," Claire said. Her companions smiled; little signs signaled her slow return to them.

Rob pulled out the edge of a small tent through a flap in the duffel bag. "We wait until morning and then hop a tour bus to Wiltshire."

"Wiltshire... Wiltshire... why is that name so familiar?" She searched her memories, and then settled on those of a paranormal detective by the same moniker. Her life as a small time reporter for a largely unread publication seemed like it had been forever ago.

Claire looked at Rob skeptically. "What's in Wiltshire?"

"Our exit to another world."

The trio slipped away from their tour group as they headed directly from their bus over to the Stonehenge Visitor Center. A burgeoning group of visitors began the next tour, hearing the guide recount the myriad of speculations regarding the ancient site's origins.

Tour groups from different agencies meandered here and there, each wearing colored lanyards identifying which group they belonged to. Rob had cashed in one of the solid gold coins from Ma Kechewaishke and gotten them an upgraded tour which provided access to the inner circle of stones, but that was not where they headed at the moment.

Claire grinned at Rob as he walked through the crowds. He blended in perfectly with the other American tourists, albeit unintentionally. The only good condition men's clothing they had remaining after his recent transformations were a crisp set of cargo pants and a collared polo shirt he'd tossed into the bag from the sporting goods store. He looked like a suburban insurance sales-man on holiday.

"Follow me." Rob brought them to the Heelstone on the north-east side of the ruins. Traffic milled about, but interest in the Heel-stone remained far less than that of the standing stone circles. Most people skirted the large rock only in an effort to get elsewhere, but some read the informational pieces describing the stone's folklore and independent history, which blamed its presence on everything from the devil to worship of the Norse Goddess Freyja.

The relative disinterest provided Rob with all the cover he need-ed. He walked around to the north side of the stone where he wouldn't be noticed; only a chain-link fence and a paved avenue lay beyond the southwest face. Rob took a hunting knife from his bag and cut his hand, letting a trickle of blood flow out.

Peeking around the corner of the stone, the girls gave him a worried look as he smeared a bloody handprint on the giant rock. The porous sarsen stone drank in the offering. Rob explained, "There's power in blood. It's a necessary reagent to many of the ancient mechanics of the Tesseract. You might say that it's what kick-starts the ancient engines."

He shouldered the bag and took Claire by the hand. They weaved their way through the crowds as they headed back towards the standing stones.

Pausing near one of the upright stone pillars, Rob retrieved a folded piece of paper they'd printed at the internet café the previ-ous evening; he stashed the folding knife out of sight. He stared at the paper and turned slightly in place while he consulted the printed star chart in an effort to orient himself properly.

"What are you doing?" asked Jackie.

"I need to get a fix on exactly where we are," he replied. "Well, not so much where we are, but how the portals are aligned. It's like a set of shifting tubes and tunnels; they all lead to the right places, but the entrances keep moving..."

"Because of the Earth's rotation?"

"Exactly. But not just that, also because of the travel around the sun." He paused for a moment and then pointed at another pillar around the circle. "That's the one we need to activate."

"It's like a key to the door, then?" Claire wondered.

"Yes," Rob replied with a smile as a swelling tour group grew closer. "And all doors lead to their fixed destination, *or* to the Prime, depending on how it is opened... except during those certain astral phases." Rob glanced over his shoulder.

Suddenly, he looked very worried. He put his hands around Claire's face and kissed her deeply. He leaned into it and they fell back slightly, resting against the pillar. Claire didn't resist; she melted into the embrace. All the emotive memories from her Prime-self coursed through her and grew more intense. Her heartbeat pounded like a drum in her ears as his soft lips pressed against hers. She suddenly realized that Bithia and Rob, Zabe, had been in love! Their passion for each other washed intensely over her—exhilarating and confusing her heart all at once.

Stunned to silence, Jackie stood there for a long, awkward moment, and then averted her eyes. Suddenly, a third wheel, she kicked a rock slightly and followed it away from the duo. She nudged it ever forward over the next couple of seconds, hoping one of the two face-suckers would come up for air.

Rob broke the embrace and immediately turned his head towards the tourists that had passed by on their way around the circle. Jackie turned to look at what had Rob's attention, but Claire still leaned, weak-kneed, against the rock. Her eyes remained closed for that moment. Rob touched her face, and she looked at him, starry eyed.

"I apologize," Rob said, and pointed to a man in a security uniform. The guard carried some kind of hand-held scanner, which he stared into with a furrowed brow. "That's Prime technology. The vyrm must know we're here, but the tech is only accurate to within a few hundred feet—they are tracking the poison they injected you with in the ether. People tend not to stare too long or too intently at gestures of romance."

Claire probed, "So you saved my life with a kiss? Is that all it was?" She tried to sort out her sudden feelings.

Time was short, and Rob evaded the question. "We have to go, quickly."

Jackie shot Claire a surprised look. Claire raised her eyebrows in response to her nonverbal question and tugged at her shirt collar as if the temperature had suddenly increased. They both spun on their heels and followed; Rob quickened the pace.

Just as they arrived at the necessary stone, they heard a whistle above the dull crowd noises and spotted the frustrated security guard; he searched vainly for his quarry amid the groups spread across the grounds. Their eyes picked out the source of the screeching signal: another security guard pointed down to the bloody handprint they'd left on that monument. He'd used a whistle to alert the other sentry.

The guard holding the scanner, the one they'd fooled with a kiss, dropped his scanner to his side and put his hand on a holstered stun gun. They knew there was only one location that their prey would be headed to.

Claire, Jackie, and Rob huddled behind the pillar. "We've got to get to the inner circle, and fast," he said as he smeared another bloody handprint upon the stone. It seemed to hum gently with an otherworldly power, but they didn't hear the sound with their ears, rather some other undiscovered sense detected it.

"But they know we're here! They'll catch us!"

"There's only the two of them... I think," Rob tried to reassure her. "I didn't expect a heavy contingent here. This portal doesn't lead anywhere a sane person would ever want to visit. We'll make it if we go quickly!"

Jackie reached into Rob's khaki pants pocket and pulled out the knife. She unfolded it quickly and decisively.

"What are you doing?" Claire demanded.

Wincing, Jackie dragged the sharp end of the knife across her palm, drawing a long rivulet of blood that dripped down her hand. "Giving you a diversion!" She turned and darted away from the stone, making a beeline towards the central circle. She kept a keen eye on the guards.

They spotted her immediately and began to hastily make their way towards her. Jackie struggled against the crowds, intentionally letting them slow her down so that her hunters would catch up.

Claire watched in horror as the vyrm closed in from opposite sides of a small crowd. They would have her in a matter of seconds.

Suddenly Jackie yelled in a loud, piercing voice, "Bomb! There's a bomb!"

Pandemonium erupted. People scattered in every direction. Others in the panicked mob took up the call warning, "Bomb! Bomb!"

The enemy agents tried to pursue Jackie through the throng, which she suddenly proved more adept at picking her way through. All of the people had one goal: to get away as far from Stonehenge as possible. Her diversion cleared the traffic and turned all watchful eyes momentarily away from the center circle.

"Come on," Rob insisted, taking Claire by the hand.

They made a mad dash towards the middle; as soon as they hit it, their bodies seemed to disintegrate in a flash of light and a wisp of ozone. But nobody was near enough to see it.

Nitthogr stormed through the stone corridor; his footsteps echoed down the hallway, announcing his arrival to his loyal army. At every station he passed, he found his loyal vyrm kneeling before his presence and whispering reverently, *"Herald of Sh'logath."*

The sorcerer strode up to General Regorik, who stood in salute, personally guarding Bithia's cell door. Regorik cocked his head. He'd hoped an opportunity to tease Caivev would have presented itself. "Your lapdog did not accompany you?"

Nitthogr grinned; "Caivev is leading a different sort of mission at this moment," he stated as he let the nearby door fall ajar. "Hello, Princess," he greeted her seditiously.

Bithia was tied to her chair at the center of the room; a vyrm psychic in each corner surrounded her. The warlock moved his face so close to hers that she could feel his breath. She still refused to look at him.

His rage suddenly overtook him, and he slapped Bithia ferociously, splitting her lip. She still would not look at him. Nitthogr balled his fists and struck her over and over, drawing blood and tears from her face. Finally, he slugged her in the belly; she gasped, choking for air.

Nitthogr stood back and admired his handiwork. Drool dripped from his petite prisoner's mouth while she wheezed in pain. Already, purple and blackish bruises had begun to swell; but she still maintained an aura of supernatural beauty and dignity. That very thing only further enraged him.

"It will never work," she coughed between ragged breaths. "The Inversion Pendant..."

He cocked an eyebrow in response.

"Because I do not hate you." The strength of her voice convinced him of her truthfulness. "The amulet will never make her *love* you because what I feel for you is pity, not despise." She let a smile momentarily overtake her in that small victory, knowing that the opposite of pity was apathy. She hoped this would be enough to free Claire Jones of Earth from his hold. "How twisted you are—she will never love you; you don't understand the concept. Because your plan hinges on so divine a notion as love, you will never succeed."

She hung her head, exhausted, expecting either unconsciousness or another furious beating to overtake her. Nitthogr fumed at her accusation and its probable veracity. He walked circles around her, staring down at her helpless form as the red haze of rage threatened to blind him. He clenched and unclenched his fists, ready to unleash a hail of blows upon her, when he caught sight of something in the corner of his eye.

Nitthogr stood up straight and stared right into the face of the nearby Vyrm psychic. He remained at attention in the corner, helping to trap Bithia's spirit in this realm and keep her eidolon from again contacting Claire Jones via one of many other avenues open to talented astral projectors. The psychic kept his gaze straight ahead. He looked at nothing in particular, staring directly through the sorcerer.

The warlock spotted it, clear as day. A tiny octagonal tattoo just behind the guard's left ear: barely the form of a serpent at this size. Nitthogr snarled. The guard broke his repose and tackled Nitthogr.

"Tarkhūn!" Nitthogr roared, igniting his hands with brilliant flames and grabbing at the spy's throat.

"Traitor!" the rogue screamed against the burning at his windpipe. Dagger in hand, the doomed Tarkhūn vyrm stabbed the Sorcerer, over and over. Each blow found its mark; the blade repeatedly buried itself deep within Nitthogr's chest.

More furious with each blow, Nitthogr's hands glowed ever more intensely until both combatants burned themselves out in a climax of rage! The Tarkhūn's body collapsed upon the sorcerer, dropping the bloody dagger even as his skull melted in upon itself, forming a viscous, red puddle, like a crude cup of liquefied meat. Nitthogr's arms fell to his sides, and he panted heavily, leaking bright crimson blood all around him.

Regorik and his troops burst into the room; the entire altercation only taking a few seconds. He slid to his master's side and flung aside the destroyed body of the spy with one powerful arm; he cradled Nitthogr in the other and checked his vitals.

"I will live," the warlock croaked, glaring at the crippled Bithia nearby. "My hate sustains me."

The vyrm captain helped him to his feet and let Nitthogr lean on his strength while they walked from the room, leaving a trail of blood in their wake. As Regorik shifted his master's weight onto two other soldiers, Nitthogr gave him one final command, breathing painfully through the spurting chest wounds. "Ready a contingent. If my brother wishes to change the rules of our game and up the ante, then we will respond in kind and visit retribution upon the Tarkhūn, demanding a payment in blood!"

Regorik nodded. His face was more serious than ever; he watched his faithful soldiers escort the Herald of Sh'logath towards the infirmary.

Vikrum Wiltshire had barely slept the last several days as he scoured the remnants of Claire Jones's Duluth apartment. He'd picked the locks to find that it had already been pretty well scavenged by the police, hospital professionals, the northern brothers from the Red Order, and of course, the cultists who had been chasing Claire.

Wiltshire was technically on vacation, and so his partner remained behind in New York. The man had a wife and family and couldn't set off on a moment's notice like Wiltshire could—even though he'd promised to pay Sexton's way.

Since his last encounter with Miss Jones, he'd been burning the candles at both ends, both pissing of Praetor Russo by killing a dangerous supernatural creature that stalked the catacombs beneath the Vatican, and taking a job for the enemy. He'd solved a case for the heptobscurantum and "saved" Bruce Cannon, extorting him for a significant amount of compensation in the meantime, making Wiltshire an independently wealthy man.

He'd had to use his vacation time to do it in order to get around Russo's orders not to take the case. He had a little more freedom now, given his financial reversals. But Wiltshire also had no intention of quitting the Order. He'd never joined them for the money—he did what he did because someone had to do it.

Russo may have been an asshole, but Wiltshire still needed him—and the access to the Order's non-financial resources such as the archives. And like it or not, Russo needed Wiltshire, too. But at least Wiltshire had some leverage now, and that gave him the opportunity to jump back into the search for Claire Jones.

The brothers of the Order in Minnesota had turned up nothing. Grandfather Tlugv had left the Superior region to go further north before Claire's life went to hell, so the Order had very little leads.

Wiltshire sighed and kicked a piece of debris across the room. He'd been told not to expect much from his peers when he visited the Keep in Minneapolis. And they'd been right. But he had to see the place with his own eyes.

"Dead ends," he mumbled, pacing around the room. News media kept the story alive, though buried in the rear pages of the newspaper. The search was still ongoing, and so Wiltshire had to assume she was still at large—still running from heptobscurantum pursuit.

An overturned photo album lay on the floor, and Wiltshire picked it up. He set it on the end table as he examined it.

The photo was of Claire and her father.

"If I was in trouble, who would I run to?" He stared at the image and then pulled up an Internet search and discovered that Sam Jones was currently directing a dig in the war torn country of Chiriqui.

Because of the conflicts, there were no flights in or out of Chiriqui where local warlords had a stranglehold on the government and on the populace. But Central America wasn't nearly as geographically large as the United States and there were Keeps in that region he could fly to which were in driving range.

With a flick of his thumbs, he booked a flight. And then he turned and abandoned Claire's apartment.

Chapter Seventeen

Claire gasped as her body simultaneously ripped apart on Earth and stitched back together on a new plane of reality. It felt like a spear of ice impaled her—but there was little pain, merely a sense of shock and intense cold that no person could prepare for.

Immediately, a hand clamped over her mouth to keep her silent—Rob's hand. She huffed repetitively and her nostrils flared as she tried to keep her heart rate under control following the portal jump. She suddenly realized that she'd been screaming. Her hot breath steamed in the vapid cold of the place; their breaths were the only nearby sounds except the faint echo of her initial cry.

As Rob released her, sure she wouldn't scream again, Claire turned a slow arc. The sickly green sky appeared dead, and the sun seemed to have collapsed inward upon itself; it more closely resembled a black-hole than a luminary body. Currently, they found themselves within some sort of ruined city. Their surroundings resembled a village market; a set of structures similar to Earth's Stonehenge surrounded them, jutting up from the surrounding foundations. Still, everything felt very alien in origin.

They walked in silence for a few minutes, getting a lay of the land. Claire kept glancing at Rob. Even in the dark and threatening surroundings, she saw his confidence brim. Her mind kept returning to that kiss. The new and sudden river of feelings it unlocked brightened her on the inside, even despite the dreary surroundings.

Everything nearby seemed painted in tones of the subdued: greys and blues, as if the spectrum of light in this place had suffered some critical breaking. The ground had cracked and peeled like old, baked mud; it crunched underfoot. Dust and soot covered everything in a thin layer.

They marched a few blocks from the portal, where a skyline opened between two broken structures. Distant mountains loomed on the horizon, but most menacing of all was the giant, obsidian polyhedron which hung in the sky.

Rob put a finger to his lips to indicate silence. He pointed upward and whispered, "Sh'logath."

The sight instilled supernatural, abject terror when looked at for any amount of time. Even catching it in the corner of her eye greatly unnerved Claire.

Sh'logath appeared to lurk on the threshold of the planet, only just coming into existence; the object shimmered glossily as if it phased between reality and nonexistence. The sky glowed red and burned around its edges, flaring as the atmosphere ignited against the almost-touch of the petrifying agod.

"This way," Rob whispered. His muted words sounded like shouts as they broke the silent, dead air of the charred planet. He led her around a corner and into a dilapidated construction, where he unzipped the duffel bag and withdrew some warmer clothing.

"Where are we?" asked Claire. But even as she asked, Bithia's memories crawled through her mind. *The ruined realm, the site of the Syzygyc War... the place where reality's destruction had been halted so long ago.*

"We are in the Desolation." He looked around with trepidation. "I believe that we are in the city of Limbus, specifically."

"Limbus?"

"The Dead City, we call it. It's the capital of the Desolation, under minority control of the ancient houses of the vyrm. But they, the Tarkhūn, are still dangerous: a ruling caste born of ancient lineage. There was a civil war many years ago. The majority of Tarkhūn pledged fealty to Nitthogr's brother. The Black, the common, proletarian class, sided with Nitthogr."

"So, we are safe here?"

"Claire Jones, you have never been in more danger than you are right now," he whispered. "The Tarkhūn have waged their own war against the blackborn vyrm and Nitthogr, but you are nowhere near safe. The Tarkhūn would gladly kill us or use us for their own plans." He did look at her sympathetically. She should have known all of this after merging with the princess, but for the vyrm poison and its psychic amnesia only let through snippets of information.

"Then why did we come here?" Claire asked fearfully.

"This is the place where Nitthogr has the least influence, ever since the majority of his followers escaped through the portals so long ago. It's the place where he'd least expect us to go. Realistically, he'd expect us to try to sneak into the Prime where I might find support among any of my remaining kin in the hill country. It's unlikely that he could have conquered them while retaining control of the castle."

"So what then? We wait in this cold, damp darkness?" The environment's creeping grey had already began to crush her spirits.

Rob shushed her. The silence cracked in the distance; stones broke off the face of a mountain and crashed ominously amid a far-off lightning storm.

"I do have a plan. But it's a very dangerous one." He had her attention. "We must keep you safe and hidden away from Nitthogr. Perhaps my kin have galvanized against the warlock—we might fight back, rescue the Princess? There is no other way... if he possesses both you and her, he will conquer the whole of reality, corrupting the Tesseract with his malfeasance. If he controls only one of you," he pointed to the hideous object in the sky, "he will destroy everything! The only way to ensure reality's survival is to protect you both."

Claire nodded, understanding that this was a last-ditch effort to save her planet, her people, and every other person in existence, too. "Lead the way," she said, emboldened.

They rose to depart. No sooner did they exit the destroyed building than a heavily armed contingent of vyrm sprang up around them with weapons drawn. They maintained a cool demeanor, neither talking nor overextending their posture.

Rob and Claire raised their hands in surrender. The vyrm leader silently pointed to the ground and held up two pairs of manacles.

"What do we do?" Claire asked. Worry permeated her voice.

"We lie on the ground and pray the Tarkhūn are merciful today." No sooner were they clapped into crude restraints than a soldier stepped over each of them and clubbed them behind the head with a retractable baton, rendering both unconscious.

Rob's eyelids fluttered and opened. His eyes hurt despite the dim quality of the light in the prison cell. Mostly the pain came from the base of his skull and radiated forward from where he'd been hit with the club. His arms, chained at the wrist, twisted behind his back, so he sat on his butt and watched over Claire.

Similarly bound, she lay on her side. Rob noticed a smile on her face; Claire's eyes seemed to move beneath their lids. She was dreaming, he deduced. He didn't know how long he sat motionless in the dead, musty air, watching Claire: a long time... perhaps an hour? His thoughts turned to the subtle differences between her and Bithia. It was his turn to smile.

"Whatever it is you're dreaming of, enjoy it," Rob whispered. "When you wake up, the nightmare begins."

For several long minutes more, she slept. Rob occasionally glanced at the vyrm guard posted just beyond the cold iron bars that locked them within their cell. Then Claire stretched and awoke with a yawn.

Before she opened her eyes she whispered, still half dreaming, "I had the wolf dream again... the old one that ends the way it's supposed to."

Rob smiled and then turned his attention to a new guard who approached briskly.

The massive vyrm leaned against the bars. "On your feet," he hissed. "The master wishes to see you."

Rob stood and helped Claire to her feet. Together, they would face the inevitable. Slowly, they shuffled out from the crumbling dungeon and onto a cobblestone footpath that wound through the city. Old statues of terrified vyrm citizens adorned the walks at random intervals; the roadside, stone figures were as common as highway advertisements on Earth.

"These vyrm are all so big," Claire whispered as a question. Most of them appeared taller and more muscular; this breed seemed more reptilian in nature. Many had necks so thick that their tendons bulged from shoulder to chin as they held their proud heads high. These vyrm would have difficulty using only makeup to disguise their appearance if they infiltrated Earth's population.

"The Tarkhūn are superior, genetically speaking," he whispered back. "A stronger, ancient breed, less diluted in the gene pool."

"And the statues?"

"Old... from long ago when the civil war originally—"

Their rear escort gave him a prod in the small of the back. The glare he shot Rob told him enough. It said *be quiet... or else*.

The trail coiled through the ashen, desiccated city. Still, there were signs of Limbus's proud and ancient origins. Here and there doors would open and close as vyrm onlookers came out to silently watch the prisoners parading by. Those openings gave tiny peeks into the vyrm living quarters; their culture blended highly advanced technology with ancient lifestyles. LED style lights illuminated the interiors enough that they could identify stone tools and other artisan items intermixed with circuit boards. Still, everything remained quiet under the pall of the sky-bound monstrosity.

Slowly, the road rose and curled around a hill. The guards lead the prisoners through a less decayed part of the city where the path climbed steeply. It emptied just outside an immense, pillared building. Claire's eyebrows rose as she took it in; it reminded her of so many Greek temples she had toured with her father.

Claire sulked momentarily as the ground leveled off at a large garden of detailed stonework. Surely her father must be worried about her. By now he must have been notified that she had gone crazy, or else he'd been told whatever story James had fed the media in his efforts to hunt her down.

Rob frowned as he looked from statue to statue in the rock garden. Not all the statues were of vyrm; some were other types of humanoids from different planes, and many of them were human. Some humans wore their garments in styles that indicated that they were from The Prime. Rob slid his hand over the form of a soldier who wore the old-style royal uniform his people wore during the Syzygyc War.

"They're so real looking," Claire noted as they passed by, wandering as if through a maze.

"They *are* real," Rob stated, prompting another shove from the guard. They continued their march in relative silence.

Vivian spotted her prey from deep inside the canopy of the jungle. Heat and humidity clung to her like a wet blanket and plastered her hair to her face and flushed her cheeks.

One of her two accomplices, both vyrm trackers, grinned at her with an arrogant smirk. Their physiology easily handled the excessive mid-day heat of Chiriqui. She grinned back at them, matching their hubris with her own; the makeup paste of the creature's skin had begun to slide like melting butter. Vivian chuckled and adjusted her position before returning her eyes back to the job. At least her other contact, a spy from the ranks of the Black who'd infiltrated this region, had figured out how to keep his disguise from liquefying in the heat.

The three lay prone on a platform they'd rigged high in the trees where they could overlook the clearing where the archaeologists worked. In Vivian's scope, she spotted Dr. Sam Jones excitedly directing the excavation.

His team had uncovered a large section of buried ruins. They'd obviously been working at a fever pitch—not just due to the civil unrest, which necessitated as speedy of a dig as possible, but also because of the enthusiasm of major discovery.

The elated look on Dr. Jones' face said it all. He'd found something big, something he didn't understand but which could rival the greatest discoveries ever made.

Vivian zoomed her scope out until the larger picture began to make sense. Her jaw dropped in wonder when she recognized the capstone. The archaeologist had stumbled onto a temple she'd only read about in ancient texts; she recognized the symbol clearly upon the unearthed peak of the ancient, pyramid-like temple.

"Kreephast. Do you see it?" She asked the local infiltrator. Her voice was barely more than a whisper.

"I do," he responded. "The Lost Temple." A moment of silent wonder passed between the three hunters... that and the realization that this was not what they had come here for. None of this would matter after The Awakening.

"Do you see what brews further south?"

Vivian scanned further, zooming her electronic crosshairs to their maximum ability. A dust cloud rose up above the verdant awning of the jungle, where she knew a large trail stretched from the main city to Jones' campsite. Intermittent breaks in the canopy gave her glimpses of the beat-up jeeps and cobbled-together heaps kept running with creative uses of chicken wire and riveted strapping.

"What is it? Locals?"

"The best I can tell," Kreephast stated, "is that they are with the rebels." He tapped the poorly sewed patch on his dark canvas vest.

"What will they do to the researchers?"

"Kill them, most likely. Nothing sends a strong message to your government like murdering Americans."

Vivian cursed under her breath. "We want Doctor Jones alive. I will go and collect him." She began creeping towards the edge of the platform. "Charobv, give me a diversion in five minutes. Kreephast, go back to the rebels, just in case. Get them to lock down this sector and control it. If it all falls apart, The Lost Temple could prove a significant asset."

The pasty-faced vyrm nodded and locked his sights onto expendable targets between the approaching rebel convoy and the exuberant archaeologist. "You'd better make haste," he chided. "The rebels are getting close, and I want to see how many of these vermin I can put down before I run out of targets or ammo."

Kreephast raised one final question before she slid down her tree. "What is our preferred method for controlling this sector?"

"Find something in their mythology or religions? Whatever. Make something up for all I care. Just keep the area secure and safe. I'm sure none of them will figure out how to get in."

Kreephast saluted and accepted the mission, as pointless as it was. It was a matter of duty for him, even though he assumed the sands of time had all but drained away with the impending coming of the agod.

Vivian returned his salute and shimmied down the tree. A few minutes later, shots rang out over and over as Charobv killed person after person. The sniper fire caused a stampede of humans, sending the panicked herd straight for the location the Dunnischkte candidate intended as her intercept point.

Claire had eluded her. But since then, every Plan B had gone perfectly, and within minutes, she would have Claire's father. If she ever reemerged, she'd have the perfect bait to catch the woman.

As the prisoners walked just a little further into the heart of Limbus, the mass of statues gave way to hundreds of waist-high pillars. Upon each rested a flat, checkered, gaming board with colored pieces. The tables hedged in the pillared building and created a border on the grounds between the building and the cliff face, which gave way to a sheer drop down into the north side of the city.

"It looks like chess," Claire observed.

Giving her a funny look, he wondering why the guard didn't prod her for speaking, too. Rob playfully wondered if Claire was trying to bait him into receiving another slap from their vyrm chaperone.

A stairway sloped upward and onto a large dais within the middle of the building. Between the pillared columns, more tables stood at random, interspersed with other, newer statues. These statues appeared more dignified somehow; most of them possessed resolute, unyielding faces: less fear and more strength and dignity.

Shuffling between the tables and talking with himself, a tall and skinny figure wandered between the tables, making move after move, playing both sides of the board until he had to take more than a moment's thought between moves, and then he simply moved to the next table. As they neared his position, they spotted the most prominent statue. Upon an elevated podium, it stood taller than anything else.

Claire noticed that the game-player was unlike the Black *or* the Tarkhūn. His skin looked less reptilian and his facial features more human. He appeared to be more of a human-vyrm hybrid.

The hybrid's tightly cropped hair ended in a ponytail that flopped slightly as he moved from location to location, each place tethered around that statue which loomed nearer and nearer as they picked through a path that led to the odd, somehow regal, figure.

"Basilisk?" Claire asked her companion. She looked at Rob, but he was transfixed by the object at the center of the room: the statue.

Rob stopped despite the shoves of the vyrm who meant to push him forward. Rob's jaw hung slack in awe and tears welled at the edge of his eyes. He dropped to his knees and bowed low to the ground in respect. Then he stood and continued the forced march.

Claire, too, stared at the statue in awe. Its face was a very near perfect copy of her father's. The man was perhaps taller, and of a larger build, but the resemblance was uncanny. His stony arms bent at the elbow and an intricately engraved kind of ancient longsword lay across his palms as if he offered it to her.

"The Stone Glaive and the Architect King," Rob whispered in awe. The guard shoved him again, but he barely noticed.

Moments later, they had walked near enough that the game player whirled around to meet his guests. He bowed to their presence in greeting. Rob returned the gesture and Claire likewise fumbled her way through, following Rob's queue.

"Greetings, son of Zahaben, and Claire Jones," Basilisk offered.

Rob could hardly take his eyes off the proud statue, however. He forced himself to focus on the matter at hand and tried to quell the righteous fury that rose up within him; he'd never dared dream of coming so close to the progenitor of the Tesseract. "Greetings, Basilisk, Child of the Agod." he managed a proper response.

Basilisk nodded to the trio of guards. The largest of them dropped Rob's duffel bag, which he'd confiscated. And then, the guards departed, leaving the humans in the hands of the vyrm ruler.

An awkward silence passed as Basilisk silently looked them over. His eyes radiated glee.

Breaking the silence, Rob asked, "Does this mean you don't intend to kill us today?"

A sorcerer in his own right, Basilisk grinned mischievously and waved a finger while hissing a word of power. The manacles fell from his prisoners' wrists. "I find I'd rather parley today. You two are potentially important pieces in a far grander game than you might realize." He wrung his hands with nervous enthusiasm. "I'm interested in seeing how your roles play out."

Basilisk stepped closer and swatted all the pieces from an unfinished game at the nearest table. He snapped his fingers emphatically and one of the statues jumped to life, startling Claire, who stood nearby. The Tarkhūn servant bowed to his master and nimbly scurried off.

Claire inspected the next nearest statue more closely, trying to discern if it too was a vyrm decoy or an actual statue. Rob also meandered through the collection, but his eyes fixed on the figure of the Architect King.

"Are these all statues?" Claire asked Basilisk, an unmistakable tone of awe crept into her voice.

Loving the flattery of her inflection, Basilisk replied. "None of these are mere 'statues,' my dear."

Rob shot her a look and a gentle nod to corroborate that fact. He drew ever nearer the king as he wandered.

"They are living stone," Basilisk explained. "It is a little talent of mine," he bragged. "My brother may have unraveled the mystery of dimensional travel via the Tesseract's vertices, but I alone deciphered the glyphs upon the Architect King's sword and learned to transmute flesh to stone."

Claire touched the face of a nearby figure. "They're alive?"

"Yes. They are quite conscious: immortal but completely immobile. Trapped with only their thoughts and loneliness, yet unable to retreat completely into their minds; they are ever present and fully awake."

"That sounds horrible," Claire lamented, sympathetically pulling her hand from the statue's face. "Then these are all your prisoners?"

Basilisk whirled around and bellowed with a supernaturally loud voice, "By what right do you touch the Stone Glaive?"

Rob quickly pulled his hand back from the blade, which he'd been inexplicably drawn to like a moth to fire. He turned and bowed apologetically. "I apologize. I never thought I would see such a grand thing in person."

Not taking his eyes from it, he whispered from the histories in a voice just loud enough to be heard. "A divine shard broken off the very engines of the heavens—the machine that churns out life and the fabric of reality. A piece of the chariot of the Creator God."

Basilisk shrugged off the breach of protocol and beckoned him to come closer; the vyrm servant returned with a large platter of exotic foods and set it on the cleared table. "Come, Zabe. Join us as we lunch. I have much I'd like to discuss."

Rob and Claire stood opposite the ruler and waited for him to reach for any of the items first. Basilisk popped a tiny fruit into his mouth and began chewing while they hesitated; he gave them an incredulous look as he did so. "If I had intended you harm, I would've done so already. I didn't bring you all the way up here to merely poison you."

The two guests politely ate from the platter at Basilisk's insistence.

"You both understand that my brother and I each have spies everywhere?"

Rob nodded.

"And yet, we still cannot see and hear everything, everywhere. So tell me Zabe, new Captain of the Royal Guard... yes, I heard of your father's heroic passing... what is your plan?"

Rob swallowed hard. "Just keep moving," he said honestly.

Basilisk moved away from the table and leaned against a statue. The rocky figure appeared to have been frozen in mid-motion, as if he'd been running when Basilisk cursed him. "That plan doesn't have much of an end-game," he observed. "You are the leader of a force pledged to protect a woman already in your enemy's custody."

"I'm routing a greater concern."

"You're willing to sacrifice the woman you love in order to fore-stall the inevitable?"

Rob glared at him.

"Oh, come now. Everyone knows about your 'secret' relation-ship with Princess Bithia."

"Sh'logath is not a great eventuality," Rob accused. "Even you, one of the Brothers of the Apocalypse, a herald of the Devourer, dare not awaken him!"

"That's quite an accusation!"

"I have heard the prophecies and I've read the scriptures that tell of your meeting with the Architect King!"

Basilisk held up a hand to silence Rob. Rob paused, cut short, and Basilisk gave a hand signal. Nearly a dozen vyrm assassins had been king as still as stone and hidden amongst the statue garden; at his signal, they stood and departed to give their leader his confi-dentiality.

His eyes counted to ensure their total privacy. "Now then, we are utterly alone. Tell me what they say on the Prime?" He turned his back to Rob and stared at his grandest prize positioned on the platform.

"They say that at our darkest hour, as you and Nitthogr led the vyrm against our forces in the Syzygyc War, the Architect King reappeared and went to you. They say that you had a conversation and that even as Sh'logath encroached upon the membrane of re-ality, he offered himself to you in sacrifice and that you accepted his terms, learning the secret to freeze people as stone in the process."

Standing still, retaining his poise, he asked over his shoulder, "Do they say anything specific about this conversation?"

"That he showed you how you still valued life—reality; that you saw the struggles of all peoples—that the struggle is worth it. They say that you saw the weakness of Sh'logath's theology: annihilation is not the answer to the eternal struggle. It's said that the King offered his life up for all others. That he would remain your hostage for as long as Sh'logath continued to slumber, but that his sons and daughters would forever rule the Prime until he one day reclaims his authority over all creation."

"Why would someone accept those terms?" Basilisk retorted. "One life for many? That doesn't make sense... if it happened as you say. I still remember when my brother and I stood together over the profane alter, inviting Sh'logath into our realm!"

"It does not make sense," Rob agreed. "Unless you, Basilisk, doubted some of the tenants of the Sh'logath cult... unless you *do* value the struggle of life which the agod promised to remove... unless there is still some shred of the old man that still remains: clinging to hope in your original faith—in the old religion of the Prime. Perhaps you were never fully converted to the vyrm ways?"

"And what if I'm not?" he snapped at Rob, who had obviously touched a nerve.

Behind them, Claire approached the central statue in wonder, taking in the glory of the King.

"And neither is my brother! He would use Sh'logath as a means to his own ends! To mingle his own blood within the line of the Architect King, as if such harlotry might be tolerated!" Basilisk stared at Claire, who fingered the hilt of the royal Stone Glaive. He paid her actions little mind. "Even though, his plans might have some merit."

"So you know he will release Sh'logath if he does not achieve satisfaction," Rob warned, curiously eyeing Claire, who took hold of the sword by the excessively long handle. "And then, all your plans and efforts here will have been for naught. The Destroyer will obliterate all existence, the Tesseract will shatter; reality—life—everything will cease, everywhere and all at once!"

Basilisk sighed, staring at Claire, who pulled the heavy sword from the hands of the statue, tugging against its weight. "If so, then all *your* prophecies will have all failed," he replied.

Claire awkwardly locked eyes with Basilisk. "I can take this? I remember only a little of the Prime histories from Bithia's mind."

"You have claim to the sword," he said matter-of-factly.

She snatched the old leather sheathe that lay at the feet of the Architect King and inserted the ancient blade. "Will this help us fight against Nitthogr?"

Rob replied, "I'm not sure. But it may be a rallying symbol. I think it will take more than an ancient sword to over-match the warlock. It may inspire my kin in the hill country, though; we *will* need to enter the Prime and rescue the princess."

Basilisk scoffed with a snort of derision. "Strong hearts are the most easily deceived; their inherent confidence is just the first lie that they will believe. All the rest that follow find root that much more easily.

"You know that you cannot defeat my brother, don't you?" He tipped over a piece on the nearest game board.

"None thought that you could ever defeat the architect king." Rob nodded to the petrified form behind him.

Basilisk snorted and replied. "I'm not sure that I really ever did."

"You'd be wise to remember that. Some have prophesied that the king will eventually throw off his stony flesh and repair all the wrongs that have infected the Tesseract. You have the power to simply release him from this stony prison and return him to his service. *He could overthrow Nitthogr!*" Rob said.

Basilisk hissed. "You have no right to make such a suggestion! That is not how the prophecy goes!" He calmed himself in the moments that followed his outburst. The vyrm ruler returned to the matter at hand. "I'm sure your next move against my brother will become apparent in due time. You'd best formulate a plan sooner rather than later."

"Tell us what we should do," Claire asked. The same fiery zeal that Bithia possessed burned within her eyes. "You've obviously got a broader view of the situation and a great talent for strategy—how else could you have defended this realm for so long against Nitthogr's army and their superior numbers: the Black outnumbers the Tarkhūn two to one!"

Rob raised an eyebrow. Clearly, the vyrm poison had not blocked all her shared memories from The Prime.

"Let me tell you a story, *Claire Jones*." He stressed her name as if to remind her that although she shared much with the princess, she was not actually Bithia. "Long ago, thousands of years before you were born, in fact, Nitthogr and I left our positions and departed from The Prime in order to explore the dimensional doors. We were pioneers! We left on commission of the royal family who sought the empirical evidence to validate what their faith, *my faith*, already proclaimed.

"We found everything to be true, and we proved it. As we continued to explore, we found new and wonderful things with every trip. And then we arrived here... before it became the Desolation. It was green and vibrant in that era. The people here, the vyrm, shared with us their fanatical faith—they truly believed. They needed no proof, no validation for what they knew in their hearts to be true: their deity, although he did not exist, was real and alive even in his nonexistence! Something in the simplicity of their faith appealed to us—their fervor, their abject devotion to their cause—even if it demanded that nonexistence meet with reality at the very cost of that reality!

"Only one could survive such an encounter, and we became enslaved to that glorious concept: that pure faith could produce a new reality. Something would come from nothing by the very fact of our dedication and devotion to such an ideal! And yet," Basilisk looked far off into the distance where the black chunk of nether hung in the broken sky.

"I don't know that we were ever fully convinced that this was best. Our zeal demanded action, but we didn't think through the metaphysics. If Sh'logath exists, then by his nature as Agod of nonexistence, then *nothing could exist!* We would invoke total annihilation. We knew this, yet in our fervor we released him, anyway; we invoked the foul ritual and called to him in his darkness.

"But then... the Architect King approached even as Sh'logath cracked the walls of reality. There were only a few options left to us, and doubt crept into my hybrid heart as the Tesseract's very designer offered us a choice. Either embrace Sh'logath or return to the service of the King!"

Basilisk stopped and stood there in silence. He moved a nearby game piece and sighed.

"Well?" Claire exclaimed. "What did you do?"

He responded with a whispered, "Neither. The game remains at a draw. I alone hold reality in balance."

"But the prophecy!" said Rob. "You cannot hold reality in the balance forever! Even if you *could*—you won't."

Basilisk gave him an accusatory look. "Perhaps you wish me to decide my fate right now? To throw in my lot with the prophecy?"

Rob threw his hands up. "No! No, I'm happy with the middle ground."

"Then what was the point of the story?" Claire asked.

Basilisk narrowed his eyes. "I did not know what to do then, and I certainly don't know what to do now." He stepped to the other side of the game board and made a move, then returned to do likewise again.

Standing there in the growing silence, Rob took Claire by the shoulders and they started to back up, hoping that this was the sorcerer's unspoken way of releasing them from his captivity. Walking backward for the first couple of steps, Rob bowed and turned to leave, picking up his duffel bag.

"You have free rein to walk about Limbus," Basilisk called out after them, "at least, for now, anyway. But let me remind you that there are far worse things dwelling in the Desolation... things that I have no control over."

They bowed again.

"Oh, and Claire Jones?"

She paused and met his gaze.

"I am very interested in seeing what move *you* make, especially now that your father has fallen?"

"What?" she yelled, growing stiff with shock. "My father is dead?"

"If not already, then he will be in short order. Caivev was sent to collect him."

Claire looked at Rob, her heart full of confusion and rage.

"Caivev is Vivian," Rob shared with her. "She's a trained sleeper agent and assassin from the Prime." He turned her shoulders back to the path, trying to get her to follow, but she meandered, distracted by the potential of such news.

They got outside of Basilisk's immediate purview and Rob pulled out the tattered, yellowed pages he'd stolen from the Grimmorium Nitthogr. "Claire? Come on, Claire, we've got to get to the next portal. We have to leave Limbus."

"My father..." she trailed off, only vocalizing a portion of her thoughts.

He took her by the hand and looked into her eyes. "And my father too... We won't let their sacrifices be in vain. We must not let that be!"

She clung to him and wept on his shoulder for a long moment, and then pushed back. "Okay. Where do we go next?"

Chapter Eighteen

"Home. My home," Rob replied. "We must enter the Prime." They skirted the edge of Limbus, passing much the same way that they came.

As they passed silently through the somber city, a darker pall fell over the land. Likely it always existed, but the further they traveled from the center of Limbus, the more pronounced it grew; with less ambient heat, the air temperature cooled the further they got from the populated parts of the city.

Rob and Claire stood at the outskirts of Limbus. A very pronounced line distinguished the borders where the cracked, parched soil of the wasteland began. Rob exhaled a sigh; his breath crystallized into frost.

High above, the nearly starless sky reminded them of the danger of this realm. The obsidian monstrosity that hung above them, scraping the horizon, seemed to devour the light from even the furthest solar bodies, sucking it all away into the nethersphere. As the unholy devourer lurked at the threshold, awaiting the profane invitation, the darkness remained an ominous reminder of the high stakes.

Claire turned to Rob, her breath also exploded into mist. "Why didn't we just go straight to the Prime from Stonehenge?"

"They would have been able to locate us immediately," he replied. "From this realm, we could conceivably go anywhere. It takes us entirely off their radar; they won't know where to begin looking—we're in the wind, so to speak."

"So then, we're going to a new portal location?"

"Yes."

"And what are the two possible locations for it?"

Rob was quiet for a moment, knowing she would struggle with the choice. "Either to a secret place on the Prime, where any of my remaining kin will have gathered... or to Earth."

Claire nodded. It was her turn to keep silent and introspective. She handed Rob the Stone Glaive. He stared blankly at her, convinced she didn't know the significance of the gift she'd given him. "And what if I wanted to return to Earth?"

"You want to rescue your father?"

Claire stared forward into the barren wasteland that stretched before them. "It doesn't matter right now. We can't do anything from Limbus."

She stepped forward, striding ahead with purpose. The ground crunched underfoot like broken glass: the only sound for miles as the duo walked ahead, into the unknown.

Victor Adams drummed his fingers on the heavy magic book which the warlock had left behind as a monument to his sincerity. None of the Illuminati could decipher the writings, and so they remained indebted to Nitthogr unless they could find another person capable of understanding the eldritch text, preferably someone who was also able to wield its arcane power.

The book lay upon the wooden table that had always been the appointed place for The Seven's meetings, except that their number was now one fewer. Adams looked down and stared at the weathered golden rings adorning his stumpy fingers.

How many men's heads had he personally caved in with the golden, skull-shaped jewelry? He'd shed much blood back when he was a low-ranking hit-man for the Persian Syndicate. That was before Nitthogr found him and made him great, before he became a part of the Heptobscurantum and decimated his opposition, seizing control of the Syndicate by his own power and the power lent him by his warlock advisor.

He gave his rings a quick polish against the breast of his jacket. Any moment now Summers' people would deliver their newest candidate, the current leader of the Ordo Templi Orientis, a man heavily endorsed by their other contacts within the Order of the Golden Dawn.

Trask had always proved a bit of a wild card in the past, and while his ideas had always seemed sound, something about the man had never quite sat well for Victor. In private conversations with his fellow council members, the other men of The Seven each agreed with the Persian mobster.

While Trask had seemed quite willing to go at odds with the sorcerer, a thing they each admired independently, the remaining six each feared that Trask had *too much* in common with James Shianan. Perhaps neither Trask nor Nitthogr had committed to the awakening ritual.

The door opened and his five remaining fellows of the Illuminati entered. Greyson and Cannon led the way. They had been in charge of the final vetting process. Cannon, an experienced assassin in his own right, was charged with the immediate elimination of any failing candidates whose vision did not align with that of The Seven. Knowledge that they even existed was too dangerous of a loose end. But this new candidate, Sisyphus, not only comprehended the writings of the Grimmorium Nitthogr, but also embraced the Heptobscurantum's maddening manifesto.

Victor raised an eyebrow when Peter Greyson and Bruce Cannon sat down. "Well, Peter?" he asked in his thick accent.

Greyson nodded with a telling smile. "Jacob Sisyphus is a true believer. He may not have the raw power at his disposal that this sorcerer, James Shianan, wields, but he understands the ways of power as a wizard."

Thomas Chelish rendered an inquisitive look.

Greyson explained further. "The power seems to indwell Shianan who controls it as it flows from him. Sisyphus wields power, too, tapping into it as he is available. He is an *educated* thaumaturge, whereas James is a natural arcanist."

The remnant nodded, each accepting that assessment. Having a powerful occultist in their group was a benefit. They feared the possibility of Nitthogr taking Trask's empty seat and assuming total control over The Seven.

As it stood, currently, Nitthogr was supposedly removed from the ruling council of seven, even if he had originally engineered its construction. He was supposed to be only a counselor and consultant. The Seven had never openly defied any direct and overt orders he had impositioned them with, but that time would come soon. He'd recently given more and more dictates to these men who were not accustomed to being controlled.

There was also the problem that they had all seen in him. None believed in his devotion to Sh'logath. Too long had they seen him make choices or give advice, which he had to defend or rationalize later.

The Persian leaned forward at the table and rapped his knuckles against the engraving. "Well... do we like Sisyphus?"

Nodding, Greyson leaned in and put up his hands to quell the excitement. "Brothers, we can't vote yet. Let's not be too hasty in calling this meeting to order; we ought to first discuss in secret our fear of James's subversive nature. We don't want to have those thoughts written into the minutes."

A collection of nods circulated the room. They agreed in unison.

Greyson took charge of the conversation as the moderator. "We haven't discussed this openly, but I believe we are all of the same thought regarding this so-called Herald of Sh'logath." He scanned the table; the other five each nodded solemnly. "We could have initiated the Great Awakening during any of the last few lunar cycles had it not been for Nitthogr's excuses. We've had the ability to collect Claire Jones at our leisure up until his personal plans exploded in his face."

"I think we can all see how thinly veiled 'his plans' are," Andrew Thornton intoned. "He's obviously working some independent scheme and using us—using Sh'logath—as a part of that."

Five of the six readily leaned forward with their hands balled in fists, ready to call for an official vote in the confidence they'd entrusted to the warlock. Bruce Cannon, however, stayed back; obviously he had more to add.

"Bruce?"

"All of this is true," Cannon said, "and yet we've all been witness to the raw power that Nitthogr has at his disposal. Can this council stand in open defiance to Nitthogr if he cleanly breaks his allegiance to Sh'logath?"

Charles Summers, perhaps the most thoughtful and atheological of the bunch, chimed in. "If our hearts are set on performing the grand Invitation and releasing Sh'logath but that results in our destruction—will that change anything?"

Cannon looked at him, confused.

"On one hand is the idea that Nitthogr has retreated from the true faith and we must usurp him to cause the Awakening. If we are destroyed because of our attempts, it will be for Sh'logath's glory. If we succeed, stopping a false prophet, it is to the Devourer's glory! If we are wrong and Nitthogr has remained true to the agod's higher plan and he is forced to destroy us in order to fulfill it, then this too glorifies Sh'logath. All roads lead to that eventual glory—Sh'logath rises, regardless!"

His occultic fervor rose up. Passion interwove his words. The six slapped their palms against the table enthusiastically.

Holding up one more finger to tick off his second question, he asked, "How will the vyrm react if we move against their leader?"

"Do we continue to need them? Enrollment into even the upper levels of the Heptobscurantum is on the rise. But there is always Vivian. She is a true adherent. She could initiate a coup against James if it becomes necessary... overthrow Nitthogr as the leader of The Black. Or else we can maybe identify one of the vyrm generals who could take his place."

The cult knew that, even though they had Nitthogr's book, they needed the back of the vyrm to accomplish their goals.

Cannon leaned forward, buying into the rhetoric. With his fist sideways, he called for the vote. "Do we continue under the thumb of Nitthogr, who we suspect may be a pretender to Sh'logath's will?"

In unison, they turned a thumb down. The vote was unanimous. Silently they stood and respectively unfolded their robes. Each pulled it over their bodies, drawing the hood around their face in order to properly convene. It was the one ritual formality the secret society held to.

Adams laid a new robe on the table and called the meeting to order. The first order of business would be to install their seventh member and ratify him as a legal member of the Heptobscurantum. Hopefully this occult magician could provide some protection against the warlock's rage whenever he returned to Earth and learned of The Seven's schismatic intentions.

He laid his arm out with fist balled up. Adams asked with his thick accent, "Jacob Sisyphus?"

Around the table each member signaled with a thumbs up.

"Greyson? Please retrieve our brother and let us welcome him to The Seven."

Day and night blended together. Very little light permeated the atmosphere deep enough to reach the cracked, alien surface of The Desolation; the eater of the light hung as a fixture in the sky. It seemed too close, an ominous reminder of the impending doom. It also remained a very real threat to their sanity, tempting their stressed psyches to break down and go mad.

Claire's feet drug heavy against the crystalline shards underfoot. Jagged stones threatened to smash their ankles if they didn't give enough attention to each footstep; the cold sapped Claire's desire to keep pace.

She stumbled and Rob caught her, kept her from falling. He pointed in the distance and pulled her behind a rocky outcropping. She lay next to him as they peered out from behind their cover. Rob pointed towards the horizon where a group of vyrm rovers wandered far ahead: outcast members of the vyrm who sided with neither the Black nor the Tarkhūn—they were either rejects, outcasts, or members of a tiny population which held to a heretical faith in the long-since-exterminated royal line: a faction which hoped in a future vyrm redeemer. This was the third nomadic group they'd spotted since their departure from Limbus yesterday. Claire barely looked at them, though. Her thoughts during this journey had gone to war against each other.

Bithia's thoughts, memories, and emotions had slowly crept back toward the surface. Claire knew that she had loved Rob far more intensely and purely than she had let him know. Her brilliantly sensual feelings toward him seemed to suddenly awaken after their first encounter with the nomadic vyrm drifters—the vyrm toxins had cleared her system, perhaps bringing through more of Bithia and making Claire blush as she shared in them.

The intense feelings waged war against her darker thoughts; they helped distract from dwelling on the unknown fate of her father. Basilisk had given her no real information. He'd only opened the door to misery and despair, poisoning her thoughts in a more damaging way than the vyrm psychics who had bitten her in the ether.

Claire glanced again at Rob. He'd explained how they should avoid any wasteland wanderers at all costs. Most of them had turned savage and feral, according to what he had read; many of the rovers had even become cannibalistic. However, most of his information regarding life on the Desolation was very outdated. No new research had been gathered since the decade following the Syzygyc War and no new opportunities for exploration of this realm ever presented itself.

Rob watched them with rapt interest. "I always thought I would become a field researcher," he whispered to Claire. "You know, if I hadn't been born into the family of the royal protectorate." He smiled boyishly. "There's just so much that we don't really know."

Leaning up against him, she merely nodded and shivered. She figured it would be quite some time before they could get moving again, using their past encounters as a guide. They had to wait for them to pass before they could risk moving again. The uncomfortable ground poked her body from underneath and the cold dirt sapped any warmth she tried to retain.

Rob put an arm around her and drew her close, sharing his body heat with her. Claire flushed as Bithia's desires invaded her thoughts... at least, she thought they were Bithia's. He rolled to his side,, and she nestled into the crook of his arm. They lay there like that for several hours until the vyrm disappeared from the horizon.

Eventually, they shook off the dust and prepared to continue the journey onward. Rob shouldered the duffel. "Have many of Bithia's memories returned to you from your dream travel? Right before our castle fell under siege, I had asked her... an important question."

"No," Claire partially lied. Many fractured images and thoughts had come back to her, but not what he was looking for. She sighed as they began trudging onward. She didn't know how to balance her own thoughts and feelings against Bithia's. The only thing that she knew for sure was that she was *not Bithia*. But whenever she looked at Rob, she felt confused, conflicted.

She stared at her feet as they slogged through the badlands. At least that kept her eyes off Rob. Claire couldn't help but feel a little guilty for experiencing the Princess's emotions toward him. Right now, she just wished that this whole experience was a bad dream she would soon wake from.

Hours passed in relative silence. The tedious monotony of it all stretched forever. Time seemed to stand still, and the constant movement and crippling cold managed to suck every last shred of energy from her.

Eventually, all vestiges of the faint daylight that guided them had completely dissipated. Rob found a broken boulder and the two travelers crept into the cleft, mashing their bodies together to share their warmth.

Claire tossed and turned throughout the night. Both the extreme discomfort and the mental confusion kept rousing her. Rob seemed to sleep just fine, she observed with ire. She squeezed her elbows in and tried to sleep in a new position. An unnerving fear kept her awake, despite the desperate need for rest. Every time she slept, her mental connection to the princess seemed to deepen.

She winced against a jagged knob in her hip and leaned more into Rob's body. Claire feared that the more she connected with Bithia, the more she would feel compelled to act on her feelings. She really *knew* Bithia, and Claire felt she might slip and lose some sense of herself and fall into Bithia's mind. Claire feared that she would either lose herself completely, or betray someone who she was growing to love like a twin sister.

Looking at Rob, sleeping as easily as he did in these conditions, Claire felt fully capable of betraying the princess—and that scared her, too.

She squeezed her eyelids and concentrated on herself. The pain and worry over her father's plight came crashing back to her. That was not a better solution.

Claire smiled. *But at least I can control it! I'm sure that I will be able to master my feelings in time.* She relaxed, satisfied that she would not lose herself entirely. Her eyelids fluttered once more, and she bit her lip to try to distract herself from the very real body heat of the man next to her, touching her. It radiated so powerfully. *But I still can't trust myself.*

She tucked her chin down and sighed, growing weary from all the mental exhaustion. Eventually, it tired her enough that she slipped into a dreamless state.

Chapter Nineteen

Bruce Cannon opened the steel door of the nondescript factory. Nestled in one of the more run-down parts of Detroit, it possessed the perfect camouflage. Cannon bid Victor Adams and Jacob Sisyphus a warm welcome as the factory belched dark smoke into the air. The active pollution was perhaps the building's only distinguishing feature as its peers in the neighborhood had fallen largely silent following the economic downturn.

"I trust you found it easily enough." He made small talk as they wandered through the facility, until the grinding noises of the work overpowered any conversation. All the workers on the floor wore a lapel pin bearing a seven-pointed star, identifying them as cultists from the Heptobscurantum.

Near a giant turbine, Cannon threw a combination of levers. A hatch hissed opened, revealing a secret passage leading below ground. As the three walked ahead, the portal sealed behind them. Behind the door, the factory noise was all but eliminated, enabling the men to speak freely.

"I think you will be quite impressed with Doctor Walther," Cannon stated. "Pietro Walther has been working in the psuedo-sciences for his entire career."

"If he's so brilliant," Adams said with a hint of warning in his voice, "then why is this the first time The Seven has ever heard of him?"

"Thornton has known of him all along," Cannon hedged. "He's financed the lab from his oil operations' R and D budget. But to answer your question, this is perhaps the first *relevant* breakthrough for our purposes. It could radically impact our chances of completing the Great Awakening, even should Nitthogr attempt to prevent us from moving forward."

The stairwell emptied out into a large laboratory. Technologies both old and new scattered the grounds; equipment and notes lay heaped over benches and desks, as if some scientific hoarder had nested below the factory.

Spotting the doctor as he worked on a project in the distance, Cannon paused with his accomplices. "I must warn you, neither Doctor Walther nor his assistants are members of the Heptobscurantum. He is interested purely in the science and accomplishment of discovery. To him, Sh'logath is an incorporeal idea... a philosophical ideal. Let us not mention the Awakening or our true purposes."

Adams and Sisyphus nodded. They followed and Cannon made introductions, which Walther largely ignored as he tinkered; he only paused to do a double take at Sisyphus, but then discounted whatever thoughts had occurred to him.

The machine he tweaked looked like a hybrid of ancient artifacts that were attached to the internals of a space shuttle; a wheeled section of carpentry scaffolding contained the body of the turboencabulator-style machine. Circuit boards hung at random places and an entire spool of industrial copper wire had been emptied; the cables wrapped all around the scaffolding and snaked away in trails across the floor.

"I assume you gentlemen are here to see my work?" He glared sidelong at Cannon. "And if it doesn't perform adequately, I suppose you will defund me and my research?"

Cannon sighed and shook his head. "For the last time, Pietro, *I am not going to pull your funding*. These men are merely here to see it. And besides, I've already seen it work. You have nothing to worry about."

Walther finally looked at his guests. He glanced again at the newest of The Seven, doing a double take. "You. Has anyone told you that you look like Jacob Sisyphus?"

The massive man only grinned through his ever-present five o'clock shadow. He ran his fingers through his thick hair and shook out his mullet. Besides the growing paunch on his belly, he was a very recognizable figure in many circles. "I should. I'm the one and only. You are a fan from the golden, glory years?"

Walther's lip curled in a smile. "I'll admit that professional wrestling has always been a guilty pleasure of mine. I met you once, you know. Recently. I was at the last event you headlined... I thought you were going to win."

Sisyphus flashed him a cocky grin. "Oh, but I am... *we* are."

Walther nodded. "I had no idea that you were interested in science."

Cannon shot Sisyphus a look of warning. Walther was not in the loop as to the Heptobscurantum's true aims.

"Always," Sisyphus merely replied. "I've never believed that this," he pinched his flesh for emphasis, "is all there is."

"Then be prepared to have that belief empirically proven." He turned to an assistant. "Mizz Heiderscheidt, a vial of blood, please?"

His aide quickly walked to a gurney nearby. A sedated man, homeless by the looks of him, lay strapped to the rails of an old medical bed. The lab assistant callously jabbed the needle into him, digging around until she found a vein, and then drew a full syringe of blood and returned, handing it over to Doctor Walther.

Her methods worked, but also demonstrated little medical training and no regard for the patient.

"Gentlemen," the eccentric scientist emphatically announced, "prepare to see the laws of reality broken." He turned, injected the blood into a catheter tube, and cranked a dial. The ancient pieces of technology seemed to vibrate and glow with a supernatural light.

Walther pulled a set of welding goggles over his eyes and slammed a large red button affixed to the scaffolding with duct tape. Three brilliant beams of energy shot out from laser projectors welded to the machine; they met at a blinding point of impact fifteen feet from the machine. Walther wheeled on an industrial dial; the beams shifted apart slowly as he turned the wheel and a triangular portal opened.

The observers' jaws dropped and their eyes widened as the triangle grew larger. Within the boundary of the energy beams, they could see another dimension.

"It's quite stable," Walther stated, taking a pigeon from its cage nearby. He walked to the portal and released the bird at the mouth of the energy gate; it flew through, crackling with a pop like static electricity as it crossed over. It immediately emerged on the other side of the portal and flew away, no worse for wear.

Walther turned and bowed. "We have broken the barrier between dimensions." He pointed to a row of whiteboards boasting calculations spanning the distance. "I have identified twenty-seven specific dimensions so far, but my figures indicate either thirty-two or thirty-three that exist. But this one," he pointed to the glowing door, "this one is the easiest to access. It is the root. We call it Prime; the rest of the realities, including our own, seem to derive from this singular plane of existence."

The gate began to flicker slightly. "As the blood diminishes, the gate loses stability." He took another pigeon and released it just as the portal flickered. The bird flew through as before, but when the signal strength slightly sputtered, the pigeon split into three pieces as if perfectly sliced apart. The dead creature fell to the burnt grass on the other side of the dimensional window. "Of course, the answer is to keep the machine powered. Feed it more blood."

The three men nodded excitedly. "Now it is *I who am a fan of you.*" Sisyphus shook the doctor's hand.

"Gentlemen," Cannon stated. "We have some business to discuss." He nodded with pleasure and bid farewell to the doctor, then he guided Adams and Sisyphus back towards the stairs.

"So," Adams began, "you will finally tell us your purpose for this meeting? How do you suggest we use this technology to our ends?"

Cannon nodded. "We know we must pull Vivian to our side and set her against Nitthogr. This is the way we do that."

"How do you mean?"

Cannon indicated Sisyphus. "For all his occult training and mastery, he cannot match Nitthogr's raw power, no offense, Jacob, but it is a fact, just as *I* could not best Vivian in a physical fight. There is some inherent strength in the people of the Prime, a kind of power."

Intrigued, Sisyphus nodded and asked, "And how does this help?"

"If you notice, this machine did not open at the portal locations, which Nitthogr seems to control. Science burrowed a way through the stuff of reality and forced open its own window. We can access the other dimensions without Nitthogr ever knowing, and we are not limited to the portal locations."

Adams followed his train of thought. "We can send Vivian through to see what her mentor is up to behind her back?"

"Exactly! She is a true disciple of Sh'logath—I am sure of it. If she sees him secretly act contrary to the part, he has publicly played for so long, she will come to our side."

"But what if she tells him of our coup instead?"

"Then he learns about it only a little earlier than anticipated," Cannon said. "Very little changes except that we potentially gain a powerful ally against Nitthogr if he has truly departed from the true faith. And if he has not, then we might also learn that, too."

His accomplices nodded. "And how do we convince her to spy on her master?"

Cannon grinned. "That part is easy. We need only tell her the truth: show her the facts and logic. These will demand that she vindicate his character. Her affection for him should motivate her. In her efforts to defend him, she will prove his defection."

Adams nodded. "I will meet with her immediately."

"Good," he replied. "I have a slightly different job for you, Jacob Sisyphus."

A pale, hollow light greeted Claire as her eyelids fluttered open in the morning. The cold had woken her; Rob's body heat no longer warmed her in its absence. She crawled out from the split in the rock and found him staring into the distance.

He turned and greeted her. "I did not think we had gotten this far yet."

She offered an inquisitive look.

"We are already well inside the Plains of Neggath."

"Is that good?"

"Perhaps," Rob said. "I've never actually been here before. I always thought it was further from Limbus, according to maps in the history books. The plains harbor many potential dangers—worse than mere unaligned vyrm rovers."

Claire dug through the duffel and sorted through the food packets. She hoped to load up on calories before the hard trek. Only a few rations remained. "How much longer until our next stop?"

"Straruck lies that way." He pointed to the horizon. "If we keep this pace, we may reach it this afternoon, even. An ancient religious university lies upon the flats surrounded by Straruck village."

Finishing a bland applesauce packet, Claire nearly choked on the unpleasant texture. "Then let's get moving. I always wanted to study abroad."

Rob smiled. "I don't think it's anything like what you would expect. Long before the wars, Straruck was a hub of philosophy, religion, law, and medical research. In fact, they say that the cult of Sh'logath formed there as a joint venture between the religion and philosophy students."

"Yeah," Claire remarked. "Sounds an awful lot like Stanford, if you ask me."

Her sarcasm didn't go unnoticed. "I have only seen stills from the war era. It appeared that the sands have laid claim to much of it. Perhaps karma has cosmically repaid them for their part in creating The Devourer? Nonetheless, I am excited to see it with my own eyes."

Claire grinned at him as they plodded onward. "You sound a lot like my father." She trailed off, thoughts turning dark.

Suddenly, both travelers stumbled, and the ground trembled. Rob's hand flew immediately to the Glaive at his back and he drew it from the scabbard. He held the bulky, engraved shard at the ready. Long seconds passed and its weight quickly tired his forearms. There were no immediate aftershocks and so he sheathed the weapon.

They traveled in silence for the next several hours until the dim outline of foreign structures became visible in the distance; they ignored the minor, intermittent quakes. Towers and buildings bent at odd and broken angles as their foundations had shifted and crumbled through the long, harsh years. The land had done much to reclaim itself from the vyrm occupation.

Cautiously approaching, Rob and Claire often stopped to watch and wait, spying out any potential enemy positions. A magnificent structure at the center of the decayed village rose above the others; it was their obvious destination. The large dome may have once been splendorous and proud. Now, a huge section of the cupola had been blasted away and age had ripped wounds across the rounded top, exposing structural ribs beneath its stucco skin.

They slogged ahead at a quickened pace. Underfoot, fine-grained sand dunes had overtaken the ankle-biting shards. The silt caked most of the larger debris to the ground. Ground tremors seemed to increase as they neared the edge of Straruck. They rumbled as if they had embodied the sickly heartbeat of a broken city.

Rob and Claire stalked silently through the maze of broken buildings. With no windows or doors remaining, there were few places for enemies to set ambushes for them. Still, despite the cover of darkness they'd had since Limbus and the promise of the Tarkhūn leader, they were reluctant to completely take Basilisk at his word.

As they rounded a final corner, they entered the edge of the central campus. Most of the buildings had been either blasted away or fallen to the extreme decay of age and neglect. Those derelicts that still remained had become nearly cocooned within the fine silica sand.

Claire almost stepped around the corner when Rob grabbed her and pulled her back out of sight. He pointed and motioned to remain silent. He pointed to several sets of footprints in the sand ahead. They watched and listened for a few moments.

Following their patrol route, they spotted a group of well-armed Tarkhūn walking their patrol circuit. The vyrm battle garb was well suited to the terrain and provided a modicum of camouflage within the rugged Plains of Neggath. They talked in a clicking kind of language.

Rob cocked his head, trying to understand it. The grimace on his face told Claire that he was unable to interpret it. "That's not the traditional vyrm tongue."

Claire felt a tingling rush in her mind. "The Tarkhūn commonly speak in a dialect of the old royal vyrm language. It was a part of Bithia's studies." She paused and listened. "They're talking about an insect invasion and the boredom of guarding the travel portal. Apparently, sentry duty is not a high calling for the Tarkhūn."

She cocked her head and blushed. "Also," she smirked, "the one talking now enjoys telling dirty jokes."

The guards suddenly started yelling and shooting at the sand. A crevasse formed near the Tarkhūn as Rob and Claire watched incredulously. A massive, grub-like worm erupted from the dune. Fiery plasma blasted from the lead Tarkhūn's pistol. It tore through the translucent skin of the writhing monstrosity.

Shrieking, the worm leveled its multitudinous bank of shiny, black eyes at the guards. With hideous antennae twitching, its jaws elongated, and it vomited forth a small army of dog-sized terrors. The heavily carapaced crawlers snaked towards their prey upon a thousand cilia-like legs. Their slimy feet crackled with a kind of necrotic energy as enzymatic electricity bounced around their millipede-like undercarriage.

Bellowing with rage, the two vyrm bravely stood their ground, blasting at both the wave of smaller crawlers and the giant parent that had carried them. One vyrm shouted a warning into the communications fob clipped on his shoulder. The momentary disruption was just enough for the swarm to surge forward and envelop him. They knocked him over, twisting around his feet.

The toppled guard screamed in anguish as the chemical electricity wreathed his body and wracked him with pain. His Tarkhūn companion quickly executed him with a single shot to the head. His communicator flooded with the sounds of another incident, and he clicked a short response before fleeing the overtaken courtyard. Smoke erupted on the far side of the campus, and the echoes of blaster fire drifted through the air. The surviving vyrm sprinted directly for the distant fracas.

Washing over the cadaver, the creatures writhed all over the dead Tarkhūn's body. Their caustic feet fed upon the flesh of the fallen. Within seconds, the teeming mass cleared away. Nothing remained of the victim except for bones and inorganic material.

Rob turned away from the grisly scene as the giant queen sank back below the sands. Her minions roamed the courtyard ahead, infesting the ground with their presence. "Carrion worms?" he wondered aloud. "They aren't native to the Desolation," he concluded. "Someone must have intentionally released them here, possibly in order to soften up the local garrison before an invasion."

"Nitthogr?" Claire asked.

Rob nodded. "I can't think of anyone else with the knowledge or means to travel the planes."

After checking the duffel bag, Rob slung the depleted sack across his chest. Their provisions had all but expired. He grabbed Claire by the hand. "If Nitthogr is here, then we shouldn't be. It's far too dangerous to risk him seeing you." He frowned into the empty duffel. "But we'd never make it beyond the Plains on this."

They skulked through the building, fleeing deeper within as the first carrion crawlers explored the doorway with curious, caustic tendrils. Sprinting through the dark halls, they put some distance between them and the invading creatures.

Pausing for a moment to breathe, Rob wiped the heavy desert dust from a sign. It showed the layout of the grounds and displayed a network of paths in washed-out lines of color. They led from building to building via buried tunnels or suspended corridors. "It's a student and visitor's guide." He traced his fingers along the faded magenta line connecting their location to the central building. "Here's our path!"

Echoes from millions of tiny insectoid feet began reverberating down the hallway behind them. Claire and Rob immediately turned a corner and sprinted forward; they ran up a winding, platformed staircase and into the next passage where a suspended causeway opened.

The suspended aerial walkway looked in poor repair. Wind had badly battered the bridge over the millennia; it flowed through gaping holes where the glass had long since broken. Rob gave the floor a couple of probing steps. Some of the alloy meshwork underfoot proved spongy; the weather of so many years had oxidized the metal, and large rust flakes took root at various intervals.

Scuttling noises in pursuit ensured they had no other avenue but this. One by one, Rob and Claire gingerly stepped along the stronger parts of the corridor, keeping to the edges as much as possible, where the structural supports proved heavier.

An immense hole had been torn from the center of the skywalk floor. The breach nearly severed the entire line; only architectural scaffolding tied the two ends of the tube together. Rob first, and then Claire, jumped nimbly across the chasm. The metal framework bounced tenuously under their maneuvers. Once beyond, they fled to the other side just as their terrifying pursuit discovered a way forward into the mouth of the metallic, skeletal tunnel.

The duo darted down the next corridor and around a bend. Claire ducked, diving into a room just in time to avoid the blaster fire from a Tarkhūn patrol. Rob leapt in behind her; chunks of plaster exploded above him as he dove forward. The echoes of the blaster fire would certainly draw more crawlers! He quickly peeked around the threshold and drew a volley of blaster fire.

"There's a whole group of them camped at the end of the hall, and two more creeping up on our position." Rob said. He grunted as his body stretched with a bone-cracking noise. His clothes split open at the seam points and his werewolf form overwhelmed the clothing's tensile strength. Reaching over his left shoulder, he drew the Stone Glaive just as the two vyrm scouts burst in.

Rob slashed the first across the chest with the blade; the sigils flashed when the keen edge tasted blood. Almost instantly the Tarkhūn turned to stone, forever immortalizing the surprised look upon his face; he fell backwards as he turned into a statue. No sooner did his body clear the doorframe than his agitated vyrm compatriots opened fire. Their burning rounds pulverized the stony form, blasting one of their own into hunks of rock and powder.

With a whirling kick, the second Tarkhūn booted Rob in the gut. The vyrm was so massive that he nearly matched Rob, even in his werewolf form. Grabbing Rob by the wrists, he dug his talons deep into Rob's flesh, keeping the blade far from his reptilian skin. The ground vibrated slightly as the whelming tremors seemed to swell; the carrion crawlers drew nearer.

Rob and the Tarkhūn struggled, crashing back and forth in the room. The walls shook, freeing chunks of plaster and dust; anxiously, Claire dodged the entangled combatants as best as she could. The sounds of the approaching crawler horde began overwhelming the sounds of their struggle. In the hallway, the vyrm opened fire, trying to turn back the larval enemy.

The insect-like worms only seemed to pick up speed, perhaps an illusion based on their increasing number as they burgeoned within the campus. They bled through the windows and other structural cracks.

"Rob!" Claire screamed as the first of the carrion worms broke the ranks of its dead brethren and turned from the small arms fire and slinked into their room.

Rob growled and opened his jaws. He quickly snapped them shut on the vyrm's face and raked his sharp incisors across the surprised enemy's eyes.

The giant Tarkhūn howled in pain, staggering backwards and rubbing his blinded eyes. He tripped over the first crawler and fell to his back, screaming in agony as the creatures swarmed over him.

Scooping Claire up in his free arm, Rob leveled his shoulder and charged through a nearby wall. He poured all of his might into ramming through and broke beyond the first wall like a cannonade, and then the second, and a third.

They stumbled through the last wall and into the corridor. Surprised at the intrusion, the encamped vyrm held their position as they poured hot fire into the living horde that pressed in ahead. The Tarkhūn hissed in surprise, but couldn't spare the gunfire to take a shot at the humanoids.

Rob roared a warning, which they seemed to heed. He and Claire turned the corner and didn't slow for anything, not even the torturous shrieks behind them as the carrion crawlers overwhelmed the vyrm force. Rob finally stopped at a darkened descent into the mouth of an underpass.

Claire nodded to Rob as if saying, *yes, I trust you*. They cautiously stepped into the shadows. Several steps in, a loud tremor shook the tunnel with earthquake malevolence, and then passed. They pressed ahead through the darkness; what little light their rear exit provided seemed to dim as it writhed with the surging, maggoty legion.

The ground erupted ahead of them as the carrion queen burst up from the ground, barring a forward escape. Rob howled as he leapt towards the behemoth, stabbing the blade deep into the beast's face. The stony wound began to spread its effect across the titan head.

Squealing with an otherworldly panic, it snapped its arthropodic head forward like a whip, dashing Rob to the ground where the Stone Glaive clattered beyond his grasp. The monster thrashed in something like a death roll; lashing ferocious circles, it shredded its own flesh, tearing the stony portion away so that it could not continue infecting the queen with the transmutation.

The tunnel shook and partially collapsed under the violence. A large crack grew ominously above the giant worm as it hissed at its enemies. Closing in from behind, the worm's children skittered anxiously toward their quarry.

Rob leapt for the ancient blade, but the queen shot a putrid secretion from her mouth; the viscous goo coated Rob's fist, sticking it to the floor.

He ripped his arm up from the ground and screamed in pain as the acidic slime smoke and sizzled, eating away his flesh. Within a fraction of a second, his right hand had been burnt so deeply that only fragments of tendon and exposed bone remained.

Rising even higher within the tunnel, the queen splayed her legs and shrieked loudly, laying claim to her prize. Her piercing shriek reverberated so loudly that the walls shook and excited her drones. They chittered and pulsed forward happily, covering over the Stone Glaive. Those closest turned to rock as they did so, but only the frenzy of the kill mattered to them.

Rob scrambled away from the powerful sword before the crawlers could reach him. The queen screeched with glee. Suddenly, the ceiling gave way and a large chunk of tunnel crushed the queen, opening the underground passage up to the sky.

With one arm hanging limp, Rob grabbed Claire with his good hand. "Come on!" he yelled, flinging them towards the ramp-like debris.

"But the sword? We can't just leave it!"

"You are more important than any artifact!" His disabled arm hung useless as he glanced backwards regretfully.

They rushed up the shifting shale slope and broke out into the sky. Below, the wounded creature screeched and flailed, collapsing even more of the ground and opening new sinkholes as Claire and Rob fled.

Leaning against the foundation of the central dome, the escapees panted for air. Claire grabbed Rob's destroyed arm near the wrist and examined it. He winced against the pain.

She looked him in the eyes, afraid her fearful face would scare him.

"Don't worry about it." Torment crept into his voice like the guttural growl of an angry canine. "It will heal."

Even as Claire watched it, she could see the flesh slowly stitching back together, regenerating at a cellular level. Rob tried to flex it, balling his raw hand into a fist. He drew a sharp, pained breath and then relaxed it, convinced of his hands' functionality, even if limited.

"This way," he said, guiding her around the building, not wanting to lose their momentum. Rob peeked through a once grand vestibule, now drained of all her glory. He exhaled his nervousness.

A mammoth, double door made of inlaid mineral and precious metals had been blasted open from the inside. It lay twisted ajar, barely clinging to its hinges. A hazy, pulsing light radiated from within, illuminating the interior with shades of brown.

"That door has remained sealed for millennia," Rob breathed. "It is the birthplace of Sh'logath. No vyrm has dared breach the chamber for respect and fear of the 'Thousand Elder's Sacrifice.'"

Rob guided her around the dome's foundation, trying to keep the building between them and the sounds of chaos and gunfire as much as possible. Creeping into the building via a crumbling access hatch, they weaved through the outer court, which gave the dome a very chapel-like motif. Creeping up a decayed stairwell, he led her to a rickety metal catwalk.

Through the broken sections in a wall, they could watch two vyrm forces battling against each other on the forsaken Plains of Neggath. Several buildings had been dashed away nearby where the ground reclaimed a large patch of flat land. Embroiled within the conflict, there, Rob spotted the vyrm general Regorik. Regorik ferociously tore his way through his enemies, and Rob wondered how long ago Regorik defected to the Black, betraying the Tarkhūn for Nitthogr.

From their vantage, they could see that both of the warring sides were flanked by the ravenous carrion worms. Regorik's army ignored them while the Tarkhūn rear guard was forced to engage them. Nitthogr's forces wielded some kind of ultrasonic emitter; whenever the worms drew too close, a vyrm scattered them with the device.

Rob tore his attention away from the battle and cleared away an aperture that lead into the main chamber. Inside was deathly silent. The stadium-like enclosure resembled a mass crypt.

He and Claire stared down at a sight that only two others had seen in thousands of years, aside from the army of the Black, which had invaded through the nearby portal just recently. Dust caked the desiccated bodies, which lay upon a thousand tables. They'd been arranged in neat rows, all seeming to point to the circle at the center.

"The Thousand Elders," he whispered. "This is where it all started... where the philosophers and religious fanatics established reality from nonreality and birthed an ageless terror—calling the ancient agod from the purely conceptual into the visceral, yet noncorporeal."

"Most of those words are antonyms of each other," Claire stated of his illogical sentence. But the side of her that had melded with Bithia's thought process completely understood what he'd said. The philosophical concept that God, as a force, must have an equal and an opposite, was mere conjecture—a falsehood according to all religious texts across the Tesseract—and yet the Thousand Elders had found a way around the metaphysical barriers. Through sheer faith they leant their flesh to birth the empirical form of the devourer: Sh'logath.

"This way." Rob grabbed a long, rusty chain that hung from the catwalk. They crawled down it, and he winced each time he had to grasp the chain with his bad hand.

Picking their way through the lines of weather-mummified bodies, Rob traced a finger across the chest of one. The dust was thinner atop the vyrm husk than it was on the table. Suddenly, the body on the nearest table drew one ragged breath, startling Claire.

The body exhaled a death rattle. Rivulets of dust rolled off his chest and settled upon the platform where he rested.

"They are in deep torpor," Rob said in awe. He examined one only briefly before continuing onward. He guessed they each took perhaps one breath every several years. "Except for that one over there." He pointed to a crumbling, mummified cadaver slumped in a heavy metal chair near the raised central stage.

Briskly, cautiously, they approached the dais. On the chair's backrest, Claire could translate the word engraved behind the corpse. "The Voice."

"This was the one who spoke on behalf of the Thousand Elders. The one who stayed back: their prophet and spokesperson. Legends say he remained in order to watch the rise of Sh'logath and instruct the followers in the rites and rituals to honor their agod. It was *he* that originally instructed Basilisk and Nitthogr."

"I guess it took longer than he thought?" Claire whispered.

As they grew near the raised steps, sigils glowed on the floor nearest them. The portal remained active, glowing with a brownish hue. Rob withdrew the frayed chapter from the Grimmorium Nitthogr. He momentarily examined it and looked at Claire.

"Claire, you have a decision to make," Rob said evenly. He didn't want to try to influence her choice with his own desires. He could not bear the guilt of any repercussions. "This door leads to a couple of possible destinations."

She could sense his thoughts. "One of them is Earth?" Her thoughts turned to her father. She couldn't stop thinking of Vivian, Caivev, torturing him.

"Yes."

Claire grimaced and blinked back hot tears. She took Rob by the hands, carefully holding the wounded one, which had almost completely healed by now. "I trust your judgment," she said, and then she embraced him, pressing her head against his midsection. "Do you still say that we must go to the Prime?"

Rob's form melted down into his human shape, seamlessly continuing the embrace. "It is the only way we stand a chance," he whispered into her ear.

"Then we go to the Prime."

Chapter Twenty

Next to the goggled Doctor Walther, Jacob Sisyphus stood at the shimmering portal alongside a trio of heavily armed mercenaries. All four wore their Heptobscurantum lapel pins upon their breast. The remainder of The Seven, except for Bruce Cannon, stood gathered behind to see their wizard off.

Nearby, a number of homeless drifters had been strapped to a bank of vertical braces, making a long chain of blood donors. They could keep the gate open as long as reasonably necessary. Catheter tubes connecting the machine to the suppliers were not easy to miss; they snaked across the floor, daisy chained together so that when one donor was drained, the next would begin to flow without a drop in supply.

Cannon descended the stairs with Vivian in tow. Vivian locked eyes with Adams; she glared at him. She had protested this mission only slightly, however, and accepted it under the premise of vindicating her precious herald in the eyes of The Seven. A small contingent of Heptobscurantum mercenaries followed them, pushing a blindfolded man forward; he was bound at the hands and gagged at his mouth.

Doctor Walther looked giddy, pleased that he could finally begin. He took up an additional control module he'd rigged to the machine since the last visit. The control board had been pieced together out of three arcade golfing machines; one roller ball controlled lateral movement of the gate on the plane it was opened to. The other rollers controlled vertical and the forward-backward movements in that space. Walther moved the portal around in three dimensions, giving them a view of a besieged, smoking castle that flew the black flag of Sh'logath.

Greyson smiled at Vivian. "Glad to see you got here as soon as possible. You came here straight from your last mission?"

Vivian positioned the man between her and Greyson. "See to it that Nitthogr's prize is not damaged. He will need this one for leverage." She spat her words with disdain.

The prisoner, Sam Jones, was manacled and blindfolded. Sweat stains clung to his neck and his hair lay lank and unwashed. He'd spent several days in transit and with little rest in the hands of his captors. A ring of duct tape encircled his head to keep him from calling for help.

"As soon as I vindicate his name, Claire Jones' father will be turned over to Nitthogr. He may prove important to the Herald's plan or function as leverage if needed." She pushed the hostage into Greyson's arms.

Greyson replied calmly. "Mister Jones will remain in the care of The Seven until your return, and maybe we can finally learn why the Awakening would require any leverage at all—especially when brute force has always proven useful, until now?"

Vivian scowled at Greyson and then nodded to Sisyphus's crew. They gave her room as she stepped near the gate. "I'll return by own methods," she told them. "I will meet you at the table, either *with* my master or *without*."

Sisyphus looked her over. They hadn't met yet. He smiled at her lecherously as an invitation. She didn't pay him any attention.

Walther turned a dial, and the portal enlarged. The blood donor closest to the machine groaned slightly and shuddered as the machine demanded more power. "Don't touch the edges," Walther warned. "Unless you don't want those body parts anymore."

Vivian dove through the gate and landed in a somersault. She sprinted off into the shadows as Walther wheeled the gate around into a relatively hidden location.

Greyson shoved Claire's father against the bed and wheeled it into the last position in a line of sedated homeless people. They all wore restraints and had been tethered to machinery via a long intravenous tube which siphoned blood to power the machine. Greyson attached Sam Jones to a monitor that tracked his vitals.

"Doctor." Sisyphus nodded and gave Walther a salute that he'd made famous in his wrestling career. He flashed him a smile to brandish his two vampiric teeth implants, and then he leapt through the portal. His team followed suit.

Behind The Seven, the first vagrant trembled and then gasped, completely drained. A beeping scanner mounted to the rack near his head flat-lined with a squeal.

Greyson hit a lever on the gurney where he'd finished strapping in the archaeologist and it flipped up into a vertical position holding him upright; only a few empty beds remained open. "I'm afraid that we don't find that leverage is as valuable of a commodity as some of our peers do, Doctor Jones." He carelessly jammed the intravenous blood tube into the wrist of Claire's father, who cringed at the piercing pain.

"I guess we shall see if you are more valuable as a battery, or as one of Nitthogr's pawns."

Rob found the particular runes required to realign the portal's target and cleaned them off. He wiped the thick dust out of the symbols' grooves so that they could be activated. The brown and amber hue shifted to a more vibrant color.

Hand in hand, they stepped into the radiant glow and evaporated into beams of pure energy. They re-materialized within a dimly lit cave where torchlight cast just enough flickering luminescence to blind them against the shadows beyond. They couldn't see the enemies, but heard the unmistakable sounds of firearms being drawn and readied upon them.

Rob and Claire threw their hands up immediately. Their hearts sent up little prayers in the hopes that the darkness did not hide the vyrm. A voice from beyond the torches demanded, "Identify yourselves!"

Rob recognized the voice. "Wulftone?" He dropped his hands. "Who else is with you?"

"It's Zabe... and Bithia?" Wulftone's voice exclaimed excitedly. Clicking sounds came as the weapons were lowered. A second later, Wulftone stepped into the light and gave Zabe a hearty hug. "It is good to see you!" He bowed low to Claire. "Princess!"

Zabe shook his head. "No. This is Claire Jones from the Earth realm."

Wulftone shot him an incredulous look. "You planeswalked?"

He nodded. "Yes. And I understand the risks."

"But how? We were hoping to trap Regorik's forces here in the slim chance they come this way. Perhaps we could trade him as a ransom. A large contingent of the Black went to the Desolation, and we thought they might return on this path—even if it's not been used since its discovery, eons ago."

Zabe pulled the battered manuscript portion from his bag. He admitted matter-of-factly, "I robbed the museum and took the forbidden Grimmorium texts." He looked around the room; his eyes had begun to grow accustomed to the light. "It's good to see that many of our kin survived long enough to flee."

"We thought you had perished during the invasion," an old man said, walking into the circle of torchlight. "If you survived, perhaps there is hope, too, for Zahaben?"

Zabe pulled his grandfather into an embrace. "I am sorry, Shardai. I was there when he made the grandest sacrifice." He held up his left wrist, brandishing the leather band embossed with their family crest.

Shardai nodded, his face weathered and tight-lipped. "Tell us about this girl, then," he said, and beckoned him to follow. "I'm sure we both have much catching up to do." They passed through a hidden passage in the tunnel, which led away from the more public cave where the portal resided at an old shrine.

Zabe told them everything while they ascended the organic, flowing tunnels that rose steeply through the ground and led to their hideout. Claire filled in the blanks where his memories were incomplete or nonexistent. They neared the end of their summary as their climb leveled off.

Pausing just long enough to stow his duffel bag, discard his tattered earth-clothes, and grab a spare tunic from one of the many barracks rooms, Zabe found a few spare rations for him and Claire. He found an adjacent room for Claire and a change of clothes before they rejoined Zabe's grandfather.

Shardai took them through a long, craggy hallway; it opened at a sharp precipice where they could look out over the sprawling landscape. It was dark here; no torches lit the mouth of the cavern. The darkness helped their location remain hidden on the steep slope. Zabe crept forward, careful not to go too far and tumble out the entry and down the rugged mountainside, and swung his feet over the ledge.

Claire and Zabe sat on the entry's lip. Shardai and Wulftone joined them on either side. Already the sky burned rubicund at the edges; the sun had begun rising with an ominous red sky. It was not necessarily an ill omen, but the view certainly emanated an ominous tone.

As the countryside came into view beneath the morning light, Zabe's spirit sank. His kin shared his pain; their hearts broke all over again each time they looked out over the destruction of their home. Claire's eyes welled up; a stinging heart-pain rang through her soul as she felt the pain—seeing the devastation through Bithia's eyes.

Just below the steep granite and sandstone escarpments that hid the caves, the once rolling hills of green had been lit ablaze. Smoke curled skyward from villages and ancestral homes that would have otherwise dotted the verdant countryside. The glowing red line crept across the land, leaving only ash and carbon in its wake.

Upon the charred terrain, the newcomers spotted prisoner camps. Their heavily armed towers were hastily constructed from the repurposed homes of these peaceful people the vyrm had enslaved. The camp towers flew the black flag of Sh'logath.

Far closer than anyone liked, the nearest internment facility boasted a swelling group of detainees within its barbed fencing. Zabe and his kin watched a burgeoning line of new prisoners approach from a more distant, burning village. They had been forced to march through the night. Several broke rank and attempted to flee; their vyrm oppressors readily mowed down the escapees with disruptor rifles.

"What can we do?" Zabe whispered in a defeated tone.

Claire put a hand on his shoulder. "Remember the mission," she reminded him, even if her strong voice almost cracked with pain. "My father... your people... keep the big picture in mind. Stop Sh'logath's reviving by any way possible, and that means rescuing the princess."

Wulftone whispered to Zabe, "You're sure this is not Bithia?"

The four nodded solemnly. Far in the distance, the royal castle stood tall; encircling the stockades, the armies of The Black camped in massive droves according to their legion commanders. Beyond that, the old, beautiful ivy had been burnt away from the scorched bastion walls. Somewhere in those heavily fortified dungeons, their princess languished in the dark.

They knew what had to be done: they needed to break Princess Bithia out of the most heavily guarded fortress in the universe.

Morning came quickly as Zabe and his men drew up plans for the rescue mission. Reports were unsure, but scouts thought that they'd spotted Regorik, back from the Desolation; they also thought they spied Caivev. Nitthogr's top agents were best avoided if possible.

Zabe's kinsmen had already planted people within each of the internment camps in order to stir up dissent and raise the hopes of detainees; hope was their most powerful weapon—even if it meant willful captivity on the part of some of their warriors. While Wulftone and Shardai hadn't expected either Zabe or Zahaben to return and lead them, they'd come up with a variety of contingency plans for their moles in the prison camps.

If they sent up a signal, the recruiters would start riots within the camps and try to overthrow their oppressors. Even if they couldn't overthrow the despots at one camp, it might draw vyrm support from other camps and enable the resistance in those other areas to rise up.

Zabe gathered the troops he'd selected and initiated them into the Guardian Corps with a simple yet sincere pledge. Some details of the mission were too sensitive to share without any troops outside the bounds of the Corps, details such as the secret passage underneath the royal throne room.

Alongside his new inductees, Zabe led the small crew of his kinsmen through a narrow shaft in the bedrock. He and the newly pledged warriors donned the pieces of royal armor and weapons collected in the secret armory maintained by Shardai; Zabe's fine plate work bore a neatly trimmed gold stripe, identifying him as one of the elite Guardian Corps. Shardai had even found a set to fit Claire's smaller frame; it had once belonged to Zabe's younger brother, who'd disappeared long ago during one of Nitthogr's mad attempts against the crown.

The tiny lights each wore on their foreheads cast eerie shadows through the jagged, natural warren that ran below the castle. The tunnel's faraway network of caverns connected to the palace's foundation by a series of nightmarishly claustrophobic, buried fissures.

Zabe kept an eye on each member of the troop. His gaze sized Claire up in her armor; light from his headlamp glinted off the armor's gilding. He nodded to her with a melancholy smile as their eyes met. "It's good to see someone in this set of mail," Zabe said, and then turned away.

Something in his voice asked her not to probe the subject deeper, and so she didn't ask about it. She merely fingered the engraved craftsmanship thoughtfully, and then stumbled, bumping into the next bend in the tunnel, which narrowed significantly. Jarik, one of Zabe's younger kinsmen, steadied her before she could fall.

After squeezing through the tight crevasse, Claire sighed and tried to regulate her breathing. She'd never been terribly afraid of tight spaces, but she'd spent enough time underground these last few days that she begun to develop a strong distaste for it. "Of course there would be a secret, underground tunnel leading to the castle," she mused under her breath. "No castle is complete without one."

Zabe looked at her curiously. He ignored the ironic trope and searched for the next turn in the damp web of secret passageways.

Fingering a carving of the royal family's crest upon the rock face, Zabe waved them forward into the dark several paces until they came to a slightly larger subterranean grotto. He pointed to the ceiling, where a large hole yawned open above them. Three quarters of the circumference were covered with wrought metal ladders; riggings for hauling freight adorned the smaller side.

He checked his timepiece as Claire, Wulftone, and the four others joined him. "The royal family sometimes used the tunnel network to transport highly sensitive items for safe storage in the vault... the Chamber of Mysteries. Only the Guardian Corps has ever known of its existence, beyond the royal family, that is."

Claire nodded. Bithia's knowledge of the place unfolded in her mind. Unused for several generations, it had kept many things safe from the public eye. One of the primary duties of Bithia's family was safeguarding the realms by locking away artifacts or items which posed too great a threat to the people across the dimensions to remain at large.

"And now we wait just a little longer." Zabe glanced at his timepiece again. "Shardai and the larger force will begin the diversion soon." He swallowed the lump in his throat. He knew that many of them would die at the hands of the vyrm so that they could have this chance at success. The last time he had been home, his father had been sacrificed; today he might lose his grandfather to the same cause.

Wulftone put a comforting hand on his cousin's shoulder. "We will succeed," he assured him.

Claire laid her hand on the other shoulder. Zabe nodded and sighed, pushing his anxiety far from his mind. He looked at his timepiece again. "Friends, are you ready to save the worlds?"

Only seconds later, the ground shook slightly with a mild aftershock from the distant explosions Shardai had detonated. Dust gently rained down on the party. Jarik spat a mouthful of dust that had caked his lips.

Silently, they jumped and grabbed the ladders, clambering up a great distance until they found a ledge carved from the heavy minerals. Overhead, an ancient stone door with a complicated system of latches forced them to remain crouched. Barely more than a slab of granite, it bore an engraved symbol of the royal family.

Zabe crouched low and groaned slightly, as if he flexed every muscle in his body. Lupine features burst forth and he grew large; his body stretched and his snout elongated as fur sprouted everywhere, rippling as he shifted for comfort in the royal armor, which had been built to stretch with the shape-shifter. The elastic joints between shield plates expanded around his bulging biceps and quads.

With one massive paw, he held the stone door. With the other, he triggered the latches, and they opened with a loud clank.

Everyone held their breath as he slowly lowered the four foot square stone. It remained fixed on a hinged side. Above them, the bottom side of the opening was covered with a large tapestry-carpet. It sagged slightly without the support of the floor to uphold it.

The tallest by far, Zabe, peeked through first. He stood and lifted the rug enough so that he could peek out. Crouching back down, he reported, "The coast is clear."

Crawling out from the tapestry, they crawled to their feet behind the pair of thrones in the center of the palace throne room. Just a little further behind them stood a huge set of double doors. The barrier glowed metallic, engraved with sigils and inset with gems. Moreso than by their immense physical strength, they were protected by old magics given by the Architect King. Even if Nitthogr joined forces with Basilisk, there was no way they could ever break it open. They needed the key: a member of the royal family.

"The Chamber of Mysteries," Claire whispered. She touched the amulet around her neck as she thought of the Architect King, and in turn, the face of her father.

"Can you sense Bithia?" Zabe asked Claire. She was critically important to locating the princess, otherwise she would've been too valuable to have brought her along. The mission rested on finding her and escaping as quickly as possible.

"I can feel her," she said. "The connection is strong, but I can't feel her like I did when we merged."

"Humph. The vyrm poison must still be interfering to some degree."

"But I *can* get a sense of her general direction. I just can't pinpoint an exact location, but I can give a kind of compass heading?"

Zabe nodded encouragingly as Claire pointed hesitantly in the direction of the Princesses' cell. "This way," Zabe said, guiding the small force down a hallway just beyond the royal chamber.

Professor Jarfig huddled in his home with his wife and two children. The head curator at the Prime's foremost museum, he lived for curiosity. His zeal for discovery and the preservation of history motivated him in all things. That same curiosity compelled him to leave one window in his home open. He'd watched the entire vyrm invasion unfold from that lonely hole.

Jarfig's wife had begged him to board it up, to collapse the only remaining access to the outside world. Their hillside, dugout home was spacious and well-appointed; they could easily wait an extended amount of time before they would need to worry for supplies. By the second day of the siege, however, she knew it was vain to continue begging him; he had already filled an entire journal with the chronicles of military activity. He actively preserved these moments for future generations and had already planned the museum exhibit. Now, he just needed the military to mount an overthrow of the sorcerer's occupation.

As a whole, his family abhorred violence. Jarfig and his wife did everything they could to inspire their children to pursuits of intellect; they took away sticks that his children might pretend were swords and forbade any kind of toy that might resemble a blaster. And *that* had not been easy. Jenner, the oldest, had always been prone to the rough and tumble and the parents had feared he might some day pursue the military or even Guardian Corps. Most of the Corps were dead now, from what they'd gathered.

Much as it sickened the family to watch the war rage on their doorstep, it satisfied them at some deep level. Their morbid curiosity demanded satisfaction in the same way that people can't look away from a grisly accident scene they pass.

So far, they'd survived weeks on end following Nitthogr's incursion to the Prime. Vyrm forces had discovered and rounded up all their neighbors, carting them off to prisoner camps. Jarfig had taken many precautions over the years, having guessed that something like this would happen eventually.

"Honey," Jarfig whispered loudly, with his face pressed into a pair of powerful, telescopic lenses. "Come quick. What do you make of this?"

She left her children to continue the quiet game they'd engaged with on the wooden, tiled floor and tiptoed over to her husband. He pointed to the anomaly and handed her the binocular device.

"It must be another of Nitthogr's evil magics," she said of the blazing beacon that hovered in the sky. It moved surely and slowly: a pulsing light in the sky.

Jarfig watched it throughout the day with intense fascination. Sometimes it was a mere sliver of light; sometimes it appeared to be a collection of strange faces contained within a burning, triangular frame.

Vyrm forces had not come near their home since the early days of the invasion and the guards they'd posted at the museum nearby did not venture out often and they never wandered far. Now, however, this magic beacon worried him; it seemed to draw nearer with each hour. And then it suddenly disappeared from sight.

Jarfig watched for a long while. He scanned his full range of vision repeatedly, but could not locate it again.

After watching and waiting through his lunch hour for it to reappear, he finally gave up on its return. The professor leaned back in his chair and set down his goggles. As nervous as the approaching irregularity made him, he felt a little disappointed to be presented with a mystery he was unable to solve.

He picked up his pen, about to record his final entry regarding the enigmatic light, when a blunt pain flashed across his face. The blow knocked him over backwards, flinging the journal from his hands. Jarfig twisted around on the floor and screamed for his family to flee.

Standing over him was Jarfig's doppelganger. He sneered down at the professor where he lay, bleeding. A group of armored men stormed through his window as the glowing triangle whirled around through the air and then enlarged.

"You're not vyrm!" he howled, noting their strange dress and weapons. "What do you want? Please, I am a man of peace!"

The doppelganger laughed and turned to the faces watching from beyond the fiery veil. "A man of peace? Well, isn't that ironic?" He gave a neck slicing motion to his accomplices.

Jarfig screamed as the alien mercenaries opened fire with their weapons, cutting down his wife and children. "No! Why?" he wailed tearfully.

Jacob Sisyphus looked down at his pathetic variant. "We only want *you*." He clubbed the Prime version of himself across the side of the skull, knocking him unconscious.

Sisyphus dragged the body outside and easily threw him over his shoulder. With an evil grin, he hopped back through the enlarged energy gate, not seeing that the oldest of Jarfig's children had escaped the massacre and watched him go with baleful eyes.

Smoke curled against the ceiling inside the spacious atrium. Zabe, Claire, and Jarik poured blaster fire from their position into a troop of vyrm sentries. They'd flanked the reptilian invaders and traded offensives with Wulftone. One side pummeled them with laser bursts and then move into a new position to take a better angle against the enemy while the others provided cover fire.

The last vyrm soldier fell and the six invaders regrouped in the middle, quickly moving ahead. They had worked to systematically clear the rooms between the throne-room and the prisoner chambers. Resistance was stiff, but not overwhelming in numbers; as long as they worked smartly, their mission remained possible. Their diversion to pull the significant forces outside the castle walls appeared to have worked.

Zabe glanced at a window up near the ceiling; the glass had been blasted out during the initial vyrm incursion. He could see smoke still rising beyond the bastions. Hopefully, the vyrm would remain preoccupied with Shardai's forces for a while yet.

"I feel her," Claire said. "I can feel her very strongly. She must be just ahead!"

"Then let's go free her," Jarik said impulsively. He kicked in the next set of doors, only to be greeted by a half dozen vyrm posted on one side of the Y-shaped junction.

The startled sentries immediately opened fire on the impulsive warrior, riddling him with blaster fire. Many shots flew wide, but so many more found their mark. Jarik crumpled to the floor, paying fully for his deadly mistake.

Leaning just over the threshold, the remaining five Guardian Corpsmen blasted anything that moved into the corridor. They mowed down the coverless vyrm with extreme prejudice; the right-most corridor—the one with the guards—ended with a brick wall that cut off any avenue of retreat for their enemies. Claire's pistol gave a shrill, dying whine as her last chargepak depleted. Zabe's chirped away with an audio warning that the power source had very nearly depleted. He dropped it into the thigh holster that was a part of his armor.

They ran ahead. As they stepped over the dead bodies and came to the locked door, Claire glanced at Zabe, the brave Captain of the Guardian Corps. Seeing him in action triggered something deep inside of her, some primal desire. She could sense his loyalty, his inner strength, and intense character. Claire bit her lip and pushed those thoughts from her heart with her mind... she didn't even know if these feelings came from her or the side of her mind where Bithia's vyrm-hobbled thoughts hung out.

With his massive, lupine strength, Zabe tore the door from its hinges and Claire watched him charge into the room. Growls and screams echoed from within; one vyrm psychic sailed airborne through the opening, flung by the werewolf. The vyrm broke against the stone wall and slumped lifelessly to the ground.

Startled by sudden action down the left hallway, Wulftone and his two men charged down the passage with blasters firing. "Get the Princess," he shouted. "We'll watch your flank!"

Claire ran to the prison door as Zabe and the princess emerged. Bithia was bloodied and bruised, but she held her head high, casting an aura of nobility and grace. Suddenly overwhelmed by an altogether different emotion, Claire couldn't help but embrace her twin like a long-lost sister.

Bithia returned the gesture. Breaking her embrace, she turned to Zabe, who melted into his smaller human figure. Bithia kissed him fiercely. "I knew you would come for me! I knew it," she insisted.

"Princess," he said, "we've got to get you out of here." The chirping of his blaster's chargepak reinforced the urgency.

She touched his face and looked into his eyes. "But first I have to tell you! The day before the invasion, you asked me a question—a question I never answered—the vyrm attack had come so suddenly..."

The reunion didn't last another second. The walls where the corridors joined ruptured in a fiery explosion of burned brick and concussive force.

An entire squad of heavily armed vyrm poured through the rift. At their head strode the red hooded warlock in all his glory. Nitthogr laughed mockingly. They were trapped in the hallway like mice in a bottle.

Nitthogr's derisive laughter turned into a genuine giggle as he glared at his prey from beneath the crimson, scaly cloak that was his off-earth trademark. The metallic gold trim mirrored his reptilian eyes; they shone with intense malice as they fell upon Zabe, who stood between the half-vyrm and the princess.

"At last," Nitthogr hissed. "Today, I will terminate the last of your wretched bloodline. And soon, everything I've ever desired will be mine!"

The sorcerer's face twisted with rage and he shouted with maniac fury. A glowing burst of energy erupted from his hands—it streaked towards Zabe, crackling with negative energy.

Claire flung herself in front of Zabe. Her heart demanded she save him! The bolt of magic energy struck her instead; she screamed in momentary pain and then surprise as the glow wrapped itself around her, enveloping her. The amulet at her neck neatly sucked the eldritch energy within. As it hung against her nape, the artifact glowed brilliantly.

Wild eyed and surprised, Claire stood on trembling legs, guarding Zabe and Bithia from the fuming warlock; Nitthogr bit his lips with such frustration that they bled. She locked her gaze with him: such hollow, hateful eyes. In that moment she knew that there was never any love between her and James—this man was empty, incapable of that ability. Now, in such close proximity to the princess, Bithia's strength had become her strength. James no longer, and would never again, hold sway over her.

Nitthogr balled his fists and then released them, regaining his composure. He dared not approach; the prize was too great to risk. If both women died, the Chamber of Mysteries—*and the Awakening of Sh'logath*—would remain forever beyond his reach.

"Claire Jones," he greeted. His words dripped with falsely honeyed words. "It is so good to see you again. I see you've discovered what I've been up to since we last parted. I think it's safe to assume that our wedding is off?"

She only glared in response, holding her arms out in order to shield her friends as much as possible. Her mind scrambled for the best course of action.

Nitthogr whirled in surprise, and just in time to erect a shimmering, magical force field. Wulftone's laser bursts would have otherwise torn through the sorcerer's face. Blaster fire from the left cut down several vyrm surrounding Nitthogr. And then the barrage ceased as quickly as it had started. Sharp whines from depleted power cells echoed down the halls.

The warlock cursed and momentarily lost his composure, commanding half of the soldiers at his side to catch Wulftone and his comrades and perform unspeakable atrocities upon them. He turned back to his primary objectives and resumed negotiations.

"I don't think that you quite understand how important you are, Claire. You are the last of Princess Bithia's variants. You see, all across the multiple realms there are many copies of you, different variants, each for different planes, in fact—"

"I know how the Tesseract works," she spat.

Nitthogr exhaled an angry sigh, trying to maintain his cool. "Then you know how important you are to my plans. I will rule all the realms, by my own hand and power. I will control the Tesseract! I will remake it in *my own* image, I will wrest the very controls of reality away from the hands of the Architect King!" Behind, his warriors seemed to shift uneasily at the omission.

"And Sh'logath will have no place in it?" Claire asked, baiting him into the trap, hoping to turn his guards against him.

Nitthogr locked eyes with Claire. He extended an olive branch. "Of course not. Why would I destroy the very thing which I am trying to create? I would remake the Prime for *our* glory—*for the glory of our family*. You would be my queen, and our children would be the new royal line. Sh'logath has given me this power—and he would have honor, of course, but he must forever remain at slumber."

A noticeable grumble murmured through the surrounding forces. Just as the first moved to aim a weapon at him, Nitthogr knocked them all backwards with a supernatural wave of energy. They all fell to their backs, and the warlock hissed a few alien words. He made a violent sign in the air as part of a spell and his forces groaned and then spontaneously combusted with eerie purple flames. The supernatural inferno immolated the pile of writhing vyrm as they shrieked unnervingly.

Nitthogr turned back and flashed his most congenial Hollywood smile to Claire. Zabe's blaster chirped, reminding the room that the warlock remained an overwhelmingly powerful force against them. They could not blast their way out of this situation—he had only a few charges remaining.

The warlock looked deep into Claire's defiant eyes. "I will even allow you to keep your father, Claire. I'm sure that by now you have suspected I would collect him. Come with me willingly and I will grant you his life as a wedding present, in addition to all the other promises I've made you. Together, we and our children will rip open the Chamber of Mysteries, lay ahold of the Tesseract, and form the grandest dynasty that has ever existed!"

Nitthogr smiled as Claire slowly approached. She glanced apologetically at her friends. The warlock held his hands out to her, beckoning her to speed along her slowly shuffling feet.

Zabe's face fell with despair at her betrayal.

"How could you?" Bithia's voice cracked. "Claire, no!"

She stepped so slowly and painfully that her gait functioned as an apology. "But, my father!" Claire pleaded with her friends to understand, backpedaling towards the sorcerer. She winked briefly, committing to the hard sell against Nitthogr.

Suddenly whirling around, Claire ripped the amulet from her neck, knowing from her merging with Bithia how the power it absorbed begged for release. She smashed the glowing artifact against her enemy, who could not touch it. It erupted with a sonic boom and a detonation of raw energy! The entire distance between them exploded. The ceiling collapsed, opening an escape access above but also splitting open an aperture below. Crumbling debris blocked the hall from the thaumaturge, who'd been blasted backwards by the impact of kinetic force.

Her ears rang, but the adrenaline would have deafened her, anyway. "Which way do we go?" Claire demanded over the shock vibrating through her head. She helped the princess to her feet, ready to sprint for the exit on legs made woozy by endorphins.

"This way," Bithia charged into the lead. Between her panting breaths, she yelled, "There is a room filled with mirrors; Zabe, you know the room! We must get to it!"

Nitthogr crawled to his feet in the courtyard where he'd been blasted to. His body smoked and the edges of his cloak smoldered with burn marks. He stumbled only slightly, a limping, seething ball of rage at losing his mark.

He screamed at any of vyrm within earshot, scrambling them to seek out the intruders. "Keep at least one of the females alive! Both if you can manage," he demanded, still hoping to fulfill his darkest desires and break his way into the royal chamber.

The warlock's chest seeped red, viscous blood. His stab wounds had reopened from the massive blast that Claire Jones had hit him with. He spat curses as he grudgingly staggered towards the infirmary to seek medical attention, shaking his head. Such wounds were beneath him.

As soon as the area had vacated, a duct grate skittered across the tiled floor, knocking over a potted shrub. Caivev crawled out of the wall and dusted herself off; glad she had been far enough from the blast to avoid the brunt of the damage.

She cast a betrayed look in the direction where Nitthogr had retreated. With much to think on, she spewed a few vitriolic insults into the air, hoping they would somehow land on her former mentor.

The Seven had been right all along. Nitthogr had played her—tried to manipulate even Sh'logath! Caivev broke into a jog, searching out the closest portal that could return her to Earth where she could confirm this news with those who were true adherents of the agod. She could confirm her fears: Nitthogr was a traitor, no longer to be honored among his own creation: the Heptobscurantum.

Chapter Twenty-One

Claire, Zabe, and Bithia fled through the fragmented cavity that opened above them. They scrambled up the debris mound and leapt to the higher floor before Nitthogr or any of his forces could react to Claire's quick thinking.

Sprinting through the complex, they rounded a corner and climbed a large, curving stairwell leading into one of the many spires. They moved into the primary citadel, a towering maze of rooms that boasted fortified minarets on all four sides.

Evading enemy sounds ahead, the three ducked into an empty room. They tiptoed through and exited on the other side, escaping through the adjacent hall where they ascended another stair.

Foraging ahead, they heard alarms blaring from outside the massive central turret.

"Every vyrm in the castle is looking for us," Zabe insisted on more speed.

"It's just ahead and up the next stairs on the right," Bithia said.

They hurried ahead and skidded to a halt in the middle of the corridor's intersection. They nearly collided with the vyrm General Regorik, who led a dozen of his best soldiers. Both parties paused, eyes wide in surprise.

Making a snap judgment, Bithia yanked Zabe's blaster pistol from his right thigh and a large combat knife from his left. She shoved Zabe down the passage on the right and fled back the way they'd come, screaming, "Get out of here!"

Regorik did a double-take. The moment demanded immediate action, and he recognized Bithia as the true princess. He ignored Zabe and Claire as they stumbled towards the stairway. "After her," he howled, whirling around the corner, needing every spare second to catch up to the escaped princess.

Zabe halted before he could climb the first step. "No! I have to rescue her!" He turned to give pursuit.

Claire grabbed him by the hand. She knew Bithia's heart and intentions *better than he did*. "She has a plan. She ordered you to flee—don't let everyone's sacrifice be for naught! Especially hers!"

He looked at her with deep, wet eyes. "No! She can't?" He saw those same strengths Bithia possessed in Claire, and yet *she was not her*.

Claire embraced him deeply, quickly, and then pulled him towards the escape.

"But the question? She finally had an answer..."

Claire began ascending the steps. Zabe paused a moment longer and then followed, hoping that Bithia had a better plan than the one he suspected.

Bithia hesitated at a corner, deciding on right or left. She darted right and could hear Regorik's troops hot on her tail. She scrambled around another turn and then slipped into a room, trying to cut across to slip out the other side, just as they had done before. *Maybe I can double back on them and still get to the mirrors?* Just before she reached the door, it burst open with the group of vyrm soldiers they'd slipped away from earlier.

She skidded to a quick stop and then sprinted back the way she'd come. Her breath came in ragged gasps, and sweat poured down her brow.

"Freeze!" the vyrm shouted behind her.

Darting for the door, her exit suddenly filled with Regorik's massive frame. She turned and retreated into the center of the room.

Regorik and his forces poured in and encircled her. The other vyrm trackers did likewise.

Bithia spun a slow circle with a knife in her right fist; the blaster in her left hand chirped. She searched desperately for an opening.

"You will not have me," she spat. She glared daggers at the enemies from her puffy, bruised eyebrows. She ignored the stinging pain from her matted, sweaty hair as it brushed her wounded eyes.

Regorik laughed heartily, his voice full of scorn. "Blip... blip... blip," he mocked, ticking off the electronic trills of the depleted blaster battery.

"I think you *will* come with us, Princess. You have one, maybe two shots left. Come with us and we'll even let your friends escape; there's nowhere for them to go but up, otherwise. But there is no escape for *you*."

"There is always another way," she shouted at him with surprising defiance. Her words echoed through the large room.

He gave Bithia an apprehensive look. "Put it down, girl."

Bithia fluttered her eyelids slowly. "Yes," she groaned.

Regorik looked at her, confused. Unsure if she was cooperating.

"Yes, Zabe. My answer was yes!" She suddenly stared at Regorik with piercing, cold eyes and flipped the knife at him with surprising force. The blade pierced his eye socket and buried itself up to the hilt, severing brain from stem and killing the unsuspecting general instantly.

The circle of vyrm charged at her, but they were too late. She had already raised the blaster to her head. "Yes," she whispered again, "a thousand times over, Zabe. My answer was yes." She pulled the trigger before any enemy could stop her.

Claire and Zabe reached the top step and launched forward, down the final hall. Only the door at the end blocked their ultimate goal.

Suddenly, Claire cried out and pitched forward. She moaned with a panicked pain, trying to still crawl forward, trying to stay on mission.

Zabe rushed to her side and rolled her onto her back. Her breath came in jagged, agonizing gulps and her eyes zipped back and forth as if she had fallen into REM sleep.

"I am... who... me... who am I..." she shot straight up and groaned against some unseen weight. "Yes!" she shouted out, and then collapsed under the strain and shock that overwhelmed her system.

Zabe scooped her up in his arms and scrambled towards the room of mirrors. Hot tears streamed down his cheeks. He knew exactly what was happening. Two of the same people on the same plane of existence and one was a prime—Claire was being psychically slammed into by the prime spirit. *That only happens if... when...*

It meant that Princess Bithia was dead.

CHAPTER TWENTY-TWO

Wiltshire arrived at the airport on a small charter. The flight bumped to the ground that made him grateful he worked for the Vatican and prayerfully hoped that it bought him a little help from the big guy upstairs.

His plane rolled to a stop at the small airport in Paso Canoas, on the south eastern edge of Costa Rica. A local guide was supposed to pick him up.

The regional Order helped Wiltshire make arrangements. They were not a boys-only club, even if the Vatican still mostly was, and female investigators were also called brothers.

Camila wasn't a brother of the order, but she was a local asset, and she had agreed to be his driver and translator. She drove an older model jeep which was plenty capable of navigating rugged terrain, but not so flashy as to attract the attention of thieves or ne'er-do-wells which had suddenly popped up all over the region near the border of Costa Rica and the war-torn Chiriqui, which was a province on south western edge of Panama.

Camila wasn't a brother of the order, but she was a local asset, and she had agreed to be his driver and translator. She drove an older model jeep which was plenty capable of navigating rugged terrain, but not so flashy as to attract the attention of thieves or ne'er-do-wells.

They didn't chat about anything serious as they bumped along the roads and back trails, which Camila knew and snuck across the border and into Chiriqui. The drive took several hours and Camila had filled up additional fuel canisters and hidden them inside a wooden crate to discourage anyone from trying to steal them.

The forest roads they took were largely untraveled and ill kept. They teemed with life. Insects buzzed, and the general sense of danger felt palpably present.

Camila got him into Chiriqui unmolested and navigated to the archaeological site. A few men with guns approached and Camila had a brief chat with them.

Wiltshire didn't understand until she began using a few words he was familiar with, religious words. Two of the three men looked very nervous and backed off. The third seemed very responsive to Camila, who'd obviously convinced him that it was eternally beneficial to him let a brother of the Red Order poke around.

The nervous duo reluctantly let them pass and the third led them to Sam Jones' quarters, nearby. The little hut was barely more than a large room with a cot and a few personal effects. The cot was overturned and his things lay strewn about the room.

"Did they sack his room, I'm guessing?" Wiltshire asked.

Camila relayed the question, and the soldier shook his head and spoke through the interpreter.

"No. It was this way when we arrived. None of us touched it... some of the men thought it was cursed. We don't get that close." The man slipped a few coins and small tools, a stapler, and a pack of batteries into his pocket. "But if you say that God is with this man, I can come in with protection."

The soldier looked around to see what else he could steal. There wasn't anything else of value.

Wiltshire rubbed his chin and muttered. "Then it looks like a struggle. Damn it. The cultists got to him first, then," he surmised.

The soldier looked out the window. A few men approached wearing militia uniforms and the patches of their local warlord. He rattled off a few quick words.

"We've got to go," Camila said.

Wiltshire nodded, and they hurried out the door, hopped into her jeep and made for the border without looking back.

As soon as they got close to the border, Wiltshire got cell service again and incoming messages beeped.

They were from Sexton. Messages came in as if his partner knew the answers to the exact questions and objections Wiltshire would have raised. *Weirdness in Chicago near Jackson Park. Something big enough to cut your vacation short over. I know, I know... when it rains, it pours.*

In her mind, Claire focused on her one task—*get out!* Nothing else entered her mind. Zabe was five feet ahead, and suddenly the pain cut through her. Every nerve ending in her body burned with lightning force.

Her mind screamed as if some cold probe forced its way inside of it, tearing open her softest, most precious sanctuary with its intrusion. In her own inner-voice, she kept hearing *I'm sorry... I'm so sorry! It was the only way to stop him.*

Claire suddenly understood. Some aspects were similar to when she'd merged with Bithia in the ether, but this was more visceral: a more real kind of merging. This time severe pain accompanied it—she felt the agony of Bithia's death and the transfer of all her life energies into Claire's already taxed psyche. Bithia's very soul had downloaded into Claire!

What is a download?

Her mind spun out of control as a split second stretched into a lifetime. Instead of Bithia sharing the memories that she chose, every part of her was dumped into Claire with traumatic force. It was as if Bithia had fallen from the sky and landed on Claire while she drove a convertible: who was steering—who was the passenger? *We're going to spin out and crash!*

Even at the mental analogy, the foreign voice wondered, *What is a convertible?*

Uncontrollable mental energy rippled through Claire's body and reached her limbs. They shook and trembled. *A seizure?* The trauma overwhelmed her, triggered a total shut down.

She saw Zabe, Rob, rushing towards her, and then both sets of eyes rolled back in her head and went dark.

Weaponless, but not hopeless, Zabe kicked the door open and rushed within. The old, dry boards splintered, and the handle clattered to the floor.

This spacious room contained nothing but sheet-covered mirrors and dust. Footprints walked in part way from when the vyrm did an initial sweep of the premises, looking for prisoners who hid from the earlier onslaught.

The center of the room was the trigger point. All thirty-two mirrors faced the one central location.

He laid Claire gently in the middle and flung off sheet after sheet until he found the one that he needed. Each mirror's frame was engraved with decorative symbols to mark the different potential gate locations in a realm; each mirror led to a separate different plane of reality. The mirror room was a nexus location. Locating Earth's mirror, he activated the portal and instinctively touched the first location he recognized.

Twitching, Claire jerked her head up, trying to continue onward. She spotted the immense mirror nearby; it rippled silver and metallic like a pool of molten mercury.

Zabe tore an old sheet into long strips and tied them to the severed iron doorknob. He glanced down at her. "I'm getting you out of here," he reassured her, kneeling by her side. "Can you walk?"

"I'm... who... maybe," she said, struggling to crawl up on her hands and knees. She stuttered and twitched like a malfunctioning android.

He helped her to her feet. Claire clung to his left side, leaning on his strength, barely able to function independently. He walked her through the mirror, slowly entering it himself. At the last second, he snapped his wrist and yanked the heavy, metal knob towards the mirror as they fell into the ether.

Just as they stretched and shot through time and space, transformed into a shimmering bolt of energy, the mirror solidified back into glass. Just in time, the knob smashed into the mirror's glass and shattered into a million pieces, prohibiting any immediate pursuit from the nexus.

The fabric of space and reality ripped open and dumped Claire and Zabe onto the ground in the middle of a huge church sanctuary; they spilled out right behind the main lectern. Overhead, the glowing, azure portal snapped shut with the sound of breaking glass, and the rematerializing duo tumbled to a stop and looked up.

It was Sunday. More than a hundred men and women were seated in the church pews. Zabe wasn't fooled for a moment. Each wore dark, uniform clothing and a pin depicting a seven-pointed star.

Zabe stood and kicked over the podium, blocking Claire from the small army, which even now leveled weapons upon them. Claire got control of her shaky legs. Both of the minds residing within her body agreed and voiced a whisper, "I think we're in trouble."

In the blink of an eye, Rob transformed. Leaping to his feet, the werewolf snarled ferociously, causing most in the congregation to take a cautious step backwards. He warned them off with a bellow of animal fury.

The man standing closest to them, the priest, dove for a nearby, knee-height table and reached under it. He yanked a shotgun free from the hidden restraints.

"Run, Claire! Run!" Rob insisted in his gravelly, lupine voice.

Claire took a step back. Her mind still reeled from the confusion addling her thoughts; it grappled with the foreign consciousness. The two minds stitched themselves together even as they fought.

The first gunshot rang out. A loud kra-boom echoed through her head and the concussive force of the nearby shotgun blast put her hair on end and snapped her to action.

"Run! And don't look back," Rob howled; he only bled slightly from the priest's scatter-shot. The chest-plate from his royal armor absorbed the brunt of it.

Claire turned on her heels and ran. She slipped behind some machinery at the rear of the church and hid as a mob tried to give chase.

Rob wouldn't stand for any pursuit. He pounced into their midst and clawed at the maniac cultists. Blood and screams spilled from the mob as they piled on top of him with a gang tackle violent enough to make Claire's Vikings jealous.

"Kill the beast," the priest howled. "This is the monster that has been stalking your children in the parks—the monster that The Seven warned us about! And somebody find that girl. *She is the chosen one!*"

The pile of cultists flipped in every direction as Rob burst upwards, casting them off with superhuman fury. He dashed ahead on all fours as the startled priest pumped two more loads of buckshot into the werewolf. Rob caught him in his claws with a vicious, whirling uppercut. He kicked the shotgun far away as the cleric collapsed in a gory heap.

He turned again to the pulsing congregation and cringed against their small arms fire. The armor turned back some bullets; many lodged in his flesh. Rob howled in pain and rage. He charged into the mob so that they risked hitting each other if they shot, but they did not stop firing. Bullets that missed their mark hit other cultists.

The horde pressed in on Rob again, just as a shimmering window between the worlds opened. Caivev—Vivian stepped through from the Prime. She shook her head in bewilderment at the scene. Noticing the familiar werewolf, she unholstered her blaster and yanked the tracking device from her belt and activated it.

Glancing at the handheld screen, she pointed to the lycan and shouted, "I've got this!" Vivian tossed the tracker to a nearby cultist. The nearby blip on the screen glowed only faintly as the tracking poison had mostly ebbed from her system. "Follow that! Capture the girl!"

Vivian turned and pumped a scorching bolt of energy into Rob's back. He howled in agony and grabbed a nearby cultist to use as a human shield. Rob stared over his prisoner's shoulder and growled at Vivian. This was not the first time they had played this game.

Vivian poured fire into him anyway, shredding the cultist, trying to burn through and into her prey. This time, the stakes were higher than ever!

The hunter with the tracking device grabbed a small crew of accomplices and stalked Claire. They moved directly towards her hiding place. Claire watched Rob, praying that he could somehow escape.

"Get out of here!" Rob yelled again. "They must not catch you!"

Claire stayed, watched, riveted by fear and hope. "But our answer was yes," she whispered. "I do!" she wiped a tear. "Bithia would have married you." She prayed that he already knew the answer to that fated question, even if it had never been voiced.

The Heptobscurantum continued to press the attack, mobbing Rob, overwhelming him. Claire's pursuit had almost discovered her; they needed only a few steps more until they'd be on top of her.

She watched Vivian level her blaster on Rob and take careful aim. Just before her traitorous friend could pull the trigger, Claire pushed a huge stack of retired hymnals down on top of her hunters before they could discover her.

Fleeing, hot tears burned her face. Claire could clearly hear the final, echoing report of Vivian's blaster as she burst through the rear exit into the parking lot. Claire didn't stop running, couldn't stop running. The fate of the universe relied on her never slowing, never stopping—never getting caught.

Chapter Twenty-Three

Jacob Sisyphus, former professional wrestler, heptobscurantum leader, and now a madcap scientist, strapped his victim down on the table. He had thought through this process quite heavily and consulted many texts, both old and new, about the procedure.

His Prime version continued to beg. Jarfig wept openly, still in shock over the murder of his family.

Sisyphus did not pity him; he hated Jarfig for what he perceived as weakness, for all those attributes that he deemed pathetic. He refused to speak to it—to even acknowledge it or dignify it with a name—not even with a pronoun. Jarfig was an *it*, not a him.

"Please," it begged. "Just kill me!"

Sisyphus had already blindfolded it. Sick of the begging, he strapped a gag in its mouth.

But he also had no intention of letting it die. Sisyphus did not want that thing's soul to transfer into his body and contaminate him with weakness; he wanted nothing to do with it but tap it for its Primal energies.

Smiling with a twisted grin, Sisyphus brandished his sharpened incisors. He believed in his ability to siphon the powerful, life energy from his Prime without extinguishing its life. It, the physical body of the thing from the Prime, was a fountain for continued, enhanced power.

Bending down near its shoulder, Sisyphus bit his victim like a vampire and drank deep.

It cried out. The gag muffled the horrific screams while the insane occultist slaked his thirst and felt the primal energies course through him. Power which he, an adept wizard, could transmute to raw, eldritch force.

"I... I have the power... the same kind Nitthogr has." He grinned and wiped the blood from his mouth and chin as he pressed a medical bandage to the wound on the thing's shoulders. "Maybe even more."

At least a month had passed since Zabe took on the entire church full of gun-toting death cultists. At least, Claire thought it had been that long. She'd been on the move ever since, never staying more than two nights in one place—and that had been only when she felt safe. But that kind of travel schedule made all her days blur together.

She'd had to resort to occasional petty thefts in order to keep moving. Claire felt bad about it, but as far as she was concerned, a few stolen wallets and a couple hundred dollars pilfered from unsuspecting folk was a small price to pay compared to the complete and total annihilation of all existence.

A wallet she'd snagged recently had a library card in it and Claire used it to get online at a mid-sized town's public library. The older model desktop wasn't anything fancy and looked more like a hand-me-down PC, but beggars couldn't be choosers, and it worked well enough for her purposes. Even better for Claire, though, it didn't have a built-in camera she'd need to cover.

She scrolled the Internet and made a mental map of all the places to avoid within a next hundred miles or so. Claire avoided anyplace that might make for a heptobscurantum trap or had surveillance equipment which could alert her pursuers.

I need more friends... allies, she told herself, wondering momentarily if that voice in her head belonged to her or Bithia. The two shared head space.

She'd come to terms, somewhat, with sharing her mind with the Princess. It was less of a battle for the driver's wheel now that some time had passed. It had become more of a road trip with a close friend, and every day they merged a little more. She was no longer Claire, not truly, but also not Bithia... Clairithia? She scrunched up her nose at the thought. Both of her minds laughed at the absurdity. *Clairithia sounds like the name of a venereal disease.*

Claire knew she needed more information in order to keep her enemies at bay. She'd been foolish enough to attend a recruitment meeting for the cult. The heptobscurantum continued growing wide and fast.

It had been a dangerous gambit, but she needed to know exactly who still chased her. They were all dangerous, but the early initiates had no real idea what they had bought into. Some of their methodology was thought control; some of their tactics focused on intentionally seeking out the depraved and unstable. But none of the early members truly knew the true nature of Sh'logath. Sh'logath was a mere concept, an ideology, like the Flying Spaghetti Monster.

The cult presented Sh'logath as the remaker of all things. He was pitched as sympathetic; a moral force that appealed to the disenfranchised, the philosophical, the holistic. She suspected that the later levels learned of the necessity of destroying all existence and killing all living things in order to do this. Agod, nega-god, and Devourer of Reality weren't terms she heard at that meeting. But they did have a free lunch, although Claire avoided drinking the Kool-Aid.

Allies... I was looking for allies, she reminded herself. The last time she'd been at a computer with public access, she'd tried to connect with her father—but he was unable to be found. Claire *did* find an article about his dig site in Chiriqui; local warlords had shut it down and taken prisoners. She had no idea how to reach him, or if he was even still there.

She'd also researched the heptobscurantum's holdings and discovered the name of Peter Greyson as the owner and CEO of the group that had shut down the data trail after the fire demon incident. The article also listed Greyson's close friend Bruce Cannon, a wealthy philanthropist, as his business's Chief Financial Officer. As soon as she made that discovery, the computer's webcam had turned itself on and the local phone rang. She hadn't stuck around to ask more questions, but learned her lesson about cameras.

That investigator, she thought. *What was his name? Vikrum Wiltshire.*

Claire typed in the information and began her search, finding several old articles about him during his days as a cop in New York City. She recognized the photos, even if he'd been much younger than how she remembered him. And then she found an article—a recent one—about a recent business arrangement.

According to the article, Vikrum Wiltshire had done some investigative work for Bruce Cannon and in exchange had been given a one percent stake in Heptobscurantum Holdings LLC, making Wiltshire an overnight multi-millionaire. She sighed, glad that she hadn't reached out to the investigator... *he's part of the heptobscurantum.*

She pushed away from the computer and logged off, noting a few stares from other patrons. She'd dyed her hair multiple brilliant colors and wore punk-like makeup, mostly smudged and faded from her frequent travels. Claire had spent two nights with a group of skater punks who'd taken her in and fed her.

They believed themselves rebels, social outcasts. She couldn't skate, but Claire people watched around them for those two days. As wildly and outlandish as they dressed, folks refused to look at them—they only saw a collection of wild, counter-cultural colors and styles. She realized that dressing for attention meant most people wouldn't, or couldn't, give her a look. At least, not in the rural areas she had kept to. Anything beyond the normal wasn't looked at too deeply; it was ignored in the hopes that it would just go away.

Claire left the library and walked towards a cafe. Everything in the town seemed like it was cloned from the other places she'd visited. She felt certain she could pinpoint exactly where the town's post office and school were, as if the town's blueprints had transferred from one community to the next.

She walked briskly past the bulletin board, peeking at the flyer over her dark sunglasses. Her face was stapled in large, Xeroxed glory with the giant word "Reward," followed by a phone number. She felt she could breathe a little easier than she had in the past four weeks, ever since she'd first fled the counterfeit church that the heptobscurantum had defiled. Other, newer posters had begun to take over wherever her face had been hung aver the last month.

Claire walked in and searched for a seat. She caught the eye of a lecherous old man who raised his eyebrows at her pink and green ombred hair and heavy eyeliner; his wife, seated across from him, noticed and smacked him with her purse, chastising the elderly man.

She slid into a booth at the mom and pop style restaurant in a tiny east-Iowa town near the larger city of Waterloo. There were truck stops nearby, making it the perfect hub for her to hitch a ride at. Claire ordered a coffee and leaned back to rest. She thanked the waitress who delivered the cup. A new appreciation formed in her for the small, out of the way places. The culture radically differed from her norm.

What is normal, anyway?

Sighing away her tension, Claire conversed with her inner thoughts, no longer frightened when they answered back of their own accord.

Oh, Bithia, how am I going to get out of here? I've got to get out of the country!

They control the entire planet, Bithia replied. *They could find you anywhere.*

Claire nodded. *But I might have a better chance further out of the way. Maybe Peru?* She'd always fondly remembered working with her father at the Huamparán dig on the Inka Road and hoped to return someday.

Or you might be more noticeable. There's only a tiny population of white females in that area.

Sighing and muttering, Claire sipped her coffee. She didn't know what to do, except keep moving.

"Are you okay, honey?" the middle-aged waitress asked her.

"Oh, thanks. I'm fine," Claire lied. She realized her inner voice had been spilling out slightly as a quiet murmur. It probably sounded like she was talking to herself. Claire and Bithia both chuckled.

Huamparán was out then. Claire thought of her father. She missed him greatly; she thought of Bithia's father and missed him, too—equally, in fact. So many had made the ultimate sacrifice: fathers, the Guardian Corps, Rob, Zahaben, Shardai, and so many more. A melancholy mood embraced her like a cold embrace as she ticked off all the names, eventually losing count, repeating Rob's name a number of times.

She smiled, recalling a memory from when Bithia was a teenager. Zabe had saved her from an attempted kidnapping by a band of Nitthogr's forces. It was the first time Zabe had done so—it had always been Zahaben before that. How he'd smiled that day; his father congratulated him and folded him into the ranks of the Guardian Corps that same day. Bithia's father had been alive then, too. So was Claire's.

Claire sighed and drained her mug. She paid in loose coins, of which she had fewer and fewer. She looked up and locked eyes with Vikrum Wiltshire.

Wiltshire cocked his head. He recognized her. *Claire Jones*. She wore makeup and outrageous hair as a disguise, but that fire in her eyes gave her away, and he knew that she recognized him, too.

He'd come to Iowa to investigate a pocket of crazed cannibals that had been reported in the city just down the road, and he'd just happened in for a cup of coffee and some pancakes. The meeting had been entirely coincidental.

Hell, it's a small world, he mused.

"Claire? Claire, I've been looking for you, and your father, for like a month now."

"Is that so?" Claire responded, standing. "I know who you work for. I read you're in league with them. The cult. You did a job for Cannon overseas."

Wiltshire tried to explain. "That? No, that was—"

Claire bolted for the back door and Wiltshire moved to intercept her, to make her understand. She'd feinted and instead whirled on a dime and took off in the opposite direction.

Wiltshire fumbled with his footing and tripped. By the time he got to his feet, the bell on the front door rang as the door opened and shut. Claire was getting away.

He dashed outside and saw her flee down the street and then duck inside a building. It wasn't a huge town, but there were plenty of places to hide at, and a few major highways intersected it. If he lost her, the trail would go cold *fast*.

Wiltshire sprinted to the building and hurried through the door of the office supply shop. A confused worker looked at him.

"The girl. Which way did she go?" Wiltshire demanded.

He pointed to a door in the middle of the building where some offices and supply closets were. Wiltshire rounded the corner and nearly stumbled down the stairwell leading to the basement. He caught his balance and turned the corner, finding a mostly empty basement with a clay floor.

There were few places to hide in the place and judging by the wooden joists overhead and the stone foundation, the building was over a hundred years old. He could tell which side the street was on because of where the water main was located, protruding up from the floor.

On each of the three sides not facing the street were rickety plank steps leading up to a "Chicago entrance." Wiltshire paused momentarily, knowing he had to pick one immediately. He had one in three odds of guessing right, and if he guessed wrong, he'd lose Claire again—probably forever.

He picked a staircase, sprinted up it and exited into a mostly sunken stairwell which he emerged from after a few more steps. Wiltshire looked around frantically, but there was no sight of her. He'd picked the wrong one.

Wiltshire frowned, and then his phone chirped. It was his partner sending him a text.

Emergency. Meet Quintin Texas. He stumbled into something huge. Big trouble in Pecos.

He bit his lip and puffed a blast of hot air through his nose. *Damn, this kid is good at running.*

"Good luck, Claire. I hope you stay one step ahead of em... but you're on your own, now."

With her heart pounding, Claire rounded a corner and exited an alleyway right as a remotely piloted drone car passed her by as it snapped images for its online mapping software. Claire froze in place and then cursed. *How could I be so foolish? I've been so careful up until now!*

She'd kept to rural areas where there were seldom security cameras and she stayed off of roads that had digital photo enforcement.

The cult had their fingers into everything, and she'd seen it first hand: the heptobscurantum recruited talented people, hackers and specialists, to accomplish their goals when their influence wasn't enough. For all of Claire's caution, after one close-call, all her plans unraveled. *I've got to get out of here—and now!*

Turning, she sprinted down the street, not caring how much attention she drew to herself at this point—speed was more important than discretion. Those photos would likely pass through facial recognition protocols and alert the heptobscurantum within seconds. Claire had to flee as far as she could as fast as she could; she had minutes at the most.

Reaching the end of the block near the two-lane highway, she darted across the street and into the parking lot of the large truck stop. Claire ran up to the bank of semi-trucks parked near the filling station and banged on doors, hoping she could convince one to give her a lift.

At the third vehicle, a door finally unlocked. Claire nearly fell off the step when the passenger door opened to her.

"Rob!" she exclaimed.

The OTR driver stared back at her quizzically. "Yeah," he said... but the accent was wrong. "Robert. Robert Schaeffer." He extended a hand. "Do I know you?"

"Oh my God," Claire exclaimed, faking the excitement, as if it was really meant for Robert Schaeffer and not for Rob, Zabe, the Prime variant. "It's me, Claire, Jones. We went to school together."

He looked at her, squinting, and then recognized her. "Oh yeah! The snake girl... archeology nerd."

Claire clambered into the cab. "Where are you headed? I *really* need a lift." She was surprised at her own emotions. When she saw him, it wasn't just Bithia's heart that skipped a beat... it was her own.

He nodded, and they pulled out as he shifted into second and turned onto the highway. "Man, do I ever remember you." Robert laughed. "You know, I had the biggest crush on you back in school, but then I got into some trouble and had to leave." The statement hung in the air as Claire applied it as an accurate assessment of her own life.

"You must be in some kind of trouble?" He didn't wait for a response before shifting the truck into the highest gear. He'd only ever helped her, ever since she'd known him.

"You might say that." She looked over her shoulder and into the side-view mirror. The filling station had shrunk behind them.

Her nerves balled up in her gut and she suddenly felt tired and heavy as the adrenaline surge began to wear off. She knew she needed to make some kind of small talk with her host: invent a story, or better yet, get him talking so that she wouldn't need to.

Claire turned to him. "It's been so long... years. What have been you up to all this time?"

"Oh, you know," he said, raising his voice above the engine noise. He patted the top of the dash. "I've just been trucking, making money. But that seemed kind of hollow and pointless after a few years."

Claire nodded, faking an interest. She fought the impulse to look away from him; his face painfully reminded her of what she had so recently lost.

"All of that changed, though. Just recently I found some purpose in my life. You might say that I found religion. Do you have anything *you* believe in, Claire?" He winked at her.

Claire stared in horror, just now noticing the seven-pointed star pinned to his trucker cap. She glanced out the window, but they were moving too fast for her to jump from the truck—that move would only cripple or kill her—she was fine with the latter, but the former would spell certain doom!

Robert picked up his CB mic and dialed in a new channel. "This is Robert Schaeffer, US DOT number one eighteen two thirty-five. Lock onto my GPS. I have captured Claire Jones."

CHAPTER TWENTY-FOUR

The air smelled musty in Claire's cell; it felt almost like it had a gritty texture. Claire assumed that her jailers secreted her somewhere below ground.

She sighed. Several days had passed since they had captured her and locked her away. *Luckily, we are not alone?* Her mind occupied itself. The only visitors had been high-ranking members of the Heptobscurantum. Daily, they left her food and literature about the cult as if they might somehow convince her to willingly surrender herself to the Great Awakening.

Today, however, none of them came. The day crawled along; Claire ignored the grumble in her belly.

Eventually, a familiar figure walked into the room: Caivev, Vivian. She strode in with her cocky attitude. "I wonder if I should thank you, Claire."

Claire barely acknowledged her presence. She only shrugged indifferently.

"You've done quite a bit to help me, you know." Vivian toyed with her. "See, I was really quite torn about the importance of the Heptobscurantum, previously; I only saw them as another of Nitthogr's puppets. I barely even credited them as true followers of Sh'logath. All I really wanted to do was complete my Dunnischkte: complete the vyrm merging, something similar to what you've done with the Princess... become both, and more, than the sum of the originals. It was my service to the agod.

"Deep down I never really thought that the Awakening would come to pass in my lifetime; I would need the Dunnischkte in order to live long enough to see it. After all, every one of Nitthogr's schemes was eventually foiled by the Guardian Corps, and so my merging was all that mattered. But now you are here and the Guardian Corps are no more; there are none left to stop us from invoking The Devourer."

She flashed a grin. "The Awakening is only a few days away. I just thought I would give you my thanks before I leave you with The Seven. The Heptobscurantum are the true believers—the faithful ones."

Vivian turned to leave. On her way out, she nodded to the seven men who entered the dank chamber.

They approached wordlessly. "I'm guessing you're either a really old Boy Band, or this Seven that traitor told me about?"

Several of them grinned. They wore either cultic garb or sharp business attire, depending on the company each had left just prior to their arrival.

"What? You couldn't come up with something more clever than The Seven? I've got a bunch of choice selections for you." She calmly rattled off a string of highly obscene expletives.

The big guy in the middle smirked ear to ear. He stood an entire head above his peers. He might have been handsome except for his dopey face and a wild mullet. "I like her," he laughed. "I can see exactly why Nitthogr wanted to keep her." He leveled his scary eyes at her. Deadpan, he stated, "But that's not a consideration for us, Princess Claire."

Claire gave him her attention.

"We need your blood for the sacrifice: the blood of the Architect King. It runs through your veins."

Is this true, Bithia?

Of course it's true. You *are the Prime now.* Claire's heart sank. Every girl dreams of being a princess someday. Claire became Princess of all reality, but at the cost of her life.

"In mere days, we will take you to this world's central Tesseract gate, a powerful nexus point of reality. There, during the solar eclipse, we will perform the rites and ritual. Your blood must be shed to release the almighty Sh'logath, waking him from his slumber in the nethersphere!"

He sounded so excited about it. He'd raised his eyebrows in expectation; the goofy grin on his face beckoned for a response, as if he expected her to yell, "hot dog! Count me in!"

Claire laughed at the incredulity of it all. "That all sounds so... incredibly stupid!"

Her captor's face fell.

"Well, at least I'll get to travel a little. You know, see the world before the end," she scoffed. "Where is this amazing, powerful, exotic location where you plan to cut me up like a chicken and dance around in my blood, or whatever? The Taj Mahal? The pyramids at Giza? Chichen Itza?"

An awkward silence followed. "Nebraska," he said flatly. "Mullen Nebraska."

Claire busted a gut. She sniggered so hard that tears flowed, laughing so long and loud that each of them, one by one, departed. The only one to remain was the tall one. She stopped her derisive laughter after the others had left, leaving only the two of them.

He held two stone tablets, each carved with tiny engravings. They were unlike anything she had ever seen in any museum or excavations previously. "These detail the process, the rites. They were taken here long ago from The Desolation." He fixed her with his dark eyes. "James had hidden them away, even copied them into his Grimmorium. I just wanted you to know how certain your fate is—it's set in stone." He smiled and gave a lighthearted laugh, as if her life meant nothing.

"I'll leave you with that hope: the hope of The Great Awakening." He turned and signaled the cultists who had waited in the shadows. They came forward and began moving the large, wrought iron cage that confined her. Scooting it across the concrete floor, they moved it to the far side of the basement, revealing more of her prison. It looked like some kind of loading dock.

They pushed the enclosure up the ramp and into the back of a semi-trailer. Crammed into the back and caged like an animal, they slowly shut the doors.

Her captor waved slightly. "Goodbye, Princess Claire. I will see you again in Nebraska."

The doors slammed with a heavy clank and the rattling of padlocks. She was sealed within the complete darkness.

Claire spent two days in the cargo box as nothing more than freight. The heat in day scorched her and she froze at night; the shaky trailer rattled her body across several states, occasionally knocking her flat or banging her into the sidewalls of her cell. The only thing worse than the jostling was the long bouts of waiting when the truck sat idling at wayside rests or roadside stops.

No doubt she was quite bruised by now. Bruises would be the least of her worries when the truck finally arrived in Nebraska. Her transit eventually slowed to a crawl, crunching gravel beneath the tires.

The parking brake hissed with a dreadful sense of finality. Moments later, the doors creaked open, letting sunlight pour in. Claire held up her hands to block the blinding rays; it had been too long since she'd last seen it.

Cultists poured into the trailer, watched over by the big guy who warned them not to let her escape—there were too many hiding places in the middle of nowhere, and all their hopes were pinned on this ritual. Claire caught her captor's name from the proles: Sisyphus.

She leaned limply against the cage, lying flaccid from fatigue and muscle soreness as much as from her abject defiance. Claire tried to take stock of her surroundings as much as possible. It was a tiny town, perhaps large enough for five hundred souls. The truck parked downtown where they had erected some kind of stage. They'd mounted an immense stone altar upon it.

Crowds filled the streets: too large of a crowd to be the local population. All the onlookers wore some kind of marking to identifying them as heptobscurantum. Claire squinted at the roofline. No building climbed taller than two stories and the downtown section only sprawled a few blocks in any given direction; rifle wielding cultists took positions atop the buildings.

Dragging their sacrifice to the altar area, Sisyphus and his adherents presented the badly disheveled girl before the other six men of the Illuminati. They nodded and her captors took her away, hauling her towards a nearby salon.

The windows had been shot out of the storefront. Claire glanced down the streets. Cultists had established a two block perimeter from the altar. They'd parked vehicles perpendicular to create barriers. Among them was the local sheriff's car; the driver's side glass appeared shattered, and the door was smeared with blood and bullet holes.

They've taken over an entire town!

Inside the beauty parlor, cultists happily made small talk, buzzing with excitement. They cleaned the chosen sacrifice, washing her body and hair, dressing her in white; women applied make-up to hide the swelling of bruises on her face and arms and returned her wild hair color to normal.

Even as they tried to engage her in conversation, Claire remained defiantly silent. A group of soldiers stood watch over her, wielding only stun-guns and retractable batons. They would not make the mistake of giving her access to lethal force, nor risk shedding her blood prematurely.

Sisyphus left Claire to rest under close watch of the guards for several hours. She tossed and turned on the camp cot, wishing she could sleep away the last moments of her life. Bithia's voice chanted a series of prayers inside Claire's head.

Breaking the eerie calm that hung over the town, a beating of drums began in the town's center. A loud voice shouted in the distance. "Bring out the sacrifice!"

Binding her hands with a silk rope, her kidnappers walked her slowly to the dais. All around her stood a mass of cloaked Heptobscurantum; each wore a mask.

With every drum beat, her stomach twisted with ulceric pain. Claire's guts tied in knots, but her head remained surprisingly cool. *The Architect King does not abandon his children* Bithia insisted. *Have faith! This cannot be the end! There are prophecies yet to be fulfilled!*

Claire grimaced in response to Bithia's encouragement. She shared all of her counterparts' experiences, memories, thoughts, and yet she was perhaps the realistic one of the two; her eyes darted in every direction, looking for any source of help or escape.

The sky burned over head and the blazing sun hung in the afternoon sky. Against the burning light, the moon had just begun to close the distance. They were only moments away from the eclipse.

Cloaked in ceremonial robes, with faces hidden behind masks of whitewashed skulls, The Seven yanked Claire up the steps and tied her to the altar. The entire town began to wildly chant some unrecognizable mantra as incited by The Seven. Six of its members sat round the altar on their knees, cushioned by a pillow at each point of the seven-pointed star. The Heptobscurantum's symbol surrounded the central altar with fresh paint. The chanting kept steady cadence with the drum.

Frenzied and speaking some nonsense dialect of the vyrm tongue, Sisyphus stood and approached the sacrifice. He wielded an oversized, ornate athame: a curved middle-eastern hook-blade.

Claire's eyes widened, and she suddenly felt her fear rise up. Terror trickled down her spine and electrified every cell in her body. Even the Bithia side of her psyche began to panic.

Sisyphus held the blade high and pointed it downward at Claire's body. The animalistic chanting reached a crescendo as the moon crested; it just began to cross over the perimeter of the sun when the crowd stopped chanting. The silence seemed to scream by comparison. Sisyphus tensed and sneered maniacally, ready to plunge the nasty weapon into his victim.

"Excuse me!" a loud voice cried out, breaking the tension's climax. The crowd seemed to collectively gasp as a man in a dirty cap and rumpled clothing ascended the steps.

All members of The Seven stopped and turned to face the interruption. Every eye in the town fixed on him. "It's the trucker," one of the men in the inner circle murmured.

Claire bent her neck and caught a glimpse of the man who approached the profane altar. Robert Schaeffer strode confidently towards her and The Seven.

One of the Illuminati stood and demanded an explanation. "We thank you for your service, initiate. But you cannot be here. You were not invited to this ritual! And you are certainly not welcome on the dais; return to the audience and be silent!" He pointed to the crowd.

Robert Schaeffer grinned with a lopsided smile. He pointed to his cap and the Heptobscurantum pin. "*Oh this*? You think I'm one of *you*?"

The cult leader pulled off his mask to better look at the intruder.

"You know, Greyson, I never liked you." The trucker pulled off his hat and released the disguise spell that had concealed him. His form immediately melted into the crimson, scaled cloak that was

Nitthogr's trademark. Hissing, he pointed one palm at Greyson and the other behind him.

A blue shield of energy rippled behind the sorcerer, catching the rifle bullets even as the rooftop snipers began firing upon him. A brilliant flash of energy erupted from his other hand, striking Greyson in the torso; it threw him across the altar, catching Sisyphus across chest and knocking him to the ground.

The wicked athame tumbled downward and caught Claire against her face, slicing her from cheekbone to chin. Blood splattered and dripped down upon the altar.

Splitting the sky behind the altar, a six-foot gash opened from the void, glowing furiously and spitting lightning. It mirrored, in amplified form, the wound on Claire's face. A rumbling groan resonated through the air: a deep, vibrating growl that emanated from within the portal.

"James!" Claire cried out as her former fiancé rushed to her side.

James drew his own sword and cut through her bonds. He scooped her up and put Claire on her feet. Maintaining the azure shield, he leapt upon the altar and sheathed his weapon. With the whizzing sounds of ricochets, bullets deflected safely away. "I'm sure you never guessed that it would be *I* who came to your rescue?"

James whirled around, blasting several members of The Seven with energy bursts as they tried to apprehend him. Noises rumbled as the agod shifted in the nether, stirring from his slumber; the sounds threatened to deafen those nearest the crack through reality.

The inter-dimensional fissure remained far too small for Sh'logath to enter through. The Heptobscurantum needed to shed much more of Claire's blood.

"You know what this place is?" James asked Claire, treating her as cordially as if they were still a couple.

"Nebraska," she spat disdainfully. Claire stayed relatively close to her surprise rescuer, but her disgust was meant more for the sorcerer than for the Midwestern state.

"Yes," James said. "But more than that... this town sits upon the most powerful dimensional door on the planet. It can be opened from any other gate if one knows how to access it, and it leads anywhere! It's one of the most sensitive points of the Tesseract!"

As if on cue, energy doors opened all around them. Vyrm warriors poured through the dimensional rifts, opening fire upon the cultists. Heptobscurantum warriors dove for cover, returning fire. Bodies fell on both sides and carnage flooded the streets.

The vyrm wore black face paint, ready for an overwhelming assault upon their earth enemies. They hissed and screeched, chasing down wounded cultists, sometimes over-pursuing and finding themselves in the crosshairs of the Heptobscurantum.

More cultists arrived from the outskirts, meeting force with force. They took defensive positions and dug in. Blazing fires erupted around the town amid shrieks and shouts of pandemonium. A propane tank exploded near the staging zone. Deep within the void, Sh'logath roared—most definitely awakened.

James grabbed Claire by the wrist. "Come! We have to get you out of here. You are the key... perhaps the most important person in the universe right now."

She shook his grasp. "I'm not going anywhere with you!"

He snatched her by the shoulders and turned her to face him. "Neither *my* plans nor *your* plans will ever come to fruition if that portal gets any bigger! That means we have to get you away from here!"

She grudgingly resigned herself to her rescuer.

James clung to her arm, pushing fighters out of the way. He blasted a nearby cultist and then threw a fireball at the rooftop sniper who had taken aim at them. The gable which hid the cultist exploded violently, belching flame and smoke.

Suddenly, a concussive burst flung James forward and into the dirt. He rolled over and scrambled to his feet, the scrape on his face leaked blood down his chin.

Meeting eyes with his attacker, James glared at Sisyphus. The Occultist ripped the skull mask off and tossed it aside. He bit through a medical blood transfusion bag and choked down the nasty, viscous fluid.

James's face twisted with rage. Sisyphus met the snarl with his own, spewing blood from his mouth. James fired a bolt of hot energy at the man; he batted it aside with his own supernatural shield.

The two titans ran towards each other. Each blasted the other with bursts of raw, primal power. They collided in a tangled mass of fists and glowing power.

Sisyphus bit James. The warlock howled with pain and scorched his attacker's face with a burst of eldritch power. They rolled across the pavement near a bouncing, live power line; the severed end writhed around the street in search of a victim.

Claire turned to flee as Bithia urged her onward. She picked her way through the pitched battle, dodging around vyrm and humans locked in melee combat. A rifle bullet ripped through the vyrm nearest her. He shrieked and fell while Claire ducked behind the nearest source of cover.

Holding her fear in check, she scrambled around, looking for anywhere she could escape to. A nearby vyrm, bleeding on the ground, took careful aim with his disruptor and shot the sniper who'd pinned them down. The cultist dropped his rifle as he tumbled over the second story ledge.

Claire tried to run, but the wounded vyrm grabbed her by the ankle. He hissed and held her fast: Nitthogr's prize! Claire gave him a swift kick to the face with her free leg and wrenched her foot free.

She turned back the way she had come from. The black tear in reality beckoned to her soul, as Sh'logath called to it from beyond. Through her blood, he'd latched onto her soul.

At Claire's left, James punched Sisyphus with a glowing fist. The occult wizard rocketed across the block and crashed through the exterior wall of the beauty salon. James turned and spotted Claire. Each of his hands clutched a raging fireball; he chucked them at random, incinerating nearby members of the Heptobscurantum as he strode purposefully towards her.

He had nearly caught up to her when another seam in reality split and parted. Stepping through the dimensional gate, Jackie lowered an intimidating plasma rifle at him, a lethal technology indigenous to the Prime. "Get away from her!" She yelled.

James sneered at her. But his smile quickly fell.

Striding through the portal behind Jackie stood Rob in his towering, lupine form. His royal armor hugged his muscles, covering sensitive parts of his tough hide which bore many new, permanent scars since his last battle with the Heptobscurantum.

Rob unsheathed his sword, drawing the stone shard from the scabbard slung across his shoulder. He pointed the Stone Glaive at the sorcerer and growled; the sigils which covered it glowed with an ancient power.

CHAPTER TWENTY-FIVE

"Jackie, get Claire," Rob said. The eclipse had taken full hold, dimming the sky, but the moon did not pass beyond. It hung in place as if staying to watch the destruction of all reality, waiting for the battle to play out below.

Jackie nodded and hurried forward, dodging mounds of burning debris. She shot off bursts of laser energy to lay cover fire and ran to her friend while James slowly turned to face Rob. Her eyes gleamed with a certain fire of confidence, as if she had done this before.

James wore an impressed grin upon his face. "How many times must I kill you?" James smiled maniacally. His smirk turned to a snarl, and he flung blazing fireballs at the werewolf.

Rob deflected them with his massive sword and charged towards the sorcerer. James sidestepped and drew his sword in response. Eldritch flame burst forth, wreathing his blade with fire.

James slashed at him. Rob blocked and their crossing blades splattered sparks across the space between them. They thrust and parried, each trying to open an opportunity for a lethal strike.

Between blows, the sorcerer scooped up the nearby athame. Fire wreathed it, too, as he pressed the attack, striking with a flurry of blows. The warlock wildly cut at his enemy.

Rob whirled around, evading the blades and seeking a new angle on his enemy. He saw an opening as James over-extended his attack. Whirling the glaive high above his head, Rob held off the killing strike when Claire shrieked nearby.

Both Rob and James froze. A tentacle shot out of the void. Greyish green, it wrapped around Claire while Jackie fired into the gathering vyrm troops, trying to keep them at bay.

Claire grabbed at anything that she could to prevent the Devourer from pulling her through the tear and into the nether. Both of the combatants rushed to her, momentarily forgetting their deep and bitter rivalry in defense of the princess.

James blasted the monstrous tendril with fire. The otherworldly appendage paid it no notice. The sorcerer hacked and slashed at it with both burning blades, but it completely resisted all of his efforts.

Rob leapt towards it, bringing the Stone Glaive to bear. He sliced downward violently. The tendril cut partially, and the wound turned to stone. The tentacle stiffened as it clutched its prey. Rob smashed it, breaking the arm to gray chunks, which crumbled like old concrete as the severed limb retreated to the negative dimension.

He rushed to Claire's side and broke her free from the stone appendage which wrapped around her. Jackie grabbed her friend. "Come on! Let's go!" They dove out of the way of a second squid-like limb that tried to seize her.

Rob sliced cleanly through those as soon as able. A blast of hot air spewed from the nether-hole and a terrible shriek echoed through the town. Sh'logath hungered desperately for Claire's blood.

Jackie grabbed Claire, and they crawled underneath the semi-truck trailer, trying to stay shielded from the vyrm onslaught. "How did you get here?" Claire exclaimed her joy more than she asked the question.

She fired a quick burst of energy into the group that got too close. "I didn't know what to do. I wandered around Europe until a very beaten-up werewolf found me. We couldn't find you, so we went looking for that stone sword, figuring we'd catch up here before Sh'logath woke up."

Claire beamed. Despite the dark circumstances, her friends' attempted rescue made everything a little brighter.

The Heptobscurantum's forces had begun to wane, even though the vyrm had stopped entering through the dimensional gates, which had winked shut. The cultists' numbers had simply been insufficient to contend with Nitthogr's.

Rob hacked at a mob of vyrm soldiers as they charged towards his friends. Each that he drew blood on froze as stone. Half of the attackers turned and fled back to the safety of the larger group, where Jackie peppered them with her assault blaster.

She changed out chargepaks with a high frequency and hoped that she had enough. The entire trailer suddenly ripped free from its position and skidded to the side, toppling to its side and crushing an entire faction of vyrm.

Jacob Sisyphus stood on the opposite sidewalk, manipulating the forces powerful enough to wield a tractor trailer as his toy. His hands glowed with energy, but his eyes looked fatigued and bloodshot. With robes tattered and torn, he limped across the street, using an eldritch shield to block the offensive Jackie tried to mount. Summoning all of his rage, Sisyphus charged ahead and punched Jackie with a wild haymaker.

Jackie fell to the ground. Her head cracked against the pavement, knocking her unconscious. Sisyphus hurled her weapon into the distance so that Claire couldn't grab it.

A cheer went up from the scattered Heptobscurantum and the remaining members of their cult targeted James, keeping him occupied with a rain of bullets. Sisyphus tried to grab Claire, but she proved more agile than suspected. She ducked and slipped away from him.

"Get her!" screamed Adams as Claire bobbed around the corner of the semi-tractor.

Sisyphus ran after her. He stepped around the edge of the cab just in time to see the werewolf charge forward with his swinging fist. The first blow stood the former wrestler up straight, and the second one drove him to the ground.

Rob picked up the wizard and shook him violently. He hoisted the robed cult leader high above his head and flung The Seven's eldritch master across the intersection, where he crashed into his four peers.

The entire battle seemed to come to a halt as Sisyphus, clearly dazed, struggled to his feet. He stood in one corner of the offensive triangle. Summers, behind him, handed the Occultist another pack of blood, and he bit into it with his one remaining false tooth. The remaining Illuminati stood behind their recharged magic wielder.

Opposing him on one side of the Mexican standoff was James: the inter-dimensional warlock, Nitthogr. On the other was Rob, the werewolf with the mythic stone blade.

Adams tried to outfox his enemies in political fashion. "Tell us, almighty Nitthogr. Why do you oppose our sacrifice of the Princess? Wouldn't it make sense that we pour out all her blood upon this altar? The moment of the Great Awakening is at hand!"

Clearly flustered by the turnabout, James shouted. "You know nothing! I am Nitthogr, true Herald of Sh'logath! Only *I* know the proper day and hour of the Awakening!"

The Devourer roared from beyond, and the vyrm shifted on their feet, uncertain of their course. They lowered their weapons ever so slightly.

"We know everything!" Adams screamed back. "Caivev..." he looked around for something. "Caivev told us..." something had distracted him, like the ear ringing of persistent tinnitus. "Caivev told us of your treachery against Sh'logath!" He looked around, pulling a foreign object stuffed within Sisyphus's cloak: a TRX718 blaster pistol.

The shrill whine it emitted had grown demandingly loud, now audible to all. Adams looked at Rob, who had flung the man at them seconds ago.

Rob stared at the blaster with cold, hard expectation. The charging port on the battery pack rapidly flashed red, right above the terminal, where a tiny metal clip had been jammed.

Boom.

The TRX718 exploded with a flash of light; its concussive fireball flattened the ragged remnants of The Seven. James shielded his eyes against the intensely bright eruption which seemed to suck all sound into the detonation. From the smoldering crater, Jacob Sisyphus struggled to rise; he shook under his own weight, and finally collapsed.

In the moment of silence that followed, jaws dropped and the faces of the on-looking Heptobscurantum members fell. A rally cry rose up from the vyrm army and they charged against their fleeing human enemy. The cultists routed in terror, scattering in any and every direction.

Rob walked towards James tentatively, like a mongoose stalking a cobra. Vyrm slinked around him, giving the sword wielding lycanthrope wide berth.

Behind the warlock, the tear through the fabric of space squirmed with the writhing of tentacles. They clawed blindly at the air in their vain attempt to pull Sh'logath into this realm.

James lifted his two blades in challenge. "I've been killing members of your family for generations now! And it ends today!"

"One way or another!" Rob howled back, bringing his massive blade to bear.

James blocked and swung while Rob dodged and parried. Rob's heavy glaive proved slower than the light blades of his enemy, but the brute force behind his blows knocked the sorcerer back with each strike. James tried to keep a tight grip on his weapons.

Rob swung mightily with a slice that could have cleaved the sorcerer cleanly through. James blocked, but the hooked athame clattered out of his hand and skittered to the ground.

Summoning his dark power, the warlock blasted Rob's face with a burst of searing flame. Rob flailed his weapon wildly, momentarily blinded.

James somersaulted away and scooped up the athame. He whirled around just in time to catch Rob's next ferocious strike. James countered with five blows of his own; the final one lodged the nasty occult blade in the meat of Rob's arm.

Rob growled in pain, recoiling slightly. He yanked the athame from his wounded flesh and threw it back at him.

The warlock ducked, and it sailed across the open pavement, lodging firmly in the spine of a vyrm who tried to pull open the semi-truck's cab door. Claire and Jackie sat inside the locked vehicle, obviously arguing with each other over how to operate the big rig.

James darted towards the vehicle, his prize threatened escape. Rob leapt over the warlock and stood between the two, barring the way yet again. James ducked the werewolf's clawed swipe that would have taken his head off. The deep cut from the athame had nearly stitched itself back together.

With a two finger strike that crackled with white lightning, James stepped inside Rob's guard and jabbed a nerve on the lycan's torso. Rob's sword arm fell dead, and he dropped the Stone Glaive, roaring as James slipped past him.

Rob swung around with his other arm and smashed the disengaging warlock with a massive blow, pivoting his hips like a baseball batter. He knocked James back across the asphalt, flinging him far over the stage, altar, and out of sight.

Shaking out the numbness from his arm, Rob picked up the rune-covered blade. He looked up and saw Claire reach over the wheel and locate the ignition.

The semi-truck chortled and belched diesel smoke. Claire revved the engine, intimidating the vyrm near the hood with the Peterbilt's mechanical thundering.

Rob circled around the truck and slew any vyrm who threatened the girls. He cleared the area immediately surrounding them and spotted a pair of enemies crawling on the roof. Using his powerful lycanthrope legs, Rob leapt clear to the top of the cab. A second later, two stone statues shattered upon the pavement beside the truck.

The air sizzled and crackled with power. A roar emanated near the altar: a different kind of rumbling from the constant screeching within the nether void.

Rob bent his knees like a surfer as he stood atop the roof of the semi. It started to bounce and lurch as Claire struggled to work the transmission and the clutch in tandem.

What dim light remained seemed drawn into the glowing orb that James held in two hands above his head. The ball of energy grew and intensified as the warlock vampirically siphoned the power from anything in his vicinity. Vyrm warriors who stood too close fell dead as the incantation sucked their life forces into the black orb of destruction.

"I am Nitthogr! Herald of Sh'logath: Beast of the Tesseract! If I cannot have satisfaction, then The Devourer shall rise!" He raved like a madman. His intentions were very clear: he would kill Princess Claire and cause the Awakening!

Guided by instinct alone, Rob flung the Stone Glaive at the sorcerer. It streaked towards him, spinning rapidly like a giant shuriken. It closed the gap in a split second and missed the mark. The blade merely nicked Nitthogr's wrist as it sailed past.

The sorcerer cackled at Rob's failure. And then began screaming. The energy ball fizzled and dissipated in a greasy puff of smoke as Nitthogr clutched his wrist. The skin cracked, turning gray. A patch of stone hardened and started spreading.

Nitthogr swiftly drew his blade and wreathed it with fire. He hacked cleanly through his arm at the joint, stemming the spread of the effect and partially cauterizing the wound with flame. He howled with pain and rage as his severed limb turned to stone on the ground below.

Rob leapt down from the roof and sprinted towards his enemy. Nitthogr's free arm grew razor claws formed of eldritch energy. He snarled, welcoming the challenge.

They collided in a flurry of slashing claws, pounding fists, and crushing knees. Vyrm flocked around them, circling the fighters; all of the Heptobscurantum had been chased off by now.

Crashing vehicle sounds echoed down the street as Claire and Jackie rammed their way through the blockade and upshifted, pouring on the gas and stomping on the throttle with diesel fury.

Nitthogr raked his claws across Rob's face. The lycan howled and grabbed the wound, exposing his midsection.

Seizing the opportunity, the sorcerer stabbed his knife-like hand deep into the werewolf's belly; just missing a plated section of armor, he found a tender target, plunging his clawed hand through Rob's thick hide and deep into his organs.

Rob clapped a taloned paw around his enemy and hugged him close so that he could not escape. The warlock could not even remove his hand. Nitthogr flailed his stump wildly; hissing, he tried to push himself free. The werewolf greeted him with a ferocious growl, spewing spittle all over the half-vyrm's face.

Sinking deep into the warlock's flesh with his own claws, Rob squeezed Nitthogr's spine in his firm grip. Bellowing with fury, he raised the sorcerer high above his head, ripping the razor-sharp arm from where it had lodged in his midsection. He turned to the nearby void and cast the flailing warlock into the vast nothing.

Nitthogr pitched headlong through the tear, shrieking curses as he evaporated into a noncorporeal essence, finally falling into the presence of his nega-god. The thrashing tentacles collapsed into the fissure and Rob stood there, staring into the maddening black maw.

A long pause ensued. None of the vyrm dared approach the creature who had just thrown their master into the emptiness.

As Rob stared into the supernatural vacuum, something passed between him and the agod, as if they'd come to some sort of understanding.

"Mighty Sh'logath," Rob screamed through the opening. "Long has my family stood between your followers and the line of the Architect King. I stand here to tell you that it will forever be so! I stand here, in my place between you and her—keeping reality a constant!"

He could hear the reply as a terrible voice in his thoughts. It reached out to him from the abyss and touched his mind with palpable horror. *You think that reality is a constant because that is all you've ever known. Prior to creation, I WAS. Your Architect King is an agod who overthrew a reign that stretched into eternity prior!*

And yet today is not the day of my waking, and even now I drift towards slumber: the blood offering too weak to sustain.

The glowing tear had already begun shrinking slowly. Rob stood in front of the rip as an accuser.

"You have heard all the words here today, testimony of your own followers' betrayal. Judge them according to your harsh standards! Your herald, Nitthogr, has long conspired against you, scheming for his own profit—*using you*, as if you were some pawn to be manipulated."

A great silence came from the grand nothingness on the other side of the diminishing hole. Suddenly, a sucking sound welled up, like a mighty wind.

All the vyrm began sliding, pulled towards the crack with a kind of electromagnetic force. Only the scaly warriors, dead and living, seemed affected. They flew towards the hole, pulled inside with increasing hurricane force. Bodies collided and clogged the shrinking portal. They snapped and cracked, popping with sickening sounds as the power of the agod pulled his forces into the void where he slumbered.

Suddenly, the hole winked out of existence with a ghastly slurping sound, followed by stark silence. The sun shone brightly. The eclipse had passed.

Rob looked down at his belly. Blood and viscera slicked his midsection. It healed slowly, *slower than normal,* he thought. He staggered on his feet and reclaimed the sigil engraved Stone Glaive.

Probably healing so slow because I'm so fatigued, he mused. Then he sank to his knees. *I just need a minute to rest.* His eyes rolled back in his head and he slumped over on his side, refusing to die but unable to stay conscious.

Chapter Twenty-Six

Sam Jones shook off the grogginess. He'd been blindfolded, and the gag was still over his mouth, but he could hear.

Something had gone wrong for his captors. Very wrong. There were frantic sounds of motion. Some things were hastily packed, and others were smashed and destroyed. And there were voices, lots of angry and confused voices. Some he recognized.

"Leave him here to die," said a female. *Vivian*, he only now recognized the voice he'd heard several times through the drug-addled haze he'd been in.

It's definitely her. I've heard it before—she was supposed to be Claire's sister-in-law.

He realized that, if he was coming out of the drug-induced coma, the medical equipment keeping him under must have been shut off or damaged.

A few moments after all the loud sounds of the evacuation had begun, they ended. Everything had gone quiet and perfectly still. All sounds of life had ceased and even the noise of things like air-conditioning or heat had stopped, leaving only an eerie stillness that completely isolated him.

Claire's father had a sudden revelation. The equipment keeping him hydrated and providing nutrients were off, and he was trapped in these restraints. *Nobody knows where I am... wherever I am.*

That led to one final, terrifying thought.

I'm going to die here.

Rob's eyelids fluttered and opened. Jackie and Claire stood over him.

Claire weaved her fingers through his wild hair. "There you are," she said warmly; her face was only inches from his. "You've been unconscious for days."

"Where am I?" Rob sat up gingerly and touched his stomach where he'd been impaled. He moved the blanket away and saw the scar tissue that crisscrossed his abdomen like lightning bolts. His exposed skin was overlapped with other scars that he'd gained since he and Claire had departed company a month ago; they cross hatched his naked body, telling the story of his struggles since her escape. "How did I get here?"

"We drove a semi!" Jackie said, true to her bubbly self.

"After the sun returned, we turned around and found you lying next to the sword of the Architect King."

Rob looked around, searching for the ancient blade.

"Don't worry. It's stashed someplace safe."

"With *someone* safe," Jackie corrected.

Rob looked at Claire inquisitively.

"It's with an old friend at the moment," Claire said. "Professor Jecima. So now you tell *us* what happened in Mullen, Nebraska."

Closing his eyes, Rob remembered every detail. He recounted his final battle with Nitthogr in front of the netherspace portal. "I stared into the face of madness and told Sh'logath to stay comfortable where he was. He's not escaping the void any time soon. Not while I'm alive."

Claire sat down next to Rob. "Then do you really think it's over?"

"The Seven might be down," he sighed, "but the heptobscurantum is probably larger than we could ever know."

Claire nodded. She'd seen that to be true during her month on the run.

"But it will certainly take them a long time to recover. Possibly years or more, I would suspect," he concluded. "If even one of the high-ranking heptobscurantum escaped the destruction, they will eventually re-emerge."

"The Prime will certainly rise from the ashes," Jackie said. She had explained to Claire already how she and Rob had helped the resistance turn the tides against the vyrm before they came to her rescue. "Wulftone certainly seems like a very capable overseer for the reconstruction efforts."

Claire caught the twinkle in her friend's eyes when she said his name. She grinned at her. *Leave it to Jackie to fall for a guy from another dimension.* The irony of that thought wasn't lost on her. "I'm glad to hear that he escaped. I didn't think anyone could make it out of that place alive!"

She tried to deflect her thoughts away from the inter-dimensional love connections that seemed to revolve around her. "There's also Basilisk, although he doesn't seem to be champing at the bit to free Sh'logath. And Vivian… Caivev, I mean. She's still out there."

"But I will always be right here to protect you," Rob said, laying a hand gently upon the side of her face, careful not to touch the long line of stitches that ran from chin to cheekbone.

Claire ignored the dull pain and leaned against him. She decided that not thinking about her feelings wouldn't help.

Claire took his hand and intertwined her fingers with his. Her heart fluttered, and all her emotions urged her to kiss him. She awkwardly brushed a stray stand of hair from her face, instead, unsure of taking quite so bold a step.

"We should get out of here." She tried to grapple with her heart's impulses. She wanted to be certain that she was not feeling Bithia's emotions—it had to be real: her recent track record with love had made her reluctant in that area. It would take some time to sort through it. "We've still got to find my father. Last I heard was that he'd been taken prisoner in Central America... maybe. I don't know, but the unrest there has finally settled down. Some kind of new leader took over there. Maybe they'll give us information."

"And don't forget that snake, Vivian," Jackie said. "Or Caivev—or whatever name she's using. She's still out there, too."

Claire nodded and then locked eyes with Rob. In that moment knew that the intense love she felt for him belonged to her and not Bithia. Bithia loved him deeply, truly. But these new feelings she had for Rob were entirely her own.

Vikrum Wiltshire and Atticus Sexton exited their rental car in the town of Pecos, Texas. *City... it's technically a city*, Wiltshire had to remind himself. He put the car into the park at the edge of the parking lot.

Sexton's mobile phone vibrated. "It's Praetor Russo." He read the text aloud.

Get to Pecos Texas. Code 16:16. Information incoming.

Sixteen sixteen was the Order's emergency code. It was only used for threat-levels of potentially world-ending impact. *Revelation sixteen sixteen... And he gathered them together into a place called in the Hebrew tongue Armageddon.*

"Tell him we're already here and already investigating it."

Sexton nodded and fired off a text.

The parking lot, cracked and faded from the harsh Texas sun, was in as bad shape as the abandoned building on the far side of the lot. It was a mostly brick affair, all faded reds and grays except where the bright yellow police tape criss-crossed the scene.

Wiltshire's phone rang as he exited. On the other end, one of the brothers from the Lake Superior region's Keep provided an update. "We got a hit on one of the people you've been searching for. Did a little investigating and got some data. I'm sending it over now," said the voice on the other end.

"Thanks," Wiltshire said and then hung up, wondering if he'd even get the chance to follow up on it if the events inside the building were as bad as expected. His phone buzzed as the data packet began downloading automatically.

"Well," sighed Sexton. "We'd better go inside."

Wiltshire nodded and followed his partner towards the derelict building and the line of police cars which were parked there. They'd been tracking down Quintin Hall for several days, following leads and picking up clues.

Apparently, Quintin had gotten involved with a nice lady who had less than nice hobbies. She was mixed up in a cult that worshiped the Black Goat. It had started as a kind of heptobscurantum offshoot and still retained some loose affiliation to it. The trail led them here, where it had apparently gone cold.

Dead and cold.

The members of the Order provided some identification and paperwork to the local law enforcement and were allowed to pass.

Inside, they found the abandoned building, much as they'd expected to. Naked walls and old concrete. Empty boxes and rooms that contained little more than dust.

And then they found what had drawn Quintin's investigation down to Texas. At the center of the room someone had engraved the seven-pointed star into the concrete with what looked like a concrete saw. At its center rose a stone column.

It was an ancient slab of rock engraved with old sigils that had been smoothed by eons' worth of weather. Dead bodies littered the scene around the stony plinth. Many were dismembered and their insides were laid open to the air. Blood had pooled within the mystic sigil cut into the floor that surrounded the stone.

Sexton's stomach groaned, and he ran to the edge of the scene and vomited all over the wall. Hunched over and with his hands on his partner, "Whatever the hell is happening here, mark my words, it's connected to the heptobscurantum and to Claire Jones."

With Claire's father still missing, Vikrum Wiltshire discovers all Hell breaking loose!
Something from beyond the Tesseract now threatens everything Claire has worked and bled for. There is a traitor in her midst—someone who has unleashed a trickster demigod. And her werewolf protector and his magical Stone Glaive can do little against an enemy who can blink in and out of existence.

There's only one way to stop Akko Soggathoth, herald of the apocalypse, and it involves traveling the Darque dimension. If they cannot collect the haunted artifacts first, the fiend will awaken his eldritch siblings... and rip open the Nether Gate, exposing the multiverse to terrors beyond our imagining!
Go grab your copy NOW!

https://books2read.com/gateofthemultiverse

WHAT'S NEXT?

The interconnected worlds of the multiverse intersect a few different literary universes. There are the Casefiles of Vikrum which quite obviously intersect the books featuring Claire and Zabe, but there is also the time mystic adventure series with an overlap from the Red Order (*The Hidden Rings of Myrddin the Cambion*) and also a fey world briefly seen in book 3, *The Architect King* where *Curse of the Fey Duelist* occurs.

Keep up to date and stay in touch with the author at this link: https://www.subscribepage.com/wolvesofthetesseract and add your email to be added to the newsletter list!

The Architect King – the Creator God. He is currently in stone form, trapped within Basilisk's stronghold at Limbus until some prophesied day.

The Black – common, lowest Caste of the species. Also called blackborn.

Chamber of Mysteries – an impenetrable vault where the arcane artifacts collected by the Royal Family are kept; also home to the Tesseract.

Desolation – a realm of the multiverse; formerly known as Edenya before the Syzygyc War ravaged the landscape.

Dimensional Inversion Pendant – a mysterious artifact made from darquematter; it alters the link between a Prime and his or her variants.

Dunnischkte - a religious ritual to gain a hybrid status between vyrm and human.

Dunnischktet – someone who has completed the Dunnischkte; he or she gains nigh immortality and the ability to shift between hybrid, vyrm, and human forms.

Frostmancer – tarkhūn with special abilities including ice/cold control.

Grimmorium Nitthogr – a journal kept by the fallen Veritas cleric Nitthogr; it is an arcane work that is the culmination of all the sorcery he learned in his earlier years before Sh'logath taught him even deeper and viler magics.

Guardian Corps – royal guards tasked with protecting the royal line and also the chamber of mysteries; some corpsmen decide to join the Veritas, a secretive monastic order drawn from their numbers.

Heptobscurantum – human branch of the vyrm's cult of Sh'logath.

Lich – tarkhūn with psychic abilities; they are always identified at a young age and pressed into service of the Sh'logath cult.

Limbus – the home to Basilisk, the recognized leader of the Tarkhūn, and the capital of Desolation.

Multiverse – thirty-three connected dimensions that can be travelled via pathways that open up based upon the astral alignment/calendar.

Plains of Neggath - region in Desolation where the Sh'logath cult birthed the great Agod; the area is a veritable wasteland and often the home of Rovers.

The Prime – the main realm of the multiverse: the ultimate reality. It also refers to a person who lives within this realm; each Prime has dimensional copies living on the different realms of the multiverse.

Pyromancer – tarkhūn with special abilities including fire generation and manipulation.

Rovers – unaligned vyrm tribes. They are typically either Seekers of Maetha or Followers of Krakkath, two different theologies that some vyrm adhere to.

The Seven – illuminati-like ruling council of the Heprobscurantum.

Shade – tarkhūn with extreme camouflaging ability; some have even gained the ability to completely shapeshift their forms.

Sh'logath – the Devourer, Nega-God, Agod of Destruction, the Reality Eater... all are names to describe the terror that lurks on the verge of reality.

Straruck – the Holy city in the Neggath region; it has holy significance to the vyrm (their religions kind of Mecca).

The Syzygyc War – the war that waged many years between the Prime and Desolation as they sought to awaken Shlogath; it was prevented by the Architect King.

Tarkhūn – high caste of vyrm that once ruled their race before a schism led by Nitthogr long ago. They are a rarer, but stronger breed. Some, who resemble member of The Black, have developed additional powers.

Tesseract – a gem created by the Architect King; it is the key to all power in reality and the embodiment of the multiverse.

Thousand Elder's Sacrifice – the sacrificial torpor the vyrm elders entered into in order to make Sh'logath real via dark rites.

TRX718 – a high powered blaster pistol.

Voice of the Thousand Elders – the chief Cleric of the Vyrm's Thousand Elders. He stayed alive and died of old age, although his spirit remains disembodied and tied to the Thousand Elders will.

Vyrm – reptilian humanoid race whose home realm is known as the Desolation.

<h1 style="text-align:center">Dramatis Personae</h1>

Andrew Thornton – A member of The Seven who rule the heptobscurantum

Atticus Sexton – A paranormal investigator and Red Order brother; Vikrum Wiltshire is his partner

Basilisk – Brother to Nitthogr. He rules the dimension known as the Desolation

Bithia of the Prime – Princess. Daughter of the Architect King and ruler of the Prime, and by extension, the multiverse

Bruce Cannon – A member of The Seven who rule the heptobscurantum. Hired Vikrum Wiltshire to save his life

Caivev – Traitor to the Prime, former Guardian Corps member. She has wanted to join Nitthogr and Basilisk as a dunnischktet and is a ranking member of the vyrm's army. Took the form of Vivian on Earth

Charles Summers – A member of The Seven who rule the heptobscurantum

Charsk – A vyrm leader

Claire Jones – Daughter of Sam Jones. Human variant of Princess Bithia

Jackie – Claire's best friend since her high school days

Jacob Sisyphus – Formerly a popular professional wrestler. He is a long time cultist and an arcane practitioner and now a member of The Seven who lead the heptobscurantum

James Shianan – A former pro soccer player with worldwide fame. His is a form taken by Nitthogr

Jarfig – Museum curator and historian from the prime. He is the Prime variant of Jacob Sisyphus

Jonathan Trask – A member of The Seven who rule the heptobscurantum. Turned out to be a Tarkhūn traitor and spy

Ma Kechewaishke – A Native American woman who helped Claire access the astral plane

Miles Jecima – A linguist with specialty in dead, ancient, and unknown languages. He is good friends and peers with Sam Jones

Nitthogr – Sorcerer and leader of both The Black and the heptobscurantum. He and his brother were, long ago, members of the Veritas—a monastic order in the Prime

Peter Greyson – A member of The Seven who rule the heptobscurantum

Praetor Russo – In charge of a large region of Red Order members

Quintin Hall – Formerly with the Red Order. He is still a paranormal investigator but has gone private. Hall remains in touch with Vikrum Wiltshire

Regorik – Lead war commander of The Black and second in command after Caivev. He is Tarkhūn

Rob – Another name for Zabe which he goes by when on Claire's Earth

Robert Schaeffer – The Earth version of Zabe. He looks like Zabe... but they are not the same person

Sam Jones – Archaeologist and father of Claire Jones

Shardai – A former member (retired) of the Guardian Corps

Thomas Chelish – A member of The Seven who rule the heptobscurantum

Victor Adams – A member of The Seven who rule the heptobscurantum

Vikrum Wiltshire – A paranormal investigator who works for the mysterious Red Order sect of the Vatican

Vivian Shianan – Works for the Special Research Division of the government which looks into paranormal phenomenon and dispels questions. Half sibling to James Shianan. See Caivev.

Zabe – Son of Zahaben. Guardian Corps soldier. Friend and confidant of Princess Bithia

Zahaben – Captain of Princess Bithia's personal guard and leader of the Guardian Corps

About the Author

Christopher D. Schmitz is an indie author from the fly-over states who dabbles in game design. He has published award winning science fiction, fantasy, and humor. He's written and freelanced for a variety of outlets, including a blog that has helped countless writers on their publishing journey. On any given weekend, he can be found at pop culture and comic conventions across the USA or playing his bagpipes for people. You can look him up at www.authorchristopherdschmitz.com.

ALSO BY CHRISTOPHER D. SCHMITZ

www.ingramcontent.com/pod-product-compliance
Lightning Source LLC
Chambersburg PA
CBHW061100190726
48286CB00006B/1814